FAREWELL,
FOUR WATERS

FAREWELL, FOUR WATERS

ONE AID WORKER'S SUDDEN ESCAPE FROM AFGHANISTAN

A NOVEL BASED ON TRUE EVENTS

KATE McCORD

A PROTECTIVE PSEUDONYM

MOODY PUBLISHERS

CHICAGO

Interior design: Erik M. Peterson
Cover design: Dean Renninger
Cover photo of flag of Afghanistan, copyright © by Andrew Dunhan / open clip art.
Cover photo of woman, copyright © by Gennadii_Afanasiev / thinkstock.com.
All rights reserved.

Library of Congress Cataloging-in-Publication Data

McCord, Kate.
Farewell, Four Waters : a novel based on true events / Kate McCord, a protective pseudonym.
    pages cm
ISBN 978-0-8024-1206-5
1. Americans—Afghanistan—Ficton. 2. Women—Education—Afghanistan—Fiction.
3. Literacy programs—Afghanistan—Fiction. 4. Literacy—Afghanistan—Fiction.
5. Afghan War, 2001—Fiction. I. Title.
PS3613.C38226F38 2014
813'.6—dc23

                                                               2014004376

We hope you enjoy this book from River North Fiction by Moody Publishers. Our goal is to provide high-quality, thought-provoking books and products that connect truth to your real needs and challenges. For more information on other books and products written and produced from a biblical perspective, go to www.moodypublishers.com or write to:

River North Fiction
Imprint of Moody Publishers
820 N. LaSalle Boulevard
Chicago, IL 60610

1 3 5 7 9 10 8 6 4 2

Printed in the United States of America

For the "Valley Team," who shared my journey;
for Debbie, who welcomed me home;
and for Amy, Ruth, and Elaine who
helped me find Christ in the loss.

PART 1

DAY 14

KABUL, AFGHANISTAN

1

Three hours and the office would close. Marie scribbled another name—another Afghan official with a title, a stamp, and a signature that she still needed. If she focused, Marie could get it done; her project would be approved and she could go home to Shehktan.

Her cell phone chirped. She glanced across the room at the broken window blinds, bars of light streaming through the gaps, dust floating thick and dry. She looked back at the young man, whose rapid directions she'd suddenly lost track of.

Her phone chirped again. Instinctively, she caught the small yellow nylon pouch tethered to the strap of her black backpack. Her lifeline. She pulled the flap, slipped her fingers inside, and retrieved the phone.

The young man took a breath and continued talking.

Marie lifted the display before her eyes. *Carolyn? She knows I'm busy. Why is she calling?* A dozen possible reasons raced through her mind. The phone rang out again.

In front of her sat a row of three mismatched desks: two laminated wood, chipped on the corners, and one scratched, gray metal.

She looked at the dirty concrete-colored computer monitors with their red, white, and blue stickers, "USAID"—gifts of the American people—attached were keyboards with grease and dust-stained keys.

Her phone sounded a fourth time.

She clutched a sheaf of papers in her left hand: written instructions, recorded in uneven black script; names crossed out, rewritten, crossed out again. Some words written in Dari, their backward-looping shapes clashing against fragments of English instructions.

The phone chirped a fifth time. *Carolyn.* It was her coworker, housemate, and closest friend in Afghanistan. *Something must be wrong.* Marie waved her interruption to the young man. "One minute."

He didn't stop.

She pushed the green button and pressed the phone to her ear. "Hello."

Carolyn's voice was rushed, unnaturally high, and panicked. "Oh, thank God you answered! Thank God! You won't believe it. I'm so glad you answered."

The panic in Carolyn's voice made Marie's knees buckle, straighten, then lock.

The young man's words fused and disappeared into the background as she tried to focus on Carolyn's scattered message. "We got a text . . . a foreigner . . . a woman . . . executed right here, on the street, in Kabul . . . Did you hear? Are you all right?"

The pale blue room with the broken window blinds, mismatched desks, and USAID hardware convulsed in Marie's peripheral vision, then settled. Marie reached for the corner of the desk in front of her. Her knuckles raked the edges of a cluster of nearly empty glass tea cups. Their smooth sides seemed to contrast with the broken cadence of Carolyn's words.

"I was afraid it was you. It's not you! Are you okay? Where are you?"

Marie pushed the desk away, fixed her eyes on the split shafts of sunlight holding dust in their slanted beams. She forced calm into her voice. "I'm here."

"Where?"

Marie narrowed her eyes, forced her knees to unlock, and slowed her words into sentences. "I'm fine. I'm downtown."

In the mismatched desks in front of her, two young Afghan clerks in Western clothing sat on half-broken chairs. A third stood silent, finally realizing his speech had been interrupted. "I'm at the Ministry of Economy getting approval for our literacy project." *Of course*, she thought. *She already knows that.* She looked at her translator. His downcast eyes testified to his discomfort. Marie realized he could hear Carolyn's side of the conversation. They could *all* hear. *A foreigner . . . a woman . . . executed . . . right here . . . on the street . . . in Kabul.*

An ugly, rough-edged word. *Executed.*

Carolyn, calling from the Kabul guesthouse, couldn't see the three young Afghan men, Marie's translator, the row of mismatched desks, the pale blue walls, or the broken blinds. She couldn't see the sheaf of papers Marie held in her left hand or the scratched instructions in black ink that told her which office to enter next. The cell phone created a context in which these two incongruent scenes—the guesthouse and the Kabul office—clashed with such force that it created a third, surreal scene in her mind. Marie stood, phone in hand, disoriented. She felt engulfed in a sudden squall of churning dust. She caught her breath and groped for something solid, something firm.

Carolyn's words still tumbled about. "Come back. Come back to the guesthouse right away."

Back to the guesthouse—now? Before finishing?

But Carolyn kept talking. "We're on lockdown. We're *all* on lockdown. You have to come back."

Another gust swept over her. "What?"

"The entire foreign community's on lockdown. Can you get here? You have to come."

It was protocol. *Lockdown; get inside the thick mud-brick walls of your compound. Lock the gate. Hide from the men with Kalashnikovs out on the street.* Marie was on the wrong side of the city, surrounded by the wrong people. Lost in a Kabul government office with three young Afghan men behind a bank of mismatched desks and her translator, Fawad. *Strangers. Foreigners. No, I'm the stranger. I'm the foreigner.* She pulled her voice tight, careful, and thin; then whispered, "Who was it?"

Carolyn still rushed her words. "We don't know. I'm trying to find out. I'll let you know. When can you get back here?"

Marie looked at the sheaf of papers in her left hand. The first were instructions; the rest were letters, protocols, and statements. Each one required a government stamp and signature. That's why she was in this office, why she was in Kabul. She needed the stamps and signatures to start their literacy project. She couldn't fly back to Shehktan until she got them. No, she wouldn't leave, not without the approval.

Fawad in his rural Afghan clothes, and the young men behind the desks in their almost Western-style jeans were all watching her silently. Waiting.

Carolyn interrupted Marie's thoughts. "When are you coming back?"

She looked at the broken and twisted Venetian blinds, the thick layer of khaki Kabuli soil that coated each thin, white blade, the sharp streaks of sun piercing the gaps, and the dust suspended in shafts of light. Marie knew the protocol for lockdown: go home immediately, stay home. But home was far away, in Shehktan, and Marie had work to do. "I don't know. I'll be there soon."

"Marie!" Carolyn protested.

Marie caught her own breath and held it a moment before speaking. "Carolyn, calm down. Tell me what happened."

Carolyn's words were still rushed; her voice, still too high-pitched. "They said it was three blocks from the guesthouse. Two or three men in a car. I heard the bullets. Lots of them. Soon after you left. But I didn't think . . . I just thought, *Oh, a firefight somewhere with the Afghan National Army and insurgents. Taliban. Not one of us.* But it *was* one of us. Can you believe it, Marie? That never happens . . . right on the street! Right here, in our neighborhood. They shot one of us right in front of the schoolchildren. That's what people are saying. That's all I know. Come back to the guesthouse. You have to. Come back now."

"Carolyn, stop. I'm at the Ministry of Economy, in the office. I'm safe here, and I have work to do. I'll call you soon."

Marie snapped her phone shut, slipped it back into its yellow nylon sheath, and watched the scene in her imagination. She shuddered. *I was there. Just blocks from where I caught my taxi. I missed it. I didn't hear the bullets. I must have passed just minutes before she was killed. I must've climbed into my taxi just before it all happened. I missed it. Missed it by only minutes.*

She looked at her translator's downturned face and followed the angle of his eyes. Fawad was studying the grimy, nearly empty glass teacups sitting on the corner of the desk. She looked up at the row of young Afghan men. They were still silent, all of them, watching her.

Finally, Marie spoke—her words sounded far away, foreign, words that came from a stranger, words spoken in a voice she could no longer recognize even though it was her own. "A foreign aid worker, a woman, was killed in Cart'e Seh."

The young men waited.

Cart'e Seh? Marie thought. *Why do I even know that neighborhood? Its geography, its shape, its residents? How did these Dari words come from my mouth? Where did I get them? Was I really speaking them? Why am I shocked? We're in downtown Kabul. Afghanistan. Things happen. Bombs in trucks go off next to convoys full of soldiers. Mines explode under vehicles and kill women and children in nearby buses. People die. Every day, we hear news reports of people killed and maimed. Why is this different?* She spoke her next sentence out loud as if to impress its truth upon her spinning thoughts. "A foreign aid worker, a woman, was killed in Cart'e Seh."

The reality settled. A solitary woman, executed at close range, intentionally killed on a Kabul street just blocks from Marie's guesthouse. Killed in an area considered safe for foreign workers. The woman's scarf, her cell phone, the aid work that she did, the welcome she had in the community, none of it mattered. She was killed, left in a pool of hot blood on a dusty Kabul street. This was a new thing. Marie shuddered.

She, too, walked those same Kabul streets. She, too, wore a cotton headscarf, long coat, and sandals. She, too, carried a cell phone. *It could have been me.* She stood unsteady and silent for several moments.

The three young men behind their dust and grime-covered desks watched and waited. Finally, the standing one broke the silence. "It's okay. Cart'e Seh is far away." His voice was gentle, soft.

Marie was not reassured. The rules had suddenly changed. Never before had an aid worker been so publicly executed. Yes, others had been kidnapped, and years before—during the wars—aid workers were killed, but that was a long time ago.

This was almost seven years after the fall of the Taliban. Since 9/11, aid workers had poured into Afghanistan. They brought medical care, education, training, and reconstruction. They were welcomed by Afghans throughout the country.

Marie looked at the sheaf of papers in her hand; half were printed in Dari, the other half in English. Project setup forms: a women's literacy project. The people in Shehktan had asked for this project. The women wanted to learn to read and the men had approved. Stamps. Signatures. She needed the approvals of government leaders in Kabul.

She checked the time on her cell phone. *Three hours and the office will close. If I leave now, I'll have to come back after the weekend. No. I want to go home to Shehktan. Start this project.*

She looked around the office. Every surface laced with fine Kabuli dust. Of the four young men, three worked for the government. Kabulis in skinny khaki and olive jeans edged with zippers and pockets in odd locations. They each wore tight fitting, polyester shirts, two with loud prints, one solid gold. All were clean shaven. One wore his hair short on the sides and back, but long in the front. His bangs fell down to his eyebrows. The other two wore their hair slicked back.

She looked at Fawad. Her translator was country, not Kabuli. He wore a crisp white *shalvar kameez,* a long shirt that fell down to his knees, with matching trousers that spilled over long, pointed black shoes. His neat beard, mustache, and carefully cut hair all looked out of place in this Kabul office. Marie watched him study three thick, fingerprint-covered glass cups that sat on the edge of the desk.

The still-standing clerk spoke in careful English. "We're at war. Sometimes these things happen. Of course it's terrible, but these things happen. Did you know her?"

Marie cocked her head sideways. She had no idea who'd been killed. "No."

"Then there's nothing to do." The young man shrugged. "We should continue."

Marie looked again at the stack of papers in her hand. She thought of the mullah in Shehktan, with his gray-and-white turban and gray-streaked beard. He was the first to ask for the project. "Our women must learn to read," he had said. "It's important. Without literacy, they're blind." When she asked if they wanted to learn, he had said they did. "Yes. Of course."

Marie had not believed him, so she conducted her own survey. She hired six Afghan women, each from different neighborhoods around the city, and sent them out to interview neighbors. The results were overwhelming. The women wanted to learn.

Marie had already raised the money for the project. She had approval from her NGO, the nongovernmental organization for whom she worked in Shehktan. All she needed were the Kabul stamps and signatures.

She made the decision that the young men behind their mismatched desks wanted her to make. She nodded, reread the instructions she'd already recorded, and asked the standing man to continue.

The room relaxed and returned to work.

The young man delivered the last set of instructions. When he finished, Marie thanked all three for their assistance, even though only one had helped. She placed her right hand over her heart, the appropriate gesture for a respectful greeting, and wished them safety in God.

Fawad turned and followed her out of the office into a long, empty, gray, tiled hallway with dull, light blue walls and rows of closed wooden doors. Marie walked several feet down the hallway, out of earshot from the office, then stopped.

"Do you understand our instructions?"

Fawad nodded. "Yes. The next office is over there." He pointed to a closed door on the right, about eight feet away. "Mari-jan. We should call Mr. Dave."

Dave was their boss, the director of the NGO for which both worked. "Yes, but I need to call Carolyn first."

"Who?"

Marie smiled. She'd used Carolyn's American name, not her Afghan name. "Nazanin."

Fawad nodded. He knew Nazanin. Carolyn, he'd never met.

Marie stepped to the side of the hallway, pulled the Velcro from her nylon pouch, and retrieved her phone. She found Carolyn's number in the list of contacts and wondered what she would say to her.

Carolyn was young, twenty-three when she first arrived in Afghanistan. Now she was just shy of twenty-five. She did her first six months in Kabul, learning the basics of Dari. When she could speak enough to get by, she moved to Shehktan and settled into Marie's house. She joined Marie in the middle of the last project, a teacher-training program that led them out to remote villages.

At first, Marie had been hesitant. Carolyn was so young, almost twenty years younger than herself and breathtakingly naïve. Marie assumed she would arrive addicted to her cell phone and the Internet. She couldn't imagine how the young woman would cope with the unrelenting summer heat or the brutal winter cold of northern Afghanistan. Marie was convinced that traveling rough roads in spring-shot vehicles and walking donkey paths would be too much for the young American woman, but she was wrong. Carolyn had done well and the Afghans adored her.

Over time, Marie grew to rely on her young companion. It wasn't just the work, although Carolyn was good at that. There was more. She had become a treasured friend. They laughed together and cried together. They shared their meals, the challenges of living in-country, and the joys of getting to know people and seeing new things. They shared their own stories and the stories of the Afghan women whose histories so often broke their hearts. They prayed and worshiped together. In many ways, they'd become closer than sisters.

Now there was a guy. He'd been in the picture since the beginning, just as a distraction at first. Marie had watched the relationship develop. More than once, she'd listened to Carolyn debate the young man's attributes, wonder what she wanted, and vacillate between hope and disregard. When Marie planned her trip to collect approvals for the new project, Carolyn jumped at the opportunity for shared travel from Shehktan to Kabul. She'd left Marie to the government work and flown on to Dubai, where her young man joined her for a week of ice cream, hamburgers, and conversation.

She had returned to Kabul giddy. He hadn't actually proposed, but they'd had the talk. Now Carolyn was proposing departure dates; before the summer when the heat saps everyone's strength, or at the start of Ramadan, when the Afghans grow short-tempered. Marie measured the time before Carolyn would leave: nine months, ten? It was too soon.

Marie sighed. Of course, she wanted Carolyn to be happy. Still, it was too soon. She pushed the green call button on her phone.

Carolyn answered. "Marie?"

"Hi, Carolyn."

"Are you on your way back to the guesthouse?"

"No. We're going to finish our work and then return. I'll call you when I head back."

"Are you sure?"

"Yes. Have you heard anything new?"

"Not much."

"Okay. Text me if you hear anything."

"Marie? Are you sure?"

"Yeah. Look, we're already here. If we're lucky, we can get the project approved today. Go back to Shehktan on the next flight."

"Okay."

Marie knew she was already pulling her heart away from Carolyn. She could hear the distance in her own voice. She would have handled the call differently, the day differently, if she didn't already know Carolyn would leave in just a few months. Surely she wouldn't have left her friend alone at a Kabul guesthouse on a day like this. The dull edge of guilt pressed into her temple. "Hey, Carolyn, are you okay?"

Carolyn didn't respond.

"Carolyn?"

"Yeah. I'm fine. I mean, no. I'm not fine. How could I be? One of us was killed. Right on the street. It could have been any of us."

Marie understood. Every day they walked past Afghan men with Kalashnikovs in their hands. They had to believe they wouldn't be shot or they couldn't do it. "Carolyn—"

"It's okay." The younger woman sighed heavily. "Do what you have to do. I'll be here when you get back. Don't worry about it. I'm safe. Just call me before you leave the ministry. Okay?"

"Yeah, I will."

"Thanks."

"Sure. I'll talk to you later," Marie said, ending the call. Then she scrolled through her contacts and placed another.

The smooth, deep bass of a man in his sixties answered the phone. "Hello."

"Dave? Marie here."

"It's good to hear your voice. I talked to Carolyn. She said you were fine, but downtown." Dave, always straight to business.

"Yeah. We're still here."

"Fawad with you?"

Marie looked over at the translator. "Yeah. We're going to try to get the project approved. Then I'll go back to the guesthouse and send Fawad home. Can he still take the bus?"

"To Shehktan?"

"Yeah."

Dave was a details man. He liked to consider every piece of information he could get. "Yes. He'll take the bus to the provincial capital, then catch a line taxi to town. It's no problem. He knows how to do it."

"I just wanted to know if it was still safe enough for him to travel that way."

"Oh." Dave's voice lightened. "Yeah. Of course." His voice dropped back down. "But you can't. That road's closed to us. Wait for the plane. Okay?"

Marie was impatient. "Yeah, I know."

"Okay." Dave's voice lightened again. He was back to collecting information. "Do you know who was killed yet?"

"No. Do you?"

"I heard her name, but we don't know her. She's with a different NGO."

Marie hesitated. She didn't know that many people in Kabul, but it was possible she knew the woman. "What's her name?"

Fawad raised his eyebrows but kept his eyes on the floor.

Dave gave the name. "You know her?"

"No. I don't think so."

"Yeah. Neither do I. But she's one of us and no one's been caught."

"What does that mean?"

"It means the killers had permission."

Marie caught her breath. *Permission.* "Government? Mullahs?"

"Yeah. Someone."

Marie looked at a chip of peeling, blue paint. "Yeah."

"Call me when you leave downtown."

"I will."

Marie snapped the phone shut, but it chirped before she had a chance to slide it back into its little yellow pouch.

"Yeah, Dave."

"Margaret and I are flying down this afternoon."

"What?" Marie stepped back against the wall. "Why? It can't affect us, right? Not in Shehktan."

"It might, Marie. I need to assess the situation. Figure out what all this means. I'm going to meet with some of the other heads of NGOs. We're staying at the guesthouse. We'll arrive this afternoon."

"You got a flight?"

"We called. They added us to the Faizabad leg. We're leaving in about two hours. Security, you know."

"Yeah, they're good that way." Marie envisioned the small white King Air that served aid workers in remote locations across the country; noncommercial, nonprofit, and invaluable. "You're coming to the guesthouse?"

"Yeah."

Of course, it made sense. This was a crisis. There would be meetings. People who knew things would collect information, talk to one another, and assess the situation. Was this a new normal or an outlier? Was it personal or random? Did the Afghan government or the religious leaders sanction the killing? And if they did, had they called for more? The foreign community would have to figure all that out. The leaders would make decisions. Of course Dave would come.

Marie nodded. "Okay. I'll see you later. Travel safe."

"Thanks."

Marie slid her phone back into its yellow pouch. She looked up at

Fawad. "Mr. Dave and his wife are coming to Kabul." She didn't say when.

The young man nodded, but said nothing.

Marie bristled. Fawad probably thought the married couple was coming down to look after the poor single women. "He has work to do here."

Fawad nodded again, but still said nothing.

"Okay, let's see what we can get done."

Marie walked from desk to desk, her stack of project papers in her hand, Fawad beside her. They walked into and out of dingy offices with threadbare, dust-and-tea-stained carpets, spring-shot sofas with blackened armrests, and Afghan men with thick beards and creased, poorly fitting suits. Marie explained her project over and over, presented her papers for stamps and signatures, and counted on Fawad to understand the next steps.

2

Finally, just before the government closed for the weekend, Marie and Fawad reached the last necessary office. A large, gold-trimmed sign marked the door. Inside, an overweight, middle-aged Afghan government minister sat behind a huge, dark brown desk, a cigarette limp between his fingertips.

The man took Marie's sheaf of papers, carelessly waved it in the air, and demanded, "Why are you working in the north? You should do a project in Kandahar. Our women there need help. You should go there and help them."

Marie stiffened. She felt her shoulders and neck lock. Was this a game? A joke? She had no idea. She thought about the woman killed. *Does he know?*

She thought about Kandahar, just across the border with Pakistan. Home of the Taliban. Outside real government control. Kandahar, where aid workers disappeared in broad daylight. Marie lived on the far side of a mountain range that cut the country and once divided its disparate tribes. If her town, Shehktan, wasn't held together by the government, it would be chaos. It would be like Kandahar.

The man in the big chair behind the big desk scowled. "Why should I approve this? You should work in Kandahar. Our women need help."

Marie looked down at the carpet. She searched for wisdom, prayed. *Is he serious?* She had all the stamps and signatures she needed except this one man's. In that moment, she chose a response. She forced a smile and looked into the man's bearded face. "Ah, Saeb, I can't go to Kandahar."

The man roared. "Why not?"

Fawad hung his head.

Marie looked across the room through another set of broken Venetian blinds. She lightened her voice even further. "They would steal me."

Marie knew the word for "kidnap," but had chosen "steal" instead. She was looking for humor and praying she would find it.

The big man scowled.

Marie waited.

Suddenly, he tilted his head back and laughed. He laughed hard and deep. He laughed from the pit of his stomach and the room rocked. Fawad jumped. Marie's legs relaxed.

The big man ripped open a drawer. He pulled a stamp and ink pad from the darkness and slammed them against the surface of his desk. He flipped the ink pad open, jammed the stamp against it, and in one violent stroke, smashed the stamp onto Marie's document. He pulled a silver pen from a wooden stand and signed the page with a flourish.

Marie breathed.

The big man stood, pushing his chair backward until it hit the wall behind him. In four quick strides, he stepped in front of Marie.

She tried not to flinch, but failed.

If the man noticed, he said nothing. Instead, he shoved the approved project documents toward Marie with his left hand and stretched forth his right to shake hers.

Marie reached for the papers, but he didn't release them. She lifted her right hand, bracing herself.

The big man engulfed it, squeezed too hard, and congratulated her on her approved project. Then he released the papers into her left hand with a firm warning. "But they may steal you in Shehktan, too. You cannot trust anyone."

Fawad winced.

The big man threw his hands in the air in mock exasperation. "This is Afghanistan!"

Rattled, Marie forced a smile. She placed her right hand over her heart, bowed slightly, wished the man God's protection, and carefully fled the room.

Once in the hallway, Marie leaned against the cool blue-gray wall and closed her eyes. The big man's warning clashing in her mind.

Fawad's words entered the swirl. "He is a very powerful man."

She whispered. "Yes, Fawad-jan. He's powerful." She stood up straight. "And our project's approved." She took a step toward the stairwell.

"Mari-jan. When will you return to Shehktan?"

Marie stopped and looked at Fawad, disturbed by his question. Instantly she imagined strangers waiting for her on the airport road. Dave's security lecture replayed in her mind: *"Never tell Afghans where you're planning to go—not the police, not our coworkers, not your friends. Even if they're completely trustworthy, they might tell someone else."* She chose her words carefully. "Fawad-jan, I will return to Shehktan soon."

The translator looked down at the gray floor.

Marie added. "My work here in Kabul is complete. Thank you for your assistance."

Fawad put his hand on his heart and nodded.

Marie would say no more.

The two walked down the concrete stairwell and stepped into a wide, tiled hall. Marie found a small, metal table inside the building's doorway. She dropped her backpack on it. "I have some calls to make, then we'll leave."

Fawad nodded.

Marie slipped the now complete papers into a plastic folder inside her backpack and pulled her cell phone back out to call Dave. She scrolled through the contacts, selected Dave, and pushed the call button. "Hey. It's me, Marie."

"Everything all right?"

"Yeah. We got all the approvals."

"You're kidding."

"Nope. All the stamps and signatures required. Everything's set."

"How did you do that? I mean, it usually takes me several days."

"It's easier for a woman, especially one who speaks Dari," she said lightly. They'd been over this before. Only this time the evidence was on her side.

Dave didn't agree, but then he'd never been a foreign woman in Afghanistan. Marie knew that the Afghan men in their offices didn't see her the way they saw men. She wasn't competition. Instead, she was their guest: helpless and vulnerable, a woman who needed their guidance and protection. That was a role they could understand.

"Well. Congratulations," Dave said.

Marie thought she heard disappointment in Dave's voice. Originally, he had wanted to send his translator alone to get the approvals. Marie had argued, as she so often did when her understanding clashed with his. In this situation, she was sure she could get the approvals herself. Dave hadn't agreed with her, but in the end he consented to let her go if she took Fawad with her. She had agreed to the compromise.

Marie thanked Dave, even though he didn't sound sincere. Their relationship was a delicate balance on both sides. As NGO director, Dave was responsible for Marie's safety—a responsibility he took seriously enough to limit her movements when he thought it best. For her part, Marie recognized his authority but often chafed at his decision-making process. She had her own perspective on what was safe and appropriate and enough experience in-country to voice her opinions. This time, she'd been proven right. Still, she knew better than to rub it in.

She stood beside the hallway desk, cell phone in hand, and looked up at Fawad. His eyes were averted. She bit down hard, pressed her lips, and turned her face away.

"Where to now?" Dave asked, clearing the air.

"I'm going back to the guesthouse."

"Good. Be careful. Text me when you get there, okay?"

"Yep. I always do. When are you arriving?"

"We're on the runway. Plane's on its way. Should be in Kabul in an hour, guesthouse in two."

"Okay. Thanks."

Marie called Carolyn next.

"Hey Marie." Carolyn's voice was weary, but lighter, more measured.

"How you doing?"

"I'm okay. Chad and Casey got here about half an hour ago, so I've got company."

"Who are they?"

"New couple from Texas. Just arrived. They're going to live here in the guesthouse until they can set up their own home."

"Our guesthouse?"

"Yeah. Dave didn't tell you?"

Marie shrugged. She didn't have the energy for the naïveté, enthusiasm, and endless questions of those at the beginning of their Afghan journey. Still, they had arrived, and she would have to engage with them. "Well, good. I'm glad you're not alone."

"Yeah, and they have a little boy. Simon. He's adorable!"

"You know Dave and Margaret are on their way, right?"

"Where?"

"Kabul. The guesthouse."

"Now?"

"Yeah. They should be there in a couple hours."

"Why?"

Marie shrugged. "Meetings. You know."

"Does Dave think this could affect us in Shehktan?"

"Maybe. He's looking into it." Marie changed the subject. "Anyway, I'm glad you're not alone. How old's the boy?"

"He's two and a half, and into everything. I found some wooden puzzles, and we're playing with them."

"Do they know?"

"Yeah. Their coworkers met them at the airport. Told them on the way."

Marie looked over at Fawad. The man was staring through the wood framed glass door toward the enclosed garden beyond. "I'm glad you didn't have to tell them."

"Yeah, me too." Carolyn slipped into sarcasm. "Welcome to Kabul. We're on lockdown. One of our own has been killed on the street, but don't worry. You'll be safe here."

Marie sighed. "We're completely safe until the moment we're not." *The problem is*, she thought, *sometimes you don't recognize the moment until it's too late.* "Listen, I'm leaving downtown. I should be back there in about forty minutes."

"Be safe."

"Will do. See ya."

She didn't tell Carolyn that she was planning to stop at the Internet café before she went back to the guesthouse. Marie knew her friend would argue and so would Fawad. She didn't want to debate it. There was no Internet at the guesthouse and she wanted to connect with her friends and family back in America. She knew they would panic when they woke up and read the news.

Marie checked her clothes, made sure her brown and gold scarf was draped properly around her head and shoulders. She didn't want to be fidgeting with her stuff when she needed to pay attention to the Afghan street.

Fawad pushed the double doors of the building open, stepped out onto a concrete patio, and walked down a short flight of steps and onto a concrete walkway lined with red rosebushes. Marie followed. They walked to a guardhouse where three Kalashnikov-wielding uniformed men waited with a notebook that contained their names and signatures. Marie nodded at the guards, looked at their guns, and felt a sharp twist of tension. She turned away and left Fawad to sign the book and chat with the men.

She stepped toward a dark shipping container, just to the right of the gate. She pulled the cloth curtain aside, leaned in, and called into the darkness. "*Salaam alaikum,* Missus. Peace be upon you."

A middle-aged woman called back, "Walaykum salaam, my friend." She was wearing an orange-and-yellow headscarf, brown jacket and matching skirt, with black lightweight trousers beneath. She stepped up to Marie, clasped her hands, and kissed both her cheeks. "Are you leaving?"

"Yes, our work is finished. We must leave now. Say hello to your family for me."

"Yes, yes. Come to my house. What kind of food do you like? I will make you lunch."

Marie laughed. She'd only met the woman in the morning when she'd stepped inside the booth to be searched. They had laughed and teased each other. Now, they acted like old friends. "I'll visit you when I come back to Kabul."

The woman smiled broadly. "Come. We will drink tea and share stories."

Marie released the woman's hands and leaned back into the sunlight.

She offered a common good-bye. "*Pahno ba khuda.* Hide in God."
The woman responded. "*Khuda hafez.* Be safe in God."

Marie turned, glanced at Fawad, nodded, and waited for him to open the gate to the Kabul street. The two stepped through and let the gate close behind them. Instantly, the muscles in Marie's hips and around her knees pulled tight. She drew a deep breath into her abdomen and took the measure of the street. Two dark Toyotas were parked in front of a wall. Four men walked from the left, toward them. They weren't together. Three wore ill-fitting counterfeit suits and pointy-toed shoes. The fourth wore a neatly pressed khaki shalvar kameez, with a black suit jacket over the knee-length shirt. He carried a black faux-leather computer bag in his hand. Marie studied the bag. *A laptop?* To the right, another half dozen men, similarly dressed and equally alone, dotted the sidewalk. She focused her breath. *Inhale, exhale.*

Across the street, two bearded men in suits walked toward the gate of a different government office. The men stopped to purchase a newspaper from a boy-vendor. In the distance, several other men walked toward the white-and-blue barricade that blocked the entrance into the street. Six Afghan police officers in dark gray uniforms with guns holstered stood around the barricade.

Marie breathed easily. The scene was normal. All was well. She followed Fawad toward the barricade. "I'll take a taxi back to Cart'e Seh."

Fawad nodded, then lowered his head slightly. "We should hire a driver for you. You shouldn't take a regular taxi."

Marie shrugged, her stomach twisting at his advice.

Beyond the barricade, the Kabul street was thick with bright yellow taxis. All private vehicles, used Toyota Corollas, or old Russian sedans, each one owned by a single family. There was no radio network linking the taxis, no central dispatch, just fathers and brothers driving the streets, picking up passengers, and dropping them at their destinations. To most, Marie was a guest, a woman to be protected and delivered safely.

Of course, Marie knew kidnapping was always a very real threat, even in Kabul, but it usually wasn't random. She'd been to the security trainings. She'd paid attention. Usually, when they take you, it's because they've watched you, tracked your movements, paid your staff for information, and grabbed you. It's not because you were walking down a Kabul street or riding in a random taxi.

In Kabul, the taxi drivers were all just normal men. Some had been schoolteachers, some soldiers, some government officials. Others were simply returnees from Pakistan or Iran. They'd borrowed money from every family member they could tap to purchase their vehicle. They worked hard to pay off the debt and support their families. Virtually all the drivers she'd met had children, most of them in school. They might wake up in the middle of the night wondering how they could get more cash, but they weren't connected to the violent factions intent on destabilizing the country. They were just men trying to earn a living on the traffic-choked streets of Kabul. Marie reasoned her way back to confidence. *I can trust them.*

Professional drivers were different. They were connected and accustomed to making a lot of money off foreigners. They could easily sell her to the highest bidder. Those men, Marie didn't trust. Still, she thanked Fawad for his advice.

Marie waited on the corner while Fawad waded into traffic. She looked down, and then behind her at a row of street vendors, mostly boys, surrounded by their newspapers and posters of military and religious heroes. The boys watched her silently, their eyes giving nothing away.

Marie stood still, her knees and hips locked.

Men and women, walking down the street, stepped around her. She tried not to watch them, pretending an ease she didn't feel. It was a chilly late October day, and some of the men wore lightweight wool blankets around their shoulders, their hands folded behind their backs. Marie peered into their folded hands as they passed: empty. Other men wore suit jackets or windbreakers over their shalvar kameezes or Western trousers, their hands swinging freely. These were easier to see. Nothing hidden.

Every man and boy on the street stared at her. Marie looked into the face of each, the memory of the morning's phone call fresh in her mind. She forced her jaw unlocked and waited.

An old Russian Lada pulled to a stop in front of Fawad. Marie looked at the driver. He wore a light brown shalvar kameez with a khaki fisherman's vest and a black, brown, and white-checked man scarf around his neck. His hair was thick, black, and curly. His close cut black beard was edged with gray. He was probably forty, no more. Marie felt a wave of nausea. She would not have chosen him.

Fawad spoke to the taxi driver, then waved toward Marie. He gave her the price and she nodded. He opened the back door and waited. Marie slid onto the red-and-black carpet-covered backseat and muttered a muted *salaam*. Fawad forced the creaking door shut and walked away.

3

Marie pushed the door locks down as the driver pulled the old taxi back into the thick traffic. She watched the man through the rearview mirror uneasily. She wondered if he knew what had happened that morning, but imagined he did. News travels quickly in Kabul. She wondered how he felt about it, what he thought. He said nothing.

She looked out the window and swept her eyes across the men

staring at her from the street and passing vehicles. She wondered if they were staring more than usual but tried to talk herself down. *No. It's Afghanistan. Men stare. Don't worry; it's normal.* But the tension across her shoulders remained.

She saw a group of men standing at an intersection, lightweight wool blankets wrapped around their shoulders, hands hidden behind their backs. She wished they would drop their hands—prove they were safe—but they didn't.

The tension in her shoulders spread to her neck. She looked from one watching face to the next, silently asking, *Are you the one? Or you? Will you try to kill me?* The back of her throat filled with acid, mixing with bitter Kabul exhaust fumes.

The driver turned down a double-walled street. Pallet-sized boxes, filled with dirt and rock, were stacked along the road. Behind them rose a high wall, crowned with concertina wire and punctuated by guard towers with high-powered machine guns. Two tan-colored armored vehicles and a jeep disappeared through a gate in the wall. The proximity of the American embassy compound made her nervous.

The driver turned onto another traffic-clogged road. The shops, filled with aluminum cooking pots, bright blue, red, and green plastics, electrical supplies, and cell phones, were all filled with men. Everywhere Afghan men watched her pass, and the question returned. *Are you the one?*

A woman in a light-blue, all-encompassing burqa caught Marie's attention. The woman held a large, brown, flowered thermos in her hand and haggled with a gray-bearded shopkeeper through the woven screen over her eyes. Marie glared at the man. *Give her her price!*

She looked back at the silent driver in the rearview mirror. Did he approve? Condemn? Was he safe? Suddenly she had to know. "Did you hear about the shooting this morning?"

The man shrugged. "She must have done something wrong."

Wrong? Really? Marie didn't believe the driver's interpretation. She turned away from the mirror, staring out the window.

They drove around a paved circle with green and yellow melons heaped into small hills—so bright, and so soft that Marie smiled a little, despite her tension. They turned along a wide, crowded road, and Marie saw the outline of a high-priced Western-style hotel on a rocky brown and black perch. *A target,* she thought. They drove past glass-faced shops, two story shopping plazas, and the wooden booths of bright tin exhaust pipe and heater sellers. Marie watched it all.

Finally, they turned down a wide paved street just blocks from Marie's guesthouse. She told the driver to stop in front of an Internet café, paid him the equivalent of three dollars, then hesitated. The driver waited silently while Marie formed her question. "Where was the foreigner killed?"

The driver motioned toward the street in front of them. "Two roads ahead."

"On this street?" It seemed too busy, too public for such a thing to happen.

The driver shook his head. "Four gates to the left."

Marie pictured the road: wide, wall-lined, and quiet. Just like the roads that led to her guesthouse. She steadied her breath and stepped out onto the Kabul street.

Marie hopped over a deep, narrow culvert filled with acrid city waste, then crossed a chipped, light-brown tiled sidewalk and pushed a glass door open. The chatter inside the Internet café immediately stopped. Marie swept her eyes past small groups of staring Afghan teenage boys. A harsh rebuke rose up from the pit of her stomach, but she ground her teeth against the words. *Boys,* she reminded herself. *Just boys.*

Marie picked up a ticket from a young boy behind a scratched wooden desk. She thanked him, then sat down on an upholstered black flowered couch while the teenagers watched her silently. The tension pulled her joints tight. *Just boys.*

She pulled her laptop from her backpack, and within minutes, she was connected. She logged onto her webmail server and began reading. Each email was the same as the previous; just the barest facts, the ones she already knew. Still, she read them all, then checked the news feeds.

Finally, she started writing. She wrote several emails; the first to Debbie, her closest friend in America. The woman would still be sleeping, but she'd read the news as soon as she woke up, and Marie wanted her to find her own reassuring message at the same time.

Dear Debbie,
I'm fine. Don't worry. I'll write more later. I love you.
Marie

She sent the second email.

Dear Mom,
I imagine you and Dad have already heard the news this morning. If you haven't, you will soon enough. Don't worry. I'm fine. Everything's okay here. I'll write you later when I have more time.
Love, Marie

The third email went out to a group of friends back in the States: people who regularly prayed for her, for the people of Afghanistan, and for the work she was doing.

Dear Friends,
You may have heard that a foreign aid worker was killed in Kabul today. I'm sad to say it's true. Please pray for her family. Please also pray for the rest of the foreign community. Pray for wisdom as we try to figure out what all this means. Pray for our security and peace.
Thanks,
Marie

When she finished typing, Marie looked around at the teenagers still huddled behind their computer screens—they'd given up staring at her. She shut down her laptop and slid it into her backpack. When she tried to stand, her knees wouldn't bend. She groaned softly, pushed her feet forward and backward, rubbed her bones, and finally stood up. Her hips ached. She paid the boy at the chipped, wooden desk without speaking, pushed open the glass door, and stepped out onto the sidewalk. She looked up, down, and across the street, measuring the scene before she walked into it.

Yellow taxis, overstuffed buses, and dusty cars rolled past, their occupants staring expressionless at her. A tan dog slept curled next to the building beside her. A dozen or more men of various ages rode bicycles between the street and the culvert. Each turned to stare. There were no other women.

Marie looked up the street. There, in the middle of the intersection, an Afghan policeman with a holstered weapon stood stock-still, his red traffic paddle hanging at his side as he traced her body with his eyes, despite her culturally appropriate clothing. She growled. A blue Toyota Corolla ground to a halt at the officer's knee, and he spun around, slamming his traffic paddle on the hood of the car and yelling into the windshield.

"Hah!" Marie snarled at him. Gone was her usual respectful demeanor. "Pay attention to your job!" Neither could hear the other's words over the distance and the rumble of traffic.

Marie locked her jaw and walked quickly across the street in front of her. On the other side, she saw an Afghan man standing on the edge of a dusty vacant lot. She studied him with narrowed eyes. He wore a long khaki shirt, matching baggy pants, plastic sandals, and a lightweight blanket wrapped around his shoulders. He held his hands behind his back and watched her. He didn't move.

Marie felt the hard edge of rage twist her stomach. She glared. *Are you the one?* When he didn't look away, Marie locked her fists, furrowed her brow, and stared as fiercely as she could, as if willing him to hear her thoughts. *What have I done to you?* Her stare, the stare of a woman was aggressive, violent, and deeply inappropriate. Still, the man didn't move. He continued to stand, stock-still and staring, his hands hidden behind his back.

All at once, the morning's terrifying events and the rage and fear with which she viewed the men in the street came together in one teeming mass in Marie's stomach. Something within her snapped. She ground her teeth at the stranger, this staring man on the edge of the dusty lot who had become the object of all her anger. Seething, she jumped over the waste-filled culvert that separated her from the lot, eyes locked on the man, who was now only twenty feet away and still didn't move. Marie planted her feet and squared her shoulders. Then she shouted at him. "What? What do you want?"

The man stepped back, shock on his face. He swung his hands forward, palms outward, empty. He waved them as if to say, "No, no." He stammered a moment, then finally shrugged his shoulders and said only, "You're beautiful. Forgive me. You're beautiful." He let his empty hands fall to his sides.

Marie stood stunned—stunned at his words, at the inappropriateness of her challenge, at the depth of her rage. In a flash, she realized she'd been looking at every man on the street as her enemy: the policeman, the taxi driver, the bearded man who haggled with the woman in the blue burqa. In fact, she had hated them. The wild intensity of the emotions she'd fought to reason away shocked her into bitter realization. She had looked at this man, this stranger on this street, with absolute and pure hatred, and she'd picked a fight with him.

A woman had been brutally killed, a foreigner, protected only by her headscarf and the goodwill of her neighbors—just like Marie—and Marie was responding with hatred. She wanted judgment, justice, retribution. She wanted her own voice. She wanted to hold an entire people guilty and condemn them all. She wanted to shake her fists at all of Afghanistan and shout, "How dare you! How dare you!" Yet how dare *she*. Responding to violence with rage, she had hated this man, one of her neighbors—the very people she had come to serve. The incongruity shamed her.

Marie felt the raw energy of blind rage melt from her muscles, leaving only weakness and a deep sense of failure. She recognized the intense darkness that had enveloped her soul, and it both sickened and frightened her. She stood, defeated, in a dusty, vacant lot on the backside of the world.

She shook her head, looked down, and turned away. *You're beautiful. Forgive me. You're beautiful.* His words echoed in her ears, shaming her.

She left the man, still standing amid the rock and dust and weeds, and walked toward her guesthouse, tears flowing over her cheeks. She wiped them away as best she could, but they wouldn't stop. A lone man walking past, gray-bearded and stooped, saw her tears and looked away.

At the corner, she turned onto a wide, unpaved, wall-lined road. One block ahead, the road abutted a traffic-clogged paved street. Just before the street, a row of wooden shacks stood perched on the edge of a deep culvert. Marie saw the dark red carcass of a fat-bottomed Afghan sheep hanging from a metal hook in front of one of the shacks. Beside the carcass, a meat seller and his customer turned to stare at her. Marie looked away. Her own guesthouse gate lay between herself and the carcass.

She walked past three wooden gates, then stepped up to a large, unmarked, gray, double gate. She took a deep breath, dried her face with her scarf, and rang the bell.

"*Balé?*"

She heard the soft voice of the guesthouse's day guard through the metal gate. "It's Mari-jan."

Immediately, the gate swung open. "Mari-jan. Welcome." The guard smiled.

Marie looked into his bearded face.

He saw her swollen eyes, recognized recent tears, and politely looked away. "Mari-jan. Welcome. Come, come. There are bad men on the street. Come."

Marie placed her hand on her heart and stepped inside the large compound. The soft scent of red roses and sweet mulberries caressed the ache in her head. She breathed. *Safe.*

The guard, a middle-aged, tall, bearded man with sharp, angular features broke into her quiet. "Mari-jan, you are well? You have had success?"

Marie nodded. She liked this guard. She had once seen him reading a small, green, Dari New Testament and thought he might be a brother, a Jesus-follower, but she'd never asked. "Yes. Yes. We have found success. Our project is approved."

"Congratulations. God is good."

Marie nodded. *Yes. God is good.* The shock of her actions on the street still shamed her heart. *I'm not, but He is.* She looked up at the large, one-story whitewashed mud-brick building on the right side of the compound. Though the thick curtains behind the wide glass windows were drawn against the midday sun, she imagined Carolyn and the new family inside. "Nazanin?" she asked, using her friend's Afghan name with the guard.

"Yes. In the big house. A family has arrived." The guard dropped his voice. "Mari-jan. You are well? You have become sad?"

Marie looked into his face. "Coco-jan, Uncle, my heart has become sad but I am well. Thanks be to God."

He pressed his hand to his chest. *"Saber."* Wait. Be patient.

Marie knew that was the word spoken to one who is grieving a loss. *He must think I knew her, the woman killed.* She felt the sting of guilt. *Still, yes, there's a loss.* She thought of the man she'd yelled at and the boys in the Internet café. She thought of Fawad chiding her on the street and the big man in the last office with the rocking laughter and dark warning. She thought of Carolyn, giddy in the glow of young love, talking about leaving Shehktan. She took a deep breath. *Yes. There's a loss. Something, but I don't have any idea what it is. None of this.* She thanked the guard for his kindness, then added, "I have become tired. With your permission?"

The guard immediately stepped back, wished Marie a good rest, and retreated through a doorway along the right side of the compound. Marie watched him disappear into deep shadows.

When he was gone, she walked quickly across the compound, between the rosebush-edged main house on the right and the row of storage rooms on the left. Just past the mulberry tree, she stepped onto a raised, hard-mud platform that faced another, smaller, mudbaked brick building, this one built against the back wall of the compound.

Through the open curtains of the front room, Marie could see white walls, a dark gray television screen, and a five-gallon water canister on top of a white plastic stand. Otherwise, the room was empty. She felt a soft wave of relief wash over her. She didn't want to see anyone, not Carolyn, and certainly not a brand-new couple with a two-and-a-half-year-old full of energy and need. She just wanted to catch her breath.

Prying off her sandals at the door, Marie stepped into a long, narrow hall and felt the cool of the deeply shaded space. She unlocked the door to her temporary room and collapsed onto the bed.

Thoughts and images tumbled within her. *A woman killed. This is Afghanistan. No place is safe. You're beautiful. Lockdown. When are you going back to Shehktan?* She sat up, found her phone, and texted Carolyn. "At guesthouse. Need rest. Will see you soon." She texted Dave. "At guesthouse." She turned her phone off, closed her eyes, and buried her face in the pillow. The clashing images immediately returned. She pushed them away. *Focus,* she thought. *Focus!* She turned her attention outward.

A child cried from the street beyond the wall; a dog barked, growled, and stopped; plates clacked against each other; she breathed; a soft, rhythmic thud sounded, then paused and began again. Marie imagined the scene beyond the wall. She pictured a woman with a green and pink scarf tied bandanna-style around the back of her head, two pink-flowered sleeves pushed up to her elbows, a thin stick in her hand, beating the dust out of a red cotton mat. Such a familiar activity—a woman cleaning her home. The muscles in Marie's legs softened. Her breath deepened.

She rolled over and studied the blue-and-white checked fabric stretched across the ceiling. She followed a seam that ran parallel to the far wall. At the corner the fabric folded neatly against the white-painted mud-brick wall. Marie studied the fold and imagined an Afghan man with a scarf tied around his waist, pulling the fabric into the corner. *An Afghan man,* she thought. *A father, perhaps.* She tried to figure out how he'd attached the fabric so tightly, so neatly.

The soft, rhythmic thudding continued. She thought about the space between the ceiling fabric and the hay-covered wooden limbs that supported the mud roof. She imagined spiders and tiny lizards living beyond the soft ceiling—a whole ecosystem separated from her by a thin sheet of cheap fabric.

Her hips relaxed against the soft mattress. *Look around. Listen. This is where you are, where you want to be.* Her head rolled gently against the pillow.

She followed a set of yellow stains that ran down from one corner of the ceiling. The roof had leaked, but it was some time before. Again, she imagined a scene: two men, one on the ground and the other on the roof, both covered in mud. One filled a bucket, the other lifted it on a rope and spread its contents across the roof. Marie thought of her own house and the older man with his son who had re-mudded her roof the year before. She had watched the bucket rise and fall through a gap in the curtain, and when the men were finished and gone, she'd climbed the wooden ladder to see their work. *Shehktan. Home.*

Her heart soothed at the images of a less hostile Afghanistan, Marie rubbed the fine Kabuli dust from her eyelashes. She looked at the white, sheer curtains covering the window beside her and the heavy, yellow drapes hooked to metal loops encircling a bronze-colored curtain rod. The beehive-shaped cap on one end was loose and canted. The cap on the other end was missing.

A small anonymous plaque hung slightly crooked on a naked nail fixed beside the window. She studied its tiny clouds and shafts of sunlight pouring over a wheat field. She tried to make out the words, but they were too far away. She rolled over, swung her feet off the bed, sat up straight, and leaned toward the wall. The title was simply "God's Promise." She lifted the little plaque off its nail and read the first sentence aloud:

God didn't promise days without pain.

Marie shut her eyes against a sudden rush of tears. An image appeared: a foreign woman walking, scarved and alone, down a Kabul street. A sudden rush of gunfire . . . a cell phone ringing . . . a blue room with venetian blinds, three mismatched desks, and watching Afghan men. She pressed her finger and thumb into her closed eye sockets, and the tears withdrew. She opened her eyes and read on:

Laughter without sorrow or sun without rain,
But God did promise strength for the day,
Comfort for the tears and a light for the way.

Strength? Where? She saw herself standing in front of the big man in the final office, the one who had mocked her, and her tension returned. She saw the boys in the Internet café and the policeman smacking the hood of the car. She saw the lone man, blanket-wrapped in the vacant lot. She looked back down at the plaque. She felt the muscles pull her hips and knees tight.

And for all who believe in his kingdom above
He answers their faith with everlasting love.

Platitudes, she thought. Tossing the plaque down on her bed, she saw the inscription in gray, swirling font on its bottom corner. Isaiah 43:2. A verse she'd memorized years before. "When you pass through the waters, I will be with you; and through the rivers, they shall not overwhelm you; when you walk through fire you shall not be burned, and the flame shall not consume you."

"Hah!" She said out loud. "I'd rather be dry and cool."

She unzipped her backpack, pulled out a yellow, spiral-bound notebook, and pressed her pen hard against the page.

October 2008
Shot dead walking down a street. When did that become acceptable? When did that become normal? I want to find out what the woman did wrong so I can make sure I don't do anything like it. I want to believe she did something wrong. Then the killing would make sense. That's foolish. It doesn't matter what she did. Killing doesn't ever make sense. And there's no guarantees here. Do everything right and nothing bad will happen? It doesn't work that way. Not in Afghanistan. Not in America. We're not in control.

She read what she had written. *Angry. I'm angry. At what? At the woman for getting killed. At the Afghans for killing her. At myself for being afraid.* She closed her eyes and spoke the next thoughts aloud. "I'm angry for being angry."

She returned to her journal. This time, she wrote a prayer. "Lord God, I'm here."

Behind those simple words, all the emotions of the day lay naked and aching. Dropping her pen, she pulled the white sheer away from the window. A skinny calico cat lay across the concrete walkway of the

40

enclosed yard. Marie called to it through the window. The cat jerked its head up, looked around and lay back down.

Marie closed her notebook and went outside into the cool afternoon air. She scooped the cat up in her hands and pressed the animal against her chest. The cat buried its head in Marie's neck and purred. Marie rubbed the back of its head between her thumb and forefinger. For a moment, she was lost in the sweetness of the cat's affection.

4

"Hey. That was a short nap." Carolyn was standing in the doorway of the main house in Western-style jeans and an orange and white T-shirt. Her brown hair hung loose over her shoulders. Marie was still wearing her long, brown Afghan coat and the brown and gold scarf she'd worn all morning.

"Yeah. I just wanted to close my eyes for a few minutes."

"Come on in and have some tea. Meet Chad and Casey. Little Simon's taking a nap, but you can meet him later."

Marie swallowed. She wasn't ready to meet the newcomers. But Carolyn, she did want to see her. "Do we have decaf?"

"Yeah. I'll make you some."

Marie nodded. "Let me change my clothes and I'll be over in a minute." She kissed the back of the cat's head, then put it down on the sidewalk.

Inside, she pulled her scarf from her head and shoulders, shook it twice, and draped it over a hook mounted on the wall. She unbuttoned her coat, shook it as well, and hung it on the same hook. Her eyes fell across her lightweight, navy skirt, the pair of thin, pajama-style tombones she wore underneath, and onto her dust-caked toes. *Kabuli dust,* she thought. *Just like Shehktan.*

In the white-tiled bathroom, she turned on a low tap and looked up at the small, round, red light on the electric hot water canister, its gauge measuring warmth. She slipped her foot under the flow. Warm water swept away the dust caked between her toes and around her ankles. She smiled. *Electric hot water heaters. One Kabuli benefit.*

Back in her room she slipped into a pair of sun-faded denim. The jeans made her feel normal, American, except they were too big. They fit once, on her last trip to the States when she'd bought them. Now, they needed a belt she didn't have. Too many fights with stomach bugs. *Central Asian weight loss program.* She smiled to herself. *At least they weren't tombones and a skirt.*

She didn't bother to change her long sleeved, light blue cotton shirt. She liked the fine Afghan embroidery around the yoke and sleeve cuffs, and besides, it was comfortable.

Marie crossed the yard and pushed open the door to the guesthouse. The kitchen was well-equipped: a U-shaped blue painted concrete counter, a real sink with hot and cold running water, a red painted concrete floor with a drain in the middle of it, and a small gas range and oven combination. Next to the door, a refrigerator hummed unevenly. On the floor beside the refrigerator sat a small voltage regulator, its relays smacking and sliding like roller skates on a wooden floor. On the other side of the door stood a small, wooden table covered with jars of Iranian jam, raw Afghan honey, Western peanut butter, and a thick towel hiding the broken fragments of the morning's fresh bread.

Carolyn was filling Marie's metal French press with boiling water from an aluminum kettle. The smell of brewing coffee mixed with natural gas, the sulfur of a match, and the damp scent of onions cooked hours before.

"Hey. I'm glad you're here. It's been a crazy day. You were successful? You can start the project?"

Marie hesitated, Carolyn's words echoing in her mind. With a shock, she heard the *you* in Carolyn's questions. *I thought it was our project. Are you leaving now?* She swallowed and looked around the room. "Yeah. It's done. We got everything."

"Thank God!" Carolyn put the half-empty kettle back on the gas stove top. She fit the strainer onto the French press and set it aside. "It's been crazy here. Chad and Casey arrived at about 10:00 a.m. Another couple brought them. They talked about a bunch of stuff and then left. Oh yeah, and we ate lunch. We have leftovers. Want some?"

A wave of nausea passed through Marie. "No, thanks. I'm not hungry. I'll eat later."

"Come on, you have to meet them. They're wonderful."

Marie followed Carolyn into a wide hallway lined with three large suitcases and two dull silver aluminum trunks. The trunks were covered with a thick film of Afghan dust. The suitcases were dust streaked but otherwise clean. The two women stepped into the sitting room. As promised, Chad and Casey were there, sitting on a sage green, 1950s-style couch.

Chad stood as soon as they entered. Casey rose more slowly. They looked for all the world like the perfect couple. Chad—tall, broad-shouldered and narrow-hipped. His hair, close-cropped and thickly curled, a beard and mustache, soft and neatly trimmed. He wore a short-sleeved orange-and-red plaid shirt, untucked over standard, well-worn blue jeans, the kind of sloppy, I'm-not-quite-clean-ness Afghans abhor. The bottom hem of his jeans curled over white socked feet. Marie smiled at the socks. *It's too early for socks. Not winter yet.* She looked back into Chad's innocent face. *He'll learn. Soon enough.*

Casey was shorter, her head no higher than Chad's shoulder. She was thin, blonde, blue-eyed, and fair-skinned. She wore a snug dark-blue T-shirt over what looked like a white tank top, the hem of white longer than the hem of blue. Her jeans were dark and tight-fitting, her socks, blue-and-white striped with small green flowers.

Americans. Marie thought.

Carolyn introduced the couple to Marie. They shook hands and sat down.

Marie knew she'd have to push aside whatever anger or frustration she was struggling with. This young couple had just arrived. They needed to be welcomed. She swallowed hard and focused on the present. "You just got in?"

Casey answered. "Yeah. We flew in from Dubai to Kabul today." Her excitement shone through her obvious exhaustion. "We got to the guesthouse this morning. Can you believe it?"

Marie guessed the young woman wasn't talking about the flight anymore. "Yeah. It's hard. Afghanistan. Anything can happen."

Casey spoke quickly. "But things like that don't normally happen, do they?"

Marie wanted to change the conversation. "No. They don't. Where are you all from?"

Chad answered. "Texas. Austin."

Marie smiled.

Casey jumped in again. "You don't like Texas?"

Marie laughed out loud. She remembered another Texan she knew. He wore brown T-shirts with a gold Longhorn silkscreened across the chest. "Are you Aggies or Longhorns?" she asked.

Chad sat up straight. "LeTourneau, actually."

"Engineer?"

"Civil." He sat up straighter. "I'm joining a water project. Wells."

Casey jumped in, her pride in her husband evident. "People need clean water to live."

"Mmm." Marie nodded. "I'm glad you're passionate about the work you'll do here. That'll help."

"Help what?"

Marie thought about the long morning ride through the crowded streets. "Help you get through the hard times."

Casey looked down at the pile of plastic children's toys in the corner of the room, then back at Marie. "What are you doing here?"

"Project management. Development."

Casey nodded, but her eyes betrayed her incomprehension.

Marie explained. "Right now, we're starting a women's literacy project up in Shehktan. I'm managing it."

"Wow, that's so cool. Women's literacy. That's great. Where exactly is Shehktan—is it near Kabul?"

Marie smiled again. "Up in the north. It's a small city, less than a hundred thousand people. More like a big town with little half-hidden villages all around it. Most foreigners in Kabul have never heard of it."

"Oh, okay, it's rural. Do you like it?"

Marie nodded. "Yeah."

Carolyn walked into the room with a metal tray covered with a plate of chocolate cream-filled cookies from a local store, the aluminum French press, a small carton of milk, a coffee cup, and a spoon.

"We're so glad to be here. You won't believe how long it took us to get here. I don't mean the flight. I mean, we came on our survey trip two years ago. That's when we decided to live here. Two years. Simon had some medical problems, nothing serious, so we had to wait until he was healthy enough. Now he's good, so here we are at last. How long've you been here?"

Marie looked at Carolyn and realized they'd already traded stories. It was her turn. "I came in '02, five years ago, almost six."

"Wow, you've been here a long time. I'll bet you know everything. Like what's going on today—do you understand it all? Our friends, the ones who picked us up at the airport, have only been here two years. They don't know what's going on. They say it's crazy, never happens. How long did it take you to learn language, anyway? Was it hard? And what about Afghan friends? I don't even know where you live—do you live here in Kabul?"

Marie sifted through the shower of questions. She wondered if it was Casey's excitement or the jetlag that confused her.

Casey jumped back in before she could reply. "Oh yeah, you live in Shehktan. I'm sorry."

Marie smiled. She slid off the chair she'd first chosen and sat down on the floor in front of the low coffee table. She pulled the French press down in front of her and waited for the coffee to brew. She wanted that coffee. She looked up at Casey, then Chad, then over at Carolyn. She didn't know where to start. "I live in Shehktan with Carolyn. We share a house in town and work together. Yeah, I speak Dari pretty well, but I'm still learning." She wrapped her hands around the warm coffee press. "And yeah." She smiled. "I have Afghan friends. Couldn't live here without them. I'm just here in Kabul to get approval for our new project; then I'm going home."

"Home, America?" Casey bit into a cookie. "Or—"

Marie smiled and shook her head. "Home, as in Shehktan."

"Oh, right. I'm sorry, my head doesn't seem to be on straight. I'm so tired, and we're just so glad to be here."

"No worries." Marie pushed the French press plunger down slowly. She could see the grounds through the plastic window clouding below the filter, then settling.

Casey caught her breath and started again. "I'm so glad to meet you. I mean, you've been here for so long. I've got thousands of questions, I don't know where to start. What should I ask?"

Marie shrugged. "Listen, I've only been here for a few years, and anyway, you live in Kabul now. There are lots of other workers here in the city; you'll meet them—maybe tomorrow morning, at 'big church.' Some have been around since the Russians. Take your time."

Casey smiled. "Big church?"

"Yeah, there's a large community here, over a hundred from all over the world. Friday is church, and here in Kabul it's big. You'll see. I'm sure your friends will take you.

Marie tilted the French press and poured its contents into a heavy red coffee mug. She added a spoonful of sugar and a dollop of milk, stirred, sipped, and smiled. *Ah*, she thought. *Coffee.* She looked up at Casey. "Don't worry. You'll figure the rest out as you go along. For now, just relax and enjoy your first day in Afghanistan." She looked across the room at the curtains tightly closed against the afternoon sun.

As if reading her thoughts, Casey gave a short laugh. "Sure picked a great first day."

Marie turned and faced the newcomers. Despite their enthusiasm, they were uneasy, and they didn't know what to think about the day's events. *Do even I know what all this means?* "Hey. You can't think about everything all at once. Just take it one day at a time and trust the people around you. You'll see. Your coworkers will help you find your way." She hoped her words were reassuring.

Casey quieted for a couple of minutes. Enough time for Marie and Carolyn to catch up. Marie filled Carolyn in on the project. They would work that together. She started to explain the setup plan but caught a warning, a doubt in Carolyn's face. "What's wrong?"

Carolyn cut a glance at Chad and Casey, then looked down at her hands.

Marie knew something was up. She waited.

"I talked to Brad this morning," Carolyn said eventually, her voice lowered.

Marie took a sip of her coffee and sat back. *Brad.* Carolyn's guy. She glanced up at Chad and Casey, who were deep in their own conversation. Marie imagined that they already knew whatever Carolyn was about to tell her.

"Uh huh," Marie prompted.

"It's just that—you know, we decided we'll get married. I mean, were not officially engaged. But we're kind of pre-engaged. You know that."

Marie felt an ache spread across her lower back. She waited.

"It's just that—with things being crazy—and I'm leaving anyway . . ."

Carolyn's words sounded painfully familiar. Suddenly Marie was reminded of Sharon, the woman who'd first welcomed her to Afghanistan, the woman who'd taught her how to walk in Shehktan. Sharon in her burgundy scarf. She looked back at Carolyn. *What did she say?* Marie poured the rest of the coffee into her cup and watched the milk change its color, as if focusing on something else would delay the inevitable. But she knew what was coming.

Carolyn took a deep breath and burst out the news. "He wants me to leave sooner than planned."

Marie stared at Carolyn, seeing Sharon instead, standing in Marie's kitchen with her burgundy scarf wrapped around her head. *"I've been accepted into the master's program. I'm going home."* Marie pushed the memory away and focused on Carolyn. "Oh."

Carolyn was clearly uncomfortable. "Well, it's crazy right now. I mean, look what's happened."

Marie watched the liquid in her cup settle. "What do *you* want to do?"

The younger woman looked away, taking in the guesthouse room. "I don't know. I mean, I want to see if things with Brad can work out." She hesitated. "And—" she sighed. "I also want to do the literacy project. I want to do it all. Marry him. Stay in Shehktan. Everything."

Marie watched tears pool in Carolyn's eyes. "Have you made a decision?"

Carolyn nodded, and Marie's heart sank. *So it's done.* "Have you told him?"

Carolyn nodded again.

Marie shivered. She saw Sharon, climbing onto the little, white plane on the dustway in Shehktan. The little door closed and Sharon was gone. She straightened her back. Sharon's departure, so many years ago, had been hard—a howling, empty space—but she'd made it. Reclaimed her Afghan life and found her own way. She'd make it again. Marie's voice drifted, just barely steady. "Okay. So you leave." She shrugged.

Chad looked down at his hands. Casey's eyes jumped back and forth between the two women. Marie realized they were watching, listening. She gathered her strength.

"Carolyn. If that's what you want to do, then do it. It's fine. I'll be sad to see you go, but really, it's fine."

Carolyn wiped the tear from her cheek then looked back at Marie. "Really? It's okay?"

Marie forced a smile. The ache in her back spread into her stomach. "Carolyn. If this is what you want to do, then I support you. Sure." She stayed in the moment. Prayed. *Oh, God. What can I say?* She felt a thick heaviness stretch across the side of her head. She breathed, thought, and added, "Have you prayed about this? Do you have peace about it?"

Carolyn nodded immediately, but Marie doubted. Still, it was Carolyn's decision and she would do whatever she could to support her. Feeling the need for a little distance, Marie rose from the floor in front of the coffee table and retook the upholstered chair she'd first sat in. The tension in her body eased.

Carolyn cleared her throat and gave words to her concern. "So . . . I guess this means you'll have to start the project alone."

Marie shrugged. "I planned the work for the two of us. I'll re-plan it for one. Really. Don't worry about the project. Just work on leaving well."

Carolyn studied her hands, and Casey jumped in to the silence. "What does that mean? I mean, how do you leave the field well? You know, we left America and tried to do that well, but that's different, isn't it?"

Marie looked at Casey, grateful for her interruption. "Yeah, it's different. When we leave our lives back there, wherever 'there' is, we're going *to* something. We're off on a mission, a grand adventure. When we leave here, it's different. We love people here, and we're pretty sure we'll never see them again. And more than that, we've changed. We're part Afghan. Our hearts live in two places. We assume we'll return to our passport countries, but when we leave here, we don't know if we'll ever come back."

"So you're leaving a project, instead of leaving *for* one."

Marie looked over at Carolyn, then back at Casey. "We don't just leave projects here. We leave our homes." Carolyn nodded.

"So . . . what does leaving *here* well look like?" Casey asked.

Marie paused and thought about what she wanted Carolyn to hear.

"Leaving well means thinking about how you leave. Praying about who to say good-bye to, and how. It means celebrating the journey and releasing the people you love and work with to God. They're His anyway." Marie paused, but there was something else that felt important. "It also means not leaving any unfinished business or half-finished conversations. You don't want to get home and realize that you never talked with that Afghan friend about what's really important to you. You don't want to wake up in downtown America in the middle of the night thinking you've left part of your story unfinished."

Marie looked over at Carolyn. "Do you have time to say good-bye to your friends?"

Carolyn perked up. "Well, I don't know. I didn't tell him when I would leave. I thought with—well, with what happened, I thought maybe a week or two. But maybe I'll need more time. I'll have to think about that."

Marie swallowed hard, feeling the blood drain from her face. "Huh." *A week? Maybe two?* With Sharon, she'd had six weeks from her announcement to their last parting at the airfield, but others left more quickly and some just never returned from a trip out of country. Still, this was Carolyn, her housemate and coworker, her friend and companion.

Marie found the ground beneath her. The decision had been made. She had to accept it, support it. And anyway, this was not like Sharon's departure. Then, she'd been new in-country herself; she didn't have a network of friends. Now she did. Now it was different.

Carolyn watched as the frown line between Marie's eyes faded. "You know, lots of people are leaving already. With the news and the possibilities, it's just too much. I'm going back to Shehktan first. I'll pack and say good-bye, but it's time. I know it's time.

Marie nodded and tried to breathe. *Two weeks is a gift. Be grateful.*

Support her. "Okay," she said, both to Carolyn and to herself. "Well, don't worry about the project. I'll take care of all that. Just . . . you know, do what you have to do."

Carolyn relaxed. "Thank you."

There was a pause while they each collected their own thoughts. Then Chad leaned forward from the couch. "Marie?"

Marie tilted her head toward him and waited.

"What if you don't have time to say good-bye? What if you have to evacuate? Leave in a rush?"

Marie scraped the rim of the coffee cup with her fingernail. She shrugged. "You cry."

No one else spoke, so Marie went on. "If you have to evacuate like that, you just do it. You grab what you can and you run. There's certainly been enough of that here. For Afghans as well as foreigners. If you don't get to say good-bye . . . I don't know. I guess it breaks your heart. But I've never done it. I don't really know. There are plenty of people around here who do. Our coworkers, Dave and Margaret, will be here soon. They had to evacuate when the Taliban swept into Kabul city. They'll tell you about it." She paused, satisfied with her deflection.

Chad leaned back, looked up at the ceiling, and said, "I guess it's best to have an exit strategy."

Marie regarded him carefully. "An exit strategy for getting out? We all have evacuation plans. I've got three packing lists taped to the inside of a cabinet door in my home. One for fast evac, one for slow evac, and one for permanent move. Plus we have an evac plan: where to go, how to get there. That kind of stuff. Is that what you mean?"

Chad raised his eyebrows. He hadn't thought about an evacuation plan or packing lists. "No, I mean a strategy for starting over someplace else."

Marie shook her head. She couldn't help her next words sounding bitter, hard and sarcastic. "Go ahead, think of an exit strategy. Develop a plan for the next chapter of your life: where you're going to live, what kind of work you're going to do, who you'll hang out with, and where you'll go to church. Do it at the end of a long day of work, when the electricity's out, and you can't think two coherent thoughts in sequence. Yeah, it doesn't work. It takes all we've got just to live here. The best we can do is think about how to serve these people—how to love them well. If we do that, we've done a lot. The rest, we'll just have to figure out when we get there." She looked over at Carolyn. "You'll figure it out when you get there. You and Brad."

Carolyn shook her head. "Yeah, I don't want to think about all that now."

Chad sat up straight, wide-eyed. "Well then—how long are you planning to stay here? What's your commitment?"

Marie laughed. "My commitment is to stay as long as I can and, hopefully, not a minute longer."

Chad considered her answer. "Then where?"

Marie smiled. "My exit strategy?"

Chad nodded.

"I mean what I said. It's impossible to think about life beyond Afghanistan when you're busy just trying to breathe through the Afghan dust. Most of us are living one small crisis to the next in absolute exhaustion. We can't even begin to think beyond that."

Carolyn stepped in. "That's the thing—you can't live in both places. It's too hard. If our head's in America, we can't really deal with the crazy parts of being here."

Chad leaned forward. "That's why you have to leave so quickly?"

Carolyn studied her hands. "Yeah, I guess so."

The foursome heard a small cry from the other room, and Casey walked out.

Marie took the opportunity to exit. "Hey, Carolyn. Thanks for the coffee; I really needed that. Chad, I know it's the middle of the afternoon, but I'm exhausted. I have to rest. See you later."

But Casey met her in the doorway, a drowsy blond-haired boy in her arms. "Are you leaving? Oh, I want to know how you got here—how you came to Afghanistan."

Marie sighed, leaning against the wall. *Might as well get it over with.* She shifted a bit to include Chad and Carolyn in her view. "Yeah. We all have a story. Mine's pretty simple. Back in the days of the Taliban, I used to pray for Afghanistan almost every day. I got to know Afghans where I lived in the States, and so I prayed for their families, too. Things were horrible here then. Heartbreaking. When 9/11 happened, I just knew I wanted to get involved. I didn't know how, so I just kept praying. It was the pastor of the Afghan–Iranian fellowship in the States who encouraged me to come here. So I did."

"Wild. That's amazing. You knew Afghan believers before you came! And you've been here ever since?"

"Mostly . . . I went home for six months once . . . I needed a break . . . I try to get home for three months every couple of years. I just need the rest. I love Afghanistan, but it wears me out." Marie took a step toward the door. She wanted desperately to leave.

Casey still had questions. "So what do you do now?"

Marie looked at Carolyn with a pleading glance.

The younger woman picked up the cue. "We were doing teacher training out in the villages in Shehktan. We trained the teachers in every village that would let us. Well, not every village. Most villages don't have schools, and some didn't want the training, but others did. In Shehktan, in the north. Now we're starting a literacy program, plus we have some smaller projects in town."

"Wow! You've been out in the villages? Our NGO director said Chad might get out to some villages, but mostly he'll stay in Kabul." She kissed the forehead of the small boy in her arms. "I doubt I'll get out much at all."

Carolyn agreed and drew Casey into a detailed story about a village hidden deep in the mountains. Marie saw the gap and quietly fled the conversation, too tired for questions and old stories.

5

Marie returned to her room, to the blue and white ceiling, the sheer, white curtains, the yellow drapes, and her yellow notebook. She pulled the drapes closed, sat down on her bed, opened her journal, and looked down at the last sentence she'd written. "Lord God, I'm here."

It read like a statement, but she knew it had been a prayer. She knew what was behind it; a cry for help, a simple, poorly articulated cry for help. Marie rubbed her temples, then her eye sockets. Her back ached, her head throbbed. *Why am I thinking of Sharon? God, that was so hard—now Carolyn. A week? Two?* She shook her head, ground her teeth, and stared at the wall. *Carolyn?*

The small plaque with its simple message came into focus. She read the words again: "God didn't promise days without pain . . . But God did promise strength for the day . . . And for all who believe in his kingdom above, He answers their faith with everlasting love." *Really? Come on.*

Instantly, she felt an internal rebuke. She sat up straight, took a deep breath, and spoke out loud. "Okay. You're here. I get that. I'm certainly here." She heard the bitterness in her voice. "Okay. Okay." She nodded her head again. "I've been here before. I know what to do. I have to break this."

She began to write:

> Father, thank you for being here, too. Thank you for this room and this solitude. Thank you for getting me back safely from the ministry. Thank you for the Internet café and email. Thank you for my friends who are just now getting up in America. Who are just now reading my email and praying. Thank you for the cat on the sidewalk. Thank

you for Carolyn and her constant joy. For Brad, who loves her. Thank you for Chad and Casey and their delight in being here. Thank you for Sharon, who met me when I first arrived in Shehktan, when I was just as naïve and idealistic as Chad and Casey are today. Thank you for carrying me through the hard times that first winter without Sharon, when it was so cold and I was so alone.

Thank you for reminding me of why I'm here. For reminding me of what I'm doing. Thank you for the quiet of this room.

She paused, reread her list, and added:

Father, thank you for the people I'll meet through this next project. Thank you for all the stamps and signatures.

Marie began to weep, not loudly, but silently, just tears. She wrote through the blur.

Father, this is crazy. I don't even know how to pray. That woman was shot dead, right out on the street. I don't even know what to feel. I was looking at everyone as though they wanted to kill me. That's not right. Forgive me. I yelled at the man in the dust lot. I'm sorry. I don't even know why I did it. I just felt so angry. Please forgive me.

And now Carolyn.

She pushed that last thought aside. It was too much. She turned the page.

What happens tomorrow? What do I do? Where do I go?

She looked at the words she'd written. Out loud, she said, "How about 76-point font written across that white wall with directions in bold?" Instead, the idea that unfolded in her mind was a question she didn't expect. "What do you want?" The question was for her. Marie started writing again, first the question, then her answer.

Father, I want to get out of Kabul. I want to go home to Shehktan. I want to see my own guards, my dogs. I want to start this new project. I want to visit my Afghan friends. I want to sleep in my own bed. I want the nightmare of this day to go away. I want to wake up in the morning and find out it was all a false report. I want to believe, when I walk out on the Afghan street, that I'll be safe. I don't want to be afraid. I don't want to see some Afghan man and wonder if he's the one who will kill me. I want to be normal. I want to drink tea in my friends' houses and laugh. I haven't really laughed all day. I want to sing. I want to forget these tears.

She wiped her cheeks and threw the notebook like a Frisbee onto her open suitcase. It smacked against the red case and tumbled on top of the pile of clothes.

Marie picked up her water bottle, stepped into the hallway, and stopped. In her mind she saw hunting dogs leaping from their kennels, barking and howling into a wind-raked night, the scent of the storm in their nostrils. Suddenly the window at the far end of the hall caught her attention. She felt the weight of the water bottle in her hand and its cool metal outline. She imagined herself hurling it through the curtained window hard, like a pitch. She could imagine the soft thud of the metal against the curtain, then the glorious crashing of shattering glass. A magnificent sound. Satisfaction.

She leaned her head against the wall behind her, closed her eyes, and pressed her lips together. *God, what is that about?* Trembling, she opened her eyes and refocused. The cool, quiet hallway reappeared. She felt the water bottle in her hand. The urge to throw it was gone.

She pushed herself off the wall and took the last two steps into the small sitting room. A simple task. She had only to fill her water bottle. She stepped in front of the five-gallon clean water dispenser, unscrewed the cap on her bottle, placed its mouth under the valve, and caught her reflection in a mirror mounted on the wall behind the dispenser.

Shocked, she thought, *Are those my eyes?* She looked again, but whatever she saw the first time was gone. A wildness. A woundedness. Its trace left only in her memory like dogs running through dark woods, baying in the distance. She pressed the valve again. Clean water sloshed against the sides of the bottle. *Breathe.*

Marie returned to her temporary room and lay down on the bed, but didn't sleep. Instead, she listened to the noises outside. Two women were arguing from the far side of the wall, their voices high-pitched and harsh, but their words indecipherable. A child wailed. Horns beeped from the distance. An Afghan pounded on a nearby gate, paused, then pounded again. She studied the cracks on the wall and tried not to think.

A door slammed beyond the wall, a car door. The electronic doorbell on the gate chimed. More voices, one male, one female: Dave and Margaret. Marie groaned.

The voices drew closer, Margaret and Carolyn back and forth. Carolyn's sentences long yet rushed. Margaret's slower and brief. The door of her building creaked. The voices shifted into words.

"Maybe two weeks. I don't know." Carolyn, never one to wait, already telling Margaret her plans. The older woman, wise, patient, asking gentle questions. Carolyn responding, half-formed thoughts articulated so clearly one would assume she had considered everything carefully. Margaret would know better.

The wheels of a small suitcase scraped the doorjamb, and the voices muted again. The metal gate outside opened and closed. Another car door shut, a different vehicle. Dave was leaving for a meeting, Marie was sure. She imagined the scene. The men would sit on Western-style furniture, drink tea or decaf coffee, and trade information: security reports, conversations with the secret police as well as the uniformed police, and foreign-based security analysts, and even the reports of local Afghan friends. They would assess the situation and make decisions. Those decisions would affect her life and the lives of the women she'd come to love and serve. She clenched her jaw. *Afghanistan!*

Beyond the guesthouse, the news of the assassination splashed across the world scene. Reporters sketched an outline of the woman's life and filled it in with conjecture. Strangers from Northern Ireland, South Africa, Jordan—nearly every country in the world posted their comments. The woman killed was judged everything from an unqualified hero to a foolish and arrogant idiot.

The victim's family made arrangements to travel from Europe to bury their daughter in the one cemetery that welcomed the remains of non-Muslims. Meanwhile, members of the Kabul foreign community prepared for the funeral of another one of their own.

Afghans who benefited from the young woman's work wept in their homes. Others, strangers and those who hadn't benefited, pronounced their own judgments.

Marie thought about all of these things while she lay, curled on a bed in a Kabul guesthouse staring at a cracked white wall. Carolyn had told her that the foreign aid community in Kabul was already reacting to the killing. Those who had been planning to leave within a few months were already buying plane tickets, packing their things, and saying good-bye. Others, who had simply had enough, were making arrangements to depart. Some aid organizations were already sending mothers with their children back to their homelands.

The other foreigners in Kabul—diplomats, soldiers, mercenaries, and reconstruction professionals—lived behind concertina wire with concrete barricades and guards. Some traveled in armored convoys, their soft bodies shelled in Kevlar, M16 automatic weapons in their hands, and heavy boots on their feet. Others lived within the walled compounds of diplomatic missions, and former Marines and soldiers who had traded their enlistments for short-term lucrative contracts lived and worked embedded with uniformed military personnel.

Marie, her friends, and the woman who had been killed came from a very different community of foreigners, a vulnerable group. They were unarmed and unprotected aid workers. They lived among the people they served, beyond the wire. They spoke the languages of the Afghans and counted on their local neighbors to keep them safe.

Marie and others like her understood the contours of Afghan reality. They knew they lived in a war zone. They understood its rules: soldiers' convoys were fair game. Body-armored weapon carriers were occupiers, no different than the Russians who preceded them. It didn't matter if they were American or English, Croatian or Norwegian. They were all the same—foreign soldiers occupying their land. Even diplomatic missions could be attacked. High-profile Afghans and foreigners with governmental influence could be bombed. But not aid workers. Those were guests, apolitical, here to help. Those are the rules of war: there are combatants and there are noncombatants. At one time, the distinction had been clear, but in Afghanistan, that was all changing.

Marie recalled a party she'd attended in 2004 held in Kabul. A mixed lot from all over the world attended, but still, they were all aid workers: UN, World Vision, Mission East, ACTED. It was the UN workers who were most frustrated. A tall, thin French woman with a clipped accent that filled the room said, "The foreign soldiers are blurring the line. They're engaging in aid work." The reconstruction work itself had become part of the war effort, a battle to win the hearts and minds of the Afghan people. Marie heard again the woman's anger. "We've all become targets!"

The bright red cross or crescent painted on a hospital no longer protected it. The cauliflower blue-on-white logo of the United Nations emblem had become fair game. Any foreign national could be kidnapped and held as leverage against the political and military powers of their passport country. The old rules no longer applied.

Others at the party blamed the desperation of an asymmetrical war: on one side stood combatants in thin shalvar kameezes and cloth turbans; on the other side, the military might of the most powerful nation in the world. Hit the target you can reach. Frustrate the reconstruction and keep the country in chaos. In the end, the foreigners will give up and leave. That was the consensus.

Since then, aid workers had been kidnapped or killed in some of the most volatile areas of the country. Marie and her community of cotton-clad sandal-shod workers knew that. But those were stories from outside Kabul, from the wild frontiers.

Today's shooting was different. This story was unthinkable.

These Afghan men had crossed another line. They had killed an unarmed, solitary foreign woman walking in her own Kabul neighborhood. They didn't kidnap her and try to sell her back for gain. They didn't pass the word to her Afghan coworkers that she should leave the country. They didn't treat her like the guest she was.

Instead, the men drove beside her on a busy Kabul Street. In the presence of dozens of schoolgirls with their UN–provided backpacks full of US–provided schoolbooks, they stopped and opened fire. They spent a magazine full of ammunition on a single, unprotected woman.

Indeed, the contours of war had changed. There were new questions that needed answering. Would they gun down blond-haired, blue-eyed Australian children on their way to school? Would they bomb the unarmed homes of Dutch or Finnish families? Would they stone the fragile bodies of American doctors, British teachers, or German project managers?

A soft thud against the door shook Marie from her thoughts. She slid her feet off the bed and pulled the door open. Margaret, her director's wife, stood calm and waiting. She was wearing a heavily embroidered, dark-blue, long-sleeved *peron* that went down to her knees and a pair of matching baggy tambones. Her gray, shoulder-length hair was loose and uncovered.

"Were you sleeping?"

Marie ran her hand through her long, auburn hair and shook it out over her shoulders. "No. Thinking, I guess."

"I'll bet. Come sit with me."

Margaret was soft-spoken and patient. She loved Jesus, her family, and Afghanistan—in that order. Her priorities were clear. She was more than willing to return to the States and the grandchildren who were growing up strangers. She wanted to know them, and the phone and Skype just weren't enough.

She also knew Marie in ways few others did. The two women, separated by almost twenty years, gathered for several hours each week to drink coffee and pray. It's not that they were friends. Socially, they had little in common. In a way, they were something more. They trusted each other. They shared things with one another that neither shared with anyone else. They communicated on a soul level, and that was a gift to each.

Marie looked into Margaret's eyes. She recognized the older woman's words as more than a simple invitation. She nodded and followed Margaret across the hall to the small white-walled sitting room. The two women sat down on red cotton floor mats.

Margaret started the conversation. "So, how are you doing?"

Marie shrugged. "On balance, okay. I mean, the news is crazy . . . but I got the project approved."

Margaret smiled.

"Is Dave considering evacuation?"

Margaret pressed her lips together. She chose her words carefully. "Of course, Dave is always considering evacuation. It's always on his list. But no, we don't think this will do it. Not for us."

Marie relaxed her shoulders. "I'm going to get a seat on the next flight north. I want to go home."

Margaret nodded. She'd known Marie for four years. Marie had already been in Shehktan for two years when Margaret and Dave arrived. Even then, the younger woman had a strong network of Afghan friends. Margaret knew Marie was happiest when safely tucked into her Afghan home, surrounded by her friends and her work. Margaret hoped that would be enough for Marie to weather this new loss, but she knew Marie would process Carolyn's departure slowly, if at all. Despite Marie's deep commitment to Christ in all things, she was more than capable of ignoring her own heart. Margaret understood that. She knew Marie wouldn't welcome her intrusion, but she'd experienced enough of her own losses in Afghanistan to know they come back to haunt you. "Carolyn talked to me."

"Uh-huh."

"So, she thinks maybe two weeks. Maybe three."

Marie nodded. "Yeah, she told me."

"I know. She said you gave her your blessing."

"What can I say? 'No. You should stay to the end of your two-year commitment. You can't go. It's all about me and I'm not ready.' That wouldn't be right."

Margaret nodded. "You did well." She thought for a few moments. "You're loving Carolyn well."

Marie caught her breath. She looked across at the corner of the room, then followed the wall up to the ceiling. She looked back at Margaret. "I'm ready to go home."

Margaret nodded.

"What about you and Dave?"

Margaret was silent for a moment. She recognized Marie's deflection and knew her friend well enough to let the subject of Carolyn's departure go. "Dave has meetings. We'll probably stay for a week or so."

"Did you know the woman?"

"No." Margaret picked some lint off her knees. "We'll buy supplies and make arrangements to have them shipped to Shehktan. I have some friends I want to visit. I don't think we'll be down here for long. Will Carolyn fly back with you?"

"Yeah, that was the original plan."

"Good."

Marie changed the subject again. "Are you and Dave going to Friday church tomorrow?"

Margaret looked up at Marie. "They're not doing big church. They're scattering."

"Scattering?"

"Small groups are meeting in each neighborhood. No big group. We're going over to the Taylor's. There's one just down the street at the Swensens'. Do you know them? "

Marie nodded. Attending "big church" was one of the highlights of her Kabul visits. Sometimes there were as many as two hundred people in the congregation. There was even a full-time pastor.

In Shehktan, worship service was different than in Kabul. Even if everyone was in town, they only had two couples, three single adults, and three children. They were lucky if they met every other week. When they did, they sang a cappella and took turns bringing a message. Sometimes they listened to a sermon downloaded online. If they liked it, they would talk about it afterward. They always prayed for one another and usually celebrated communion, which Marie loved. Their gatherings were sweet, and her little community was precious to her. But the big gatherings in Kabul were a treat. She could stand and sing out. She could get lost in the worship and talk to people she only saw once or twice a year.

"No big church?" Marie asked.

Margaret just shook her head.

"Yeah, I know the Swensens. Their house is just a block and a half away. I'll go tomorrow and take Carolyn." Marie tried to excuse herself. "I want to call for a flight."

Margaret pulled her back. "Marie, tell me—This is a lot to deal with, the murder and then Carolyn leaving. It really is." The older woman took a deep breath and pressed, "How are you feeling about all this?"

Marie clamped down her jaw and willed herself not to cry. When she thought she could, she began speaking. "I—I don't even know, exactly." Her words were clipped and hard. "The murder? It's like a bolt of lightning ripped through a tree just outside the house, and the branches have broken through the walls." As suddenly as she had called the image into being, it shocked her into silence.

Margaret nodded.

For a few moments, Marie considered the dark gray face of the silent television on the far side of the room before stating, "And all I can think about is—thank God it wasn't Carolyn or you or Dave. Thank God no one's calling my parents or posting my face on the Internet." She dug her hands into her pockets. "And that just feels, I don't know." She looked around the room as if searching for the words.

Margaret sat patiently.

Finally, Marie found words. "Lousy. Selfish. Angry. Lots of stuff. That's a start on how I feel."

"Well, that's a pretty good start."

"Hey, I did it without cursing." Marie smiled.

Margaret laughed. "Maybe if you'd cursed, you could have finished."

Marie leaned against the blank white wall. Sighed. "Mostly I just can't make sense out of it."

"And Carolyn?"

"Yeah . . . I can't even think about that." Marie winced and shook her head hard. "What can I do? She's leaving."

"Well, that's true."

"I'm going to call for the flight." Marie turned abruptly.

Margaret let her go.

Marie retreated to her room and booked seats on the Saturday northbound flight. She sent Carolyn a text with the details. *Yeah. Home. That makes sense.*

She looked at the small battery operated clock in her room: too early for dinner. She unfolded her laptop, opened her project plan, and went to work. Something she could accomplish.

6

The rest of the afternoon slipped by quietly. At 6:00 in the evening, Margaret called Marie to dinner. Marie spent another twenty minutes wrapping up her work, then headed over to the larger house. Margaret was a wonderful cook, and Marie looked forward to the meal. She found the kitchen thick with the aroma of garlic and onions. Through the hallway, she heard voices and silverware scraping glass plates. She followed the sound into a large, dull teal room with a dining table surrounded by a dozen chairs. The conversation stopped.

Dave was seated at the head of the table, his neatly combed gray hair and matching beard made him look the part of the elder statesman. He wore an Afghan-style fisherman's vest over a long-sleeve, button-down tan shirt. Margaret sat beside him. The new little boy, Simon, banged on a wooden high chair, his face smeared with brown sauce. Casey wiped a dark smudge from her shoulder while Chad, looking like he'd just walked off a movie set with his hair in perfect disarray, stopped in mid-sentence. Carolyn, her back to the doorway, her brown, wavy hair loose over her T-shirt, glanced at Marie over her shoulder.

Marie smiled, greeted everyone, and slid into an empty chair. The conversation continued, with Chad peppering Dave for information and Dave responding in his usual slow, measured way.

"The men were not apprehended. The assumption is that they will never be caught. Someone powerful, perhaps the government, perhaps a local religious leader is probably protecting them. The current thinking is that it was personal, not random, but we really don't know."

"How does all that affect us?"

Dave took a deep breath. "From a security standpoint it's hard to tell. If it was personal, it probably won't happen again. If the religious leaders called for the execution, well, then—" He hesitated, then went on. "It'll happen again."

Chad nodded.

Margaret stepped into the conversation. "From an emotional standpoint, of course, it affects us all greatly."

Marie heaped Afghan rice on her plate, then added several spoonfuls of stir-fried vegetables. The food was warm, but no longer steaming. She realized she was hungry.

Dave continued his explanation. "What's happened will shake the confidence of the foreign community. Already, many families are leaving Kabul. Others will leave as soon as the school semester ends."

"Their NGOs are sending them home?"

"No. Not necessarily. Each family, each single makes that decision on their own. Anyone can leave the country at any time." Dave looked straight at Carolyn. "Contracts, commitments, don't matter. It's important to do what you sense God is leading you to do, when you sense it." He turned back to Chad. "Some families are making that decision and leaving, not only for their physical safety, but also for their emotional health."

Carolyn took a deep breath and felt the affirmation of his words. Dave's blessing mattered.

Chad considered Dave's explanation. "So people decide on their own if they want to stay or go?"

Dave shook his head. "Not entirely. People can leave anytime they want, but if they stay, they're under the leadership of their NGO." Dave looked at Marie this time, then continued. "The NGO director can decide that everyone needs to leave. Each organization will measure risk. For now, movements are restricted. Your NGO director will tell you what you can and cannot do." Chad nodded, apparently satisfied for now.

Dave directed his attention toward Marie. "How're you doing?"

Marie was grateful to realize she'd missed most of the conversation. "Fine." She wasn't in the habit of speaking deeply with Dave and certainly wouldn't do so in such a large gathering. "Just glad I got the project approved."

"Yeah. I'm impressed. Congratulations, again."

This time, his words sounded more sincere to Marie. "Thanks."

Chad waited for a gap, then returned to his questions. "How long have you and Margaret been working in-country?"

"We first came in the summer of '79, fresh out of college. I had studied accounting. Margaret had a BS in sociology. At first, we were involved in a guesthouse for foreigners here in Kabul. We were young, and the people who came were young. Mostly hippies following the drug trail. They washed up on our doorstep, broke and broken. We did what we could to help them find the ground. Some of them came to faith and returned to work in Afghanistan."

Chad laid his fork down on his empty plate. "You've been here since then?"

Margaret laughed lightly. She picked up the conversation from Dave. "We watched the Russians invade in the winter of 1979–80. Those were difficult days. We had our first son here in Kabul. Our second child was born in Pakistan."

"That's crazy." Casey jumped in. "You had your baby here?"

Margaret smiled. "In those days, it wasn't so crazy. This was a different country. Freer than you can imagine."

"But it disintegrated," Dave interjected. "We stayed until just after the Russian withdrawal. When the mujahedin war started, we went home."

Margaret collected the empty plates. "We stayed in the States for two years."

Dave added, "When things settled down, we returned to Kabul. Unfortunately, the Taliban came."

Margaret jumped in. "That was enough."

"Margaret and the kids evacuated to Pakistan first. I stayed for a couple of months, then followed. We stayed in Pakistan for a few months and went home from there. Got our kids off to college and assumed we would live out our lives in the States."

Marie just watched, knowing how the story went. Casey prompted, "But—?"

"But then the Towers went down," Margaret said. "That changed everything."

The group sat with that understatement for a moment, thinking about how the tragedy had affected them individually. Chad rubbed his beard. "I think if we have more children, we'll leave for the births, but we're hoping to be here for a long time."

Dave asked, "What do you think is a long time?"

"Well, we're not short-termers."

Out of the corner of her eye, Marie caught Carolyn stiffen.

Chad went on passionately. "We're here for the long haul. We're going to dig in, learn the language, live in community with Afghans. We want to make a difference. We're committed to sharing God's love through our actions *and* our words. I'm joining a well project. We're getting clean water to Afghans in the rural areas. It's just amazing to me that people still die for lack of clean water. It's so important—a basic necessity."

Dave smiled, nodding. The young man was talking more to his own heart than to the group around the table.

Margaret chose encouraging words. "That's a good objective. A good motivation."

Chad went on. "Of course, if the country descends into complete civil war and everyone leaves, we'll have to leave, too."

Marie smiled. "So that's the exit path?"

Chad's words turned into a lecture. "If we have to leave, I'll resume my career in the States, and then we'll look for somewhere else we can go. It only makes sense to have an exit path. A plan. Eventually, the foreign troops will leave. Perhaps Afghanistan will continue in peace. Perhaps not. If it does, we'll stay. We're in for the long haul."

Dave rubbed his beard. "All war in Afghanistan is regional."

"What do you mean?"

Dave explained. "We used to be able to travel from Kabul to Shehktan by road, but now the area forty minutes from our town has turned into a war zone. It may or may not stay that way. In the meantime, our town remains in peace, secure."

Marie added. "The country is divided into more regions than you can imagine. One can descend into chaos while another does not. If you're in the area that turns to chaos, you have to leave. There's nothing you can do about it. Meanwhile, another part of the country could be vibrant, stable, and growing."

Chad squared his shoulders. "We'll stay as long as we can. If we have to leave one part of the country, we'll move to another. That's all."

Margaret spoke her next words slowly. "It's not so easy, Chad. We don't live in Afghanistan as much as we live in our town, among our neighbors. Moving to another part of the country means starting over, setting up another house, starting new projects, and building all new relationships. It's incredibly difficult."

Marie immediately thought of all her friends in Shehktan: foreign and Afghan. The thought of leaving them all wrenched her stomach.

Margaret added a gentle warning. "How long you stay is probably out of your hands."

Chad bristled. "Of course, God is in control. Our lives belong to him. But we'll do our part."

Marie finished her food. She added her plate to the stack in front of Margaret. "I don't know if God is in control." She spoke softly. "I don't know that I can say that gunning down a woman on a street is God's work. There's something in his sovereignty that allows our free will. But our free will does not equal his will. Not when it includes something he expressly forbids." Marie took a sip of water and went on. "You're right, Chad. Our lives are in God's hands. And, we live in a country brutalized by war, poverty, jealousy, and hatred. Somehow, those two realities coexist."

Carolyn found her voice. "And it's not always God's will that we stay."

Chad stammered, "Of course—of course not. Sometimes God calls us for a season. But Casey and I are here until he calls us to leave."

Dave spoke the final word. "We all are."

With that, Margaret pushed her chair back, stood up, and took away the dirty plates. Marie followed her into the kitchen with the empty glasses and nearly empty serving bowls. By the time they reached the sink, Casey had joined them.

Marie filled a bucket with warm water and soap, then began washing each dish and placing it on the drying rack.

The newer woman was ready for a new conversation. "Wow. I'm exhausted. Jet lag, I guess. Simon isn't sleeping well. I just want to hear something good about this country. Tell me something good."

Margaret began drying the plates. When she finished each one, she handed it to Casey to put away in the cabinet. "Oh, there are wonderful things about this country. For me, it's all about the people. I'm sure it's the same for Marie."

"Absolutely," Marie agreed.

"Then tell me a story," the younger woman pleaded.

Margaret looked at Marie.

Marie spoke without turning her head. "A few months ago an Afghan friend of mine called me. His brother's child was sick and wasn't getting better. They had taken her to the local hospital and the main hospital in the provincial capital, but it didn't help. They gave the kid all kinds of medicines, wide-spectrum antibiotics that undoubtedly did more harm than good. Nothing. My friend asked me if I would help. I have a fund for just this sort of thing."

"A fund?"

"Yeah. I have a special fund to help people in need. My friends from the States donate money to it. Let me tell you, they give a lot of money. They care."

"Wow, that's cool."

"Yep." Marie handed another plate to Margaret. "Anyway, we sent the child, her mother, and her uncle—her mother's brother—to Kabul to Cure Hospital. They diagnosed tuberculosis. They said the child's abdomen was full of it. They put her on the right medicines and within weeks, the child's health improved. Now she's doing great. You know what that means, don't you?"

Casey slipped the last of the clean plates into the cupboard. "What?"

"We saved a kid's life. That's an amazing thing. I never saved anyone's life in America. Here, stuff like that happens often." She paused for a few moments then added. "It's a privilege. Really. To be able to help someone in that way."

"It happens a lot?" Casey was intrigued.

Margaret added her story. "Last year my house helper asked me to look at a neighbor man. He was in his mid-thirties, but he was weak. He couldn't get off of his cotton mat. He probably weighed ninety-five pounds and his skin was yellow. We got him down to treatment in

Kabul. Now he's cured, and he works with his brother and provides for his family."

Casey began putting glasses away. "So you saved his life, too?"

"We did our part." Margaret nodded. "Marie's right. It really is a privilege to be able to help people when we can. We've been able to take food to drought-stricken villages and blankets to people whose households were swept away in floods."

Marie said, "But those aren't our projects. Those are just things that come up along the way. Things we can help with because we're here and we have resources and we know people well enough to answer the phone when they call. Last year, when the winter was so hard, we provided coal and firewood to the poorest of the poor in our town. Most of those families didn't even have glass in their windows. Just plastic or blankets. It really is a privilege."

Casey nodded, wanting more. "And what about faith? Have you seen anyone come to faith?"

These were not the stories they shared openly. Marie chose her words carefully. "In Kabul, there are a lot of Afghan Jesus-followers." She thought of the day guard and wondered, again, if he was one of them. "Some came to faith in Pakistan or Europe and brought their faith back with them. Others came to faith here. Many gather in groups. They stay segregated—men together with other men and women with other women. The women are quieter. But yes, there are Afghans who follow Christ."

"And where you live?"

Marie continued. "Our area is highly conservative. It's as conservative as the Taliban, but there are believers. Not a lot, but a few. They keep their faith a secret; but for some, their faith is strong."

"Do you talk about Jesus with them?"

Margaret nodded.

Marie answered. "Some, but not all. It's up to them. If they want to talk about faith, and a lot do, we talk about faith. If not, we don't."

Casey was exasperated. "Do you share your faith at all?"

Both Marie and Margaret laughed. Carolyn joined their laughter from the doorway. This time, she answered. "I work with Marie, and I can tell you, she talks about her faith all the time! The thing is, Afghans are always talking about God, so we talk about God, too. They know God through the Prophet Muhammad. We know God through Jesus. I don't have the language Marie does, so I can't share as much, but I try. They're always interested. Well, not always, but often. Marie shares Jesus stories, and our Afghan friends love them."

"But do they come to faith?"

Marie could hear the frustration in Casey's voice. She turned, leaned against the sink, and met that frustration head-on. "We can't ever really know what's going on in someone's heart. We share stories. We pray and bless people. We help people wherever we can. We watch them face new situations with different attitudes and we think, 'Ah, the stories are influencing them.' We listen to them tell one another about Jesus and we think, 'Ah, they like Jesus.' Sometimes, we listen to their declarations of faith and we think, 'Look, they've committed their lives to Christ.' The truth is, we never really know. Even when we see them gather together, trade the stories with one another, listen to Scripture, or read it together, we don't know for sure what's going on in their hearts."

"It's very conservative in our town, and Carolyn and I have worked mostly out in the villages," Marie said. "It's not like Kabul. Here, there are whole families of believers. They gather in groups and their neighbors know who they are. Shehktan's not like that." She launched into a story.

"A couple of years ago, a young man stood up and publicly declared his faith in the Honorable Jesus Messiah—that's one of the ways we refer to him here. His family beat him so badly he almost died. He ran away to Pakistan, but a year later came back to Kabul. He has no relationship with his family. So, when it comes to talking about Afghans and their faith in Christ, we try to protect them. Those stories belong to them. Someday, they'll tell them."

Marie continued, "We do see the influence of Christ there. It's small, new, perhaps a mustard seed. But it's real. These are things we trust God for. In the meantime, yes, we're quite open about who we are and what we believe. And yes, our neighbors welcome us." With that, Marie turned around and focused on scrubbing the rice pot clean. As she scrubbed, she realized that the dull pain on the side of her head had almost vanished.

Margaret stepped into the silence left by Marie and Casey. Her voice was gentle, patient. "Casey. Right now, you and Chad must learn to live here. You have to learn how to be a woman, a wife, and a mother in this entirely different culture. The first six months are usually the most difficult. Over time, you'll learn language and get to know people. You'll find your own way. If you love Christ and love your Afghan neighbors, you will share things with them that will bless their lives." She paused.

Casey nodded thoughtfully.

Margaret went on. "If you keep your focus on loving Christ and your neighbor, you'll do well. It sounds simple, but really, that's all there is to it."

Marie rinsed the pot and handed it to Margaret. She dried her hands on the tail of Margaret's dishcloth, said good night, and left the three women talking in the kitchen.

7

That night, Marie slept fitfully. The first time she awakened, it was to the sound of a motorcycle roaring past the gate. She sat straight up, strained to hear across the darkness, but there was nothing. Even the dogs were quiet. The electricity was off, the transformers silent, and the stabilizers still. The silence felt like velvet, fine and soft.

She slid back down under the covers, pulled the blanket up over her shoulders, and willed herself back to sleep.

The second time she awakened, it was to the sound of gunshots. This time, her eyes snapped wide, but she didn't move. Again, she stretched herself into the darkness, into the quiet of the night. This time dogs barked in the distance. She tried to distinguish one bark from the other. She counted them silently, lost count, strained again to hear, and started over counting. This time, she just listened for the unique barks and marked them on her fingertips. *Six.* Six dogs running the neighborhood, barking in the night. No gunshots.

Again, she willed herself back to sleep.

The third time she awakened it was to the sound of a helicopter. She spun onto her back, fast and hard. She attempted to peer through the cloth-covered mud roof. She counted the beats of the spinning blades. *Two.* But she couldn't see them through the cloth ceiling and mud-covered roof. She looked at the drawn curtains; still, no line of sight. She focused, framed words inside her mind. *Helicopters. Middle of the night. Kabul. Normal.*

The battery-operated travel clock read 3:17. She sighed, put the clock down, and pulled the blankets up over her shoulders. She drifted into broken, confusing dreams.

In one, she was packing, but she couldn't get to her clothes. Her Shehktan driver, Faiz Muhammad, was there. She pleaded with him to help her, but he wouldn't. "No Mari-jan. The flood has come." She ran to the gate and tried to open it. He begged her, warned her, yelled at her, but she wouldn't listen. She pushed the gate as hard as she could, but it wouldn't open.

In the next, she was trying to walk up a hill, but her sandals kept sliding off. There was a wind, swirling, dust-filled. She couldn't see. Her long hair was loose. It snapped like heavy cords across her cheeks and eyes. She kept trying to tie her scarf, but the wind ripped it from her hands.

In the last dream, she was hiding in a dark room when the walls and ceiling trembled, buckling inward. Just as they were collapsing around her, she jumped out of bed with a gasp and raced for the door, but smacked into the wall instead. The shock jolted her fully awake.

Just then, the mullah sang out his pre-dawn call to prayer.

Marie stood still, hands against the cold wall, naked feet pressed into the carpet-covered concrete floor. She oriented herself. *Kabul. Guesthouse. Dream. Cold.*

She returned to her borrowed bed. She wished for another blanket or better yet, for her own bed. She waited for the mullah to finish, then closed her eyes and finally, slept.

The cell phone woke Marie. "Hello," her voice cracked.

"Marie. It's me, Carolyn."

"Hey."

"Were you asleep?"

Marie rubbed her eyes and rotated her head to release the night's tension. "Yeah." She looked at her clock 8:11. "I didn't sleep well."

"Me neither. Sorry to wake you. Want me to call back later?"

"No. What's up?"

"Well, I was just wondering if we were going to fellowship. It starts at ten o'clock."

"I'll be out in a minute. Put water on for coffee?"

"Sure. I'm making breakfast. Everyone else is gone."

Marie nodded. "Great. I'll be there in a couple of minutes." Her eyes fell on the small plaque with its shafts of sunlight, clouds, and earth. She read the first sentence again. "God didn't promise days without pain." *No. He promised tribulation. Floods and fire.* She pulled her eyes off the plaque.

Within minutes, she was dressed and walking across the compound's sidewalk to the main house. She pushed the kitchen door open and smiled at the warm aroma of breakfast. Carolyn stood behind the stove, the handle of the pan in one hand and a black plastic spatula in the other. "Hey, want some pancakes?"

"Absolutely."

"Coffee's over there."

Marie found the French press, pushed the plunger down, and inhaled the warm scent of fresh coffee. She remembered fragments of her dreams—packing, walking, hiding. She found a cup and poured it full of steaming black coffee. She looked into the pan and let images from the previous day play through her mind. Phone calls, ministry officials, Fawad and the stack of papers, the man on the street . . . Carolyn's announcement. A wave of nausea swept through her. She swallowed hard. "How did we get pancakes?"

"I found some mix in the cabinet. Just add water and eggs. Can you believe it? Everything's available in Kabul." Carolyn flipped the pancakes onto a waiting plate.

"Syrup?"

"Well, no. But there's honey and peanut butter."

Marie smiled. "Perfect."

The two women carried their plates into the dining room, sat down at the empty table, and ate. *Pancakes,* Marie thought. A simple treat.

As soon as they'd washed the dishes, Marie returned to her borrowed room. She was hungry for solitude, for a space to settle the unease in her body. She picked up her Bible. The embroidered strip of Afghan cloth that marked her page opened to Psalm 139. She read the entire psalm, then found her little yellow notebook and started to write.

> Lord, you know me. You know me inside and out. You know my sadness and my anger. You know my love. You know my confusion and my commitment. You know everything about me.

She looked across the room at the wall she'd banged into just hours before. She rubbed her eyes. In the last dream, the ceiling and the plastered mud walls buckled, the hay-covered ceiling limbs split, the blue-and-white checked fabric tore.

Marie looked into the Bible open on her lap. She reread the psalm, put her pen to the paper, and wrote what she knew to be true verse by verse, truth by truth, each in her own words. She spoke her last sentence out loud. "You're here with us, here and now." She looked around the room. The walls and ceiling stayed where they belonged. She drew a breath, deep and solid. "You're here with me." Her words echoed, sounding empty. "I know you're here." She searched the corners, the cracks, the yellow drapes. She searched her open, red suitcase, the wall hooks that held her brown coat and matching gold-trimmed scarf. She shook her head, reread the psalm, and returned her pen to the page.

> You're here. I don't know where, but you're here. You have to be.

She pulled a blanket up around her shoulders and rubbed the tension from her hands. She turned the page.

> You know what's next. You knew yesterday when Carolyn called. You were with us both. We're never alone, even when we feel alone. You're with us. You're with me here in this room.

She took a deep breath, rubbed her stiff hand again, and kept writing.

> You're with our Afghan staff and the teachers we taught and the women we visited in the villages. You're even with the men who drove through the street with their Kalashnikovs,

the ones who killed your beautiful daughter. You saw what they did. You know why they did it. You told us not to kill and you saw them kill. No matter how justified they think they are, you call it sin. Wrong. Evil. Horrible. And no matter how many bullets they fired, how hard they tried to destroy one of your children, they couldn't do it. She's yours. Even now, she's with you. No pain. No trauma. All that's gone. You were with her on the street, and she's with you now."

Marie lifted her pen. She was shaking.

You're here with me. No matter what happens, you're with me. No war, no geography can tear me out of your hands. Whether I'm here or back in America, I'm with you. No matter how bad things get, no matter what happens, you're still here and my soul is safe in you. Yeah. You know me and you love me. And you love the taxi driver I rode with yesterday afternoon. You love Fawad. You love the man on the street. You love Dave and Margaret and my guards.

The faces of Afghan friends and strangers filled her mind.

Even now, you're pouring your love on my friend, Zia Gul. You're sharing your truth with Aziza. You're with Khadija. You know the women who will come to our new literacy classes. You see each one. You've known them forever. You've loved them forever. None of us is alone. You sent Jesus to prove it. You ache to bring us all home.

She felt a hot tear slide over her cheek.

You know who hates us. Who lies and wants to kill us. Someday, you'll hold them to account, but not today. Today you let everyone do what we want—even our enemies—but not forever. Someday, you'll say "enough."

Oh God, please protect us. Protect me. Help me to walk in this crazy place: the good, the bad, the dangerous, the kind. Help me to bless them all. To love them the way Jesus did.

Father, please help me to live here.

Marie dropped her pen on the blanket. Her hand ached, but her heart felt lighter, easier, stronger. She looked at the clock. Nine forty-five. Within moments, she met Carolyn waiting for her inside the gate. "Pray before we go out?"

Carolyn nodded. "Yeah."

The two women bowed their heads and lifted their hands, palms upward in front of them. The day guard joined them and immediately lifted his hands as well. Marie prayed in Dari, committing their short journey and their lives into God's hands. When she said "Amen," all three passed their hands over their faces and closed the prayer.

Marie looked at the guard. He was smiling.

Marie stepped in front of Carolyn, leaned through the gate, and surveyed the street. She looked to the left. Three small children played on the edge of a mud culvert filled with dark water. The sharp stench of its raw sewage burned the air. A teenage boy pedaled a bicycle, another boy perched sideways on the rack over the back wheel. The chain scraped rhythmically. A blue-shrouded woman disappeared around a corner, the long, pleated back of her burqa floating gracefully as she walked.

Marie looked to the right. A shopkeeper stood beside the suspended carcass of an unrecognizable animal. Beyond him, thick traffic on the paved road moved slowly past.

Marie stepped out. Carolyn followed her. The two walked side by side between tall, khaki-colored mud-brick walls interrupted by small, wooden gates and large, colorfully painted metal double gates. As they neared the first corner, two Afghan women in their light blue burqas stepped through a wooden gate and onto the street. One held a corner of the back hem of her burqa over her hips, hiding the clothes she wore underneath. The other displayed a long, purple-and-black shirt and matching baggy trousers beneath the thigh-length, front hem of her richly embroidered burqa. Marie looked for the eyes of each through their woven screens, and she placed her hand on her heart and greeted them. "Salaam alaikum."

The women returned her greeting.

Marie continued speaking to them in Dari, asking the customary greeting questions. "How are you? How are your children? How is your health? Are you well?"

The women giggled. One lifted the front hem of her burqa above her face and draped it over the thickly embroidered pillbox crown. Her dark eyes shone with delight as she gave the courteous reply, "Come to my house. Come have tea."

Marie again put her hand on her heart. "May you live forever. You are kind. Good-bye."

The woman laughed again as she pulled the front of her burqa back down over her face, and the two continued on their way.

Marie and Carolyn walked through a wide empty intersection. On one corner, a storefront had been turned into a training center for tae kwon do. Marie could see a group of boys through the blue-tinted glass and quickly looked away. She knew better than to stare.

Half a block up the street, a brown metal gate opened, and a foreign man with a bicycle disappeared inside. Marie and Carolyn walked toward the gate. When they arrived, the guard welcomed them. Though he was young, he had managed a thin mustache. He didn't know Marie or Carolyn, but he knew they belonged. They each exchanged greetings, and the two women walked across the courtyard to the main building.

They stepped out of their sandals at the door and left them among an odd collection of boots, sandals, clogs, and sneakers—the footwear of foreigners. They entered a large sitting room already packed with members of their Kabul community: young adults with blue eyes, light-bearded and clean shaven men with small children in their laps, mothers with their sons and daughters gathered around their knees. There was no furniture, just brown-and-gold cotton mats on the floor, their matching pillows leaning against the pale yellow walls.

Marie and Carolyn greeted those they knew and those they didn't. They picked up song books from the pile on the floor and sat down, side by side, on a cotton mat. Marie tucked one heel against her thigh, planting the other foot flat on the floor and hugging the knee to her chest with her hands as she waited.

She felt the cool damp of the room and smelled shampoo and soap and the musky odor of human sweat. She listened to the murmur of voices in hushed conversations, not all in English.

A young German man with a guitar began to play. The room settled. He called out a number, and Marie found the song in the book she held. She joined the voices of her companions. As they sang, she glanced into the faces of those who sat across from her. A man cradled his small child in his arms. A young husband held his wife's hand. A young woman held the hand of her closest friend. Marie watched them. *These believers have chosen to stay, and the staying is full of sorrow and fear.*

Marie listened to her own trembling voice as it mingled with the trembling voices around her. She saw tears and realized she had her own.

After the song, a middle-aged Swiss man stood in their midst and prayed; his words, humble, tender, and full of faith, fell gently across the room. He sat down. The young man with the guitar strummed a chord, then called out another number. The group sang again. When they finished singing the guitar fell silent. The young man invited everyone to pray as they were led.

Their prayers began.

"Father, you are our God, and we worship you."

"You are great. Greater than everything we face."

"You created the earth and everything in it."

"You are the King of all kings."

"The great and mighty One."

"You inhabit eternity."

"We praise you because you're here with us now."

"We pray for our friends and our families. Comfort the people we love."

Their prayers continued, some in American English, some British, most in the stiffly accented phrases of a second language. Finally, silence settled over the room. The young man with the guitar called for yet another song, and the community sang, their voices thick with emotion.

The Swiss man stood. He called another man to step forward. Marie looked around. A man rose from his place. He was tall, muscular, short-haired, and bearded. Marie guessed him to be in his mid-thirties. This man she did not know.

He stepped forward, a Bible and a sheaf of paper in his hands. He bowed his head. The Swiss man placed his own hand on the man's shoulder and prayed for the message he would bring. When he finished, the community drew Bibles out from their purses or backpacks and onto their laps.

The man called out a passage and began to read 1 Peter chapter 1. His accent was thick, but his words were clear. "'Peter, an apostle of Jesus Christ, To those who are elect exiles of the Dispersion in Pontus, Galatia, Cappadocia, Asia, and Bithynia,'—and Afghanistan—"

Exiles in Afghanistan.

"—according to the foreknowledge of God the Father, in the sanctification of the Spirit, for obedience to Jesus Christ and for sprinkling with his blood: May grace and peace be multiplied to you." The man repeated: "May grace and peace be multiplied to you." He paused, looked around the room and spoke again. "To you, to us, foreigners in Afghanistan, exiles from our homes for the sake of the gospel; may God give us grace and peace."

Marie received the words, feeling them. *Grace and peace.* She looked around the room. She watched a young father lean over and kiss the top of his small child's downy head. The toddler slept peacefully in his arms. Grace and peace.

The speaker called out to the room. "Someone please read the next three verses."

A middle-aged woman with a thick German accent formed the words and lifted them into the room:

> Blessed be the God and Father of our Lord Jesus Christ! According to his great mercy, he has caused us to be born again to a living hope through the resurrection of Jesus Christ from the dead, to an inheritance that is imperishable, undefiled, and unfading, kept in heaven for you, who by God's power are being guarded through faith for a salvation ready to be revealed in the last time.

The woman fell silent. The man waited for the precious words of Scripture to settle into the shaken hearts of his brothers and sisters. Marie leaned back, rocked her head against the cool mud-brick wall, and felt the words cascade gently over the rough dry rocks within her soul.

The man spoke. "We have been born again. Our hope is alive. Jesus is risen. Our inheritance cannot be destroyed; it cannot be defiled; it will never fade. It belongs to us. This promise is for us, today. For us, the brothers and sisters who have given our lives to come with Christ to Afghanistan."

He spoke about "our young sister," the violence of her death, and the magnificence of the inheritance she had already received—an inheritance still waiting for each person who sat together in that yellow-walled room. He talked about Christ, his love, and his worth. He talked about the Afghans, whom Christ also loves. He talked about Christ's presence in the community's midst and the importance of looking to him in the place of brutal loss. Finally, he prayed for the community and sat down.

The room stayed silent for several moments. The hard edges of Marie's sadness gradually softened as her resolve was restored. Her own journey with Jesus made even this trial worth it. The soft chords of the guitar swept into her thoughts. Hearing the thick voices of men and women shape and breathe words full of sadness and strength, she added her own: "I surrender all; I surrender all."

A shaft of midmorning light illumined the tear-streaked faces of two young women. Marie felt her own tears. She unlocked her hands, opened them palms upward in front of her chest, and half whispered the next line of the song. "All to thee, my blessed Savior, I surrender all."

The young man with the guitar continued to play, and the community sang the chorus through a second time, their voices rising together in trembling resolve.

Marie felt the weight of the moment, a sacredness born of a faith woven too tightly to be torn by fleeting violence. She looked into the faces of courageous brothers and sisters who faced anew the challenge of such costly surrender. She voiced her own surrender, strengthened by the certainty that nothing was concrete except Christ himself—and that He was worth it all.

Around the room, men and women wept and trembled, yet none pulled away. Each had counted the cost before they had left their home country. Still, there was no way for them to know the full price of commitment. That day, gathered as a community of faith, the people once again opened their hands before their God. They once again gave him everything they had, all that they were.

Marie left the gathering both awed and humbled. She knew Christ had been with them; he had received their offering and met them with his own. Their worship was a declaration of the faith each would walk out in the days and weeks to come.

Marie stepped through the gate, back onto the Kabul street. She looked over at Carolyn, walking silently beside her. *Two weeks,* she thought, realizing with an aching heaviness that her own journey in Afghanistan would cost her more than she could ever imagine. She wondered if she would remember this moment, this morning, this sacred meeting with the living God. She prayed silently. *Father, please. Help me.*

The rest of the day passed quietly. There were phone calls, text messages, fragments of news to be collected, good-byes to be spoken, but no more explosions. Marie thought about walking to the Internet café. She wanted to email her friends back home, her family, but the risk seemed too high. They would all have to wait, though she knew they would be watching the news or trying not to. She prayed for their peace.

That night, the electricity went off again. The guesthouse and neighborhood quieted. Marie slept soundly in the velvety, machine-free darkness and awoke at the sound of the mullah calling out morning prayers. Stretching, she realized she had slept through the entire night. A gift.

PART 2

DAY 12

SHEHKTAN, AFGHANISTAN

8

A soft knock on the gate and quiet voices woke her. Marie recognized the voice of the night guard greeting the day guard with his familiar salaam alaikum and asking a cascade of friendly questions. She rolled back to sleep.

At 7:30 a.m., she got up, dressed, tossed her nightclothes into her suitcase, and zipped it shut. Her backpack was already packed. She pulled the sheets and pillowcase off the borrowed bed and left them in a pile on the floor, tossed her damp towel on top, pulled on her long brown coat, and carefully wrapped her brown-and-gold scarf.

Shehktan. Home. She was ready.

In the cool Kabul morning, the soft scent of wild roses from the guesthouse garden filled her head as she dragged her suitcase to the gate and dropped her backpack on top of it. The guard stepped out of his own little house and met her. After they had exchanged morning greetings and plans for the day, the guard disappeared through the gate and went off to the main road in search of a taxi willing to take two foreign women across the city to the Kabul airport.

Marie stood within the gate and listened. A car rumbled across the dusty, rock-strewn street. Another car honked in the distance. A boy sang. She peered through the small opening in the gate but couldn't see anyone. She caught the morning song of birds and found them in the mulberry tree in the center of the compound. The calico cat she had seen the day before sauntered toward her, and Marie scooped it up, holding it against her chest, and listened to it purr.

"You, little one, are a gift to me." Marie whispered while rubbing the back of the cat's head and continuing to speak to it. "I've enjoyed you. Don't eat all the birds. Stay away from strangers." Marie smiled and recalled the phrase a friend in America put on the bottom of her emails. "Don't run with scissors, okay?"

Carolyn emerged from the big house, bleary-eyed but ready to go. She wheeled her black carry-on suitcase to the gate, threw out some apologies, and settled down to wait.

"No worries. The guard went for a taxi. He's not back yet."

"I talked to Brad last night. He's so excited I'm coming home. He's planning a party. I think—maybe we'll get engaged then. Isn't it wonderful?" Carolyn didn't wait for Marie's answer to that. As if seeking a safer topic, she asked, "Do you think we could have a good-bye party in Shehktan? Would they like that?"

"Absolutely. They'll love it. We'll make *palau* and buy some cakes." Marie imagined the warm aroma of rice spiced with cardamom and cumin. She saw young women carrying large, silver trays piled with clear glass cups and thermoses filled with hot tea. "Yep. Aziza will help, and Khadija. Zia Gul, too."

"We'll have music and dance, like at a wedding?" Carolyn was delighted.

"Oh, yeah." Marie smiled, picturing the joyous dance of sparkly clothed Afghan women.

Just then the two women heard the sound of car wheels on the rock and dust outside the gate. A set of brakes screeched. A car door creaked hard on its hinges, then clapped shut. Marie rubbed the back of the cat's head, set it down on the concrete, and turned to open the gate. "They'll bring you gifts—some small things, maybe some big ones. They'll also say really touching things, like eulogies. They'll talk about how wonderful you are. Then they'll cry like crazy 'cause you're leaving."

Carolyn sighed.

"Don't worry. It'll be beautiful. So yes, we'll have a good-bye party—we'll have to. You've been part of their lives. They love you."

Marie and Carolyn stood on the side of the dusty street while the guard gently placed both suitcases into the trunk of a very old, barely yellow Russian taxi. They spoke their good-byes, lifting their hands and allowing the guard to pray for their journey. Marie loved this simple blessing, the prayers of Afghans spoken on her behalf. Sometimes, those praying were pure Muslims, men or women who feared God and cared for the guest in their community. Other times, they were Jesus-followers, brothers and sisters with whom Marie experienced a kinship that transcended the shared blood of humanity.

At *amen*, the two women slid onto the red carpet-covered backseat of the taxi. Marie spoke a gentle salaam to the driver as she locked the door next to her. The man responded, pulled the car into gear, and drove down the dusty street.

Marie studied the driver through the rear view mirror: warm skin the color of roasted wheat, dark eyes, heavy brows, angular cheeks, and a shock of wavy black hair. She looked at his colorfully embroidered kandahari cap—the front cut out, a red four-cornered flower embroidered on a black background across the flat top. *Pashtun. Maybe twenty-five at most.* She spoke. "Sir, thank you for taking us to the airport."

The driver looked into his rearview, smiled slightly, and nodded. He tilted his mirror to get a better view of Marie. He studied her carefully, then approached his question. "You were praying, yes?"

Carolyn shot a glance at Marie.

Marie only smiled. "Yes. With the guard." Then she added. "We believe in God. We believe our lives are in his hands."

The driver raised an eyebrow, glanced down at the road, and returned his eyes to the rearview. "You are Muslim?"

Marie smiled again. She prayed silently. *Father, what should I say?* She offered a reply she thought the driver would appreciate. "We believe there is one God."

"Praise be to Allah!" The driver responded, using the Arabic phrase.

Marie agreed, but instead of *Allah* she chose the Dari name for God. She wanted the driver to know she believed in God but not to assume she was a Muslim. Then she added, again using the Dari phrase, "We are submitted to God."

"Good. Very good."

Marie sensed an openness in the driver. No hostility. She took the plunge. "We are followers of the Honorable Jesus Messiah. He is our Savior and our Master."

The driver shot a glance into the rearview mirror, clenched the steering wheel, and looked back down to the road.

Carolyn tensed. "Marie." She whispered in English. "What if?"

Marie waved away Carolyn's fear. "What can we do? Hide? How is that right? Anyway, he should know us as people, just like him." Silently, she prayed. She wondered what the man would say next. When he remained wordless, she offered another subject. "Are you from Kabul?" She knew that was always a safe question.

The man lightened his grip on the steering wheel. "No. My family is from Helmand Province."

"Oh. I'm sorry." Her voice was weighted with genuine compassion. "There is war there, no?"

The man looked again at Marie through his rearview mirror. His eyes softened. "Yes. It has become bad."

"Are your parents still in Helmand?"

He waved his hand. "No. We came to Kabul three years ago. This is my father's taxi."

"Good. That's very good. You're safe."

The driver laughed. "Who is safe in Afghanistan?"

Marie sighed, nodding in agreement. The paved street was dense with traffic. Along the edges, men leaned on wooden carts piled high with potatoes, onions, or tomatoes. Other men, wrapped in thin wool blankets or zipped Western jackets, wove their way through thickly packed carts. A group of women in blue burqas slipped into a cell phone store.

Carolyn prayed silently and watched Marie.

Marie thought through their journey ahead: the checkpoint outside the airport, the walk across the parking lot, the ticket and body check at the door, the long, narrow lobby area where a man would meet them. He would lead them through the airport to a building beside the terminal. There, they would weigh their baggage and board a white jet with non-commercial markings. As soon as the engines turned, she would call Faiz Muhammad in Shehktan. An hour later, maybe two, they would land at the dusty runway just outside of her town. Faiz Muhammad would be there with the SUV, waiting. They would ride for twenty minutes and then be home.

The taxi driver interrupted Marie's thoughts. "Where are you from?"

Marie looked into the rearview. "America."

The man scowled, then asked, "What city?"

"Outside of Washington, DC."

"The capital?" Now he was interested.

"Yes, the capital."

"Do you go to the White House?"

Marie imagined herself sitting on a carpeted floor in the West Wing, Afghan style, sipping tea with the First Lady. She laughed. "No. I don't know the president or his wife. They have never invited me for tea."

The driver joined her laughter.

Their conversation slipped into ease. They asked about one another's families and talked about the topography and climate of one another's homelands. The driver asked Marie a common Afghan question. "Which is better? Afghanistan or America?"

Marie smiled and responded with an Afghan proverb. "To each person their own homeland is best."

The proverb delighted the driver. "You are wise. How did you learn our language?"

Marie shrugged. "My friends taught me."

He raised his eyebrows. "You have friends who speak my language?"

Marie knew he was thinking about Americans. "Yes, I have many Afghan friends. They still teach me your language. They are very kind."

He laughed again, then returned to his first subject. "Really, you are not Muslim?"

Marie kept her voice light. "Really, I am a follower of the Honorable Jesus Messiah."

Carolyn winced.

"Why? You are a good person. You should be Muslim." His question revealed both confusion and care.

Marie smiled, placed her hand on Carolyn's, and answered the driver gently. "I cannot be Muslim."

"But why not?"

Marie considered her response. Just then, they passed a huge pile of cut wood and a large scale with two dishes, one for the wood and the other for the weight. Marie looked at the scale, remembered the Afghan understanding of God's judgment, and responded to the driver's question. "Because, sir, someday, I will walk across the bridge between this world and heaven."

The driver picked up the well-known Afghan explanation. "Everyone will cross the bridge. Each one will stand before Allah. He will weigh their good works and their bad works. He will judge us all." He watched Marie for her reaction.

She nodded. "Yes. I will stand before God. He will weigh my works. But when he judges my works, he will not see my sins. He will not see my bad works. He will only see my good works and me. Then he will welcome me."

The driver checked the traffic, clutched the steering wheel, and shot back to the rearview mirror. "You have no sin? You have no bad works? You have only *sawab*? And you are not Muslim?"

Marie answered gently. She waved her hand to include the people on the side of the road. "Everyone has sin. Everyone has bad works. Everyone has good works. God will judge everyone."

The driver accepted the explanation. "Then Allah will judge you."

"Yes. God will judge me. God will judge me and see that I am completely innocent. He will see that the Honorable Jesus Messiah has taken all of my sins. He will welcome me. That's why I'm a follower of the Honorable Jesus Messiah. He took my sins."

The driver slapped his hand on the wheel. Carolyn tensed again, but Marie could see that he wasn't angry as much as confused. "No. That's not possible. Each person must stand before Allah. Every work they have accomplished is written in the book. No one can take your sin. Allah will judge you."

Marie looked back out the window. She thought she had said enough. She prayed. Finally, she looked again at the driver in the rearview. "Maybe. Or maybe, that is our choice."

The driver shook his head hard, then smiled. "You are a good person. Are you helping our people?"

Marie nodded. "Yes. I am starting a literacy project for women in Shehktan."

"See, you are a good person. You are our guest. Please do not be angry with our conversation."

"Thank you sir. May God bless you and your family with peace and success."

"Thank you."

The conversation was over, and it had ended well. Marie was both relieved and grateful. She looked at Carolyn, smiled, shrugged, and said only, "We're almost to the airport. Everything's fine."

Carolyn relaxed. "I don't know how you do that. I can talk to our friends, but complete strangers? It just intimidates me."

"Easy." Marie responded. "I just say hello, pray, and see where it goes."

A few minutes later, the two climbed out of the taxi. The driver pulled their suitcases from the trunk and set them down on the sidewalk. Marie drew a handful of Afghani notes from her pocket and handed them to the man.

He protested. "It is nothing." Meaning, you needn't pay for this ride. "You are our guest."

Marie countered. "You have gone to trouble. You've been kind. Please." She held out the folded money to the driver.

Again, he protested. "It's nothing. You are our guest."

Marie recognized the polite response for what it was. She reached inside the passenger side window, placed the folded money on the seat, and explained. "Gasoline is expensive, and you have taken trouble. You are kind. Hide in God."

The driver placed his right hand on his heart, bowed slightly, and responded with his own good-bye. "Be safe in God."

He drove off just as Marie and Carolyn entered the first checkpoint.

The two women smiled and endured their way through each checkpoint, each thickly clotted crowd of waiting men, and across each open space. In the main airport terminal, a middle-aged Afghan man with a clipboard led them to a small outdoor waiting area with a luggage scale and a wooden bench. On the tarmac sat white passenger planes bound for Dubai or Mumbai, an old Russian turboprop routed to Islamabad, and their own small white twin-engine King Air. In the distance, Marie could see two large military cargo planes with Afghan flags stenciled on their tails and a row of matching dark green attack helicopters—a dramatic example of the typical Afghan intermingling of civilian and military.

Marie and Carolyn weighed their luggage, sat down on the bench, and waited for the rest of the passengers to arrive. An hour and a half later, they boarded the small white plane, buckled their seat belts, and headed home to Shehktan.

The aircraft banked hard and lifted above the harsh line of dark brown mountains surrounding the city of Kabul. The brown hills around Kabul city gave way to the jagged outlines and snow-covered faces of the Hindu Kush. Warriors from Alexander the Great onward braved the desolate heights of that Central Asian mountain system. Many died along the way. The name itself means death: *Hindu*, the people of India; *kush*, "to kill." Stunning and terrifying, like Afghanistan itself.

Marie thought about her first trip through those mountains. It was deep winter when she arrived in Afghanistan almost six years earlier. Sharon and her driver, Faiz Muhammad, had met her at Kabul airport and taken her to the guesthouse. Sharon was the long-termer then, experienced and weary from the journey. They had spent three days cooped up in the guesthouse waiting for the road north to open. After the first day, Sharon had said, "Enough questions." Marie had wanted to know everything about Shehktan: the projects, the life there, the Afghans. Sharon had told her to wait. "You'll see when you live the life." Marie had held her tongue. And waited.

When the road opened, Marie and Sharon had climbed into the back of Faiz Muhammad's SUV and set out. *Glory*, Marie had thought, seeing the mountains for the first time. With their jagged black peaks and brilliant white faces, they were stunning. Sharon had only smiled.

Four hours northward, traffic had stopped. Two trucks lay over-turned in the middle of the road just beyond the exit of the longest section of the infamous Salang Tunnel. The SUV sat, engine off, inside the fumy darkness. A group of Afghan women, from the backseat of the vehicle beside them, rolled down their window and called out their greetings to Sharon and Marie; only Sharon could reply. The women gave them each a glass cup of hot tea poured from a thermos and a piece of hard morning bread. Marie had looked down at her tea, ached for a bathroom, and listened to Sharon's smooth Dari and easy laughter. When the tunnel cleared and the vehicles moved, Sharon had waved good-bye to their temporary neighbors and turned to Marie. "This is Afghanistan. I told you. You just have to live it."

Now, from her seat in the little airplane, Marie took in those same snow-laced mountains as they gave way to lower, softer brown hills. Their crevices were veined in darker brown rushing rivers, outlining pools of startling green cultivated fields. Marie traced the angular outlines and surrounding walls of a village nestled into the hills. She remembered the faces and voices, rooms and foods of hidden Afghan communities she and Carolyn had visited on their last project. She searched for some familiar landmark and spotted a cluster of tiny bright red flecks on the brown landscape below. *Red-scarved girls? Grave pennants?* She'd seen both. Marie thought of Sharon's advice. "Yep. You just have to live it."

9

The aircraft descended sharply toward a thick, serpentine river surrounded by clusters of green trees and browning rice fields. Dark smoke from a conical oven rose in columns. A bright yellow tractor crawled in a tight circle against dirt, the husks of freshly cut rice beneath its tires. Marie could make out the shape of a group of men, each in a shalvar kameez, some leaning on long-handled tools.

She could see the one paved road that ran across the town from the western outskirts of wooden shops to the denser center of one- and two-story concrete buildings. Orange, red, and green awnings lined the bazaar, forming a bright backdrop for the thin wisps of gray smoke rising from kebab- and palau-houses. She located the bank with its guard shed, then the corner towers of the small German base. Two blocks farther she saw her own wall, the enclosure full of fruit trees and rosebushes. *Home.*

The aircraft banked hard over the town, then arced southward toward a set of soft brown rhythmically undulating hills, their pockets dark in rounded shadows. Marie saw the walls of a village cut into the edge of the hillsides. Beneath the village, a dark river serpentined through cultivated fields. *Perhaps, someday, I'll get there.* She saw a cluster of bright red, deep green, and black flickering against the brown earth. *Grave markers for sure this time. Martyrs.*

In the days before the Twin Towers went down, before the Americans invaded Afghanistan, Shehktan was a battleground. The Taliban had their Pashtun fighters on one side, the Northern Alliance had their Tajik and Uzbek fighters on the other. The town of Shehktan had fallen. Talebs ruled the streets. Women hid in their compounds; men grew their beards and submitted to the Taliban, but not in the villages. In the villages, the battles raged. And before the Taliban, the Tajik and Uzbek villagers fought one another for land, water, and women. War in Afghanistan is always regional, and every family has a story.

Marie sighed.

The aircraft banked again, and a short, dusty landing strip appeared. Marie located the single-level concrete building beside the dustway and the dark SUV parked beside it. She reached across the narrow aisle to Carolyn, touched her arm, and shouted over the engine's roar. "Faiz Muhammad's here. He'll drive us home." The wheels touched down in a cloud of Afghan dust.

Marie unclipped her seatbelt and waited. The copilot, a young man with sandy blond hair, crisp, white shirt, and navy-blue slacks pushed himself into the low cabin. He leaned toward the door, unlatched it, pushed it forward, and unfolded the small metal ladder. Marie and Carolyn followed him onto the dustway. The man opened a small door at the back of the aircraft, pulled out their suitcases and backpacks, and set them down on the khaki-colored earth.

Marie and Carolyn grabbed their gear and stepped down to the tarmac.

Walking toward them was Faiz Muhammad, a tall, middle-aged bearded man with a deeply lined face and soft eyes. He wore a tan pancake-shaped wool *pakol* cap, and a purple-checked man-scarf around his neck. A camel-colored shalvar kameez and fisherman's vest hung on his thin frame. His calloused feet were shod with simple, plastic sandals.

Marie had known Faiz Muhammad since the day she first arrived in Afghanistan. She trusted him completely. It was his responsibility to take care of her, and he did. He knew everything about Marie's and Carolyn's movements, who their friends were, what they desired from the bazaar, and how their moods rose and fell throughout each week. He treated them like they were his nieces. In his own way, he loved them. With that love and care, he welcomed Marie and Carolyn home. Each pressed her right hand against her own heart. They would not touch regardless of how close they had become.

Faiz Muhammad was accustomed to Marie. She spoke his language well and understood his culture. She made her own decisions but looked to him for advice. He appreciated her wisdom and care. Besides, when his small son was sick, she paid for the boy, his mother, and his brother to go to Kabul for medical care. Faiz Muhammad was sure that gift had saved his son's life.

Carolyn was younger than Marie and, so, in Faiz Muhammad's Afghan logic, required more care. To him, she was like an urban child living with distant relatives in a village. She was naïve and delightful. Her laughter, bubbling over so often from the backseat of his vehicle, enchanted him. Her occasional tears broke his heart.

The two women slid into the backseat of the SUV while Faiz Muhammad fit the suitcases into the back and stacked the backpacks carefully on top. He slid into the front seat, put the vehicle in gear, and listened contentedly to the sound of Carolyn's happy English chatter.

Marie listened too. Occasionally she answered a question or smiled and nodded in agreement. Mostly, though, she watched the terrain through the window beyond Carolyn. The low airport building, empty as always, gradually faded from view. Three boys, each with a long, thin stick, guided a flock of fat-bottomed sheep and shaggy goats across the road toward the hills on the other side. A low, mud-brick wall, its top edge uneven from rain, snow, and disrepair, gapped the width of a donkey cart. The roughly tilled dark earth lay beyond.

Carolyn chattered on about all the things she wanted to do—who she would call first, who she would go see.

Marie breathed the cool, clean air of Shehktan, grateful for the absence of dense Kabuli exhaust fumes and the odor of refuse produced by too many people living too closely together. As the driver banked around a deeply rutted curve, a small village with tall khaki-colored walls came into view. Marie wondered if her new literacy program would take her within those walls.

On the far edge of the village, she heard rushing water and the rough rumble of a machine. Mud-brown water cascaded down a six-foot cataract, slowly turning the wooden blades of a small hydroelectric generator. *Afghans are resourceful*, she thought.

At a small wooden shed built against a wall on the edge of the village, a boy-vendor sat surrounded by four other boys and shelves full of basic household supplies: pink toilet paper, blue-and-yellow boxes of matches, white bags of salt, and dull amber blocks of cheap all-purpose soap.

Faiz Muhammad slowed down behind a small boy leading a donkey draped in rice stalks. The young boy tugged his gray donkey beside the wall and the SUV passed.

The dirt road turned and descended toward town. The walls disappeared, and the vehicle drove between wide open fields with short, brown stubble. In the distance gray-black smoke rose from a large dome-shaped oven. Beyond that, a battered, yellow Russian tractor drove in tight circles over a pile of raw rice. Half a dozen men with handmade shovels or wooden pitchforks stood around the circle. They turned and stared at Marie's vehicle as Faiz Muhammad slowly drove by. Marie looked away.

Carolyn continued talking. She was planning her good-bye party. They would buy wedding decorations from a local store and festoon the room with glittery ribbons. Marie smiled and offered to take pictures. Carolyn went on.

The open countryside gave way to light brown mud-brick walls punctuated by rough, wooden gates. Marie watched five boys crouched on the ground, beside a wall playing marbles. When the vehicle approached, the boys jumped and chased it down the street, shouting and laughing.

The mud walls gave way to glass-windowed shops housing tailors and pharmacies. Other vehicles appeared and disappeared: a blue Toyota Corolla, an improvised motorcycle rickshaw with a burgundy booth mounted on a two-wheel axle, a wooden donkey cart loaded high with tan bricks, another carrying a small pile of fine, gray sand.

Marie smiled.

Faiz Muhammad pulled behind the brick-laden cart. He waved at the bearded driver and his skinny, laboring, gray donkey. The man sat at the front of the cart, his reins in one hand and a long, thin stick in the other, his feet draped over the harness bar, his purple-checked scarf startlingly bright against the dusty, faded surroundings.

They entered the town proper, drove past its small concrete hospital, and stopped at an intersection cornered with low glass-fronted buildings. Faiz Muhammad waited for a gap in the traffic, turned right, and passed a domed mosque under construction.

Marie broke into Carolyn's plans with a question. "Faiz Muhammad-jan, who has paid for the new mosque?"

Faiz Muhammad stroked his beard. "A rich landowner, Ahmad Rasul Khan. It is sawab for him. Allah is great."

Marie looked over at Carolyn, but the younger woman was still lost in good-bye party visions. Marie looked back at the mosque. Two men perched on the edge of the dome, carefully tiling its curved face. She imagined the beauty of the final structure shimmering in the Afghan sun.

They drove past a wide, dusty park surrounded by a low, concrete wall. A group of young men played soccer, the tails of their shalvar kameezes floating behind them as they ran. In the distance, small clusters of men sat on scraps of red carpet, drinking tea, and lazing in the sun. There were no women anywhere to be seen in the park. That space belonged to men.

The SUV reached the small German military base and turned onto a dust-and-rock road. Marie looked up at the watchtower. Three guards. Two held automatic weapons; the third leaned against an empty window frame and smoked a cigarette. Their uniforms identified them as Afghans. They were the first level, the perimeter guard. Behind them was the next level, a set of German guards.

From a cross street, Marie spotted the rusty-gray gate of her friend Zia Gul and smiled. *Soon.*

Beyond her friend's gate, a three-story concrete house, still under construction, rose a full story above its tallest neighbors. Marie looked at its gray pillars, wide porches, and flat roof. She called out to her driver. "Faiz Muhammad-jan. Whose house is that?"

The man smiled wryly. He gave the name of the local head of the Ministry of Health.

Marie matched his smile. "He has become wealthy."

The driver shrugged. "He is a government minister."

The SUV bounced along the wide, rough, tree-lined road. *The autumn rains will fall soon, and the road will turn to mud,* Marie thought.

Faiz Muhammad turned into a narrow, dusty alleyway cut down the middle by a muddy, unlined culvert. He stopped at a group of young boys playing soccer in the alley. He honked the horn and waited until they collected their ball and retreated into the frame of a gate.

He drove another twenty yards, stopped, and beeped again. Marie and Carolyn waited in the back seat. The gate swung open and a rough-shaven middle-aged Afghan guard stepped into the alley, followed by two midsize dogs, one black and one golden. The man was one of their home guards, Omed. He was wearing baggy khaki trousers over dark-brown work boots, with a red T-shirt that read *Iowa State* and *42* in gold.

Grinning at his eclectic outfit, Marie slid down from the vehicle to greet Omed, and he threw his calloused hands open. "Mari-jan!" Marie rubbed the dogs' heads and rushed through her standard greeting questions. After Faiz Muhammad retrieved the bags, the two men clasped hands, touched cheeks, and exchanged their own greetings.

Marie and Carolyn, their dogs entwined around them, stepped through the gate and into the shade of a tall pear tree. The guard followed with their suitcases, closing and locking the dark green metal gate behind him. The rough rumble of the SUV motor was muffled as they stepped into the soft silence of the walled yard. Marie felt her shoulders loosen and relax.

The front yard was crowded with fruit trees: almond, peach, plum, and a pear still heavy with fruit. Beyond the trees, a wide, shallow concrete porch, roofed in thatch sheeting, spread out before the front door.

Crossing through the door into a wide hall, Marie and Carolyn unwrapped their headscarves and hung them side by side on a set of crowded wooden pegs. They pried off their sandals and kicked them onto the floor beside a pile of dress shoes, house sandals, and slippers.

Marie slipped her feet into fleece booties and padded down the hall to her room. Everything was as she had left it. The bed, a foam mattress on the floor, still unmade. The desk, crowded with scraps of paper, an MP3 player with a set of battery-operated speakers, and a scattered pile of colored markers. A small heap of laundry tumbled over a large, aluminum trunk.

She took in her familiar pictures on the wall. There was a landscape of a mountain village; a framed photograph of her parents in the home of her youth; her sister and brother-in-law on the deck at their new home, two children in their arms; a poster of a farm scene from Maryland, and another of the Blue Ridge Mountains in western Virginia; a burgundy-framed photo of her with Carolyn, their arms draped around three smiling Afghan women. Marie smiled, thinking about them, her closest Afghan friends.

Aziza, the oldest of the three, had worked for Marie's NGO since before Marie arrived. Sharon had hired her; Marie had inherited her. Aziza was wise, experienced, and strong enough to get things done when the doing seemed impossible. Marie relied on her. Plus, Aziza called herself a Jesus-follower. Marie was never really sure about that, but Sharon had been, and that was enough for her.

Khadija was the youngest of the three and much newer at the office. Marie had hired her after Sharon left and before Carolyn arrived. Khadija had learned English in Shehktan, and she knew how to use a computer. She was bright, energetic, and optimistic. She was also devotedly Muslim. She had a deeper commitment to doing the right things the right way than Aziza did. Sometimes the two women clashed, but their differences complemented each other well. *I'll see them tomorrow,* Marie thought, smiling.

Marie planned to see Zia Gul, the third Afghan in the photo, today. Zia Gul was Marie's closest Afghan friend. Marie had known her since she first arrived, and she loved the woman deeply.

Marie unpacked her things, found her coffee and French press, and padded into the kitchen. Within minutes, the comforting aroma of brewing coffee filled the air. Carolyn appeared, an MP3 player plugged into her ears and a sketchpad under her arm.

Marie interrupted the younger woman's music. "I'm going to send some emails, then visit Zia Gul."

Carolyn nodded.

"Want to come?"

Carolyn shrugged. She always wanted to go visiting with Marie, but this time she guessed Marie would want some time alone with her friend.

Marie returned to her room, set her coffee cup on the floor next to her bed, and unpacked her laptop. She flipped the switch on the backup power supply and watched the tiny red and green lights on the wireless router blink into life. She settled down. The router connected to the satellite dish on the roof and then to the world beyond Shehktan.

Marie began to write. She sent a short update to a group of praying friends, then a note to her parents. Finally, she settled her heart and wrote to her closest friend in America.

Dear Debbie,

I'm home. Praise God! It's quiet here. The dogs are outside watching our house. It's a little gray, so I can't see the mountains in the distance very well—just outlines, but it's lovely. The leaves on my trees are starting to turn brown. The rains will come soon and everything will turn to mud, but not yet.

I'll start the project tomorrow. I can't wait.

Kabul was crazy. You heard the news, I know. So many people have left. Others are leaving soon. I don't know most of them. Kabul is like a world away, even though it really isn't. Except that Carolyn's leaving. She's getting married. Or, she thinks she's getting married. I hope it works out.

Right now she's out on the back porch in the garden. Our roses are still in bloom. Can you believe it? Do you remember the picture? The whole backyard is full of roses. Our guards take care of them. They're mostly red, but some of them are white. Anyway, Carolyn's out there with her MP3 player and her sketch pad. She's leaving. And I was just getting used to her. Hah! It hasn't even been two years yet. Yikes, this place is going to be empty when she goes. We don't have anyone coming, either. So it'll just be Dave and Margaret and me at the office. Argh!

The Dutch family and the German doctor are still here, but I don't see them very often. It's been so nice to have another single woman to go out visiting with. Well, I wandered around alone before she came. I can do it again. Anyway, I have a new project and I can't wait to start it!

The Kabul thing was crazy. Nobody really knows why it happened, but it seems like it was personal. I really don't think we have anything to worry about up here. I mean, we have the normal Afghan stuff, but nothing specific, at least as far as I know. Still, it kind of made us all crazy.

I know it makes you crazy. I'm sorry. I'm sure I won't be over here forever. It's a window. It'll close. I just want to stay as long as I can. I really like it here and I like what I'm doing.

I'm going out to see Zia Gul after my coffee. Do you still have her picture? She's getting gray streaks in her hair and little crow's feet around her eyes. I should get you another picture. Her oldest daughter is studying for the entrance exam to university. I love it that my closest friend wants her girls to be educated. Did I tell you Zia Gul's husband got a night letter about that? He doesn't know who posted it, but it said he's not Muslim if he sends his daughters to school. He doesn't care. He's sending them to school anyway. I love that.

Well, I guess that's it. Tell me what's going on your way. Send my love to everyone and don't worry. I know, worrying is your job, but don't worry. Just keep a light on for me.

Love ya,
Marie.

Marie pressed the send button and took a deep breath. She scanned the contents of her inbox: security reports. She skimmed through each one. Two Afghan police officers were killed at a checkpoint in Baghlan. She pictured the map. *Baghlan. Too far away to worry about.* A roadside bomb hit a convoy including the governor of Kunduz. No one was killed, but several were injured. Marie looked at the name of the district. *Forty minutes away. Okay, that's not too close.*

The next report got her attention. *Shehktan?* Police raided a house and seized weapons, bombs, and bomb-making material. Two men were killed. She took a deep breath and read the report a second time. *Bomb-making equipment? Who did they want to bomb?* She rubbed her temples. *Dave will read this. He'll figure it out.* She sighed and pressed delete.

Marie closed the computer, put it on the shelf, and prepared herself to reenter the Afghan world beyond her gate.

10

Marie met Zia Gul the month after she arrived in Shehktan, and the two immediately connected. In those days, Zia Gul was lonely. She had moved to Shehktan from Kabul three years earlier when her husband decided it was time to return to his family's land. Unlike most older women in Shehktan, Zia Gul was educated. She had studied to the twelfth grade and would have finished university had war not intervened.

Zia Gul's marriage was a love match, one of the few Marie knew of in Afghanistan. She had met her husband during their first semester of university in Kabul. He had been smart, kind, and good-looking. She caught his eye, too.

They hadn't spoken at all until the second semester, and even then it was nothing more than a nod and a mumbled salaam. When the vicious civil war that followed the Russian withdrawal descended upon Kabul, Zia Gul's father died, and her education came to an abrupt end. That's when the man she would soon marry took action.

He tracked down Zia Gul's uncle and found the young woman's brother through him. Though the brother was only twelve at the time, the suitor did what was right. He visited the brother, sat with him over cups of tea, and asked for the girl he had so admired in his university classroom.

The brother balked. In Afghanistan, the ideal marriage match is between first cousins; this man, though a Tajik like himself, was not a family member. The boy didn't even know the suitor's family, who were all from Shehktan, not Kabul. He had no idea if the man was decent or his family honorable. Still, war was in the city and times were hard. The boy's father had already died and his mother was weak. Zia Gul was old enough to marry and clearly wasn't going to continue at the university. There were three younger sisters to help the mother, so Zia Gul wasn't needed at home. So went the boy's reasoning. He consented to give Zia Gul to her husband.

For the young woman, it was a glorious day. Not only had she already seen her husband, but she liked him too; and she'd secretly hoped he would come for her. That was ten years before Marie and Zia Gul met. In the intervening years, children were born, the Taliban took Kabul, the Americans came, and her husband decided to take his family home to Shehktan.

For Zia Gul, it had been a heartbreaking move, meaning the loss of her mother, her sisters, and the other women she had grown up with. Her husband said this would not be a problem; the women in his large family in Shehktan would welcome her. And they had tried to, but Zia Gul was literate and they were not. She was city and they were small town. She was an outsider and they were insiders. In the end, the move left Zia Gul lonely after all.

When Marie arrived in Shehktan and went looking for a language tutor, she had found Zia Gul, or rather, Zia Gul's oldest daughter had found her. Marie was walking alone around the neighborhood, praying for the hidden families behind each wall. As she walked, she averted her eyes from every man who came near her and smiled a friendly salaam to every woman or child within earshot.

Zia Gul's oldest daughter heard her salaam and immediately invited the foreigner to her house for tea. Often, women or children invited her to their homes for tea, but usually just once. "Come to my house for tea; may you live forever," and that was all. Marie knew not to accept such limited invitations. Zia Gul's oldest daughter had been different. Her invitation was insistent; she'd taken Marie's hand and refused to let her go. "You must come. My mother is waiting." Marie followed the girl.

When they entered the girl's compound, Marie saw Zia Gul crouched on the hard dirt at the far edge of a naked yard. The woman stood, soapy water dripping from her forearms. Marie looked at the shallow aluminum basin at the woman's feet, its wet clothes still set-tling into soapy water, and felt the shock of embarrassment.

Zia Gul was not embarrassed. She was delighted.

Before the end of their first cup of tea, Marie had hired Zia Gul to be her language tutor. The arrangement had been fruitful. Marie learned the Dari language and Zia Gul made a little money. But more than that, the two women became friends. They shared their lives with each other. When Zia Gul's husband traveled, Marie slept between her friend and the children so the woman wouldn't be alone. When Sharon left, Marie found refuge in Zia Gul's friendship. Together, they struggled to make sense out of the world around them.

Along the way, Zia Gul met Christ. The journey had not been easy.

At first, Zia Gul liked Marie's faith and the stories she told. She liked the teachings and works of Jesus. She thought he was a great and kind prophet. In those early days, their conversations helped Zia Gul be a better Muslim. But during the second year of their friendship, things changed. Zia Gul worked hard to find fault in everything Marie said and did. She pushed Marie to convert to Islam and correct her life choices and the culture from which she came.

Marie was patient.

Sometime early during the third year, Zia Gul's attitudes shifted. One day, Zia Gul defended Marie and her faith to a group of neighborhood women. Marie watched and wondered, but said nothing. Later, Zia Gul herself explained the goodness and love of God to a woman whose husband had taken another wife. Marie listened, prayed, and continued to wonder.

Finally, one stiflingly hot afternoon, Zia Gul spoke openly. She had had a dream. A being of light had entered her dark room. He sat on the floor beside her head, stroked her hair comfortingly, and invited her to come with him. "I knew it was Jesus. I just knew." That was all the explanation Zia Gul offered.

It wasn't that she claimed to have become a Christian—she wouldn't use that word to describe her identity. Nor had she discarded the religious practices that were such an important part of her life. She continued to pray five times a day and to fast through Ramadan. She continued to call herself a Muslim. But her faith had clearly changed. For Marie, Zia Gul had become much more than just a friend. She had become a sister, an Afghan with whom Marie genuinely shared her faith.

Of course she would visit Zia Gul first.

Marie tied her hair up and gathered her things: keys, cell phone, identification, a handful of Afghani notes, a prepaid cell phone refill card, and a cloth envelope with several one-hundred dollar bills. *Insurance.* She pinned the envelope inside her long skirt, packing everything else into her black backpack.

She put on her long, brown coat and wrapped her brown-and-gold scarf around her head. She slipped on her sandals at the door, walked across the yard, and found Omed. When she told him her plans, he was delighted. From his perspective, women should visit women. It's good for their hearts. He wished her well, following her to the gate along with the dogs. Marie paused, closed her eyes, took a deep breath, and prayed silently before stepping into the Afghan world. Immediately, the stench from the open culvert stung her nostrils.

Half a dozen small children ran to her hips. They tugged on Marie's coat and held their hands out to shake hers. As they sang out their salaams, Marie forgot about the culvert's stench. She touched the head of each child, smiling and returning every greeting. She cradled the chin of the most bashful child until the little girl looked up at her with wonder-filled eyes. Marie didn't know her, but she picked her up in her arms and kissed her grimy forehead before setting her back down in the alley. The little girl immediately jumped behind a small boy, but she trailed Marie awhile along with the others. Eventually the presence of an old man warned them away, and they left her.

At the end of the alley, a group of teenage boys clustered around an equally young shopkeeper. The wooden stall he called a shop was far too small for such a group, so the boys spilled out onto the street. As she neared the boys, her presence excited them. A few called out in bad English, "Hello, mister! Hello, mister! I fine. Thank you."

Marie locked her jaw and kept walking. These young men were violating their own cultural rules. They were rude beyond measure, but not dangerous. Still, Marie knew it wasn't appropriate for her to talk to them.

But the boys followed her, tripping over their English. They wanted her attention, her voice, her language, anything. They were simply bored, and she was entertainment.

Marie knew how to respond. She held her head high, her spine straight, and her shoulders back. She chose words for her own heart only. Necessary words. *They're boys. Annoying, but not evil. A little dangerous, not much. Just boys. Bored. Obnoxious.* She relaxed the grip of her hand around the strap of her backpack and prayed. *Lord Jesus, you're right here with me, walking beside me, down this street, between these walls, between me and these boys. I'm yours. Not theirs. I belong to you.*

The boys crowded around her closely now, demanding her attention in their broken English. The tension in the back of her jaw grew, tightening her throat. She continued her silent fervent prayer. *Father, I don't like the way these boys are treating me. I want them to go away. They're too close. Please don't let them touch me.*

The boys gave up on English and switched to Dari. "Why won't you talk to us? Don't you speak our language? Don't you speak English? Talk to us!"

Marie kept her head high, her eyes averted, her back straight, and her shoulders square. She walked slowly, careful not to step into the boy in front of her. The bitter tension clenched her stomach.

The boys broke off, tossing their final harassments at her and returned the way they'd come. Marie breathed deeply in shaky relief, but for her the ordeal wasn't over until she prayed for the boys. *Father, I forgive these boys their rudeness. I forgive them their arrogance. I forgive them this harassment. I pray you would forgive them too. I know you know each of these boys by name, that you love them and you're calling them to yourself. Show them your love and your mercy.*

She turned onto Zia Gul's street and greeted three Afghan women shrouded in dull gray-blue burqas. They returned her greeting and immediately invited her to tea. Marie thanked them but went on. As she walked, she looked up the road and saw the upper story outline of the new concrete house she'd seen earlier with Carolyn and Faiz Muhammad. It looked out of place on a street lined with twelve-foot walls and one- and two-story mud-brick homes.

She stepped up to Zia Gul's gate and found it latched but unlocked.

Knocking hard, she pushed it open and stepped into her friend's yard. Immediately, she felt at ease.

Zia Gul heard Marie's salaam and met her friend at the door of the house. The two clasped hands, kissed one another's cheeks, and exchanged greetings. Zia Gul pulled Marie into the cool darkness of her home, and Marie felt the warm welcome of sweet friendship. They settled down on burgundy, cotton floor mats in a pale green room and began trading their news.

A woman had come with three of her relatives, all dressed in their finest clothes, to request Zia Gul's firstborn daughter in marriage for the woman's son. The number of women and the fine clothes they wore marked the visit as an official proposal. Zia Gul knew and respected the family, but her daughter was too young. "I told her she would go to university first. She must pass the test; that's all. Or else I will give her in marriage."

"What's she doing now?"

"Studying." The two women laughed.

Zia Gul asked Marie about the Kabul trip.

Yes, it was successful. Yes, she was glad to be back in Shehktan. Yes, Kabul is crowded and dirty. Yes, there are too many cars.

Zia Gul's daughter brought the women glass cups, a thermos full of steaming green tea, and several small dishes of candy, raisins, and almonds. She exchanged greetings with Marie, then disappeared.

Zia Gul shared her news about a cousin of her husband who had been in an accident in the mountains that separated Shehktan from Kabul and more about the family that had come for her daughter. Marie told Zia Gul about her trip to the Kabul Ministry of Economy and the man who told her she should work in Kandahar. The women laughed.

Marie knew there were two subjects she was avoiding: the death of the foreigner and Carolyn's imminent departure. At least for a little while, she wanted to forget them both.

The conversation drifted and the afternoon slipped gently away. At four o'clock, Marie knew it was time to go. She sighed, gathered her backpack, and asked permission to leave. Zia Gul rose with her, and the two women walked to the gate.

Just inside the yard, Zia Gul caught Marie's hand. "Mari-jan, you must be careful."

Her tone startled Marie.

"My husband says there are bad men here. He says I should tell you."

Marie studied her friend's face. She assumed outsiders had come into Shehktan looking for trouble. "Have they come because of me?"

Zia Gul shook her head. "When you were in Kabul, the police killed two brothers. Uzbeks. They said they were making bombs. They said they had guns and bombs in their house."

Marie remembered the security report. "Uzbeks." *Locals.* She listened carefully.

Zia Gul released Marie's hand. "The men have become angry. My husband says you should be careful. You should not trust anyone. People here are not good."

Marie nodded. She'd heard this before. She knew Afghans didn't trust anyone who wasn't part of their extended family. Usually their concerns were based on prejudice more than fact. But something was different here—men had been killed. She wanted more information. "Does the family of the two brothers live here in Shehktan?"

"Yes. Yes." She told Marie the name of the neighborhood, on the east side of town, as well as the name of their home village, north of the city. "My husband says you must be careful. The men have become angry."

"The Uzbek family? Angry with who?"

Zia Gul shrugged. "They are fighting with another family. They have all become angry. You must be careful."

Marie took her friend's hands, kissed her cheeks, and thanked her. She asked her to thank her husband, as well. "Trust in God, my friend."

The street was quiet when Marie emerged through Zia Gul's gate. A group of boys played marbles next to a far wall. Three teenage girls in the black slacks, long black jackets, and black headscarves that marked them as students chatted as they walked. At the corner, a burgundy-cabined motorcycle rickshaw with a young driver bounced loudly and disappeared.

Marie thought about Zia Gul's warning. She knew that security assessments were always an uncomfortable mix of intuition and half-baked information. Perhaps this warning was just an Afghan husband's overreaction. Then again, perhaps it was more than that. She pulled her phone out of its yellow pouch. Although Dave was still in Kabul, she knew she had to call him. He was their NGO director and would need to assess the situation.

Dave listened to Marie's story and thanked her for the details. He had already read of the incident and assumed the Uzbeks would take revenge. After all, their men had been killed and that would not be accepted. Still, their battle was with the government and he didn't think it affected them.

Marie wasn't so sure. She trusted Dave, but still couldn't let go. It was the husband of her close friend who had provided the advice. That was important.

All Dave said was, "I'll check into it, but don't worry."

There was nothing to do now except pay attention, and Marie was good at that.

At Marie's corner, the teenage shopkeeper was gone. In his place, a black-bearded man with a light blue turban sat on a wooden crate beside a gray-bearded man wrapped in a lightweight, wool blanket.

The two looked away respectfully as Marie passed by. Her alley was empty and quiet.

She pounded on her own green metal gate, and Omed and her dogs welcomed her home. She released the tension she had felt again on the street, something more than the low-grade tension she always felt as a foreign woman on the streets of Afghanistan. Inside the house, she found Carolyn stirring scrambled eggs into a pan of fried onions, garlic, and peppers. The two chatted, but Marie kept the latest piece of news to herself. She would talk to Faiz Muhammad and listen to his council. She would watch and pay attention. Dave would investigate. No reason to worry Carolyn—not yet, not until they knew something concrete.

The two women carried their thick glass plates, heaped with steaming food, into the living room and sat down on the dark green raw cotton mats stretched across the swirling red, gold, and black carpet.

Marie looked around the living room as they ate. It was Carolyn's room.

The women shared the space, but its décor had been Carolyn's doing. She had a flair for color and design, and it showed. Before she arrived, the room had been simple, almost stark. Now it had pale yellow walls covered with large framed photographs: a few landscapes, and several personal portraits of shy Afghan children, laughing Afghan girls, and serious Afghan women with their arms draped around Marie, Carolyn, or both.

There were bright white shelves built into the walls filled with books, knickknacks, and DVDs, most of them Carolyn's. The deep window ledges and wooden window frames were also painted white. The curtains were simple, dark green panels on café rods, with white sheers behind them.

Darkness descended and the ceiling light switched on. The neighborhood generator had started. The two women talked about their trip, how good it was to be back, and what they had planned for the next day. Their conversation was light, easy. They each avoided their shared troubling subjects. After the meal, Marie retreated to her room with a novel she'd picked up at the Kabul guesthouse.

At 9:30 p.m., as usual, the electricity from the neighborhood generator went off, and the neighborhood settled into thick, quiet darkness.

Marie slid under her covers. Holly, the small, golden dog, curled in a ball on the back porch, just outside her window. Jake, the larger black dog, paced the inside of the yard. His presence comforted Marie and her neighbors, too. Women there were vulnerable and it was the job of men to protect them. Marie's neighbors wanted her protected just as their own families were protected. After all, she was their foreigner, their guest. She belonged to them.

Marie knew the velvet silence of nighttime in her neighborhood. She knew the middle of the night cries of neighbor's babies, the predawn call to pray of the local mullah, the sunrise crowing of roosters, and the braying of donkeys dragging loads through the early morning street. She knew the voices of the children who played in the alley, the clanging of the pots and pans from the neighbor's yard, the banter of women behind their walls. Her little house in Shehktan had become her home, and she was comfortable there. That night, she slept soundly.

DAY 11

CHAR AB, AFGHANISTAN

11

In the morning, Marie awoke refreshed, focused, and ready to work. Faiz Muhammad picked her and Carolyn up at 8:00 a.m. The three drove to their NGO office in silence. Marie thinking about the project setup, and Carolyn thinking about announcing her departure.

Their NGO office was located on the far side of town, its gate marked with a small, hand-painted blue-on-white sign. At the gate, Faiz Muhammad honked, and the office guard opened the double gate. The driver pulled in and parked the vehicle.

Climbing down from the SUV, Carolyn put her hand on the side of the car and teased Marie. "In America, I'm going to drive my own car!" She was already mentally leaving.

Marie shrugged. "You'll pay insurance, too."

Carolyn laughed. "Small price to pay for freedom."

In truth, Marie loved driving. She hated that she wasn't able to drive in Afghanistan, but that was only one of the many activities forbidden her. Riding a bicycle, walking unmolested on the street, swimming in the river, wearing a T-shirt or shorts, untying her hair in public, shopping—doing anything—at whim . . . The list was too long. Carolyn was right about the freedom outside Afghanistan, of course. And now that it would be hers again soon, she could afford to think about it. Marie couldn't.

"I'll catch up to you," Marie said, waving Carolyn on and turning to their driver. "Faiz Muhammad-jan, I have a question."

The man slid out of the vehicle. "Go ahead, Mari-jan."

Marie watched Carolyn walk across the gravel parking area toward a one-story mud-brick building fronted by a wide, uncovered concrete porch. When Carolyn entered the building, Marie turned back to Faiz Muhammad. "I've heard news."

Faiz Muhammad nodded and waited.

"Is there talk?"

Faiz Muhammad locked the SUV. "What kind of talk?"

Marie studied his face. He seemed unconcerned. "There was a problem when we were in Kabul. Yes?"

The man nodded. "Perhaps."

"Two men were killed. Uzbeks. Yes?"

"Yes. There is always trouble."

Marie chose her words carefully. "Is there something we should worry about?"

The driver tilted his head backward, his eyes hooded. "Perhaps." He looked straight at Marie. "We will watch."

Marie nodded. "Thank you. You will tell me, yes?"

The older man placed his hand on his heart. "Of course, Mari-jan. Don't become sad."

Marie smiled and walked away. *Watch and wait. That's all we can do.*

She slipped out of her sandals at the doorway and stepped into a long, narrow room full of mismatched desks, black fabric chairs on silver pipe frames, and a small white conference table. The pale blue walls were covered with maps, two dry-erase boards, and a half-dozen framed posters printed on thick, plastic-covered paper. The posters, each from a different project, showed photographs of grim village men, smiling children, and baby-carrying women.

Marie's favorite was a poster of a tiny old woman sitting in a wheelbarrow, clutching its upper rim, while a black-bearded man pushed it along a rutted path. The old woman's eyes were wide with equal parts of fear and delight. Marie had snapped the photo herself. It was the day of her first solo village food distribution. With Sharon temporarily out of the country, Marie had done the job alone. She had insisted that every recipient on the elders' list come in person. Three were missing. The elders had argued, but Marie wouldn't relent. A few minutes later, the woman in the wheelbarrow arrived, obviously unable to come to the meeting or anywhere else without assistance. Marie snapped the picture and accepted her own embarrassment.

The old woman hadn't complained about the wheelbarrow ride. Instead, she simply sat quietly on the edge of the platform, surrounded by bags of rice and flour and cans of cooking oil. In the end, she had cradled Marie's face in her hands, kissed her forehead, and spoke blessings over her life.

Sharon had printed the poster as a joke, but Marie loved it. It reminded her of her stumbling efforts and the grace Afghans so often showed her. It wasn't the first time she had been wrong in Afghanistan, nor would it be the last.

Carolyn stood at the far end of the room with Aziza and Khadija. The women greeted Marie, and the four settled down around the white conference table to collect one another's news.

Carolyn wanted to go first. She was sure her coworkers would be delighted that she was finally to be married. She was only twenty-four, but that was old by Afghan standards.

But Marie gently waved her off. "The classes first, okay?"

Carolyn nodded, and Marie addressed the women in clear but simple Dari. "The government has agreed to our project."

Aziza, the eldest, her hair now henna-dyed, clapped her hands. "Congratulations, Mari-jan. We will start right away."

Khadija nodded her agreement.

"Good." Marie went on. "You know how it will work?"

The women nodded, but Marie continued anyway. "We'll start by funding up to twelve classes. Each class will have twenty students, seventeen to seventy years old. Okay?"

While Marie talked, Khadija poured tea from a thermos. She placed a glass cup in front of each woman. Marie thanked her and continued.

"Each teacher must have a certificate of graduation from grade 12. She must have the agreement of the head of the household to hold the class in her home. And she must have the signature of the neighborhood elder. Yes?"

Again, Aziza responded. "Yes, yes Mari-jan. We understand. We have classes ready."

Marie knew that her Afghan coworkers had already passed the word. "And are all the teachers grade-12 graduates?"

"Yes, yes, Mari-jan." Aziza swore by God, jumped up from her place, and returned with a stack of stapled, smudged, rolled, and crumpled pages. "Six classes have become ready." She laid six packets in a row on the table in front of Marie.

Marie picked up a package and studied it carefully. The first page included a list of twenty-two handwritten names. Marie could read printed Dari fairly well, but the handwritten version differed greatly, and it mystified her. She handed the page to Aziza and asked her to read the names.

"Khorshid, daughter of Amid Ahmad. Khalida, daughter of Taleb Muhammad. Gul Afruz, daughter of Taj Muhammad. Bibi-jan, daughter of Masoud Agha. Mujghan, daughter of Amanulla."

Marie smiled at the recitation of women's names followed by their father's. She wanted to meet each woman, talk to her, get to know her. "They know I'll check on all the classes? They know I'll talk to the students, yes?"

Aziza responded quickly. "Yes, yes. We have permission."

"Good." Marie took the list of students from Aziza, counted the names, and turned to the second page. That page was also handwritten in Dari, but it contained a blue circular stamp with a signature written across it. Marie handed it to Aziza to read.

"I, Ahmad Rasul Khan, Elder of Char Ab, give my permission to . . ."

"Thanks." Marie didn't need Aziza to finish reading. "And they know we will provide the materials: books, notebooks, pens, pencils, erasers, a dry board, and dry markers?" Marie was careful to list out exactly what the office intended to purchase. Without such clarity, the participants would expect more. Marie didn't want to encourage disappointment.

Again, Aziza nodded. "Yes, yes. They have become happy."

"Good. We'll start visiting the teachers this afternoon." She picked up the first stack of pages. "This one first. Where is it?"

Aziza looked at the page. "Char Ab. It's a village outside of town. Not far."

Marie felt a dull thud against her chest. Zia Gul's words came back to her. *They had guns and bombs. Their village is north of town.* She looked at Aziza. "Char Ab?"

"Yes. It's the village of our office night guard. This is his family."

Marie knew the guard, but not well. "Is it north or south of town?"

Aziza seemed to pick up on Marie's concern. "South. It's safe. Peaceful. These are good people."

Marie nodded. "Are the rest here in town?"

"Yes, yes. All of them except this class."

"Good." Marie stretched the tension out of her neck. "We'll visit Char Ab this afternoon." She slipped the sheaf of papers into her backpack. "Tomorrow we'll visit the rest."

Marie glanced at Carolyn and smiled. "Okay, your turn. Are you ready?"

Carolyn ran her thumbnail across each fingernail, carefully pushing the cuticles back. She didn't know where to start. Aziza, Khadija, and Marie waited. Finally, Carolyn looked up. She took a deep breath and began. "I have a fiancé. I will become married." She stopped.

Aziza's eyes lit up, but Khadija cocked her head sideways. Carolyn did her best to explain the situation in her very limited Dari.

"When is the engagement party?" Aziza assumed Carolyn would go home for the large party that would mean a formal engagement contract. Carolyn looked to Marie for help.

"They want to know when you're leaving. They'll expect you to leave right before the official engagement party."

"Oh." Carolyn looked down at the glass cup of bronze-colored tea before her. She thought for a minute. She hadn't yet purchased the tickets but wanted to leave soon. "Two weeks."

Aziza and Khadija gasped. This was not the answer they were expecting. In Afghanistan a bride was expensive, and a young man needed time to gather enough money to marry. It should take a year, or at least six months. It shouldn't happen quickly.

Khadija immediately started crying. She blurted out her words in Dari. "But you just came!"

Carolyn sat up straight, wide-eyed and confused. "But I'm getting engaged." Her voice sounded like a plea.

Aziza took control of the situation. "Yes, yes. A girl must marry. It's the will of Allah. Your parents have agreed. Now, you must go." She shot a warning look at Khadija, and the younger woman immediately wiped her tears and stopped crying.

Marie placed her fingertips gently on Carolyn's knee. She looked into the young woman's concerned eyes and spoke to her in English. "You did well. It's okay."

Carolyn nodded, relieved, but of course the conversation wasn't over yet. For the Afghans, it had just begun. They wanted to know everything: whether he was a relative of hers, what family he was from, whether he was literate, what he did for a living, even how much he was paying for her.

Marie rose from the table. She had other things to do. Even if she hadn't, she admitted to herself, she would have made something up. Carolyn was leaving, and there was nothing she could do about that. *Char Ab,* she thought and immediately translated the name: *Four Waters. A village.* She smiled.

After lunch, Marie and Aziza slid into the backseat of Faiz Muhammad's SUV. Carolyn had wanted to go with them, but Marie refused. "You're leaving soon. It's not time to start new relationships." The truth was, Marie was already starting over herself—a new project, in new neighborhoods, with new Afghans. Without Carolyn. It made sense.

Aziza gave Faiz Muhammad the location. He nodded and drove out of the gate.

The meaning of the village's name had stirred her imagination. *Four Waters.* She asked Faiz Muhammad if it had been named after four rivers or four wells.

"Char Ab is an old village, but it's small," Faiz Muhammad said. "Now there are many people. They came during the mujahedin war, when the Taliban destroyed the Shamali Valley."

He was referring to the attack of 1999, when the Taliban chased the people of the Shamali Valley from their homes and destroyed their houses and crops, as well as the rich irrigation system that had kept the valley green and fertile throughout the long Afghan summers. Most of the displaced had fled to Kabul, but many moved northward first, to refugee camps in the mountains. After that, they disappeared. Some, Marie realized, had settled in Char Ab. "And the name?"

Faiz Muhammad glanced in the rearview mirror as he drove southward along the unpaved road beyond the town's walls. Ahead of them lay a row of soft brown hills, their faces scooped by eons of wind flowing across the Central Asian plains. "There are four waterfalls. Small, but they always have water. It flows from the rock. There is one river. They are still moving the river to flood the land."

Marie imagined the waterfalls cascading down deep chasms cut into the hillsides and flowing into a rich, fertile valley. She imagined a once fairly straight river rerouted with shovels and picks into a serpentine path. She wanted to know more about Char Ab. "What do they grow?"

"They are harvesting rice now."

"Do they grow rice twice a year, or just in the second planting?"

"No. They grow wheat for the first planting. They grow rice for the second. They are farmers, Tajiks from the Shamali Valley. They are good people."

Dusty, barren, uncultivated fields stretched to the right and left of their vehicle. On both sides of the road, green, black, and red pennants of martyrs' graves floated in the breeze. This was the battle line Marie had seen the day before from her seat on the small, white plane from Kabul. "Faiz Muhammad-jan, whose graves are these?"

The man cocked his head and pointed to the left side of the road. "Ah, Mari-jan, those are the martyrs from the Taliban. They came out of the town to attack the village." He pointed to the right side. "Those are the Tajik martyrs. They threw rockets at each other. Many men became martyrs."

Aziza lifted the thigh-length front of her burqa and draped its embroidered hem across the thick pillbox cap that bound the cloth to the top of her head. "One was my uncle. He left two small children."

Marie looked at the dark strips of cloth gently rising and falling above the dusty field. *Such violence. Such loss.*

Faiz Muhammad turned the SUV onto a deeply rutted dirt road. He glanced in the rearview as he drove. "This road has no gravel. When the rains fall, it will become closed."

Marie understood. There was no roadbed. Now, at the end of the long, dry summer, the road was hard, solid under the wheels of the SUV. But with the fall rains, the road would turn to mud, and after each rain they would have to wait until the ground dried or froze. They would still get through, but not whenever they wanted. Winter was another matter. If the snows came heavy, they wouldn't get through until spring. Marie felt the vehicle rock beneath them and held onto the seat back and the door handle.

They passed an Afghan teenager, dressed in a filthy shalvar kameez with a man-scarf draped over his head. The boy leaned on a tall stick, and around him a herd of sheep and goats grazed.

They drove across a rickety, wood-planked bridge, without guard-rails, and so narrow it was only visible through the front and back of the vehicle. Some thirty yards beneath, a narrow river tumbled between steep rock walls. Marie waited until they were over it before asking another question. "Does the river flood when it rains?"

Faiz Muhammad kept his eyes ahead. "This area doesn't flood when the rains come. It floods when the snows melt in the mountains. No one has information. If they hear the flood, it's too late." He went on to tell story after story of hidden villages swept away in sudden floods. In the end, he reassured the women. "The Shamalis are smart. They know about water. They build their villages on rock, above the river."

"And their farms?"

"They build their farms next to the river, of course. They move the river to flood the fields." Faiz Muhammad turned the vehicle sharply and drove along the crest of a steep hill. "Look."

Marie leaned past Aziza. The hill fell sharply just on the left side of the vehicle. Beneath them lay an irregularly cut patchwork of brown and green fields dotted with the small figures of men and donkeys. A deep, brown waterway wound through the fields. At the back of the fields stood several small mud huts, their roofs covered with tangled brown brush—the huts the farmers stayed in when the work in the fields required all their time and strength. Beyond the huts sat a large conical oven from which dark gray smoke swirled and disappeared into the bright afternoon sky.

Marie's eyes followed the smoke and only then noticed the village cut into the hills above the cultivated land. The village was long and narrow, its walls and houses wrapping around the curves of the hillsides.

Several colorful patches of red-and-black carpets outlined distant tan roofs. Small patches of bright red, orange, and deep blue clothing hung in the bright sky to dry. Marie saw a tiny outline of light blue floating along a hillside path and guessed it was a woman walking to her neighbor's house.

Dark gray, rocky peaks, their creases full of snow, towered beyond the village's rounded hills. The view was breathtaking. Marie pulled a small camera from her backpack and snapped several pictures. Then she drew her cell phone and checked for a signal. Surprised, she said, "Faiz Muhammad, they have cell."

He laughed. "Of course. This is a big village."

Marie looked at Aziza. "Are you sure they have a teacher?"

Aziza only shrugged.

Faiz Muhammad responded. "Yes. This class came from the night guard. The teacher is his brother's wife. She is from the town. She is literate."

"She finished grade 12?"

"She is very intelligent."

Marie considered the certificate in her sheaf of papers and asked again. "What grade did she finish?"

Faiz Muhammad took a deep breath. "Mari-jan. Why should I lie? This teacher is very smart. She has finished grade 10. She is the only woman in the village who can read. You must accept her."

Marie looked at Aziza.

The woman responded. "I didn't know. There is a certificate. See. It has the teacher's name." She took the papers out of Marie's hands and showed her the certificate.

Marie locked her jaw and pressed her lips together.

Aziza protested. "The teacher is the night guard's relative. How could I know?"

Marie shook her head slowly.

The deeply rutted dirt road descended sharply toward the near edge of the farmland. Marie grabbed the headrest in front of her to hold herself steady. She looked at the men working in the fields beneath them. Out of the corner of her eye, she saw Aziza pull her all-encompassing burqa back over her face. She looked up at the mountains beyond. "Beautiful," she whispered.

If there's only one woman who can read in the entire village and enough adult students who want to learn from her, why not? This had been Marie's simple plan: invite teachers to assemble their own classes, pay the teachers, provide the materials, and check on the classes from time to time. If the students kept coming, the teacher was obviously good enough.

The vehicle continued to descend. They reached the narrow valley floor, crossed three smaller wooden bridges, turned sharply, and stopped near a group of men standing in front of a low, mud hut.

Faiz Muhammad jumped out of the SUV first. He exchanged greetings with the men and motioned for Marie and Aziza to join him. He introduced the two women, but only Marie spoke. The group encircling Marie grew from five men to twelve men, then sixteen; then Marie stopped counting. Instead, she focused on counting her breaths. She held her place in their midst, but felt the muscles in her hips and knees pull tight. She didn't like being surrounded by such a large group of men. They could do anything to her, and neither she nor Faiz Muhammad could stop them. She would have to trust the Afghan men who had led her to this community.

12

Most of the men standing before Marie held some kind of farming implement—a handmade shovel, a rough-handled sickle, or a wood-tined pitchfork. Each studied Marie carefully as she and Aziza stood with Faiz Muhammad. Marie tried to avoid their eyes and focused instead on the man who seemed to be in charge. She hoped he was the elder who'd signed the agreement paper. He was not. In fact, he was the village mullah.

Marie showed him the stack of smudged pages she'd brought with her. The mullah read them carefully before returning them. He placed his hand over his heart, bowed slightly, and spoke gently. "Teacher. Welcome. We are at your service."

Marie thanked the man for his hospitality. Silently, she prayed it would continue.

The mullah chose an old man to guide the women up the hillside to the teacher's house. The two women left Faiz Muhammad with the rest of the farmers and followed the old man up a steep donkey path crisscrossing the scooped face of the hill. The first half of the climb, ending at a low, stone wall, took twenty minutes. Marie was winded by the time they reached the wall. Beside it, a thin waterfall tumbled downward along the face of the rock and pooled behind a partial dam made of boulders.

The old man stepped gazelle-like across the dam. He stopped on the other side and turned to watch Marie and Aziza. When the two women didn't move, the old man stepped back into the middle of the dam, unwound the purple-and-white checked scarf from his neck, and tossed one end to Marie. She grabbed it.

The old man held the cloth steady as Marie stepped carefully toward him. When the scarf fell slack, he jumped to the far side of the churning pool. Marie released her end of the scarf, turned, and reached out a hand for Aziza.

Aziza took Marie's hand, pressed the screen of her burqa tightly against her face for better visibility through it, and joined her coworker on the boulder. Marie turned carefully, received the man's scarf again, and stepped to the other side. Aziza followed.

The old man climbed the steep embankment before them and waited on a pathway that rose sharply along the low stone wall. Marie turned and helped Aziza again, her dress shoes worthless on the steep village terrain.

The old man climbed on top of the stone wall, crouched down, knees against his chest, and waved for the women to pass. He would not enter the walled enclosure of the house. Marie thanked him for his assistance and silently hoped he would wait until their business was complete.

The sloping field beyond the wall was brown and dotted with ragged grass. A donkey, one foot staked to the ground, munched on what looked like a weed. Beyond the donkey, on the far side of the field, a dozen or so chickens pecked at the dust.

The entire first level of the house had been built with stone. The bottom was mostly open and served as a barn, its dark caverns filled with hay. The top level was built with mud brick. Marie saw a large glassless window in the middle of the top level and waved toward the faces of a dozen or more women who leaned out toward them. The women waved back. Marie looked at her companion. "Aziza-jan, we have students."

Aziza was already exhausted from the walk up the hillside, and her pointed beige dress shoes cut painfully into the sides of her feet. "*Qaashlaqis.*" *Villagers.* It was not a compliment.

Despite her years of working with Marie's NGO, Aziza still looked down on those Afghans who lived their lives in remote, mountain-bound villages. She was from the town of Shehktan, where water was easily available and women paid neighborhood hairdressers to cut their hair and midwives to deliver their babies. Life in the far-flung villages of greater Shehktan was hard, limited, and short.

Marie continued to climb the hillside. "Yes, villagers. Village women who've never had the opportunity to learn to read. This is a good thing."

Aziza didn't respond.

An older woman with a brown, deeply lined face met the two visitors. The three clasped hands and exchanged greetings. The woman introduced herself simply as Madar-jan, meaning "mother." She was the eldest woman in the household.

As they walked through the barn level, Marie asked the woman to explain the different relationships in the household and village. The teacher, the woman explained, was her daughter-in-law. She had acquired the girl from a cousin who lived in town. The girl had been expensive, but she was a good girl and well worth it. The guard at Marie's office was her son.

"He's Shamali?"

The older woman raised one eyebrow. "We are Tajiks. Our family has been here, in this village, since the days of the king."

Marie heard pride in the woman's voice and thought she knew its cause. The woman was saying, *We are Tajiks, the second largest ethnic group in Afghanistan. We're not Uzbeks or Hazaras or Pashtuns. We're different than all of them—better. And we're not just Shamalis, refugees from the Taliban. We belong in this land, here in Shehktan. It's ours. We settled here when there were kings in Afghanistan.* In truth, Marie had no idea what the woman implied by her declaration, but the guessing made her smile.

What she did know was that the Tajiks had been in Afghanistan since before history. They dominated in the north and held the line against the Taliban conquest, a fact for which they were fiercely proud.

She also knew they were native Dari speakers, unlike their Uzbek neighbors who spoke Dari in public but Uzbek in their homes, neighborhoods, and villages. They married their own, were buried in their own cemeteries, and prayed in their own mosques. Their identity was clear and, to them, deeply significant.

Marie still wanted to know about the Shamali connection. "I heard the people in this village are Shamali." She tossed her question out lightly, hoping not to offend.

The older woman nodded. "Yes. Our family is from the Shamali Valley. When war struck, our relatives came here. Now there are many of us, but I was born here."

Marie and Aziza followed the woman up a narrow, hardened-mud staircase and stepped onto a small landing. Light streamed into the space through a tall, wide gap in the hallway wall. Through the gap, the rock wall of the hillside lay less than four feet beyond. Beneath it, the family had cut a deep culvert to divert water falling off the hillside. Between the culvert and the house, a well-worn rocky path led downward toward the far end of the house.

On the landing, Marie slipped out of her sandals, grateful for the hiking soles that had served her so well on the steep path. She pushed her sandals against the far wall next to a pile of plastic sandals and pointy-toed shoes. On the wall above the shoes a collection of light blue, blue-gray, and white embroidered burqas hung from a row of wooden dowels. The sharp pleats of the burqas created a dense pattern of blue, gray, and white stripes. Marie wanted to take a picture but stepped aside to allow Aziza to add her own blue burqa to the color-saturated wall.

The older woman pulled a dark brown blanket aside and ushered Marie into a room packed with curious Afghan village women, all standing, smiling, and staring at her.

"Salaam alaikum." Marie called out with her own genuine smile.

The women responded in near unison. "Walaykum salaam."

Aziza stepped into the room beside Marie and nodded to the gathering.

A youngish woman with startlingly light gray-green eyes and a brilliant pink-and-green–trimmed headscarf stepped forward. Marie immediately offered her hands and felt the woman envelop them in her own larger, rougher fingers.

The woman was probably nearly thirty, although she looked ten years older. She was slight of build but stood just taller than Marie. Her cheekbones were high and already lined. She wore a long-sleeved dress with dense purple flowers on a black background. The dress fell mid-calf, and beneath that she wore lightweight black tombones, a village woman's typical clothing.

The young woman explained her qualifications. She had been educated in the town before the Taliban finally defeated it. Then, she fled with her family to the mountains, where the government was in control.

The "government" she was referring to were the Afghan leaders, including President Rabbani, a Tajik who fled to the protection of the Northern Alliance when the Taliban established their government in Kabul. In the refugee town, there had been a school for girls where the young woman had worked as a teacher. She taught girls in the first through third grades. She liked it, and she was good at it. She was prepared to teach this class.

Marie realized the woman was closer to twenty-five than she had guessed, and she said nothing about having graduated twelfth grade. Still, Marie accepted her qualifications. This was Shehktan, after all; and not only that, it was a Shehktan village, remote and isolated. Besides, the women were eager to learn.

Marie and Aziza walked around the circle of the room, clasping each woman's rough hands, kissing cheeks, and inhaling the dark, damp breath of unbrushed teeth. Marie hesitated in front of a short, fat, gray-haired woman and addressed her by title. "Mother-jan. You will learn to read?"

The entire room erupted in laughter. The older woman released Marie's hands, slapped them gently, and teased her. "Have I become too old?"

Marie smiled. "Of course not, Mother-jan. I'm glad you're here."

The woman nodded, but pressed her brows downward in a scowl. "I will learn." It was a statement of will.

Marie liked it. "Good. I will celebrate."

When Marie and Aziza had greeted each woman in the room, the teacher invited them to sit down on the floor in the corner farthest from the door—the place of honor. Marie sat down next to the old woman who had slapped her hands, leaned against the cool, mud-brick wall, and waited.

The other women sat down around the edges of the room. Each leaned against the wall behind her, folded knees just inches from her neighbor's. Three women sat hip to hip on the deep, stone windowsill. The room was full, with eighteen women including the teacher, at least four under the age of seventeen. She wondered how they had known she was coming and shook her head. *Afghanistan. Always a mystery.*

Marie introduced herself, and Aziza explained the project slowly and clearly. "We would like you to learn to read and will help you do that. Your men are farmers. Your land is good. We will help you learn to read." Then, she answered their questions.

"Yes, we will provide books, notebooks, pens, pencils, erasers, and pencil sharpeners. No, we will not pay you for coming to class. Yes, we will pay your teacher."

Finally, with all of the questions answered, Marie asked the women to introduce themselves. Each gave her name, her father or husband's name, and the number of sons and daughters she'd given birth to. Even the younger women—some of them not even seventeen years old themselves—announced the births of children who were still small. Aziza checked the list for each woman's name and marked her in attendance.

A young girl of about nine entered the room with a large aluminum tray. She knelt down on the carpet before Marie and Aziza and placed three glass cups of pale green tea on the floor.

Marie looked at the three cups and realized that the third was for the woman she had called Mother-jan. Clearly she was a woman of honor, either because of her age or because of some familial status in the village.

The girl retreated and the introductions resumed.

Finally, all eyes turned to the old woman. She sipped her tea and enjoyed the attention. Then she sat up straight, stretched her hand against her chest, and announced herself. "I am Bibi-jan, daughter of Masoud Agha, the founder of this village. I will learn to read."

Marie smiled. So the woman she'd called "Mother-jan" was indeed a woman of status and undoubtedly great influence. From then on, Marie directed her questions first to Bibi-jan and then to the teacher. Her first question was simple: "How many days a week will you have class?"

Bibi-jan responded. "Six days a week. Everyone will be here." The finality in her voice offered no option for discussion or disagreement.

Marie continued. "Good. What time will you meet for class?"

Bibi-jan's face clouded. She thought for a moment and then said, "After lunch has been served and put away. Before dinner must be prepared."

Marie smiled and nodded. That was enough for her. She dismissed the students with a short speech and promised to return on Saturday with the class materials.

Every woman in the room except Bibi-jan and the teacher rose to her feet. Marie and Aziza clasped hands with each student and said good-bye. Finally, the room nearly empty, Marie and Aziza gathered their things to leave.

The teacher stopped them. "Wait. You cannot go. You must eat."

Marie protested until Bibi-jan commanded. "Sit down."

Marie and Aziza looked at each other and decided to obey. Clearly, the older woman was accustomed to authority.

The girl who had brought the tea returned with another aluminum tray. She unrolled a brown cloth across the woven carpet in front of Bibi-jan, Marie, and Aziza. On that, she laid a shallow bowl with three eggs still simmering in three quarters of an inch of oil. She broke three large pieces of cold, whole-wheat flatbread and placed one on the fabric mat in front of each woman. She added a small silver dish of powdery white salt and retreated.

Bibi-jan waved at Marie. "Eat." She broke her own piece of bread and dipped it into the oil and egg.

Marie hesitated.

The old woman rebuked her gently. "Eat. This is good."

Marie nodded and directed her next words first to the teacher. "Teacher, you are very kind. You have taken trouble. Thank you." Then added. "Bibi-jan. With your permission?"

Bibi-jan waved again, her mouth full of egg, bread, and oil.

Marie explained. "I'm a follower of the Honorable Jesus Messiah. God says that we should thank Him for the food we eat."

Bibi-jan stopped chewing and studied the stranger in her midst.

Marie explained. "It is your custom to pray after you eat, yes?"

Bibi-jan swallowed and nodded. "Yes. We Muslims pray after we eat."

Marie continued. "Yes. And it's our custom to pray before we eat. With your permission?"

The old woman tilted her head back. "You are Muslim. We are all Muslims. You have become confused."

Marie spoke gently, calmly. "Bibi-jan, I am a follower of the Honorable Jesus Messiah, and it is my custom to pray before I eat. With your permission?"

The old woman looked at the teacher, then at Aziza, who accepted the question and offered her explanation. "My coworker is from

America. She is not Afghan. She is Christian. She believes in one God. She prays before she eats. With your permission?"

Bibi-jan assented despite her confusion. She watched and listened while Marie lowered her head, raised her hands palms upward, and prayed. "All powerful God, your name is holy. Thank you for this food. Thank you for this house. Bless the class that meets here. Bless this village with peace. In the name of the Honorable Jesus Messiah. Amen."

Bibi-jan slapped the floor with her right hand. "You see. I told you you're a Muslim!" She tore off another piece of bread and jammed it into the bowl.

Aziza rolled her eyes, but Marie shrugged.

The four women chatted about chickens, cows, milk, and yogurt until the eggs were consumed and washed down with tea. Marie again requested permission to leave. Permission granted, she rose from her place, clasped Bibi-jan's hands, and bid her good-bye. As she turned to leave, she remembered another question. "Teacher, are there any other literate women in this village?"

The teacher cast the question toward Bibi-jan.

The old woman shrugged, waved her hand dismissively, then responded. "My daughter-in-law. She reads. I will read better."

Marie was surprised. "How did she learn to read?"

Again, the old woman waved her hand as if to dismiss the young daughter-in-law. "She learned in school. She's from the town."

Marie immediately wanted to meet the young woman, but thought better than to ask for an invitation. It was far too late, and they needed to get home before dark.

She thanked Bibi-jan and said good-bye again before following the teacher down the narrow staircase and across the cool, hay-strewn barn. She was grateful for a chance to talk to the woman alone. "Teacher, thank you for choosing to teach this class."

The woman nodded, but didn't respond.

Marie continued. "Do you know Bibi-jan's daughter-in-law?"

The woman stopped, turning and nodding slightly. "She was my neighbor. When we were small, we played together." Floating hay-dust and deep shadows obscured the woman's face, though not the soft sadness in her voice.

Marie tilted her head sideways, parted her lips as if to form a word, then changed her mind. "May God give the friend of your childhood peace and health."

The woman's head fell. She stood silent and still for a brief moment, then looked straight into Marie's waiting face. Her next words were weary and tinged with only the slightest hope. "Thank you."

Descending the steep path beside the cascading watercourse, Marie held on to the low stone wall as Aziza slipped on the gravel behind her but stayed upright. The old man was gone from the boulder dam, but in his place a boy waited. When he saw the women, he jumped to his feet and assisted them across the dam the same way the old man had. The boy left them on the other side.

When the path widened enough for the two women to walk side by side, Marie took advantage of the opportunity to speak privately. She wanted Aziza's advice. "Aziza-jan, my friend told me that there is a problem in the town. Do you have news? What is the talk?"

Aziza considered the question. "What kind of talk?"

"Something about the police arresting or killing two Uzbek men. Is there talk?"

Aziza nodded. "Yes, yes. You were in Kabul." She rushed through the account. "The police wanted to arrest some men. They went to the house and the men refused. They had guns and shot at the police. There was a fight. The police threw a rocket. Two boys were killed. Uzbeks from the north. Many men are angry. There was a protest. Did you hear?"

Marie shook her head. "On the street?"

"No, no. Their elders went to the governor. They had become angry."

Marie looked down at the cultivated fields, then up toward the plateau beyond. "What happened?"

Aziza shrugged her shoulders. "How should I know?"

"Is it finished?"

Aziza stopped, grabbing Marie's elbow as she spoke. "I don't know, Mari-jan. They are Uzbeks. Their hearts are hungry. They want everything, but they cannot have it. They rob people on the road to Tajikistan. They take girls by force. They are *very* bad people."

Marie winced at the generalization. Aziza, she knew, was Tajik, the stronger of the two groups in their area. She also knew that there had been bad blood between all the ethnic groups of Afghanistan since before anyone could remember. Still, the generalization was harsh. Marie spoke quietly. "May the great God of the universe show us all the way of peace."

Aziza locked her jaw but then relaxed. "You have spoken right. We must find peace." She let go of Marie and continued down the path. Marie followed her toward their waiting vehicle. Faiz Muhammad watched them descend.

The three slid into the vehicle and returned the way they had come. They drove for almost twenty minutes before reaching the outskirts of Shehktan itself. Five minutes later, the driver pulled to a stop in front of a narrow wooden gate. Marie gave Aziza instructions for the next day, said good-bye, watched her coworker disappear through the gate, then settled in to the quiet of the drive.

The bright orange sun slid gently behind the walls of her neighborhood. The sky's evening light gray melted into a deep blue. In the near darkness, Afghan women floated before her mind's eye. Tall women and short, skinny, and round: pink-on-green flowered scarves, gray ones with white stripes, brown ones with gold trim, bright yellow, pale blue. Dark brown eyes glowing in bright laughter. Heavy brows, creased temples, high cheekbones, narrow jaws. She heard their voices next—

open and loud, shy and soft—with words that were alternately sharp-edged or smooth, clear or indecipherable. Each face a human being; each human a woman; each woman a story; each story a mystery.

And the village, that beautiful village with dark water and patch-work rice fields; men with shovels and pitchforks and scythes; an old man and then a boy bearing a checkered scarf; cascading water splashing, bouncing, swirling wild; a gray donkey, an open stone barn, a window frame with a view of the world; scooped, rhythmic brown hills crowned with snow-laced peaks.

Char Ab. Marie smiled. *A good name, Four Waters.*

13

When Marie entered her home, she heard Carolyn singing softly from the kitchen. Marie paused in the hallway and felt the back of her neck tense. *Carolyn, how can you leave? It's too soon. Please.* She walked quietly into the kitchen.

Carolyn turned, abruptly stopped singing, and smiled. "Hungry?"

Marie nodded, dropping her backpack and sitting on the wide kitchen window sill. She was spent—out of energy, out of words. The things she had seen, the people she had met, all crowded beside her in the tiny, white-walled kitchen. She rubbed the dust from her eyebrows and eyelashes. "Yeah. I need to bathe."

"No problem. I'll send the guard for bread later. Sound good?"

Marie nodded and pushed herself up. She filled a bucket with water from the kitchen tap and placed it on a round grill mounted directly to the top of a red gas bottle. Boiling water for bucket baths wasn't something Marie thought about, just something she did here where their little house didn't have enough electricity to support a water heater.

Twenty minutes later, Marie returned, her long hair soaking wet, her skin blessedly dust-free. The two women carried their evening meal into the pale yellow sitting room. Marie unrolled a brown plastic tablecloth on top of the Persian carpet. They sat down on the cotton floor mats and settled into their dinner.

The house was their shared sanctuary. Marie had moved into it just three months after she'd arrived in-country, living there alone before Carolyn joined her. It was her haven. Quiet, peaceful, and—most importantly—Afghan-free.

Here, she left her scarf hanging on the hook in the hallway. She let her hair down. She wore T-shirts and sweaters and abandoned her long skirts for blue jeans or lightweight linen slacks. Here, she could be her American self.

The house had been hers until Carolyn came and filled it with new colors and conversation. Carolyn, Dave and Margaret had said, was too young to live alone. Not like Marie. Not like Sharon, the first single woman to live alone in Shehktan. Initially Marie had objected to the idea of Carolyn living with her, but it wasn't a request. Now, though it hadn't even been two years, Marie had to admit to herself that she couldn't imagine the place without her young companion.

Carolyn always wanted to know everything about Marie's day—the places she'd visited, the people she'd met. Carolyn loved the exploration. She loved meeting new people and listening to their stories. She loved the play and the laughter, the easy banter of Afghan women. If there was hard stuff, Marie took care of it. If there were difficult conversations, Marie took the lead. If there were problems, Marie figured out how to fix them.

Marie was the manager, Carolyn the expert. It was Carolyn who had the degree in education, the one who had actually been trained as a teacher. She wrote the teacher training material. That was her skill, and she was good at it.

Carolyn had wanted to do a literacy project since before she even moved to Afghanistan. There, her desire for it only grew. Every village she and Marie entered was full of women who had never learned to read. Most of the older women were at the level of complete illiteracy. They were unable even to conceive of a symbol representing a word. The younger village women were different. They had seen their children's schoolbooks and learned to use telephones. For them, symbols meant something; they just couldn't translate them.

Marie hadn't been convinced that the Afghan women wanted to read. She certainly didn't think their men would allow it. But when the mullah came and asked for literacy classes, Carolyn talked her into doing an assessment. After that, Marie designed the program, raised the funds, and collected the necessary approvals. Still, it had been Carolyn's dream. Now she was leaving, just as her dream was becoming reality, and she wanted to know everything.

Marie felt the dull edge of guilt press in. Perhaps Carolyn should have gone with her. What harm would it have done? She swallowed a mouthful of hot soup and summarized. "They have a class and the mullah and elder's permission, and they fed us fried eggs swimming in oil."

Carolyn laughed. When they'd walked the villages to do the teacher training project, they'd practically lived on fried eggs and oil—that, and sour yogurt. "I thought all the classes were going to be in the neighborhoods."

Marie nodded, swallowing. "Yeah. I think they all are, except this one. We went out to a village about a half hour south of town. Char Ab. It's beautiful."

"They have a teacher?" Carolyn was incredulous. They had visited so many villages locked into the mountains, yet they had never found a woman educated enough to teach a literacy class.

"Yeah. Sort of. Not really. A woman's daughter-in-law. She was a teacher up in the mountains during the war."

"You're kidding. Who brought that class?"

"The night guard. And check this out—they're all Shamalis."

Carolyn thought about that. "Shamalis? Refugees?"

"Yeah, a bunch of them. Most, I think. They came up during the war, but there was already a village of relatives out there. And get this." Marie put on mock airs. "I met the daughter of the founder!"

Carolyn joined the game. "Did you get her autograph?"

"Nope, but when she learns to read and write, I'll get it."

The two women laughed. Carolyn was curious. "She's a student?"

"Yep, and let me tell you, she's committed. Old, too."

"Why?" It was not common for older women to want to read or—more to the point—believe they could learn. This one was unusual.

Marie shrugged. "I don't know. It turns out her daughter-in-law is somewhat educated. Maybe she just wants to be smarter than her."

"Two women in the village are literate?"

"At least. But I don't think the daughter-in-law is all that literate. I think she's probably semiliterate. Maybe educated to fourth or fifth grade. I don't know; I want to find out. Maybe Saturday, when I take the materials."

Carolyn looked across the brown floorcloth at Marie. If Marie was going back to deliver the materials herself, it meant there was something in the village that had piqued her interest. "Why that village?"

Marie swallowed a torn fragment of soup-soaked bread. "I don't know. Maybe I'll just send the driver. I haven't decided, but I want to go. Bibi-jan—the old lady—is a riot. But there's something going on there. I'm not sure what yet."

Carolyn finished her soup. "Did they try to convert you?"

Marie smiled. "No. Bibi-jan thinks I'm a Muslim."

"What? You told her that?"

"No, of course not. I don't want her to expect me to be a Muslim. I'd fail a thousand ways. I told her I'm a follower of the Honorable Jesus Messiah, and Aziza told her I'm a Christian."

"So . . . how'd that work?"

Marie swallowed another piece of bread. "She just doesn't understand."

"Huh." Carolyn tried to picture the scene. "Well, how could she? She's never met a Christian."

"Nope."

Carolyn nodded. "Did you tell any stories?"

"Not yet, but I'm going back. I hope." Marie was ready to change the subject. She asked Carolyn how the good-bye was going.

"I hate this. I mean, I do want to go home. But when I think about leaving and never seeing these people again . . . " Her voice trailed off.

Marie waited. She tried to think of something helpful to say. *"You chose to leave"? No. That doesn't matter; even if you choose, the leaving is hard.*

Carolyn saved her from the need to respond. "Besides, I just don't know if I'm going to marry Brad." She hesitated, looking up. "You realize that, don't you?"

Marie nodded. "You can decide that later. You can't let the Afghans influence you. It's got to be your decision. Yours and Brad's."

"Yeah, but what if it doesn't happen?"

Marie stopped eating. "You're not jinxing it. It doesn't work that way. In America, we have a process. Here, there's a different process. You're not going to know if you'll marry your guy unless you go home and figure it out." She waved her hand. "You're not lying. You're just caught between cultures. They're translating. Making sense." Marie shrugged. "Let them."

"But what if I don't marry him?"

Marie mopped the last of her soup with a piece of bread. "They'll be disappointed, if they find out." She thought for a moment, then added. "You could tell them you're going home to negotiate a possible marriage with Brad."

Carolyn laughed. "I did! After you went back to your desk, but they didn't believe me."

Marie sat straight up. "You're kidding? What did they say?"

Carolyn shrugged, still laughing. "They thought I got my pronouns wrong. They just corrected my Dari."

The women laughed deep and hard.

The only window their Afghan friends had on American society was through them, and that was like looking through water glass, distorted by Marie and Carolyn's efforts to fit in with their Afghan neighbors. Of course they wouldn't understand what Carolyn was doing. How could they? They had no template, no pattern to fit Carolyn's utterly American perspective on the best way to choose a husband. Being truly recognized, understood, and known as inheritors of their own culture was a desire impossible to experience in a context of forced marriages and bride prices.

"They're throwing me an engagement party instead of a good-bye party," Carolyn said, marveling. She knew the Afghan engagement party, an absolute requirement in the Afghan marriage process, served as the formal contract between the two families. "Brad's not even here. Do you believe it?"

"You can take a photo of him and hold it on your lap." Marie pictured Carolyn, dressed for a wedding, holding a printed picture of her fiancé on her lap and laughed even harder. "They're blending cultures. They love you, and that's how they'll show it. Your parents aren't here, so they'll give you an engagement party." Marie imagined her own Afghan party outfit: royal blue and bright white fabric covered in sparkly plastic beads. "When is it? I'll wear my sparkles and dance." She lifted her hands in the air and rocked her shoulders into the elegant Afghan dance she loved so much.

Carolyn laughed. "Soon. Next Friday, I think."

When they were finished eating, Marie retreated to her own room, grateful for the laughter, but even more so for a little solitude.

DAY 8

SHEHKTAN, AFGHANISTAN

14

Over the course of the next two days, Marie and Aziza visited five new literacy classes, all of them in town. Faiz Muhammad delivered the needed supplies, Khadija typed the names and locations of each class, and Marie prepared her English version of the report required by the governor. Meanwhile, Aziza and Khadija also planned Carolyn's engagement party, Dave and Margaret continued their work in Kabul, and Shehktan remained quiet. No one else mentioned the angry Uzbeks or the young men who'd been killed. Marie took the quiet as a good sign.

On the third morning, Marie waited with Carolyn inside the green metal gate of their compound for Faiz Muhammad to pick them up. Jake and Holly, Marie's dogs, nudged her thighs. The morning chill cut into her fingertips and toes. She looked down at her sandals. *Shoes soon. It's almost cold.* Her thoughts filled with the day's plan. *Visit a class; make sure it's going well. Lunch at the office. Give Fawad the interim report.* She looked up at the gray sky. *Rain?* She groaned. *Saturday is Char Ab. Please let the weather hold.*

Carolyn interrupted her thoughts. "Marie. How long do you think you'll stay?"

"What?" The question surprised Marie.

"I mean, do you think you'll live here forever; I mean, like until you retire?"

"You know we have no idea how long we'll be able to stay." She heard a set of brakes grind, then the quick, sharp pop of Faiz Muhammad's horn. She opened the gate. "Anyway, I hope to stay as long as I can. I like it here, and I like what I'm doing. I think it matters."

Carolyn followed Marie through the gate and into the backseat of the SUV. "But what would you do? You know. If you went home?"

"You sound like Chad and Casey." Marie locked her jaw. Through the vehicle's window, she watched two small school girls emerge from a gate, one carrying a tiny, blue plastic chair. She turned toward Carolyn.

"Look. It's taking everything I've got to just make it through each day. I can't think about America!"

Carolyn looked down and braved another question. "Would you take me to a class today? I really want to see one."

Marie hesitated.

"It's my project, you know."

Marie nodded. "Sure. We'll go this morning." She called out to the driver in Dari. "Faiz Muhammad-jan, Nazanin will go with me now to visit a class." She chose a neighborhood.

"Balé. Yes, Mari-jan. That's good."

Carolyn smiled.

Faiz Muhammad reached the end of the alley, paused, and pulled out onto the wide, mostly empty mud and stone road. Marie looked toward the left. Two men talking: one on a motorcycle, one on foot. Several clusters of school boys; a bearded man wrapped in a tan blanket. She looked to the right and saw three adult men sitting in a shop. She couldn't see the old shopkeeper, but was sure he was there. Beyond the shop, a man in a turban walked down the street, followed by three burqa-draped women. Something was in his arms. Perhaps a baby.

Faiz Muhammad drove past the man.

A baby, yes. Wrapped in a blanket. Sick, maybe. Marie looked up at the looming three-story house on Zia Gul's street. "Faiz Muhammad-jan, they've painted the new house."

The driver looked across the tops of the wall. He could see the third story and half of the second floor. "Yes. It has become beautiful." Then he spoke the words necessary to deflect his compliment: "In the name of God."

The outside walls had been painted bright pink. The pillars were canary yellow, and the concrete edges of the second floor porch and rooftop platform were orange.

Marie leaned over toward Carolyn and whispered, "It looks like a Pakistani wedding cake."

Carolyn giggled and rolled her eyes. "Maybe my wedding cake will look like that."

Fifteen minutes later, Faiz Muhammad pulled the vehicle to a stop in front of a low wooden gate mounted into an otherwise nondescript mud-brick wall.

Marie pounded on the gate, pushed it open, and stepped into a narrow courtyard festooned with clotheslines, two of them draped with bright women's and children's clothing, and a third with dull brown men's clothing. Several small girls played hopscotch in a corner. The frames of their blocks cut into the hard dirt. The girls looked up, wide-eyed. One disappeared into the house, and Marie and Carolyn followed her.

A moment later, Marie slid out of her sandals and stepped into a room ringed with Afghan women in colorful dresses, black tombones, and mismatched loose scarves. The teacher stood in front of a white dry-erase board set on top of a dented aluminum trunk. She had drawn four Dari letters across the top of the board with a red marker. Another woman, a student about thirty, stood beside her, her fingers still pointing to the second letter.

Twenty-one dark pairs of eyes watched the American women as Marie greeted the class and then the teacher, clasping her hands and kissing her cheeks three times.

"*Khosh amadid*," said the teacher. "Welcome. We are practicing letters."

Marie stepped back and looked at the board. She picked up a blue dry-erase marker, carefully traced each letter, and pronounced its name. A collective *Ah* swept through the room. Some of the older women clapped. They loved hearing the foreign woman read their own letters.

Marie smiled and sat down on the red-and-black carpeted floor beside the oldest woman in the room. The woman objected and offered Marie her own place, the seat of highest honor. Marie gently refused, accepting the second-highest place in the room, and by doing so honored both the teacher and the older woman. Carolyn sat beside her.

Their entrance had distracted the students. "Please," Marie said. "Continue."

The teacher nodded and told the woman at the board to read the next letter. She did, speaking carefully and clearly. When she finished, she took her seat, and the next student arose. This one also stood before the board and read the four letters. The next, the next, and then the next followed until they reached Carolyn. The young woman whispered her panic to Marie. "I don't know the Dari alphabet."

"I know. Don't worry." Marie directed her next words to the class. "This is my friend. She's only visiting." Then she laid her hand gently on the knee of the older woman who sat beside her on the floor. "Your turn, Mother-jan."

The woman smiled, pushed herself up off the floor, stepped slowly to the board, and read the letters. It was a beautiful sight.

Carolyn grabbed Marie's arm. "This is perfect."

"Yeah. I'm glad you dreamed it."

When the class was finished, the students and teacher moved into a circle around Marie and Carolyn. They were full of questions, first for Marie. "How many children do you have?" "None?" "Why not?" "You're not married?" "Where's your father?" "Has he become dead?" "Do you have no brothers?"

Marie knew this conversation. Afghan marriages are arranged, and hers had not been. Therefore, male relatives must be missing. "Yes. I have brothers. And my father is alive, thanks be to God."

At the reference to God, the women whispered among themselves. Marie caught fragments—*God, believes, faith*. She waited while they digested the fact that she was not an infidel.

The women returned to their purpose. "Then why aren't you married?"

"In America, we have a choice. We decide if we will marry or not. And we decide who we will marry . . . if they want to marry us."

The younger women laughed like small children. The thought of a girl approaching a boy embarrassed them. The older woman sitting beside Marie had a different perspective. She slapped Marie's knee. "Ah, that is a good way."

One of the younger women in a black headscarf disagreed. "The Glorious Quran says a girl must marry."

Marie smiled and nodded. "Yes. I believe it does, but I do not follow the Glorious Quran."

A collective gasp filled the room, and incredulous responses tumbled one on top of the other. "What?" "But you must." "It's good to marry." "It's the law." "You must follow the Glorious Quran." And finally, "You're a Muslim, of course." At that, the women settled down and waited for Marie's response.

Marie chose her words carefully. "I believe there is one God. I follow the Honorable Jesus Messiah. He did not marry, and He does not command us to marry."

The women fell into deep conversation among themselves. Marie was, to them, incomprehensible, yet they liked her. She spoke their language, wore their clothes, and smiled when she talked. She gave them their literacy class. She must be a good woman. But how could she not be a Muslim? Who would not be a Muslim? But she's a foreigner. She's an American. Americans are not Muslims. Americans are Christians. America is a Christian country. In the end, they settled on that inter-pretation, then decided Marie should convert.

One of the older women posed the solution. "You are a good woman and you live here now. You should become a Muslim. That would be very good."

All the women in the room agreed, their concern obvious.

"I can't become a Muslim." She smiled and shrugged her shoulders. "It's just not possible."

Again, the women fell into conversation among themselves. They'd never met anyone who wasn't a Muslim. Then again, they'd never met a foreigner. They had no idea what a Christian was except that it wasn't a Muslim. And of course, they had heard of the Honorable Jesus Messiah. He was a prophet. Maryam, the virgin, was His mother. Still, why couldn't she become a Muslim? Did her father forbid her?

Marie and Carolyn watched and listened.

Again, the same older woman put forth the question. "Why can't you become a Muslim? We are Muslims. It's easy. Just say this." The woman recited the Arabic words of the *kalameh*, the Islamic statement of faith. "There is no God but Allah and Muhammad is his Prophet." Then she added. "Just say that."

Every woman in the room agreed.

Marie smiled, put her hand on her heart to show respect, and tilted her head slightly sideways. "I can't say that."

"Why not?" echoed from scattered voices across the room.

Marie was patient. "Because if I say that, you will think I'm a Muslim. And I'm not a Muslim. I'm a follower of the Honorable Jesus Messiah. He is my Savior and my Master." Marie didn't wait for the women to collectively consider her response. Instead, she went on. "God is the God of all. We are all born of Father Adam and Mother Eve."

The women immediately agreed.

Marie continued. "God has given us two great commandments. The first: love Him with our heart, mind, and body. And the second: love our neighbors as ourselves."

This time, the women did consider. They considered and agreed that the foreign woman had spoken wisely.

Marie added to her explanation. "You are my neighbors now, you are learning to read, and I have become happy."

The women clapped their hands together. "Yes, yes. This is sawab for you. It is a good work. Allah is pleased."

The room settled and the oldest woman summed up the conversation. "You are our guest. Please, drink your tea."

Marie had forgotten that a girl had placed a glass cup of green tea before her. She lifted the cup and leaned back against the cool wall. When she returned the cup to the floor, the women resumed their questions.

"Are men in America allowed to have many wives?" "No?" "Oh, that's good." "Our men can have four, and we hate it." "Where is your mother?" "Is she alive?" "Do you miss her?" "How many brothers and sisters do you have?"

When they thought they knew everything there was to know about Marie, they turned their attention to Carolyn, but still directed their questions to Marie. "Is she your daughter?" "Your sister?" "Why is she with you?" "Why doesn't she speak Dari?"

To this last question, Marie turned the conversation to Carolyn. "She does speak Dari. She understands your words. She can answer for herself."

Surprised, the women turned directly to Carolyn. "Are you married? Why not?"

Carolyn tried to explain her upcoming engagement, but the framework was too confusing. In the end, the women decided that Carolyn's father had chosen a husband for her and had called her home to marry. They thought that was very good indeed.

Marie shrugged. "They don't understand, but they're happy for you. Good enough."

Carolyn laughed and nodded.

The women turned their questions back to Marie. "Why do you wear a scarf if you're not a Muslim? Do Christians cover their heads?"

Marie smiled. "In my country, I don't wear a scarf."

The women shuddered. "You go about with your head naked? That's very bad."

Marie kept smiling. "It's a big world. Full of different countries. Each country has its own culture. In our culture, most women don't cover their heads. If a woman is Muslim, she may cover her head. She can do that. America is free."

The women agreed that was a good thing. A Muslim woman must cover her head. "But why do you let men see you naked?"

Marie laughed. "I don't. I wear clothes. All the time."

At that, the women joined Marie's laughter. The idea that any woman would walk around completely naked was simply ridiculous. Who would do that? Marie was delighted—she had found humor with these precious women.

When the room settled down, Marie explained. "You cover your head to show that you're submitted to Allah, yes?"

This time, the oldest woman spoke. "Yes. It's commanded in the Glorious Quran. And if a man sees a woman's hair, he will lust after her, and she will become guilty of sin. A woman must cover her hair."

Marie nodded. "That's good. You should not tempt another person to sin." She went on. "I am a follower of the Honorable Jesus Messiah. He told us a story. May I tell you?"

For the women, stories were wonderful, and a prophet's story, even better. They nudged in closer around Marie and Carolyn.

"One day, the Honorable Jesus Messiah was teaching a group of people. They said his teachings were wise. Master Jesus told a story. In the summer, a man built a new house for his family. He dug a trench. He didn't want to use stones; they were too heavy and expensive. So he built his walls right on top of the dirt. He built a roof. Then, his family moved into the new house. They laid carpets and lived in the house."

The women shook their heads. They knew the man wasn't wise. That house was dangerous.

Marie continued. "The man's neighbor also built a house for his family. He dug a trench. He bought big rocks, and he split the rocks and pushed them into the trench. He built the bottom of the wall with the rock. The work was very hard and took much effort and time. When the base of the house was finished, the man built the walls with baked bricks. Then he built a roof and moved his family into the new house. They laid carpets and lived in the house."

This time, the women were satisfied with the man's efforts. That was the right way to build a house, and they knew it. So far, Jesus' story made perfect sense in the context of their lives.

Marie continued. "When the fall came, the rain fell. The wind blew. The first house moved. The bricks separated. The roof fell down."

The women gasped.

"Don't worry. The family escaped." Marie knew that wasn't in the Bible story, but she hadn't meant to imply that children had died. "But the neighbor's house stayed strong. Do you know why?"

They did. The teacher said, "Because the man built on rock," and the rest of the women agreed.

Marie closed the story. "The Honorable Jesus Messiah said that if we hear his words and do them, we will be like the man who built his house on the rock. I am a follower of the Honorable Jesus Messiah. I show that I am submitted to God by trying to do the things Master Jesus Messiah taught." At that, Marie leaned back and sipped her tea.

The women talked among themselves. "That's a good story." "This foreigner is wise." "She is a good woman." Finally, they turned their attention back to Marie. "Why do you wear a scarf here?"

Marie shrugged. "Because it's your culture and I respect you."

The oldest woman slapped Marie's knee. "Hah! You are a good woman. Come to my house; have tea. My daughter-in-law will make you lunch. What kind of food do you like? Come."

Marie laughed, thanked the woman for her invitation, and encouraged her to live forever.

One by one, the women took their leave. It was time for them to cook the midday meal for their families. When most had left, Marie checked the teacher's attendance roster and thanked her for her work. Then she and Carolyn stepped back onto the street.

Marie looked left toward the corner and immediately stepped back, feeling the closed gate against her shoulders. Something didn't feel right, but she wasn't sure what. In a climate of constant security updates and veiled dangers, she had learned to go on instinct. She looked left again, this time catching sight of two boys emerging from another gate, just before the intersection. Marie looked past them to the corner, now empty.

Carolyn sensed her alertness. "What is it?"

Marie looked up and down the street. "Nothing, I guess. I just thought—" She shrugged.

"Did you see something?"

She thought she had seen someone at first, a young man on the corner. He'd looked vaguely familiar, but then disappeared. But perhaps not. She wasn't sure. She looked back at Carolyn and smiled. "Nah. Just paranoid, maybe."

The two women slid into the back seat of Faiz Muhammad's waiting SUV. The driver was smiling. "They have students?"

"Oh, yes," Carolyn gushed. "A full class. And they're wonderful."

"Yes, I think the teacher is doing well," Marie said.

Carolyn chattered on. "That was so much fun. Those women are just beautiful! I love this project. I'm—well, I'm so glad you're doing it."

"Yeah, me too. It's a great project, and the women seem to love it." She thought immediately of Bibi-jan in Char Ab, and the scoop-faced hills and cultivated fields below. Then she remembered the corner behind them and the young man who stood still beside the wall. She was sure she'd seen him before. "Faiz Muhammad-jan?"

"Yes, Mari-jan."

"Did you see a young man standing on the corner behind you?"

The driver looked at Marie in the rearview.

"Maybe he had a motorcycle?"

The driver looked back at the road. "No. Did you see someone?"

Marie shook her head. "I don't know. Maybe."

"Don't worry. Trust in God."

Marie accepted the driver's words as the end of the conversation, but not the end of the subject. She knew he would be on the lookout for a man and a motorcycle. If someone was watching them, he would find out. She relaxed and pushed the thought aside, replaying the class gathering in her mind. It had been fun, and the women were beautiful. *This is a privilege.*

Carolyn questioned her about the incident, but Marie waved it away. "Nothing to worry about. Kabul's got me a little jumpy, that's all." She remembered Zia Gul's story. *The men have become angry. You cannot trust anyone.* She looked over at Carolyn and smiled. *No need to worry her. She's leaving soon.*

The two women rode the rest of the way to their office in silence.

15

After lunch, Marie finished her interim report for the literacy project. The local government required the update. She printed her English language pages and added the Dari-typed list of participant names and class addresses that Khadija had prepared. Fawad, the office translator, would prepare a full Dari version and submit it to the government.

Marie slipped on her sandals at the door and stepped out onto the wide porch. The hills and cultivated fields of Char Ab were far behind her, but she would go on Saturday. She looked up at the sky. *Gray.* Shehktan hadn't seen rain since the spring. It would come soon, and when it did, the road to Char Ab would turn to soup.

Marie walked along the concrete porch beside the building to the men's office. Inside, she found Fawad, the engineer, and the office bookkeeper, each behind his own metal desk.

They all stood and offered Marie their salaams.

The engineer, a gray-haired man of about fifty, engaged Marie in conversation. "How was your journey?"

Marie realized she hadn't seen the men since her return from Kabul. She shared details from her experience at the ministry before stepping up to Fawad's desk.

The younger man looked up, but the engineer kept speaking. "Do you have news from Mr. Dave?"

Marie hesitated.

"When's he coming back?"

Avoiding the question, Marie looked down at her bright-red toes against the cold, carpeted, concrete floor. *Winter's coming quickly.* It was office policy to limit communication about foreigners' travel plans. "Tomorrow, maybe Saturday. I'm not sure." She lied. She knew Dave and Margaret were booked on the Sunday flight.

"Good. I have a report for him."

"I'm sure he'll be happy." Smiling, she turned her attention to the translator. "Fawad-jan, I too have a report." She handed the sheaf of pages to the man, then noticed something different about him. "You have new clothes. Congratulations."

Fawad chuckled, opened a desk drawer, and tossed a piece of wrapped candy to Marie. "Yes. This suit is from Turkey. It's very nice."

She could tell by the creased lapels and puckered sleeve heads that the suit was a locally made counterfeit. "Congratulations." Still, she was sure it was expensive and wondered how the young man could afford it. She unwrapped the candy and popped it into her mouth. "This is the literacy report for the ministry."

Fawad flipped through the pages. "Thank you. I'll translate it."

"Thanks. Could you check to see if everything you need is there?"

Fawad read. "These are the class addresses?"

Marie nodded. "Yes. We've started five classes. We'll start more next week. They'll go on the next six-month report."

Fawad stroked his short black beard. "You have a class in Char Ab?"

The engineer looked up at Marie from his desk.

Marie felt the cold from the concrete floor under the thin carpet sting the soles of her bare feet. "Yes."

Fawad looked at the engineer.

Marie followed his eyes. "What's wrong?"

Fawad hesitated.

The engineer answered. "Nothing, Mari-jan. The commander of Char Ab, Ahmad Rasul Khan, is a friend of the local governor. The governor will become happy."

Marie turned the name over in her mind. *Ahmad Rasul Khan.* Had she heard that name before? *What did Bibi-jan say?* Marie recalled the older woman's words. "I am Bibi-jan, daughter of Masoud Agha, the founder of this village. I will learn to read." She looked at the engineer. "The commander of Char Ab?" Something in this new piece of information required her attention, but she couldn't put her finger on it. "Engineer Khan, how does that affect us and our project?"

Fawad studied his hands.

The engineer spoke. "Ah, it's nothing. Sticks and fists. Words. Arguments. It is like a dust-wind. It will pass."

Marie paid attention. "Who is arguing?"

The engineer tried to wave away Marie's concern. "Mari-jan, it's nothing."

The young office bookkeeper clarified. "The Uzbeks the police killed are enemies of that commander." He followed his words with a glance at Fawad, who stiffened but said nothing.

Marie froze. "What?" Zia Gul's story crashed into her thoughts. "The brothers with bombs and guns?"

The young bookkeeper nodded.

The engineer jumped back in. "Mari-jan. It is nothing. A small thing. You must not worry. They are men. They will come to agreement."

Marie narrowed her eyes. She wondered if Dave had this information too. "So, let me see if I understand. The elder of Char Ab is a strong man. He is a commander. He has his own soldiers."

The engineer laughed. "Every commander is a strong man. Every commander has soldiers. Mari-jan. This is Afghanistan. Don't worry."

Marie smiled despite the sudden rush of fear that tightened her chest. "Thank you, Engineer Khan." She looked down and suddenly felt the cold that seeped into her feet, making them ache. She looked back up at Fawad. *Isn't he Uzbek?* "Fawad-jan, are those men your relatives?"

The young man shook his head. "No, no. They are a different family. This is nothing. All will be well."

Marie nodded, unconvinced. She considered the report she'd placed in Fawad's hands: names of each participant, addresses of each class. Information. Far too much information to hand over, but there wasn't much she could do; the government demanded it. She remembered the security protocol: *Vary your movements. Never announce where you're planning to go.* She nodded to herself. *I do that. No worries.* She looked across the desk at Fawad. "Is the report complete?"

Fawad rubbed his beard. "Yes. I think so. When will you give me the locations of the rest of the classes?"

Marie caught the edge of yet another vague concern, but lost it too quickly. She shrugged. "In six months, with the next report."

Fawad inhaled slowly. "You should give me the addresses and student names as you start each class. The government wants to know where we are working."

Marie nodded. His request sounded reasonable enough. "Sure. No problem. I'll ask Khadija to give you each class list as soon as we receive it. Okay?"

"Yes. Thank you."

Marie bid the men good-bye and returned to the women's office. Her thoughts retraced the conversation. *The leader of Char Ab is a strong man. A warlord? Is that Bibi-jan's son? Brother? Uncle? He is a friend of the governor. Is that good for us? Bad? The Uzbek family with their bombs and guns are arguing with the commander. Does this matter? Is it sticks and fists, or guns and bombs? The police found bombs.*

She met Khadija just inside the door to the office. "Fawad wants the locations of each class and the names of the students as soon as the class begins. Okay?"

"Yes. No problem. I'll type the list and give it to him."

Marie returned to her desk. She pushed aside her concerns, opened her email application, and composed a message to her friends back home.

Dear Friends,

Exciting news! We started the first neighborhood literacy classes this week. Next week, we'll start more. The women have a real desire to learn. I asked them why they wanted to read. Here are some of their responses . . .

"I go to town to visit a doctor, but I can't read the signs. I don't know where the doctor is. I have to ask someone."

"I want to read wedding invitations for myself. If I can't read, I have to wait until my son comes home and ask him to read it to me."

"I want to read the Glorious Quran and learn about my religion."

"I want to read the names of the medicines doctors give me for my children."

They all said it's good to read. They said, "When a

person can't read, she is blind." They're excited to learn.
Please pray for these beautiful women and their new classes.

Marie knew the events in Kabul were still a major news story for
her friends in the States. For her, the Kabul trip and everything that
happened there seemed like a lifetime past. Since then, Carolyn had
announced her departure, Marie had started a new project, and now
there was some kind of local security problem that might or might
not be significant. She wasn't ready to write about Carolyn or this
unknown trouble; she just didn't know what to say. But Kabul . . .
Was that just last week? God, I'm spinning. She took a deep breath and
began to write again.

> As you can tell, I've returned safely to my home in
> Shehktan. Everything here is quiet. Kabul is far away. Still,
> the events of last week have left us all sad and shaken.
> Please pray for us as we continue to live and work here.

That was enough. Marie pressed send, grateful for the satellite
mounted on the office roof. *Later,* she thought, *I'll talk to Dave. He
has to know we're connected to one side of the feuding families. God, please
don't let this matter.*

That evening, the autumn rains began to fall.
Marie sat in her room and watched the ground outside her window
soften. She thought it unlikely that the road to Char Ab would hold
after even a little rain. It might take days to dry enough to travel.
Marie had hoped to deliver the supplies to the village herself. She
wanted to visit Bibi-jan, the teacher, and the women of the village.
She wanted to see the cultivated fields, those scoop-faced hills, and the
snow-laced mountains beyond them. She sighed.

When the electricity cut out, Marie lit a gas lamp and unrolled a map of the town with her literacy classes marked on it. She knelt down over the map and read the names of each highlighted neighborhood. She mentally identified which teachers and which rooms full of women belonged to each neighborhood. The village of Char Ab was the outlier and the easiest to recall. The others blurred together.

Marie prayed for each neighborhood by name. She prayed for the teacher, the male householder who had offered the use of his home, and the neighborhood elder who had approved the class. She prayed for the students. Those whose names or faces she remembered, she held individually before God. The rest, she simply prayed for as a group.

The excitement and anticipation of the women encouraged Marie, and she felt good about being able to do the project. But she would be doing it without Carolyn, and Marie already missed her companionship. They had worked together for over a year. Marie knew that wasn't a long time, but it had been intense. They had lived together in an isolated corner of Afghanistan and shared in a community of less than twelve other foreigners. They had walked the hills together and slept in village mud houses together; shared the affliction of giardia, mosquitoes, the unrelenting summer heat, and the brutal winter cold. They had laughed together and lived together in a country not their own and found so many blessings in the journey.

Marie closed her eyes. A scrapbook of mini-video clips unfolded before her of Carolyn and herself. Soaking wet, shivering side by side, a single wool blanket wrapped around their shoulders; an Afghan woman placing hot cups of tea in their trembling hands. A Christmas Eve when their community swelled to eighteen with out-of-town visitors, singing Christmas songs a cappella from printed sheets of paper. Carolyn laughing with a blue-eyed young Dutchman, who had left just after the younger woman arrived. Carolyn sharing the Christmas story with an Afghan neighbor, the women and children gushing with delight over the sugar cookies the women had baked together for the occasion. A party, the two of them sparkling in their Afghan wedding clothes. The women clapping while they danced.

Marie forced her mental screen to go blank—she knew better than to allow her mind to wander down that road. It was too hard, too lonely, too sad. She pushed herself off the floor, stood in the middle of the room, lifted her hands, and prayed for Carolyn, for Brad, and for their future together. She prayed for Carolyn's reentry into the United States, for her adjustment, for the fun of normalcy. She prayed for Carolyn's heart, for the loss she would experience when she left Afghanistan behind. She prayed for wisdom, for grace, for Carolyn to live a healthy, full American life with Afghanistan still pulsing in her veins.

Enough. Enough.

Marie opened her eyes and looked straight into the small burgundy framed photo on her wall. Carolyn, Marie, Aziza, Khadija, and Zia Gul, arms wrapped around one another's shoulders, all smiling in dappled, tree-filtered sunlight.

Marie forced her head to turn from their faces. *Focus on the future. Don't hold on to the past. It's not yours anymore. You don't get to keep it. Celebrate what's been and move on.*

A cold, steady rain fell throughout the long night, and by the morning, every unpaved street in Shehktan had turned to thick mud. The road to Char Ab melted into soup.

DAY 7

SHEKHTAN, AFGHANISTAN

16

In the morning, Marie looked out at the gray sky and soft ground of her back yard. She wondered when the road to Char Ab would be firm enough to travel. Saturday, when she had planned to go, was only two days away. She pushed herself out of bed.

In the kitchen, Carolyn had placed a kettle on the stove and began listing her soon-to-be-realized blessings. "Paved streets, central heating, hot water on demand, 24/7 electricity, hot showers, washing machines, clothes dryers, supermarkets, my own car!"

Still bleary-eyed from sleep, Marie pushed the images away and smiled at her young friend. She knew Carolyn's dreaming was part of her journey—a healthy mental projection before a life-tearing physical and emotional extraction. Still, it did her own heart no good to contemplate what she didn't and wouldn't have.

After morning coffee, Marie told Omed to install the diesel heaters in each room and cover the thin windows with sheets of plastic. She put away her sandals and dug her socks and cleated, slip-on winter shoes out of the aluminum trunk in her bedroom. The rain had come, and with it the change of seasons. The long, dry summer was over. It was time to prepare for the short days and brutal cold of Shehktan's winter.

The day passed slowly. At lunchtime, the rain resumed.

After lunch, Marie donned her long brown coat and matching scarf, unfolded her black umbrella, slipped into the black leather winter shoes, and headed out to Zia Gul's house.

The alley outside her gate was deep with mud but otherwise empty. Marie lifted the bottoms of her thin black tombones and walked slowly, careful to keep her clothes as mud-free as possible.

At the corner, Marie nodded to the old gray-bearded man in his wooden shop. "Cold has come," she said, in as light a voice as possible.

The old man pulled his blanket tighter and nodded, grim-faced.

The late fall rains were a precious gift to a thirsty land full of farmers and herdsmen. She also knew the rains meant cold and mud—and soon, hunger. She understood that most Afghans would keep their heaters stored away until the cold became unbearable. Even then, they would balance the cost of fuel against the price of bread. Like her neighbors, Marie had learned to fear the brutal, unrelenting winter cold. Unlike them, she could afford to install her heater, fill it with diesel, and warm her space.

The rain-filled street was deserted. Afghans knew enough to stay out of the cold rain. She clenched her teeth. Aware of the slick mud under her feet, Marie walked carefully as the rain beaded off her umbrella.

Marie found Zia Gul sitting on the swirling red carpet in her pale green room. She was helping her oldest son with his math homework.

Zia Gul rose quickly, obviously delighted, and pulled Marie into the room. "Mari-jan. Where have you been? It's been almost a week and you haven't been here."

The boy scooped up his papers and disappeared.

"I am not without work," Marie said.

"You work too much." Zia Gul laughed. "You should come to my house. We should drink tea. Where have you been? And look, you're wet. You will become sick. Sit."

Marie sat down on a burgundy cotton floor mat, careful to keep the mud-stained edges of her clothes from soiling Zia Gul's carpet. She told her friend about the literacy classes.

Zia Gul asked, "Where are they? How much do you pay? I will teach a class."

"Okay, can you find twenty students?"

The only answer was the sound of her friend's sigh.

The eldest daughter entered the room carrying a large silver tray with a black thermos and two glass cups, and several small dishes of raisins, nuts, and salted chickpeas. The girl placed the treats on the floor between the two women, filled the cups with steaming green tea from the thermos, and retreated.

Marie told Zia Gul about the village, its farmers and cultivated fields, and the trek up the hillside and across the waterfall. She told her about the class and the teacher.

"You must be careful, Mari-jan. There are many bad people here."

Marie nodded. "The village has welcomed us. The daughter of the village founder is in our class."

"She's a student?"

"She's old. Her hair is white. But yes," Marie nodded. "She's a student."

"Can an old woman learn to read?" Zia Gul laughed.

"If she wants to."

The thin afternoon light cast dim shadows across the pale green walls. Outside, a donkey's hooves splashed and clacked through the mud. Marie didn't hear the scrapes and creeks of a cart. *It's alone,* she thought. *Probably guided by a boy.* Marie finished three cups of tea and decided to break the subject she'd hidden the week before. "My friend Carolyn is leaving."

"Who?"

Marie remembered. "Sorry. That's her American name. Nazanin."

Zia Gul looked directly into Marie's eyes. "Nazanin is leaving? Why? Has her father told her she must come home?"

Marie laughed. "No. In our culture, Nazanin is an adult, even though she isn't married. She must make her own decisions."

Her friend filled their tea cups from the thermos. "Then why is she leaving? She doesn't like Shehktan?"

Marie traced the outline of a carpet-flower with her thumbnail. "No. She is becoming engaged."

Zia Gul clapped her hands together. "Congratulations. That's good. Very good. A girl must marry. You should marry. Allah says you must marry."

"The Honorable Jesus Messiah didn't marry. He doesn't command us to marry." Marie tilted her head just slightly backward as if to say, "What do you have to say to that?"

Zia Gul responded. "Acht, you are Jesus-follower. You do not know the Glorious Quran. You must marry."

"You're confused." Maria was always baffled by her friend's capacity to mix Christianity with her own culturally defined Islam. "Anyway. Nazanin is leaving."

Silence fell in the room. Marie returned to outlining flowers in the carpet with her thumbnail. Zia Gul sipped her tea. Finally, she asked, "Will you be alone?"

Marie nodded. "Mr. Dave and his wife will still be here."

Zia Gul tilted her head sideways. "You will live alone again?"

Marie could only manage a nod.

"You will become sad. It's not good to be alone. You must not be sad. You must come here."

Marie smiled. She remembered the warmth of Zia Gul's welcome in the dark days after Sharon left. At that time, she was still new in-country. Her language skills were limited and her friendships few. *Never mind,* she thought. *This will be easier. Now, Shehktan is home.*

She turned the attention back to her friend. "You are alone."

Zia Gul bristled. "How can you say I'm alone? I have children. I have a husband."

"But you miss your home. Your family, your friends."

Zia Gul nodded. "Yes. My family is far away. What can I do? I am here."

Marie knew the loss of their families was a thing they shared. She let her eyes wander across the now-silent room to the mint green drapes that hung across the windows. One of their brackets had separated from the mud-brick wall. The rod tilted slightly downward under the weight of the drapes.

"It's not good for you to be alone." Zia Gul's voice was soft, gentle, and concerned.

"Zia Gul, my friend. You know I am never alone."

Zia Gul waved Marie's words away. "I know. I know. God is everywhere, closer than the vein in your neck. Your family is not."

Marie prayed silently. *Father, what should I say? How can I explain that Jesus is with me, even here, even in this room? How can I say that, when she knows how lost I was after Sharon left?*

Zia Gul stepped into her own story. "When my cousin became married, her husband took her to Iran. She has become lost to us. What can we do? A girl must marry. It is her fate. We were students together. She was my best friend. Now, she has become lost to me."

Marie nodded and sipped her tea.

Zia Gul went on. "My brother went to Dubai for work. Sometimes he calls me on the phone. When I hear his voice, I become happy."

"When was the last time you saw him?"

Zia Gul counted the years silently. "Six years. Yes, it has become six years. He has two children now. I do not know them."

Marie heard the heavy sadness in her friend's voice and thought of her sister's small children. She didn't know them, either. "He is well, yes? His family is well?"

"Very well. He is an engineer. He builds office buildings and stores.

I think he has become wealthy." Zia Gul thought for a moment, then added, "But I cannot see him."

Marie considered her friend's words. "Do you pray for him?"

Zia Gul looked straight into Marie's eyes. "Of course. Of course. I pray *namaz* five times a day. I'm a good Muslim."

"I know." Marie spoke softly. "But you pray for him? In Dari? By name?"

Zia Gul nodded. "Yes. Especially during Ramadan when I'm fasting. It's important."

Marie scooped several salted chickpeas from the dish and dropped them into her mouth. They were soft from the humidity, and stale. She swallowed hard. "I pray for my mother and father, my brother, my sister and her family. I love them. I miss them. I know that God is with them, so I pray for them. I pray they won't be afraid and worry about me. I pray they have good health. I ask God to show them the right way to live. I ask Him to show them the path of righteousness. I ask God to give them joy."

Zia Gul studied her friend. Finally, she said simply, "God is everywhere."

Marie remembered an experience. *Perhaps,* she thought, *it will help us both.* "Saturday, when I came to your house, a group of young men followed me on the street. They were impolite. Disrespectful. I didn't like it."

Zia Gul immediately jumped in. "Young men must learn respect. If they are without education, they are without respect. They must learn."

Marie went on. "I didn't like it, so I prayed."

Zia Gul looked down at the carpet between the two women. They had talked about prayer many times before. In the beginning, Zia Gul had carefully instructed Marie. "There is a time to pray. One must first prepare, then spread out a prayer mat. Finally, one can pray."

Over time, though, Zia Gul had learned a different way. She knew that her friend prayed whenever she wanted, wherever she was. She also knew that Mari-jan prayed in her own language about the things that were important to her. And now, the two women often prayed together to the Honorable Jesus Messiah. Zia Gul loved praying with Mari-jan and she loved Jesus, but she was still confused by the differences in their spirituality.

Marie continued. "I talked to God while I was on the street. I knew God was with me. I knew Jesus was beside me. I knew I wasn't alone."

Zia Gul rubbed the edge of her jaw, then spoke. "Of course. God is everywhere."

Marie prayed silently. She didn't know how to explain what she meant. After a moment, she changed directions. "Zia Gul-jan, why do you pray namaz?"

"It is the command of Allah. We must pray namaz five times a day, unless we can't. You know."

Marie did know. She knew more than that, too. Like the fact that if a woman was unclean, she couldn't pray. She would have to make up the prayers later. Still, Marie was looking for more than a commandment. "But how do you feel when you pray namaz? Do you like it?"

"Of course, of course." The woman spoke more loudly now, confidently. "It is a blessing. Sometimes my children are here. Maybe they are playing or fighting. I wash myself. I roll out my prayer mat and I pray. They don't interrupt me. They see that I have become busy." Zia Gul paused.

The afternoon light melted from the rain-filled sky, leaving the room in gray shadow, as Marie waited.

"It's good," Zia Gul finally responded. "I like it."

"But why?" Marie asked.

"When I pray namaz, I know God is near."

Marie clapped her hands together. "That's it. When I pray, I know God is near. I know God is with me. My heart becomes filled with peace. It's good."

"Yes, it's good. But on the street?"

"Yes, on the street." Marie nodded. "When the boys harassed me, I prayed. I felt God with me. My heart became calm."

Zia Gul nodded, then looked toward the darkening window. "It has become late. Stay for dinner."

Marie smiled and pushed herself up from the floor, ready to leave. "You are kind. With your permission?"

Zia Gul joined her. "It has become dark. I'll send my son with you."

At the doorway, Zia Gul and Marie held hands and spoke their blessings. Zia Gul prayed for Nazanin and Marie. Marie prayed for Zia Gul's family. They kissed each other's cheeks and said good-bye.

Marie followed Zia Gul's son through the rain and mud back toward her own house. The two didn't speak. Marie thought about her conversation with Zia Gul. *How do I know God is with me? I pray. I'm sad, angry, excited, maybe just bored. Then I pray and I remember— God's with me. I feel His presence.* She chided herself. *But really, most of the time I just forget. I work. I get busy. I live here like I'm alone. Most of the time, anyway.*

Marie felt the mud slide under her shoes. She felt the fabric of her skirt and tombones between her fingertips, the weight of their hems heavy with mud. She observed the back of the boy who walked in front of her. Dutiful. Proud that he was old enough to walk a woman through the darkness to her home. She smiled and began to pray.

Lord Jesus, thank you for this boy who's happy to walk me home. Thank you for this evening darkness. Thank you for my friend Zia Gul and the gift she is to me. Thank you for Carolyn and my little house. Thank you for the village and the work we're doing in the neighborhoods.

Yes, she thought. *You are with me.* She went the rest of the way home, aware of Christ, walking beside her.

In the kitchen, Carolyn was cooking lentils steeped in Afghan spices. The aroma was warm and welcoming. "The sitting room's a mess. I started packing. I hope you don't mind."

Christ is with me, right here in this kitchen, right here in this house. Christ was with me before Carolyn came, and he'll be with me when she leaves. Marie took a deep breath. "No problem. Maybe we should eat in the kitchen."

Carolyn pulled bowls from the cabinet. "But there's no heater in here, and I warmed the sitting room."

In one corner of the sitting room, a tower of books threatened to fall onto a shorter tower of DVDs. In another corner, a pile of books lay in a casual, rounded heap. Marie looked around. "What are you doing with all this stuff?"

"Those books." She pointed to the canted tower. "I'm going to send to a friend in Kabul. You don't read them, right?"

The chaos in the room scraped at the edges of Marie's line of sight.

"And those I'll take home." She pointed to another pile. "I want them. I'll pay the extra weight. I just don't know . . ."

Marie realized her friend had changed subjects. "What did you say?"

"I just don't know if the plane will be able to land." Carolyn continued, "I mean, with the rain."

"Don't worry. It'll dry out. Did you book the flight?"

"Yeah. I called today."

Marie startled, inhaled deeply. "For when?"

"Next Wednesday."

Marie forced a grin. *Wednesday. So very soon.*

"Dave and Margaret are flying in. We're going to have my good-bye party at their house on Sunday. You'll come, yeah?"

"Sure." Marie looked at a pile of books and DVDs.

"My engagement party is tomorrow, you know."

"Yeah, of course, I'm going."

Carolyn flapped her hands in the air. "Sparkles!"

"You getting excited?" Marie couldn't help but smile.

"Yeah! I'll see my parents. Spend a couple weeks with them in Colorado, then go out to see Brad."

"That's good. It's good you have a plan."

Carolyn laughed. "Yep." The younger woman went on to describe all of the things she wanted to do in America. Her journey in Afghanistan was coming to an end. The life she'd given up in America was once again becoming possible. She needed to envision her future, to mentally move into it.

Marie listened and tried to encourage her without allowing Carolyn's dreams to pull her own heart away from Afghanistan. When their meal was finished, Marie left Carolyn to her dreams, collected and washed the bowls, and retreated to the privacy of her own room.

17

That night, Marie slept fitfully. Her room was cold. A gusting wind rattled the windows and awakened Jake and Holly in the yard. Marie switched on her headlamp. One o'clock in the morning. She swung the light around the room. Nothing. A thick nausea heaved and tumbled through her abdomen. She pushed herself up. There was nothing there. Nothing but biting cold and sickening anxiety.

What is this? What's going on?

Wind and cold. *Winter's coming. So what? I've done this before.* Uzbeks and Tajiks, men with guns, police, rockets. *Was there a man watching us the other day?* Protests. Arguments. Sticks and fists. *What's it got to do with us?*

The dogs barked again.

I'm paranoid. It's just Kabul—the killing. I'm on edge; it's nothing. Carolyn's leaving and I'll be alone. That's all. I'm just on edge.

Marie drifted back to sleep, but awoke again, startled.

She remembered a half-awake dream. A wind was blowing, hard. She was walking, head down, shoulders pressed against the wind.

Tree branches split and tore past her face. Shots of lightning exploded around her. She pushed the dream-memory aside. The nausea in her stomach spread to her head. Pounding blackness. She rubbed her temples and closed her eyes.

Marie awakened again, this time with the mullah calling out morning prayers. It was still dark. She pulled her headlamp over her head, switched it on, and pushed herself out of bed. The nausea in her stomach had faded to a dull ache, but the headache remained.

It was Friday, the Afghan Sabbath and the day of Carolyn's engagement party. Marie would have the morning to herself. She made her coffee in silence, wandered back to her room, lit the heater, and pulled the blanket around herself. She opened her Bible and looked for help.

Early in her Afghan journey, the psalms became dear to Marie. She learned the difference between praying about protection from your enemies when the worst they ever do to you is lie, steal your credit card information, or gossip about you. It's something entirely different when war lies minutes away and people wander around wanting to kill you—or worse. Marie took comfort in the psalms. She read them in order, each morning speaking the text out loud.

She read Psalm 146 now, softly, the words of praise and truth filling the darkness in her room.

Praise the LORD! Praise the LORD, O my soul!

Marie willed her voice above a whisper.

I will praise the LORD as long as I live; I will sing praises to my God while I have my being.

She looked around her room. Everything was as she'd seen the night before, except that the windows still rattled in the wind and the diesel in the heater canister now burned into echoing flames.

Put not your trust in princes, in a son of man, in whom
there is no salvation. When his breath departs, he returns
to the earth; on that very day his plans perish.

Marie thought about her staff, her driver, and her guards; she
thought about Dave and the security reports and the German soldiers
in their small base two blocks away. She rubbed the side of her aching
head.

Blessed is he whose help is the God of Jacob, whose hope
is in the LORD his God, who made heaven and earth, the
sea, and all that is in them, who keeps faith forever; who
executes justice for the oppressed, who gives food to the
hungry. The LORD sets the prisoners free; the LORD opens
the eyes of the blind. The LORD lifts up those who are
bowed down; the LORD loves the righteous.

She looked through her window and imagined the world beyond,
Jake and Holly pacing the yard. The old man in the shop wrapped in
his thin blanket. Zia Gul, cold in her heater-less rooms and outdoor
bathroom. She remembered her dream, her shoulders pressed against
the wind. She read on.

The LORD watches over the sojourners; . . .

She stopped, repeated the line out loud, then repeated it again.
"The LORD watches over the sojourners . . . The LORD watches over
the sojourners."

She looked at her black backpack sitting on the floor. She closed her
eyes and whispered her prayer. "Father, are you watching over me?"

The room was silent. It had grown lighter, but not warmer. Outside
the window was gray, rainless. She read the psalm again, more slowly
this time. She drew its encouragement deep into her soul and pulled

the blanket tighter, then read it a third time. This time she prayed, *Father, what do you want me to know this morning?*

Immediately, she thought of Carolyn. She looked back at the psalm, rubbed her temples, sighed, and began to pray, her words settling into the corners of the room and soothing the rough edges of her heart.

Heavenly Father, I'm yours, and I want to look to you in everything. Help me look to you. Help me remember to praise you. you're right here with me. You watched over me last night. You're here with me now, and you'll be with me through this day. You know where I'm going and all the things I'll do. I can never be torn away from you. I belong to you now and forever. Marie drew strength in the dim cold morning light.

I will praise You. You are the great and mighty God of the universe. You are the King of America and Afghanistan. You're greater than our president and you're greater than the Taliban.

I can live here because you're with me. That's the only way I can make it. Help me know your presence here. But even when I don't feel you, remind me you're with me. You're right here, right in this room.

The room felt empty. Still, she clung to what she couldn't see.

I'm attached to people, that's for sure, but you're the One who helps me stay here. You're the One who will tell me when to leave. You're the reason I came. Not Carolyn. You're the One who keeps me standing, keeps me walking. My trust is in you. Only you.

Marie rubbed her eyes between her fingertips and her thumb, and wondered if she really believed the words she was praying. Could she hold on to them, or were they slipping away faster than she could speak them?

I need you. Can't make it without you. Everything's swirling and I don't know what's going on. This is just killing me. I'm trying so hard to put one foot in front of the other, keep the focus on the work, do the right things. But it's hard. I keep thinking about that woman in Kabul and how hard it will be to live here without Carolyn. I keep thinking about those brothers and their angry family. And now—I think there's someone watching me. God, I can't figure any of it out.

Kabul, Carolyn, violence in her community, a personal threat. *It's killing me.* She had admitted it—the bitter fear and aching sadness beneath each rocking fragment of reality. The honest writing; her own heart's struggle acknowledged and offered in prayer. *This is where I am. God. This is where I am.*

Nothing had changed in her room, but somehow, she felt warmer, lighter, safer. With closed eyes she continued praying softly and poured her heart out—everything she felt, the people she wanted to see, the questions that haunted her. Marie prayed until the morning light glowed strong in her room and the diesel heater had warmed the space enough to invite her out from under her blankets. *Carolyn's engagement party.*

⁂

Marie's Afghan party clothes were folded neatly on a back shelf in her room. She shook them out and smiled at the brilliant fabric. The outfit was a two-piece set: a long sleeved blue-on-white paisley shirtdress and matching royal blue tombones. Bright silver and blue sparkles trimmed the cuffs, yoke, and hem of the long shirt.

Marie dug through the clothes piled on the shelf until she found the brilliant blue and silver headscarf that matched the outfit. She braided her hair, dusted silver sparkles into her eye shadow, and painted her lips bright red.

Aziza hosted the engagement party at her house. She had transformed her largest room into a wedding hall with shiny blue and yellow streamers festooned from corner to corner and bright red and gold spirals pinned to the thin ceiling fabric. She had stretched a dark brown tablecloth across the floor and covered it with plates of raisins, cakes, and nuts; and she'd decorated it with pink, white, and blue paper flowers.

The women gathered: Aziza, Khadija, Zia Gul, the cleaning lady from the office, Carolyn's language tutor, neighbors, and friends.

They ate heaping plates of rice and lamb, drank tea with milk, and told bawdy stories of men and the things they liked. The younger women blushed; the others mocked. Carolyn and Marie pretended an ignorance no unmarried American woman has.

When the meal was finished and the brown floor-cloth rolled and put away, the guests offered their gifts: sparkly scarves, carved figures, beaded necklaces, and photographs of themselves smiling beneath green trees or surrounded by pink and white roses. Carolyn accepted it all, loved it all.

Marie whispered in her ear. "This is the way you should leave. Celebrating."

"This is amazing!" Carolyn's smiling eyes met Marie's.

And the women danced. They had no borrowed singer or tape player, so they put their own hands together and set the beat. The older women sang songs of love and babies, of clean water and warm sun, of the foolishness of men and the wisdom of women. The young danced first.

Each woman, one at a time, ankles together, arms stretched out, head thrown back—danced wild, full, and free. And everyone else sitting around the plastered, yellow-painted mud walls clapped the rhythm and howled encouragements. It was pure joy.

When Carolyn finally joined the others, the women howled and shouted out their wedding night advice. Carolyn understood few of their coarse words but grasped from their gestures the erotic meanings. She blushed in genuine embarrassment and fled the dance floor. The older women howled with delight; the younger ones hid their faces behind their scarves and snickered.

Marie watched, smiling, the palms of her hands burning from the clapping. She ignored the purpose of the party, and focused instead on the beauty of the room, the brilliant clothes of the women, their shared laughter, and, of course, their dance. This was an Afghanistan that would never make it onto the evening news. It was a female celebration unrivaled by anything she had experienced in America. Marie clapped; she danced, laughed, joked, and played with joy. This was the Afghanistan she loved most.

At the end of the day, Marie and Carolyn hid their sparkly clothes beneath long, dark coats. They double-wrapped their faces with their headscarves and pulled sunglasses over their eyes. They wouldn't display their colored lips or sparkly shadowed eyes to any Afghan man. Like the first names of girls, women's finery was private.

They said their good-byes, and climbed into the back of Faiz Muhammad's SUV. And then, after the joy and exhaustion of the celebration, Carolyn wept. Marie searched for words but could find none. Instead, she collected Carolyn's presents, took her hand, and cradled it in her own.

That evening, Carolyn continued to pack her things. She had decisions to make: what to take, what to give away, what to leave behind. Marie looked out at the gray sky and wondered if the weather would hold. For both, the wait was excruciating.

PART 3

DAY 5

CHAR AB, AFGHANISTAN

18

Marie awoke with the morning call to prayer. She jumped out of bed, wrapped her blanket around her shoulders, and stepped out onto the back porch where Holly and Jake jostled her for attention. Marie shivered, scratched their heads, and peered into the darkness. No rain. If the roads were passable, she would make the trip to Char Ab.

After lunch, Faiz Muhammad loaded a set of class supplies into the SUV. When Marie slid into the vehicle alone, he hesitated.

Marie guessed. "I'm going alone."

Faiz Muhammad looked at Marie through the rearview mirror, his eyes hooded, but she could see his eyebrows raised just slightly. "Aziza-jan is not going with us?"

"No." Marie smiled. "I think she is tired of visiting villages."

Faiz Muhammad shrugged. "And what's that?" He pointed to a long, one-inch thick stick that Marie had brought with her.

"A stick." Marie smiled. She didn't know the Dari for *walking stick*. "It will help me cross the little river beside the wall."

Faiz Muhammad laughed. "You are a shepherd now?" It wasn't a compliment.

"Hah! I am a woman and the paths in the village are difficult."

Faiz Muhammad, still laughing, put the SUV in gear. It was a beautiful day, soft in the gray light, and he knew the trip would make Marie happy. As they drove, Faiz Muhammad talked about the village and the kinds of crops the men farmed.

Marie only half listened.

The road out of town was firm, solid despite the rains. The surface had been scraped, then covered with layers of rock and sand. By local standards, it was an improved road. They drove straight toward the soft brown hills of Char Ab, past barren, uncultivated fields dotted with the graves of martyrs, their faded pennants standing still in the quiet afternoon.

Faiz Muhammad turned the SUV onto a deeply rutted dirt road. The vehicle slid, rocked, hesitated, then slid again and came to a stop. He jumped out of the SUV, adjusted the wheels to four-wheel-drive, and started again. This time the vehicle stayed on the road.

He stopped again and got out just before the rickety wood-plank bridge. Marie slipped out of the vehicle behind him and snapped a photograph of the hills, their scooped faces filled with crescent shadows. The dark rock mountains beyond crowned the soft curves of the hilltops in white-on-black. She took a few pictures of the bridge and another of the river rushing beneath it. *Char Ab. Beautiful.*

Faiz Muhammad checked the surface of the bridge and pronounced it safe, and the two climbed back into the vehicle. They drove slowly across the span; the planks and the round trunks of narrow trees that filled the gaps buckled violently but held. Marie held her breath. It was a long way down.

On the far side of the bridge, the road turned sharply and plunged downward. The SUV held firm until three quarters of the way down, then it slid sharply sideways. Faiz Muhammad shifted gears, rocked the vehicle up onto the side of the road, and jammed it around a deep, soft pocket. He spoke without looking in the rearview mirror. "The road is soft. The village is becoming blocked off."

"We have to get them started. When the snows fall, we won't get through." Then she added. "They'll have to do the best they can alone."

Faiz Muhammad drove the SUV up the next incline and the road stabilized. He turned again along the edge of a steep cliff. Marie looked out the window. She traced the deep brown serpentine water-way beneath her. The tight curves were still outlined with bright green growth, but the last of the patchwork fields had been harvested. The cone-shaped oven where they'd cook the rice was cold, its plumes of dark smoke gone. Marie searched the outlines of the small buildings for the men, but saw none. She asked her driver.

"They are home, or they have gone to town. Or they have gone to the city."

Marie wondered what the men did in the wintertime when the fields were sleeping, but she didn't ask. Instead, she studied the village cut into the hillsides straight across from the plateau beneath their wheels. Four torrents of water rushed downward from the face of the hills. *Char Ab. Four Waters.* She looked at the valley, found the place where they'd parked their vehicle the last time, and traced the trail she followed up to the teacher's house. She found the outline of the teacher's wall and the dark eyes of the woman's open-faced barn. She couldn't see the donkey or the chickens but knew they were there somewhere, blending into the brown earth.

She looked across at the other houses. She wondered which, if any, belonged to Bibi-jan.

Marie asked Faiz Muhammad to stop. She jumped down from the vehicle and snapped several more pictures of the village wrapped around the hillsides and the magnificent, jagged mountains beyond.

When she was finished, Faiz Muhammad gently guided the vehicle downward and pulled to stop at a small building on the far side of a narrow wooden bridge. On this visit, no one came to meet them. They had arrived alone.

Faiz Muhammad grabbed the dry-erase board and led Marie up the path to the teacher's house. The edges of the pool at the base of the small waterfall were trimmed with thin, scalloped shelves of ice. Faiz Muhammad crossed the dam easily. Marie struggled, just managing with the help of her walking stick.

By the time they reached the top of the wall, the teacher's son had arrived to meet them. Perhaps the boy had called out their arrival. Or maybe a girl had seen Marie and her driver through one of the windows, now covered in plastic. Somehow, they knew she'd arrived. Faiz Muhammad handed the dry-erase board to the boy and returned to the vehicle to wait.

In the dark barn, Marie met the teacher with three light kisses and followed her through the barn, up the narrow, mud-brick staircase, and into the room that served as their classroom.

On the far side of the room, Marie sat next to the plastic-covered windows that once overlooked the long, narrow valley. She missed the beauty of the view, but, shivering against the damp chill, she was grateful for the plastic. The teacher draped a thick wool blanket over Marie's folded legs and disappeared.

A poster of Ahmad Massoud—the Tajik military and political hero who had been assassinated a few days before 9/11—hung on one of the unpainted walls. In the picture, he held a small red flower in his finger-tips and looked kind and concerned. Marie had lived long enough in Northern Alliance territory to know better than to question the man's honor. He was a hero, even if he was a warlord. Marie thought of the grave markers along the road. Half held the remains of men who had fought beside this hero of the north. The rest marked Taliban graves, strangers from the south. *War. So much war.* She thought of the Uzbek brothers and wondered where their graves were. She thought of funerals and wailing mothers and the stories so many women told of sons and fathers and husbands lost. *So many dead.*

The remaining walls of the room were naked mud brick, marked by several seasons of winter fuel smoke. On the far wall, a dull white cotton cloth with once-blue flowers hung from a rope curtain rod. Marie guessed it hid a set of wood shelves built into the thick wall.

The plastic across the window was outlined with thin strips of wood nailed directly into the wall. There was no wooden window frame or glass—comforts too expensive for many Afghan families. Instead, the plastic sheet over the opening bowed and snapped in the light afternoon breeze. Across the doorway, the colorful light-weight fabric had been replaced with a brown wool blanket. Marie remembered emerald green with tiny red and white flowers. Now, there was faded, smoke-stained brown. She wondered if she remembered correctly.

The teacher entered the room with an aluminum tray bearing two cups of green tea, its leaves still swirling, and a small metal dish of pistachios in their shells. Looped over her wrist was a tall pink thermos. She sat down with the tray on the floor in front of Marie.

Marie started the conversation. "Please forgive me. I could not come until today."

The teacher wasn't at all concerned. "Yes. The road became mud. It could not be used. All of the men are in town."

"What are they doing?"

"Selling things. Drinking tea. Talking." She chuckled.

Marie joined her. "Yes, the men say the women sit in their houses and gossip. Perhaps the men sit in their shops and gossip, too."

The teacher pulled the tail of her scarf over her mouth and laughed hard and long.

A small boy entered with a box of narrow first-grade reading books. He dropped them on the floor and disappeared again.

Marie looked back to the teacher. "Do the students still want to learn to read?"

The woman was enthusiastic. "Oh yes. Oh yes. They are waiting for you to come. They think they have become forgotten."

"I'm sorry. I did not forget."

"Yes, yes. The rain fell and the road became mud."

Marie was curious about this woman. "Please tell me, Teacher, why do you want to teach this class?"

The woman picked at the fringe of her scarf. "If we cannot read, we are blind," she said.

Marie had often heard the saying.

The woman went on. "I can read. Women bring me things to read. I read for them. But I cannot go to town with them. It's too far and I have small children. They want to read for themselves."

"How many years did you go to school?"

"I went to grade 10, but the Taliban came before grade 10 became finished."

"Your father sent you to school?"

She nodded. "My brother. My father died."

Marie uttered the customary words of comfort spoken to the grieving: "May God forgive him."

"Yes. Thank you."

The women sat in silence for several moments, each drinking their tea, until the teacher continued. "They told my father he was not Muslim if he sent his daughters to school."

Marie nodded and remembered the night letter Zia Gul's husband had recently received. He'd scoffed at it and sent his daughters to school anyway. Marie knew such threats were common and often serious. "Your brother made you stop going to school?"

"Yes. It was very difficult then. The Taliban were everywhere. During three years, I studied with a neighbor. My mother gave her milk—we had a cow."

Marie wondered if this woman had been to an actual school at all. "What grades did you study with the neighbor?"

The teacher rose from her place on the floor and pulled aside the faded white curtain, lifting a small aluminum box from the shelf hidden in the wall. She put the box on the floor, unlocked it with a key from around her neck, and opened it. She reached into the bottom and pulled out a stack of reading books. She laid the first five books in one pile in front of Marie. "These, my neighbor taught me." She laid another six in a stack next to the first. "These, my cousin from Kabul taught me."

Marie studied the woman carefully and looked at her books. She wasn't sure what to ask next, but it didn't matter; the woman had a story and she wanted to share it.

"My aunt came to live with us in the days of the Taliban in Kabul. My uncle worked for the government. They killed him. My aunt came here with my three cousins. Two other cousins stayed in Kabul. We have not seen them."

Marie ran her fingers along the spines of the reading books. "Do you know where they are? Your cousins?"

"One cousin went to America. He lives there. Sometimes he calls my brother."

"And the other one?"

The woman looked down and shook her head, snapped her tongue against the roof of her mouth, and said, "We have not seen him. We do not know where he is. We do not know what he has become."

Marie leaned back and sipped her tea. She thought about the story and remembered the father. "How did your father die?"

The woman shrugged her shoulders. "He was mujahedin. Sometimes he came to help us. Then, he did not come. Someone told my brother that he had become martyred."

Instantly, Marie saw the grave pennants fluttering in the breeze. The teacher's story was all too familiar. The years of war had robbed so many of so much. Again, Marie spoke the common phrase of comfort. "May God forgive him."

The woman nodded and encouraged Marie to eat the small round pistachios in the dish.

Marie complied. She wondered if the teacher would succeed, if the students would learn. "May God give you and your students success."

The teacher lifted her hands, praised Allah, and passed them over her face.

At that moment, the boy returned with a box containing pens, pencils, erasers, pencil sharpeners, and markers for the board. He dropped the box in the middle of the room and again disappeared.

Marie finished her tea and placed the nearly empty cup back on the aluminum tray. She returned the tiny bowl of pistachios, as well. "Teacher, with your permission, I would like to visit Bibi-jan. Is it possible?"

The woman slid the aluminum box back onto the shelf behind the curtain. She nodded. "Yes. It's not far." Then she added, "My son will take you." The woman disappeared. A few minutes later, the same boy who had carried the school supplies up the hill entered the room and nodded. Marie rose and followed him. Neither spoke.

The boy pulled open a wooden shutter from the window at the top of the stairs. He stepped out onto a narrow path paved with round uneven river rock. Marie followed. On one side, the path was walled off by the house; a rock cliff rose steeply on the other. Marie held on to the rock walls and tried to keep up with the boy.

The pathway ended abruptly at a low rock wall with a mud roof. The roof was built directly into the steep edge of the hillside. The boy jumped onto the flat roof and Marie followed, careful of the soft, slick mud under her feet. At the far side of the roof, she stepped back onto the path. It was firmer than the roof, but it was narrow and difficult. The steep hillside along which they walked disappeared beneath them. If she slipped, nothing would stop her fall. Still, Marie could see the face of the hillside that she admired so much from the ride out to the village.

Suddenly, Marie's phone rang. She stopped and pulled it from its yellow nylon sheath. Security required her to keep her phone available at all times, check the messages when they appeared, and answer it when it rang.

"Hello, Marie. Where are you?" It was Margaret.

The brown, patchwork valley lay beneath her. Beyond that, a steep cliff rose to the plateau she had been driven along before. "I'm in

Char Ab, the village." Then she added. "Standing on a path cut into a hillside."

"Beautiful." Marie could hear the smile in Margaret's voice.

"Well, we just landed. We're on our way back to the house. Come see me. Okay?"

Marie leaned into the steep hillside. "Welcome back. I'm glad you're here."

"Marie, are you okay?"

In the excitement of the day—the teacher's story, the muddy path beneath her feet, and the prospect of drinking tea with Bibi-jan— Marie had forgotten everything that troubled her. Now, at Margaret's question, the rough-edged fragments of too many heartaches pricked her chest. Marie locked her jaw. "Yeah. I'm fine. I'm in the village. I'm fine."

"Good. Come see me tomorrow. We missed our prayer time last week. Come, okay?"

This time, Marie heard concern in Margaret's voice. "Yeah, okay. Nine o'clock. I'll be there."

Marie clicked the phone shut and slid it back into its yellow pouch. She looked up and felt a cold breeze blowing down the hillside from the mountains beyond the village. She shivered. The boy was standing fifty feet down the path where it disappeared around a ridge on the hillside. Marie took a deep breath, picked up her walking stick, and followed him.

19

The narrow path turned steeply upward along the hill face and disappeared again on the far side of yet another ridge. Marie leaned into the hillside, her sense of balance confused by the sloping plains of terrain. At the far side of the second ridge, the path again cut upward. Above her, three wide two-story buildings sat on a shelf of land cut into the hillside. In front of the second building, there was a long narrow porch covered by an overhanging mud roof. Above the porch, a row of large windows sealed in glass faced the valley.

Between the first and second house, a four-bay, one-story barn opened to a circular, nearly level field where three gray donkeys and two skinny brown milk cows grazed. A low, rounded wall separated the field from a grove of fruit trees, their leaves mostly brown in the late autumn. Marie could see the tops of the trees, but their trunks were blocked by the tall, arcing mud-brick wall. In the land of straight walls, the rounded contours of Bibi-jan's walls surprised her.

Marie followed the boy through a wooden gate that led to the or-chard. She breathed the dark, warm scent of rotting leaves and looked around at the small, densely planted trees. *This family has money and workers,* she thought. A creek cascaded nearby, but she couldn't see it.

She stepped through the back gate of the orchard, found herself in a narrow alleyway between two tall walls, and followed the boy toward the left, then through yet another wooden gate, this time entering the courtyard of the house. Before her, the wide mud-roofed porch welcomed her.

Marie heard a deep, familiar, raspy voice call out to her.

"You have become late. Where have you been?" Bibi-jan stood in an open casement window on the second floor.

"Salaam alaikum, Bibi-jan." Marie put her hand on her heart and asked all the obligatory Afghan greeting questions. "How are you? How are your children? How is your family? How is your health?"

Bibi-jan just waved the questions away, not even bothering to re-spond with her own. "Welcome, welcome. You have become late. Where have you been?"

Marie jammed her walking stick into the soft mud beneath her feet. "A long time ago, there were roads, but the water came and swept them away. Now, they are slowly returning."

Bibi-jan threw her head back in playful mockery. "The road became lost. You should have brought it back with you. We have been waiting. We have become tired of watching the road."

Marie opened her hands wide. "I have come. See. I am here."

The older woman stood straight up in the window, pressed the heel of her hand into her thick hip, and called out a challenge: "Where's our class?"

"If I tell you will you welcome me?"

Bibi-jan threw her head back and laughed. Her belly shook in rhythm, and Marie knew she'd made a new friend.

"Come. Drink tea. If there is a class, tell me."

Marie scanned the face of the house. She saw a young woman standing to the right of the porch, just inside the shadow of the barn. Marie studied the woman as she walked toward her. She was young, perhaps not more than twenty. She wore a charcoal, cotton scarf edged with narrow silver stripes that sparkled despite the deep shadows of the barn. Her eyes were wide-set and dark brown, cheekbones high and strong over a straight, angular jaw. Marie guessed she had a full set of teeth.

She looked at the young woman's clothing: a light green, flowered long-sleeved dress shot through with deep-green vines, dark-green tombones. *This woman has style,* Marie thought. *And her husband has money.*

Marie looked back up at the older woman. "There is a class, Bibi-jan." Marie motioned to the boy who still stood just inside the wall. "This boy has brought all of the supplies. Everything is ready, Bibi-jan. Only you are missing."

Once again, the old woman threw her head back and laughed so hard her whole body shook. Between the waves of laughter, she directed Marie. "Come in, come in. Drink tea, drink tea. My daughter-in-law waits for you."

Marie put her hand on her heart and leaned forward in a playful bow.

"As you wish, Bibi-jan." She pulled her walking stick out of the thick mud and walked across the flat courtyard toward the young woman. Marie reached out to the woman and received a limp hand and a muttered salaam in return. The woman held her left hand across her mouth and gazed at Marie's cleated slip-on shoes and long, thin walking stick.

She led Marie through the hay-littered barn, past two light brown, bony-hipped cows. One of the cows swung its head over its pen and nudged the young woman's shoulder as she walked by; she absently stroked the cow's long cheek and let it go.

Marie remembered the two cows in the yard. *Four cows? This family is wealthy.* She tried a question. "Do you take care of the cows?"

The woman only nodded and kept walking.

Marie followed her up a narrow, mud-brick staircase built into the back wall of the barn. The staircase led to a wide, windowed landing with a wooden shelf covered with shoes. Marie slipped out of her own shoes and lifted them onto the shelf with her toes. She leaned her walking stick into the corner beside two light blue burqas, each suspended from hidden hooks.

The young woman opened a carved wooden door, stepped aside, and waited for Marie to pass through.

Marie traced a carved flower with her fingertip as she passed through the doorway. *Wealth*, she thought, and greeted the older woman. "Salaam alaikum, Bibi-jan." She held out her hands as she spoke and was welcomed into Bibi-jan's home.

Marie sat down on the carpeted floor and leaned against the cold, white-painted wall. Immediately, the younger woman stepped into the room with a large red cotton pillow and jammed it between Marie and the wall behind her. She returned a few moments later with a matching cotton floor mat. Marie stood and waited for the charcoal-scarved woman to unfold the mat on the floor, then sat down again.

The young woman returned a third time with an aluminum tray

of tea, a thermos, and three dishes of treats: dark raisins, almonds, and pistachios. Each time the young women entered the room, she muttered "Salaam," and each time Bibi-jan ignored her.

Marie fell into an easy conversation with Bibi-jan. The older woman was strong, the undisputed power of the household. Marie was her guest and, therefore, someone to be honored. But more than that, it was obvious that Bibi-jan liked Marie. The young foreigner matched her humor. She was a distraction from the boredom that had become Bibi-jan's life. Marie was an amusement. And besides, she was no threat to the household balance of power. Immediately, Bibi-jan demanded to know the status of the class and once satisfied, found nothing else of interest to discuss.

Marie took the gap in the conversation. "Who is the young woman?"

Bibi-jan waved her hand dismissively. "She is my daughter-in-law." Then she added with obvious disgust. "She has not learned how to work."

The cry of a baby came from another room.

Bibi-jan called out loudly. "Shukria! Shukria! Bring me my son!"

Shukria, Marie thought. *Now I have a name.* A moment later, the young woman appeared with a still-crying baby in her arms. She placed the child on Bibi-jan's lap and sat down on the floor next to the door.

The old woman continued to direct her conversation toward Marie. "This is my son. Allah is great."

"Your son?" Marie didn't believe it. Bibi-jan had to be too old to have children.

"Yes. My son. Praise be to Allah!"

The boy settled peacefully into Bibi-jan's arms, but only for a few moments. When he squalled again, Shukria rose from her place and knelt on the floor next to her mother-in-law. She neither reached for the child nor withdrew from him, but simply waited.

Bibi-jan placed the boy into the younger woman's arms and dismissed them both. Shukria returned to her place inside the doorway, pulled open her shirt, and began to nurse the baby. He calmed immediately.

So the child is Shukria's, yet the mother-in-law claims him. There's a story here. Marie wanted to find it, but that would take tact and patience. "Bibi-jan, you said your father is the father of this village, yes?"

Bibi-jan sat straight up and spoke with confidence and obvious pride. "Yes. My father built this house. I was born in it. My father cut the first fields in the valley below us. My father cut the river to water the fields. My oldest brother is now the Khan Khel, the landowner. He owns most of the land you see. My father is the father of this village."

Marie listened carefully. *"My oldest brother is now the Khan Khel, the landowner." Perhaps the commander. Bibi-jan's brother.* She studied the older woman. Now she had another question to ask, but again, she chose to wait.

"And your husband?"

The woman looked through the glass casement window toward the plateau on the far side of the valley. "Gone. *Shahid.* A martyr."

The graves with their red, black, and green pennants floated before Marie's eyes. She looked at Bibi-jan's downturned face and remembered the expected response. "May God forgive him."

Bibi-jan nodded her acknowledgment but said nothing else.

"How did he die?"

This time, the older woman looked straight into Marie's eyes. She thumped the palm of her hand against her own chest. "My husband was a commander. He defended our village, first against the government, then against the Russians, and then against the Taliban. He died a martyr. He was a good man."

Marie knew better than to get mixed up in an Afghan's interpretation of history or politics. Instead she asked what she thought was an unthreatening question. "How many children do you have?"

The old woman threw a glance over her shoulder at Shukria and the now-quiet baby in the young woman's arms. She waved her hand and Shukria rose, placed the baby in Bibi-jan's lap, and retreated to her place by the door. Bibi-jan cradled the child closely. She called out to the young woman. "Bring food for our guest." Immediately, Shukria disappeared.

Marie asked her question again. "Bibi-jan, how many children do you have?"

"I have eight sons and four daughters."

"Praise to God." Marie affirmed the gift.

The woman nodded.

Marie hesitated, then asked. "Where are they now?"

Again, the woman kept her eyes fixed on the baby in her arms. "My daughters are married and gone."

"And your sons?"

"Gone."

"Gone?"

Bibi-jan carved her words sharply. "Six sons have been taken by God. Shahid (martyrs). Two sons remain." She rubbed her hand across the baby's forehead. "This one and his father."

Grandmother. The fullness of the story settled slowly into Marie's heart. Bibi-jan had lost six sons. Martyrs. That meant they'd been lost in war. Again, she thought of the graves on the far side of the river. This time, she chose her own, non-Afghan response. "May God comfort you with His peace."

For the first time in their conversation, the older woman's eyes were soft, round, and heavy. Her words followed, "Allah is merciful." She returned her gaze to the baby in her arms.

Shukria entered the room with a rolled piece of brown-and-gold woven cloth and a bowl of bright white yogurt. She unrolled the cloth on the floor in front of Marie, revealing a large broken piece of flat, whole wheat bread. Marie thanked the young woman, but she only nodded, retreating again to her place inside of the doorway.

Bibi-jan waved at Marie. "Eat, eat." Once again, her words were rough and sharp.

Marie nodded, looking down at the food and then at Bibi-jan. The old woman was clearly in control here. Marie looked at the child in Bibi-jan's arms and wondered how the grandmother had become the mother. She looked at the young woman in the doorway and began to guess at the cause of her status. These things she would have to learn, but for now, there was the matter of yogurt and fresh bread. "Bibi-jan, with your permission?" Marie raised her hands to indicate prayer.

The old woman waved her free hand as if she were throwing flour onto a ball of dough she was kneading.

Marie lowered her head and prayed. She asked God to bless the household, Bibi-jan, the baby boy, and finally Shukria. She thanked God for the food, passed her hands over her face, and began to eat. The yogurt was strong and sour, just the way Marie had come to like it. The bread was heavy and rich. Heaped with yogurt, it was perfect.

Bibi-jan had no questions for her guest, no curiosity about Marie or where she had come from. Instead, she talked about the flour that had been ground from wheat her family had grown and harvested in the fields below. She talked about the yogurt her family had prepared from the milk provided by her cows. Marie guessed the old woman no longer worked at all. She had a daughter-in-law and a son, and apparently she lived in a compound now owned by one of her brothers. Still, in everything Bibi-jan claimed ownership, possession, and responsibility.

Marie listened, asked about the seasons, the harvest, the availability of clean water, and the challenges of snow in the deep winter. Bibi-jan was delighted to describe her village and the life her people lived there. Occasionally, Marie slipped a glance at the silent woman curled just inside the doorway. She thought she'd once been beautiful, but now her most remarkable feature was sadness. She sat wrapped in it, alone.

When Marie had finished the last of the sour yogurt and had placed the remaining fragment of broken bread in the middle of the floor-cloth, Bibi-jan waved for Shukria to remove the remains. The younger woman immediately complied and disappeared from the room.

Marie thought of Hagar and Sarah, but in this scene, her hostess would be Sarah, and that wouldn't be a good story. She prayed and decided to make up her own story. Leaning her back against the heavy red pillow, Marie said, "Bibi-jan, with your permission, I would like to share a story."

"Ah, a story! A story is good. Go on."

Marie sipped her tea and began. "Once there was a man who planted wheat in a field next to a river. He broke down the wall of the river and flooded the field with water."

Bibi-jan nodded—this was exactly what a man must do.

"Summer came and the river became dry."

Bibi-jan frowned—this was a problem.

"So the man dug a well."

Bibi-jan interrupted. "He's a wise man."

"The man worked for a long time. It was summer and the sun was strong. He dug a deep well. He had to break many rocks to get to the water. In the end, he put his bucket into the well. He tasted the water, but it was salty."

Again, Bibi-jan frowned and offered a solution. "He should dig another well."

"Yes." Marie agreed. "But the man was angry and he did not want to dig another well."

Bibi-jan leaned forward, enveloped by the story.

"Instead, he watered his field with salty water. The wheat turned brown and died."

Bibi-jan slapped her knee. "He is an unwise man! Everyone knows the wheat will become dead."

"The man became angry. He cursed the field."

Bibi-jan shook her head; she knew that was a very unwise thing to do.

"The next year, there was water in the river, but the wheat did not grow."

At that moment, Shukria reentered the room and took her place inside the doorway.

Marie looked up at Shukria, smiled, and spoke directly to the young woman. "Shukria-jan. You have taken trouble. Thank you."

The young woman pulled her scarf over the lower part of her face and pulled her knees in front of her chest. Both Marie and Bibi-jan watched her.

Marie finished her story. "If we want the wheat to grow, we must give it good water."

Marie understood how to make a point in the Afghan storytelling culture; Bibi-jan knew the story was meant for her. And yet, it had been a clever story. She threw a challenge at Marie. "My brother says you Jesus-followers believe in three gods. Why do you believe in three gods?"

Marie quickly tried to recall her previous conversation with Bibi-jan. *What did I say? Nothing, right? I just prayed for the meal. I told her I was a Christ-follower.* She looked at the old woman. *So she has talked to her brother about me. The landowner? Is he the commander?*

Marie didn't want to stir up trouble. She considered her words, then said, "God our God is one." She looked directly into Bibi-jan's face. "He has given us two great commandments; love Him with everything we have." She looked toward Shukria's folded form beside the door. Bibi-jan followed her eyes. "And the second commandment. We must love our neighbors as ourselves." Marie smiled at Shukria, then returned her gaze to Bibi-jan. "We are all children of Father Adam and Mother Eve. We all belong to God. We are all neighbors."

Bibi-jan's jaw set fast and hard. Her eyes narrowed.

Marie backed up, deflecting attention from the message she had intended to deliver. "I am an American. I am a follower of the Honorable Jesus Messiah. You are an Afghan and you are a Muslim. You follow the Prophet Muhammad. We are both children of Father

Adam and Mother Eve. We both belong to God. You and I, Bibi-jan, are neighbors."

Marie's final words broke the tension. Bibi-jan slapped Marie's knee. "Yes! Yes! There is one God." She spoke the Muslim statement of faith in Arabic. "There is no God but Allah, and Muhammad is his prophet."

Marie responded gently, aware that her words would travel directly to the leader of the village. "Bibi-jan, may God bless you and your home with peace."

This time, the old woman smiled. She would have to think about Marie's story later. For now, she was pleased with her guest. "Stay the night. I will cook you meat."

Marie smiled. "You have taken great trouble. You are kind. With your permission?" She pushed herself up from the floor. "It has become late. The road to town is long."

Bibi-jan handed the baby boy back to Shukria, stood and engulfed both of Marie's hands in her own. She allowed Marie to kiss her cheeks three times, and then she placed her hand on Marie's cheek. Stroking Marie's face gently, she said, "You must come. Tomorrow. You must come. Come for lunch. Tomorrow. I will cook you meat."

Marie understood the invitation was more a command than a request. "If the rain does not fall, I will come soon." She didn't promise a day.

Bibi-jan threw her head back. "Hah!" Then playfully slapped Marie's cheek. "Tomorrow. Come tomorrow!"

Marie nodded. "If the rains do not fall. I will come soon. And I will visit your class."

The old woman hit Marie on the shoulder. "And you will see we are smart students. Our teacher is good."

Marie smiled and stepped through the carved door and onto the landing at the top of the stairs. Shukria immediately followed. Marie slipped into her shoes, grabbed her walking stick, and allowed Shukria to lead her down the stairs, through the barn, past the cows, and across the ringed courtyard.

The teacher's boy still waited at the gate.

Marie turned, took Shukria's limp hand, and caught sight of Bibi-jan standing at the window, watching. She spoke her blessing of good-bye to Shukria and released the young woman's hand.

Shukria whispered. "Please come back." Immediately, she turned and walked quickly toward the barn.

At the window, the form of Bibi-jan had vanished. Marie followed the teacher's son through the gates, across the orchard, and down the steep pathways back to her waiting vehicle.

The boy left her as soon as Faiz Muhammad appeared in view. He, too, was waiting alone.

20

Marie slid into the backseat of the SUV. Faiz Muhammad shifted into gear. He drove across the small bridge and turned the vehicle up the steep hill that led to the plateau across from the village. The SUV slid sideways and stopped at the ledge. Marie looked down the hillside. She wondered if they slid down, would they stop before they fell into the river.

Faiz Muhammad shifted again, this time easily pulling the vehicle off the edge of the hill. He drove the rest of the way up to the plateau without difficulty. The man was a good driver.

When they reached the plateau and the SUV was stable, Faiz Muhammad asked Marie about the village, the class, and the people she visited.

She told him the class would start the next day and they would have to come back in two days. She had been invited to lunch. The driver smiled. He knew it was not good for Marie to be alone. "Your eyes are shining."

Marie chuckled softly at the Afghan expression. *Your eyes are shining.* Then she thought. *They probably are.* Still, she had more questions than she had answers. "Faiz Muhammad-jan, what do you know about this village?"

The driver glanced at Marie through the rearview mirror and shrugged his shoulders

"Faiz Muhammad-jan, do you know who the commander is? The Khan Khel, the landowner?"

"Yes. Aga Rasul Khan."

Marie noted the respect with which her driver spoke Ahmad Rasul Khan's name, using *Aga,* a word of honor. "I think I had tea with his sister." Faiz Muhammad shot a glance at Marie. "What do you know about him?"

The driver chose his words carefully. "Mari-jan, Aga Rasul Khan is a very strong man. You must be careful."

"Thank you." Marie wondered how the commander had reacted to the presence of a Christian foreigner in his village. "What kind of a man is he?"

Faiz Muhammad shrugged. "He is a strong man. He is wealthy, but his heart is not hungry. He is a man of honor."

The expression *hungry heart* described a person who was greedy, who takes what he wants from whomever he wants. Bibi-jan's brother was not such a man. Instead, he was a man of honor. Marie thought of the office engineer's words. "Faiz Muhammad-jan. Aga Rasul Khan— he is a friend of the governor, yes?"

"Yes. He has many friends. The head of the Ministry of Health is his cousin. The governor is a relative."

Marie envisioned the minister's pink, yellow, and orange house just two blocks beyond Zia Gul's. *So they're related.*

Faiz Muhammad interrupted her thoughts. "He helps people. He is building the mosque in town."

Immediately, the large brick dome of the new mosque appeared in

Marie's imagination. She remembered the workmen on the face of the dome and the gold-colored tiles they held in their hands. She nodded. The pieces of the story were coming together. "Faiz Muhammad-jan. He is arguing with an Uzbek family, yes?"

The driver nodded again. "They are bad people. Their hearts are hungry."

Marie pushed his judgment on the people away but kept the realization that her favorite village was involved in whatever dispute brewed in her community. She would have to tell Dave, explain the situation to him. He would collect information, assess, and make decisions. She looked out the window, across the plateau to the village beyond. He might say she couldn't go back. He might demand they abandon the class.

She pushed the thought aside and chose a new question. "Faiz Muhammad-jan. Do you know his nephew? I think he is the son of my friend." Marie watched her driver in the rearview.

"His nephew?" Faiz Muhammad studied the road. "I think he has many nephews. His family is large."

"Maybe. My friend, the commander's sister, said that all of her sons died. Shahid, martyrs. She has one son remaining. Do you know about him?"

Faiz Muhammad shook his head.

Marie looked out the window. She could no longer see the outline of the village, just the hills and the snow-laced mountains beyond them. She inhaled the sharp, cool, clean air and thought she could taste snow. "She has a daughter-in-law," Marie said. "I think there is a story there. She says the son of her daughter-in-law is her own son."

"This is not a problem." He snorted and waved his hand. "If she has lost sons, she will find new ones."

"How does an old woman find new sons?"

Faiz Muhammad shrugged. "If one wife has no children and her sister has many, she may receive a child."

"And a grandmother?"

"Yes. And a grandmother."

Marie puzzled over the relationships as Faiz Muhammad pulled away from the plateau and descended into the difficult ravine with its soft mud basin. This time, he pulled off the road before he reached the bottom and rocked quickly up the other side.

Marie formed another question. "Faiz Muhammad-jan? I think there is a story. Can you find out for me?"

"Story about what?"

"About the sister of the commander, and about her son, and about her daughter-in-law. Can you find out?"

Faiz Muhammad was noncommittal. "Maybe." He turned the vehicle toward the tall wooden bridge. The water beneath them rushed, churned, and crashed below, nearly exploding between the steep banks of the river. Marie felt the beams beneath their wheels buckle. *Someday, this bridge will collapse. I hope we're not on it when it does.* She breathed a prayer of thanks as the SUV rocked off the bridge and onto solid ground.

The first cluster of red, black, and green grave pennants came into view. Several were surrounded by small black steel fences. Marie watched the pennants float in the late afternoon breeze.

The two drove the rest of the way in silence until they reached Marie's road. Just before they turned into her alley, Marie saw a young man in a brown, Western-style jacket and blue jeans standing on the opposite corner. She called out to her driver. "Faiz Muhammad-jan, do you see that man?"

The driver stopped abruptly, shifted his rearview, and searched behind them, but the man was gone. He shook his head. "Did you see someone?"

"Yes." Marie felt a hard knot in her stomach. "I think . . . he looks like the same man who was outside our class the other day."

Faiz Muhammad shrugged. "Perhaps."

By then, the sun had settled behind the town walls. Marie's green gate appeared black in the evening's shadow. As she jumped down from the vehicle, Faiz Muhammad asked his own question. "Is Nazanin leaving us?"

Marie realized she hadn't thought about Carolyn since she entered Bibi-jan's house. That had been a gift. "Yes. She is becoming engaged. She will leave soon."

The driver rubbed his beard. "She is a good girl. It's good she marries."

Marie gritted her teeth against the Afghan assumption that all girls must marry, but she knew her driver meant no offense. She wished him safety in God and stepped through her gate. She pulled open the door to her house. Once again, Carolyn was cooking. Once again, she was singing. Marie shook her head hard, dropping her bag. She walked back out to the porch and sat down on a wicker bench. Her dogs immediately joined her, each pushing the other for more attention. Marie scratched their necks, grateful for their faithful affection.

She listened to the quiet. No singing. No boys shouting in the alley. No plates clacking together from next door. Only the dogs' huffing, clawing, and pushing. The leaves on the fruit trees had faded, their brown hands twisted but still clinging. The light was nearly gone from the evening sky, but no stars appeared. Marie felt the cold, damp air in her sinuses and lungs. She exhaled steam.

She heard a television from the guard's house across the yard. The light on the porch and another near the gate snapped on. Electricity. The small pools of light, dense with moisture, were weak. She pushed the dogs away and went inside. Carolyn stood at the stove, frying peppers and onions in garlic and oil. The younger woman leaned her face into the steam, inhaled the garlic and leaned back. "Wouldn't broccoli be nice?"

Marie winced. Broccoli wasn't available in Shehktan, but it certainly was in America.

"Or green beans?"

Marie snapped. "You've got to stop doing that. I just can't handle it!"

"I'm sorry. I'm—I'm sorry." Carolyn stepped back.

Marie took a deep breath. "No. I'm sorry. It's just that . . . I'm not leaving."

Carolyn stepped away from the stove and pulled plates out of the cabinet and silverware from the shelf. "I know." She spoke softly. "I'm sorry. It's just—" Her words trailed off.

Marie saw a bowl of beaten eggs and poured them into the pot. She finished Carolyn's thought. "It's just that you're leaving and it's hard and you'd rather think about the good stuff you're walking into. Yeah?"

Carolyn shrugged. "I guess so. Yeah."

Marie nodded. She stirred the eggs. "I know. I mean, I think I know. But I'm not leaving." She shrugged. "I have to stay."

"You want to stay."

"Yeah." Marie watched the eggs harden into brown edged clumps. "Yeah. I want to stay. This is my life—but it's not that I don't *miss* America, and the broccoli, and the green beans, and the freedom to drive myself around. It's just that I'm *here*." Marie imagined the tiny faded pennants clinging to the grave markers on the road to Char Ab. Suddenly she saw a dust storm, its force tearing the cloth, trying to pull the pennants from their posts. She shook the image from her mind and sighed. Her voice softened. "I'm trying to keep my head *here*."

Carolyn stacked the plates, silverware, cups, and a small dish of salt onto a round aluminum tray. "I know. I'm sorry."

"Yeah, me too." Marie relented. "I know this is what you have to do. I know it's the right thing. I'm trying to deal with that. It's just, you know, hard for me."

"You want me to pretend I'm not leaving?"

"No. Of course not. Just try not to drag me into America. It's just not good for me."

"Okay . . . I'm sorry."

The two women ate their evening meal in awkward conversation. Carolyn tried not to talk about America, and Marie tried not to talk about the village literacy project. After dinner, Marie retreated to her room. She sat down on her bed and began to write.

> Carolyn's leaving. Okay. I can handle it.
> The bridge is crumbling. God, please don't let it collapse under us.
> The village is haunting. Something's there. Shukria, beautiful.
> Bibi-jan. She's got something. Can I help? Can I find the right stories? Defuse whatever that something is even if I don't understand it?
> And is someone following me? Crazy. Maybe.
> The whole thing is crazy. Uneven. Crumbling.

Marie looked for a metaphor, something to capture the chaos she was feeling.

> I'm walking down the street in the wind. My backpack keeps sliding off my shoulder and the wind keeps blowing my scarf off. I can't hold it all together. It's raining and it keeps raining and it keeps raining and the wind is blowing. Everything's turning to mud. Deeper than it's ever been. I keep trying, but I can't move forward. The wind is too strong and the mud is too thick. And the rain keeps falling.

She stopped, rubbed her eyes, looked around her room. *I can do this. I can do this.* She returned to her journal.

> Slow down. Breathe. Focus. Take an inventory. Give thanks.

The project. It's wonderful. It's working. The classes are learning, and I get to visit. I'm getting to know a whole new group of people. Women, lots of them. They're welcoming me. I'm hearing their stories. It's good. It's really good.

And Char Ab—amazing, beautiful. Privilege to go there. Something's going on. Can my stories help?

Marie leaned her head back against the cold wall. She pulled her blanket up around her shoulders. *Focus. It's too much. I can't hold on to everything. Focus on the literacy classes. Let the rest go.* She thought back through her day, allowing the faces and the voices of the women to float into her mind. She heard, again, conversations. She saw rooms, curtains, carpets, the barren fields on the way to Char Ab, the grave pennants floating in the breeze, the scoop-faced hills, and the snow-laced mountains. *This is what matters. Hold on to it.*

DAY 4

CHAR AB, AFGHANISTAN

21

The mullah's morning call to prayer woke her. It was early, still dark. Marie closed her eyes and walked through the day's plans. *Visit Margaret, lunch with the staff, check on one of the in-town classes. Any one; doesn't matter which. Okay, I can do this.* She sat bolt upright. *Good-bye dinner for Carolyn! Tonight.* She groaned. *I'll have to tell Dave about the village.* She knew Dave might do anything. He could brush it all off as nothing. He could say, "These are our classes. We'll continue. Their local conflict doesn't have anything to do with us." *Or,* Marie thought, *he could say, shut it down. Stay away. No more trips to Char Ab.* Marie lay back down and forced herself to be silent, but sleep wouldn't return.

She got up, made herself coffee, and returned to her room. Wrapping herself in blankets, she opened her Bible and settled her heart into truth.

An hour later, she rose, dressed quickly, and headed on foot to Margaret's house. She hesitated inside her own yard, praying silently before pulling the gate open. The alley was deserted. She walked its length, careful of the dark brown, overflowing gutter water, aware of its stench.

She walked to the edge of the intersection and looked around. *The old man in his little store. Who's that with him? Short hair. Mustache. Blue-gray shirt and trousers. Police? Hands on his hips. Bulge in the back of his shirt. A gun. Police.*

The officer turned and watched Marie pass.

Marie looked the other way. A young man squatted on the ground beside a mud-brick wall. He was wearing blue jeans, a button-down plaid shirt, and a short brown jacket. He had pointed shoes and a sloppy haircut. And Marie was sure he was the same man she'd seen the day before. Her stomach clenched. *Perhaps he has a friend here,* she reasoned. She fixed his image in her mind and kept walking.

She walked all the way to Margaret's gate, but just as she reached for the bell, she changed her mind. *I'll be here tonight, anyway. I don't want to talk right now.* She thought about going back to her own house, but she knew that Carolyn was there, packing. She thought about going to the office to work on the budget, but decided it could wait. What she really wanted was to go to Char Ab. *Sure. Why not?*

She texted Margaret, "Must work. See you later." Then she called Faiz Muhammad and asked him to meet her at her alley. Along the way, she looked for the young man with the brown, Western-style jacket, blue jeans, and pointed shoes. He was gone.

At the village, Bibi-jan was waiting for her. "I knew you would come today." She enveloped Marie's hands in her own, allowed her guest to kiss her cheeks, and pulled her into the sitting room. "You will eat lunch. It will become ready."

It was only 10:45 in the morning. Marie knew it was early enough for the family to prepare sufficient food to include her in their meal. Otherwise, they would serve her someone else's portion. *Besides,* she thought, *Bibi-jan's family isn't so poor they can't feed me.* So Marie agreed.

"My driver's down in the valley."

Bibi-jan waved her hand as if to brush away the dilemma. "This is not a problem. He will eat with the men."

"I thought the men were all gone."

Again, Bibi-jan waved her hand. "They were gone. They have returned."

"All of them?"

"Do you want to talk to the men?" She chuckled.

Marie's face turned crimson and she shook her head.

Bibi-jan mumbled something about work in town and more work in the provincial capital—business to be attended to, gatherings and discussions.

Marie remembered her driver. "The car is cold inside."

Bibi-jan slapped Marie's folded knee. "Bah! He has become welcome. It's not a problem." Then she chided Marie. "We are good people. We will not leave a guest in the cold."

Shukria brought a tray of teacups and treats and a thermos full of green tea.

Marie stood and greeted her as soon as she entered the room. Shukria allowed Marie to collect her hands in her own and kiss her cheeks. She muttered "Salaam," looked down, and said nothing else, then she disappeared.

Marie offered the first conversation. "Is there a literacy class? Will the women become literate?"

"Of course!" Bibi-jan feigned offense and again, she slapped Marie's knee. "Our teacher is good and we are intelligent."

Marie asked about the other students. Bibi-jan answered without interest, and Marie realized she had something else on her mind.

"Mari-jan?"

Marie cracked open a pistachio, then looked into the older woman's face.

"Where do you get your money? Does the president of the United States pay you?"

Marie smiled. She knew the concerns behind the question. *Are you a spy? Do you work for the US government? Are you dangerous for our village? Can we trust you?*

"Bibi-jan, the government of the United States does not give me money. Instead, I give the government money. I pay taxes." At this, Bibi-jan laughed out loud. She knew exactly what taxes were. She also knew that no fool pays them.

"The money for the literacy class comes from people just like you, men and women who work hard. They give a little money every month. There are many of them, so there is enough money. There's not a lot of money, though."

Bibi-jan thought about this for a few minutes, then leveled her next question. "Why do they give this money?"

Marie wasn't sure how much she wanted to tell Bibi-jan, because it was likely that whatever she said, the older woman would relay it to her brother, the village commander. "Bibi-jan, my friends give money for the literacy classes because they know me. They trust me to use the money. They trust me not to steal it. They are good people. Their hearts are not hungry."

The older woman listened carefully. Finally, she asked, "But why do they give money to help us?"

Marie observed through the large, glassed casement window: the plateau and the cultivated valley with its serpentine river beneath it. She looked back at Bibi-jan. "They are all followers of the Honorable Jesus Messiah. They know God has given us two commandments: love Him, and love our neighbors. They believe you are their neighbor. They want to help you. So, every month they give a little money. There are many of them, so there is enough money."

Bibi-jan considered Marie's answer without satisfaction. "You should build a school here. You should build a center for men and women to learn. You should build a storage building for wheat and rice. You should give us a machine to grind the wheat. Now, our men must travel to grind wheat. You should do these things." At that, the old woman was pleased.

"May God give you a school, a training center, a storage building, and a grinding machine," was all Marie said.

Bibi-jan laughed. "You should give us these things!" She slapped Marie's knee again.

Marie shrugged her shoulders and responded, "My friends are not rich."

That reply, Bibi-jan accepted. In Afghanistan, everything is based on relationships and apparently, Marie's weren't very good. She commanded Marie to drink more tea, and the two women fell into an easy conversation. The older, delighted to teach her foreign friend about her village; the younger, delighted to learn.

Bibi-jan explained her family's history. "We were a small village. My father, Masoud Agha, owned all the land. Now it belongs to my brother."

Marie interrupted. "Ahmad Rasul Khan?"

"Yes. He is my brother and he owns all this land." With that, the older woman waved her hand as if to include everything.

Marie nodded. "Is he here now?"

Bibi-jan shook her head. "No. He is in town. He has business."

"Oh. May God give him success." Marie wanted to ask more about the man's business, but thought better of the question.

Bibi-jan thanked Marie. "Yes. He is a good man." Then she went on with her story. "Many of our relatives came in the days of the Taliban. It was the time of the early wheat harvest. They had no sandals on their feet. They had become tired and hungry."

"They were refugees?"

"Yes." The older woman went on. "Many people came. They were family, so we welcomed them. What could we do?"

Marie cracked open pistachios and listened.

"They slept everywhere: in sitting rooms, on barn floors, in field sheds, even out in the open under the night sky. The women gathered water from the river and carried it up the hill. They cooked rice and baked bread for everyone. They took care of one another's children. Those girls who were old enough were married as soon as possible. It was better that way.

"The men worked side by side, harvesting wheat, threshing it, and carrying it to the mill. They dug trenches from the hard summer ground and the harder rock base. They laid foundation stones and mixed mud and straw into bricks they laid out on the hillsides to dry. They built houses, one room at a time. They dug wells deep into the rock.

"That summer and the following fall, everyone worked hard. If they could survive the first winter, they would live. Some didn't. The old, sick, and weak died because of diarrhea and fever. Some of the smaller children stopped growing. Their wheat-colored skin faded to yellow. When a child stopped breathing, the men carried him away and the women commanded the mother to be silent and to work. There was too much death.

"Winter came. The snow fell. We gave what we could." Bibi-jan waved the entire story away as if to say *enough*. She sat straight up and announced with surprising strength in her voice. "We are the people of Ahmad Rasul Khan. We are Afghans. No one fed us. We worked hard. We take nothing that is not our own! Now we will learn to read!"

Marie sat bolt upright at Bibi-jan's words: *We take nothing that is not our own . . . We take nothing that is not our own,* echoed through her thoughts.

"We will learn to read." Bibi-jan declared again.

"You take nothing that is not your own?"

"Of course not. We are good people. We work hard."

Marie looked straight into the older woman's eyes. "Does someone say you take what is not yours?"

"Bah! They are liars. Their hearts are black. All of them."

Instantly, Marie thought of the Uzbek brothers, the engineer's words, Zia Gul's warning. "Who?"

Bibi-jan looked out the window toward town. "They are bad people. We have not sinned. We are good."

"Who, Bibi-jan?"

The woman waved her hand at the town. "They want war. They are bad."

"The Uzbeks?"

"Bah! They are bad!"

Marie followed Bibi-jan's eyes as she glanced in the direction of the distant town. "Your brother, Ahmad Rasul Khan, is fighting with the Uzbeks?"

Bibi-jan nodded. "They are very bad. All of them. Their hearts are hungry."

Marie winced at the generalization. Just then, Shukria entered the room with her baby on her hip. She placed the boy on Bibi-jan's lap and retreated to the doorway.

Marie looked at Bibi-jan, then at the boy, peaceful in the older woman's arms. She looked over at Shukria, sitting in the doorway. She whispered her next question. "Bibi-jan?"

The older woman looked up.

"Is Shukria-jan Uzbek?"

The older woman locked her jaw and narrowed her eyes. "She is worthless. She cannot work." Bibi-jan didn't answer Marie's question.

Marie caught her breath. She turned toward the younger woman. She noticed her wide set eyes and light skin. *Perhaps she is Uzbek.* She looked back at Bibi-jan and wondered. There was a story here, and it wasn't good.

Marie leaned back against the wall and gazed out the window. She struggled to breathe. *I am sitting with a family who is feuding with another tribe. That can't be good. And I'm sitting with two women who hate each other.* She prayed silently, then made a decision. "Bibi-jan.

With your permission, I would like to ask your daughter-in-law some questions."

The older woman simply waved.

Marie called out to the young woman in the doorway. "Shukria-jan, please, come and sit here."

Shukria looked to her mother-in-law for permission. The older woman ignored her, so Shukria stepped forward. She sat down on her shins beside and just behind her mother-in-law. She waited, head down and patient.

"Shukria-jan, I hear you are literate?"

The younger woman nodded.

Bibi-jan pulled a piece of thread from the end of her scarf and began flossing her teeth.

Marie drew a thin, first-grade reader from her backpack, opened to a page in the middle, and asked Shukria to read.

The young woman accepted the small booklet but looked to her mother-in-law before reading the words.

The older woman focused her attention on the awakening boy, still wrapped in a heavy blanket on her lap.

Shukria read the words softly, but quickly and cleanly.

Marie nodded, thanked her, and opened a third grade reader.

Again, the young woman read softly but skillfully.

Marie had two more books in Dari, the book of Psalms and the New Testament. She wasn't sure she should reveal them, but those were the only Dari texts she had that were written at a higher level than third grade. She chose Psalms first. She opened the small booklet without regard to the psalm she chose.

Shukria took the booklet and began to read. "To you, O LORD, I call; my rock, be not deaf to me, lest, if you be silent to me, I become like those who go down to the pit." It was Psalm 28. This time, the young woman read haltingly, tripping over the dense and rich Dari poetry.

"Hear the voice of my pleas for mercy, when I cry to you for help, when I lift up my hands toward your most holy sanctuary. Do not drag me off with the wicked, with the workers of evil, who speak peace with their neighbors while evil is in their hearts." Bibi-jan interrupted her several times to correct her faulty pronunciation.

The stumbling rendition, with Bibi-jan's harsh corrections, was painful to bear. Marie thanked Shukria, retrieved the book, and returned it to her bag.

"What is that?" Bibi-jan's curiosity was awakened.

Marie responded casually. "It is *Zabur*, the book of Psalms." She waited for Bibi-jan's reaction before pulling the last book out of her bag.

The older woman simply watched her.

Marie broached a question. "Do you like it?"

The boy squirmed out of Bibi-jan's lap and reached for a half-full cup of tea. Shukria grabbed him and pulled him back to safety.

Bibi-jan nodded slowly, considered, and finally responded. "Yes. It is a prayer."

Marie agreed, still hesitant.

"Can you read our language? Can you read that?"

"Slowly. The psalms are hard. They're poetry. I read them the way Shukria does. The book of the Honorable Jesus Messiah is easier."

Bibi-jan's eyes widened. Even Shukria looked up. Marie pulled a small, dark green New Testament from her bag and showed it to Bibi-jan.

The old woman removed the book from Marie's hand. She studied the printed words on the cover but couldn't read them. "The book of the Honorable Jesus Messiah?"

"Yes. The *Injil*, the New Testament." Marie took the book back from Bibi-jan. "It's harder than the third grade reader. It's easier than the Psalms." She looked at Shukria. "Will you try a sentence?"

The young woman glanced at Bibi-jan. This time, the old woman nodded.

Marie opened the book and handed it to Shukria.

"Where does it begin?"

Marie couldn't read the words upside down, but she could see the bolded headings. She picked one.

Shukria began to read. This time, although she read haltingly, she could manage the text. It was the Dari translation of Luke 11:37–41.

"While Jesus was speaking, a Jewish mullah asked him to eat with him, so he went in and sat down at the floorcloth. The Jewish mullah was surprised to see that he did not first wash before eating. The Master said to him, 'Now you Jewish mullahs clean the outside of the cup and of the dish, but inside you are full of greed and wickedness. You fools! Did not he who made the outside make the inside also? But give as alms those things that are within, and look, everything is clean for you.' "

"Hah!" Bibi-jan interrupted. "They should clean their black hearts!"

Marie took the book from Shukria and folded it into her bag. She ignored Bibi-jan's accusation. "You read well. You have studied?"

Shukria looked straight at Marie, blinked her eyes hard to say yes, then looked away.

Bibi-jan began firing questions. "Who is this Jesus?"

Marie understood. Bibi-jan knew the Honorable Jesus Messiah, son of the Virgin Maryam, but a man with no title was not recognizable. She explained. "You call Jesus the Honorable Jesus Messiah. In the Injil, he has many names: Prophet, Savior, King of all kings, Master, Teacher."

Bibi-jan interrupted. "What is a Jewish mullah?"

"Like a Muslim mullah. Except, a Jewish mullah teaches the law of Moses. A Muslim mullah teaches *Sharia*, the law of Muhammad."

"Why does the Prophet Jesus Messiah speak to Jews?"

Marie shrugged. "Because the Honorable Jesus Messiah was a Jew."

Suddenly, Bibi-jan told Shukria to check the food. The younger woman left the room, and Bibi-jan stared through the glass window. Something had caught her attention and Marie thought it best to wait. Finally, Bibi-jan broke the silence. "Well, his idea is wise. Of course, we must wash the inside and the outsides of cups." She waved her hand as if to say *enough*.

22

Marie accepted the closure of Bibi-jan's questions about Jesus. "Bibi-jan, your daughter-in-law reads well. She has studied."

Bibi-jan locked her jaw. "She's lazy." The edges of her words were sharp and jagged.

"You chose her, yes?"

In Afghanistan, the boy's mother is usually the first to choose and approach the mother of the prospective bride. It's important that it happens that way because the bride will live with her husband's family. She will spend more time with her mother-in-law than with her husband. A mother-in-law must choose carefully.

Bibi-jan threw her head back and spit her response. "Na!"

Marie watched carefully, aware that she stood on the edge of the story. She thought of Zia Gul's story—the fact that her brother hesitated because the suitor was not her cousin. "Is your daughter-in-law family?"

Again, the woman hurled her response. "Na!"

Marie allowed the room to settle. "Forgive me, Bibi-jan. I am a foreigner. How did Shukria become your daughter-in-law?"

The old woman poured the cold, leaf-filled remains of her teacup into the base of the aluminum tray. She filled the cup anew from the thermos, the hot liquid rising in a small cloud between the two women. She sipped her tea, waved away a thought she hadn't uttered, and finally settled on a phrase. "*Ba zur.*" By force.

Marie had heard this phrase before, usually to describe situations where a stronger man had demanded a weaker man's daughter for a bride. She had heard it from families who had lost their daughters and from the women themselves who had been taken by force, sometimes too young, always against their will. She formed her question carefully. "I'm sorry, Bibi-jan. I don't understand."

Just then, Shukria stepped into the room with a large silver pitcher and matching basin. She knelt first before Bibi-jan, poured warm water from the pitcher over the older woman's hands, and collected the residue in the basin. She handed Bibi-jan a towel, never looking into the older woman's face. When Bibi-jan was finished, she waved the young woman away, and Shukria knelt before Marie.

Marie spoke as the warm water cascaded over her open palms. "Shukria-jan, you have taken trouble. You are very kind. Thank you."

The younger woman blushed and retreated with the pitcher and towel.

Marie didn't pick up the previous conversation. She thought she would learn more in time. Instead, she returned to the parable of the cup. "In America, where I'm from, there are many people who look good on the outside. Their works are good. They go to church. They read our Holy Book. People think they have honor. But some do not. Some are cruel and hit their wives. Some have hungry hearts. They steal things that do not belong to them. The outsides of their cups are clean. The insides are dirty."

Bibi-jan exhaled heavily. "It's like this in Afghanistan. Some men care only for themselves. They steal land and water. Their hearts are black. Foreigners give money to build bridges, but these men take the money. The bridge does not become built."

Marie considered Bibi-jan's response. She wondered if there was a real bridge that hadn't been built or if there had been land lost or blood spilled over land kept.

The old woman continued. "In Afghanistan, we are all poor." Suddenly, she slapped the floor. "Where is the money?"

Marie, startled, sat straight up. She wondered if Bibi-jan was asking her the question or if, instead, she was directing her question to those who would never give an answer. Marie pushed away the wanted bridge, the land, and the water. She sidestepped the opportunity to accuse and condemn. Instead, she chose another familiar Afghan phrase. "God sees."

Bibi-jan completed the sentences. "Allah without eyes, sees." She placed her fingertips on her eyes. "Without ears, hears." She placed her fingertips on her ears. "Without mouth, speaks."

Marie nodded. "And on the day of judgment, God will judge."

"Yes."

Marie tilted her head sideways, studied the old woman's face, and softly added. "All people."

Bibi-jan caught the warning in Marie's words. "Yes."

Shukria entered the room, and unrolled a brown-orange-and-yellow striped cloth on the floor between Marie and Bibi-jan. She retreated, and a moment later returned with a tray heaped with plates of steaming rice.

After the lunch, Marie and Bibi-jan left Shukria and walked down the path to the teacher's house. Along the way, Bibi-jan clapped Marie on the shoulder. "You must come tomorrow!"

Marie grinned. "May you live forever, Bibi-jan."

"Hah! You must come. We are having a celebration. There will be meat."

"What are you celebrating?"

"My niece is getting married. Tomorrow night is the henna party. You must come!"

Again Marie smiled. "I can't come at night, Bibi-jan. The road is long."

"Bah! You will stay the night!"

Marie laughed, then sighed. "You are kind."

The older woman regarded her guest. "It's fine. Come for lunch. We will celebrate!" With that, she turned and continued down the path to the teacher's house.

Marie followed. Once inside, Marie greeted each student, trying to remember their names and enjoying their inquisitive banter. She sat through the first part of the class. Satisfied with its progress, she bid the group good-bye and returned to Faiz Muhammad who waited in the valley with his vehicle.

Marie slid into the backseat. "Faiz Muhammad-jan? Did you eat lunch?"

"Of course, of course. This is a good village. These are good people."

Marie was relieved. She didn't want to think of him sitting in the cold, hungry and alone.

"Is there a class?"

"Yes. There is a class. There are many women. Maybe eighteen. They are learning."

"Good, good."

They drove up the steep hill to the plateau opposite the village. The road was solid, firm. Marie shivered and looked out at the mountains behind the distinctive hills of Char Ab. The lace was gone. Snow had fallen and only the rough outlines of black rock proved the mountains' presence.

The window glass thickened with steam from Marie's breath. She rolled her window down and shot several pictures of the village, its hills, and the distant mountains. *So harsh. So lovely.*

The plateau gave way to the ravine, now solid beneath the SUV's wheels. The ravine gave way to another ridge, then the frighteningly fragile railless bridge. The bridge gave way to the open fields punctuated by pennanted graves. The fields gave way to walled neighborhoods.

Faiz Muhammad looked at Marie through the rearview mirror. "Mari-jan? Where have you gone?"

Marie focused. "What?"

"You have gone somewhere."

"Yes. I was thinking."

Faiz Muhammad drove for several moments. "What were you thinking about?"

Marie responded. "I have learned many things today."

The driver looked at Marie in the mirror.

"I learned that the commander himself is fighting with the Uzbeks who were killed while we were in Kabul."

Faiz Muhammad nodded. "Yes. That's true. The men are all very angry. It isn't good."

Marie looked out the window at the walls that lined the road. "Is this a problem for us?"

"Perhaps."

"I also learned that the sister of the commander has a daughter-in-law taken by force."

Faiz Muhammad turned the vehicle onto the wide tree-lined road that led to Marie's alleyway. "Yes. By force."

Marie studied his face in the rearview mirror. She realized he had acquired information. "How?"

Faiz Muhammad shrugged his shoulders. He sketched the story without any trace of judgment. "There was a fight. Two boys. The nephew of the commander was hurt. He became lame. The sister of the other boy was given. It's *wali*." Law.

Marie's stomach wrenched. She tasted again the rice she had eaten with Bibi-jan. "Were the boys enemies?"

"No, no. They were friends. Schoolmates. There was a fight. The commander's nephew fell. His foot became lame."

"And the sister was given as payment?" Marie swallowed hard.

"Yes."

Marie imagined Shukria, innocent in every way, taken to a family who didn't want her. "And the friend?"

"The brother?" Faiz Muhammad looked in the rearview mirror.

"Yes. The brother of the bride."

"He was one of the brothers killed by the police when you were in Kabul."

Marie gasped and turned her head to examine the walls lining the entire length of the road; twelve-foot high mud-brick walls, only interrupted here and there by wooden or metal gates. Behind each wall, a compound with houses. Houses full of women, girls, and children. Houses full of stories.

She looked at a group of men huddled together in a wooden stall. A bank of boxes full of candy, cookies, cartons of juice, potatoes, and onions in front of them. What stories did they have? She exhaled loudly and spoke her next words more to the walls than her driver. "I could live here for thirty years and never really understand this place."

Her mind wondered to Carolyn going home, spending time with her young boyfriend, and deciding whether or not she wanted to marry him. He would be doing the same. If they chose to marry, they would plan their wedding together. They would choose a church, a banquet hall, and their first apartment. They would live separately from the families of both. They would build their lives together. They would go through hard times and good, and if they were lucky, they would love each other for the rest of their lives.

She thought of Shukria. Bibi-jan. The relatives of the two brothers who were killed. Ahmad Rasul Khan and his people. Two families locked in a bitterness that had already cost the lives of two brothers and the futures of two women.

Well, at least, she thought, *it has nothing to do with me.*

As soon as she stepped through her gate, Marie saw the boxes piled on the porch. She looked at the Omed, her guard.

"They are Nazanin-jan's. Tomorrow they will be sent to Kabul," he offered by way of explanation.

Marie nodded. *Perhaps,* she thought. *Carolyn's finished packing.*

Marie opened the front door of her home, stepped into the hallway, took off her scarf, and hung it on a set of now-empty hooks mounted on the wall. Carolyn had favored bright colored scarves. Now the colors were few and dark. Marie felt the last traces of strength slide out of her body.

She stepped out of her shoes and pushed them against the wall. Again, the space looked empty. Gone were Carolyn's stylish black leather dress shoes, her beaded sandals, and her simple brown clogs.

The house was cold beyond its temperature.

She looked at the closed door to Carolyn's room. She must reclaim that space to live comfortably. Before Carolyn came, Marie had used the room as an office with a lovely, dark brown desk and a shelf for her laptop custom-built by a local carpenter. Now, that desk was pushed against a wall in her own crowded bedroom. She would move it back to the space from which it came. She would purchase a good office chair from the one furniture store in town, move all of the electronics—the transformer, regulator, voltage divider, truck batteries, charger—everything back into Carolyn's room. She chided herself for calling it "Carolyn's room." Out loud she said, "That room will become my office again. This house will become mine."

She stared at the closed door as if by simply willing it, the room would transform itself and the house would settle into a new normalcy. She would be able to live whole and at peace.

She heard a noise—a scrape, then a thud. *Ah,* she thought, *maybe Carolyn's not finished packing after all.* She didn't knock. Instead, she walked into the sitting room. Pictures vanished from the shelves built into the walls of the room. Her books and the rows of plastic-cased DVDs were also gone, packed into boxes to be shipped to Carolyn's friends in Kabul. All that remained was one shelf of cardboard-sleeved old videocassette tapes that Sharon had left behind. *Ah, Sharon. You left, too.* She had no TV or video player. *Why do I keep them?*

Marie felt the dank emptiness and dropped her backpack on the dark green cotton floor mat just inside the door. She scooped up the entire row of videocassette tapes, cradled them in her arms, and carried them outside to the burn barrel. She knew they would create horrendous black smoke, but she knew she must burn them anyway.

At the front door, she paused, looked down at the labeled boxes, then back at the house. She declared in a loud tone, "This will be *my* house again, and I will live here."

Back in the sitting room, there were gray outlines on the walls where Carolyn's pictures had been removed, leaving intrusive and unwelcome rectangles.

The kitchen was as it had always been. Marie filled the kettle, put it on the stove, lit the gas with a match, and stepped back. "This *will* be my kitchen again."

She left the kettle on the stove, grabbed her backpack from the sitting room, and opened the door to her own room. It was small and crowded. Marie slept on a foam mattress she'd purchased in Kabul and had delivered in the luggage area of a bus. She loved her bed, piled high with thick, fuzzy blankets from neighboring China. Carolyn had tried to convince her to buy a bed frame and give up sleeping on the floor. "This is Afghanistan," Marie declared. "Sleeping on the floor is normal." On cold nights, she would fill her bed up with hot water bottles. An hour later, she'd curl up in their warmth.

Marie pulled the large silver aluminum trunk away from the wall, opened it, and retrieved her water bottles from the bottom. One was old, faded pink and purchased at someone's garage sale in America. She tucked it into a light green fleece bag. The second water bottle was red with a wide mouth that never belched boiling water on her hand when she filled it. That one came from Germany, a gift from Sharon that first winter when Marie couldn't get warm. It had a bright red fuzzy cover on it that felt soft against her skin.

In the empty kitchen she filled them from the kettle and tucked them into her bed. It was early, but the bottles would still be warm when she returned from Carolyn's good-bye party.

She filled the kettle again, returned it to the stove, and dumped coffee into her French press. *Tea is for Afghan homes.* The warm smell of the dried coffee grounds softened the ache behind her eyes.

23

When Marie returned to her room, her eyes fell on a landscape photograph she'd taken from the side of a dirt road. The photo was stunning; brilliant green rice fields in the foreground, undulating light brown hills in the middle distance, startling white-on-black jagged peaks behind, all beneath a brilliant evening sky. She'd had a local computer shop print the picture on glossy paper, and she had mounted it in a brown frame with gold stripes. *Shehktan.*

She retrieved the picture from its hook, carried it into the sitting room, and hung it on the wall within one of the dust-stained frames that so offended her earlier.

The water in the kettle boiled. She filled her French press and carried everything needed back to her room, lit the diesel heater, and returned to the aluminum trunk that contained her winter supplies. She pulled out her long, navy blue winter coat, a pair of boots for trudging through the snow, and a set of down booties for sleeping through the worst winter nights. She hung the winter coat on the wall hook—which just that morning had been crowded with Carolyn's blue, gray, and black long coats—then tucked the boots against the wall where Carolyn's dress shoes and beaded sandals once rested.

She stepped back and regarded her work, nodded, and said out loud. "This *will* be my house again. I will live here."

Marie heard Carolyn singing softly behind her closed bedroom door. She put her hands on her hips and stared at Carolyn's door, its white-painted wood silent in reply, and she was suddenly grateful that it was two weeks and not four until she left. The separation was heartbreaking. *When it's over,* she thought, *I'll start again.*

In her room, Marie found a deep blue heavy winter scarf, a black watch cap, and a pair of matching black fleece gloves which she carried into the hall and filled the hooks where Carolyn's teal, pink, and brilliant blue scarves once hung.

She glanced toward Carolyn's door. Her young companion was on the other side, sorting clothes and making decisions: take this, give away that. She stepped back into the middle of the hall and looked around. Empty. Achingly empty and too quiet.

In her room she opened a small wooden box on her desk, retrieved the MP3 player she rarely used, turned it on, and selected random play. She plugged the battery-operated speakers into the jack and pushed the volume up just high enough to fill the space in her room. Rosanne Cash's voice jumped from the speakers. "I stand here by the Western Wall / Maybe a little of that wall / Stands inside of us all."

Marie stepped back and listened. "I shove my prayers in the cracks / I got nothing to lose / No one to answer back."

No. That can't be. She pushed the advance button and Emmylou Harris's voice floated into the room. "Keep me in your prayers tonight / I'll be weary upon that road / I know the finish line's in sight / But I still have a ways to go."

The room felt better, full, the awkward echoes gone.

Marie curled up with her hot water bottles under the warmth of her thick Chinese blankets and waited for darkness to fall.

An hour later, Marie heard a knock on her door, then Carolyn's voice, tired but still edged with excitement. "Hey, you ready to go?"

"Yeah, couple minutes." It was time for Carolyn's good-bye party, the gathering of the few foreigners in town. They would eat, talk, and observe the departure of yet another of their own.

Marie forced herself out from under her thick Chinese blankets. She shed her long Afghan skirt and her black cotton tombones, pulling on Western jeans and a tan sweater. She grabbed her black backpack and stepped into the empty hallway. The coat and scarf hooks, full of her own deep colors, looked satisfying, complete. *I can do this,* Marie thought. *It's not like it was when Sharon left. I'm different now. This is my home.* She slipped her long brown Afghan coat over her shoulders and wrapped her head in her brown, gold-trimmed scarf.

She met Carolyn and Omed inside the gate. The three walked the wall-lined blocks to Dave and Margaret's house—Omed in front, Marie and Carolyn trailing. It was already night, and the overcast sky offered few stars. But even if the moon had been full, Omed would have had to lead them, because women had no business on the street alone after dark.

For Marie, a night-shrouded Afghan street was always an unsettling experience. She searched the shadows for unexpected movements or shrouded forms. A group of men passed by the threesome, silencing as they drew near. Omed greeted them casually and accepted their greeting in return. Marie and Carolyn, their light faces far too bright between their dark headscarves and darker long coats, hid beneath their scarves. The men passed and Marie breathed in deeply.

On the street in front of Dave and Margaret's double gate, a single white bulb spread a pool of weak light across the dark mud. Marie stepped into the light, then looked up and down the street. No one. Omed rang the bell. A moment later, Dave's guard opened the gate. They traded the usual greetings and stepped aside to allow Marie and Carolyn to enter. The guard welcomed them, congratulated Carolyn on her engagement, and asked after their families. The greetings complete, Omed returned to Marie's house, and the two women knocked on Dave and Margaret's door.

The house was a two-story concrete structure with a wide entrance hall and a full basement. Marie had lived on the top floor when she first had arrived in-country. Now, that space was used mostly for storage.

A small blond boy with sparkling blue eyes answered the door. He threw himself into Carolyn's arms, climbed down, and grabbed one hand of each woman, pulling them into the hall. There they shed their shoes, scarves, and long Afghan coats before entering the large, Western-style living room.

A single man, two couples, and three small children welcomed them. That was Shehktan's foreign community: seven adults and three children. In that mix, Carolyn had been a gift.

Marie looked around the room. How different it had been when she first arrived, back in the days before Dave and Margaret inherited the house from a previous aid worker and made it their own. None of the people who filled the room now had been in Shehktan then, except Marie. Everyone else from that era was gone. Marie pushed the thought away and focused on the people before her.

First, the single man. He was deeply introverted, a middle-aged German doctor. He'd spent most of his adult life working in post-conflict zones across the world. Now he trained Afghan doctors in their small Shehktan hospital. Here he was known as just Doc.

Then there was the young Dutch couple, Edmond and Tanja, with their three far-too-energetic blond boys. They'd only been in Shehktan for a year, but before that, they'd worked in Kabul. They spoke Dari well and understood clearly the world in which they lived.

Finally, Dave and Margaret. They'd been in and out of country for over thirty years, but they had been in America when Marie landed. She remembered when they first arrived in Shehktan. They were seasoned, wise, and mature. They both spoke Dari nearly fluently and settled easily into the community. Still, Marie hadn't warmed to them right away. Dave was a stickler for details, full of structure and rules. Margaret was very quiet. Besides, at that time, Sharon had left only a couple of months earlier, and Marie was focused on finding her own way with Afghans.

Marie shut her eyes tightly. *Too many good-byes.* She remembered when the young Englishman with a quick laugh and a passion for board games packed up his Settlers of Catan and returned from whence he'd come. There was an older couple, Michael and Ruth, who ran a community health project; Rebecca, a single woman who taught nurses and health workers; another, Amy, who ran a midwife training project.

And of course, there was Sharon, who had taught her how to walk in Shehktan and whose departure had left her lost and alone. Marie shuddered. She saw them all, crowding into Dave and Margaret's Western-style living room. She forced herself into the present time, the present room, and greeted those who were still there even as she pushed away the memories of those who had gone away.

The good-bye dinner was a custom, an informal ritual to celebrate a shared journey. Marie understood its importance. *We have to leave well,* she thought. This simple observance—a meal shared and prayers offered—marked the ending of a journey well walked.

Marie looked at Carolyn. *Not even two years.* She sighed. *Still, one of us. Always will be.*

She left Carolyn to explain her future plans to the others and followed Margaret into the kitchen. Making preparations was something she could do.

Margaret watched Marie gather plates and silverware for the dining room table. She stopped Marie at the kitchen door. "Marie? How are you doing?"

"Fine."

Marie knew Margaret wanted something more than that. But she thought if she spoke her feelings into words, they would never stop. And behind the words, perhaps tears would fall. And that wouldn't be good. Not now, not when the house was full. Not when Carolyn was just a few days from leaving. Certainly not when she had to tell Dave about the village. So instead of speaking, Marie just shrugged and disappeared into the Western-style dining room. She took her time setting the plates and didn't return to the kitchen until she could find nothing else to do with the table and its contents.

Margaret was waiting for her. "You know, Marie, when Caitlin was born, Dave and I were at the hospital."

Marie recalled the photograph: Dave, Margaret, a clean-shaven young man, an exhausted young woman, and a tiny pink-blanketed baby. *Caitlin.* She nodded.

"I'll tell you, something happens when a woman holds her first grandchild. It's amazing. You just fall in love." Margaret handed Marie a large glass pan of chicken in a thick cream sauce and covered with crushed almonds. Warm, heady steam enveloped Marie's face. She carried the food into the dining room and returned to the kitchen.

Margaret continued her story. "We stayed with my daughter and son-in-law for three weeks. Can you believe it? Of course you can. I've told you this story before." She handed Marie a large clear glass bowl filled with a pasta salad that smelled like pickles and onions. Marie delivered the bowl and returned again.

"Now here's the part I didn't tell you. I just wanted to wail when I gave that baby back for the last time. I mean, that's my granddaughter. She's so far away. Her mom puts her in front of the computer, but she's just fourteen months. She doesn't understand."

Marie didn't want to think about any of this, but Margaret kept talking. "On the way back to Afghanistan, a friend of mine gave me some unsolicited advice. I probably looked at her the way you're look-ing at me." Margaret shook a wooden spoon in Marie's face, and the younger woman tried to smile.

"I didn't ask and neither did you, but it was good advice, so I'm giving it to you." Margaret pushed the wooden spoon into a bowl of carrots steamed with a touch of nutmeg and cinnamon. She handed the bowl to Marie, but didn't let go.

"I want you to do this, Marie. Will you promise me?"

"Deliver the carrots?"

Margaret pressed her lips together and threw Marie the most experienced "mother look" Marie had ever seen her give.

Marie stood up straight, locked her jaw, and forced an apologetic smile. "Okay. I'm sorry. You're telling me something important and I'm making a joke. I'm sorry."

"That's better. Now listen. This is hard. I know that. You know it too. And it'll pass. You know that, too. Listen to me, okay? You're grieving."

"Yeah, yeah, of course, but it happens all the time. People leave. It's not like anyone died." Marie stepped back, still holding the steaming bowl of carrots in her hands.

"Look, Marie, it's still a deep loss. We don't just grieve when people die. We grieve when we lose people or situations, jobs, houses. We grieve when we leave our grandchildren behind in America. We grieve when we say good-bye to our friends and family. We grieve when we leave Afghanistan, and we grieve when we lose our friends here. You're grieving, and that's hard. Now go put those carrots on the table. I have more to say." She dismissed Marie with a slight wave.

Marie walked out of the kitchen and slowly put the bowl onto the dining room table. She hesitated until she heard Margaret call from the kitchen. "Marie, there's more."

Marie socked her hands in her jeans pockets and waited. She knew there was no more food to put on the table. Everything was set. Margaret had something to say, and she would have to stand still and listen.

"I told you my friend gave me advice. It was good advice and I want you to do this. Okay?"

Marie raised her eyebrows and tilted her head sideways as if to say, "Perhaps."

Margaret spoke slowly. "After Carolyn leaves—the next day—take some time off, sit down, and write a letter that you will never send. Write the story of your time together. How it affected you. All of it.

the bad, the easy and the hard. Write everything you rite as if you're telling the story to someone who's never of you, someone who's never been to Shehktan. Do ?"

Marie nodded. She knew Margaret would accept only one answer. "Yes."

"Then, when you're finished writing, go back and ask God where he's been with you; look for him. Ask him to show you, specifically. He will, you'll see. And that will make all the difference. Do you understand?"

"Yeah, sure."

"Marie. Do this."

Marie nodded, but everything in her said, *Forget it. Push it all aside. Don't think about it. Reclaim the house. Keep working. Just keep moving forward. Don't reflect. Reflecting is hard. Don't look back.*

Margaret persisted. "It's important, Marie. If we can find Christ in our experience, we can make it. It's not that everything will magically become easy—it won't. At least, it rarely does for me."

Marie thought about her prayer times. *Aren't I already doing that? I pray, anchor my heart in God, and everything seems okay. Then I get up and the world comes crashing back in. What's the point?* She snapped out her question, "So why do it?"

"Because Christ is enough. Because he's more than enough."

Marie bristled. "Come on, Margaret. I know God is with us. All the time. I get that. I know he's working things out. Bringing good. There's nothing wrong with my theology."

"Marie!"

"I know this stuff."

Margaret reached out and gently took hold of Marie's shoulders, looking straight into her eyes.

"Marie, your mind knows this stuff. Your heart doesn't. Until your heart finds Christ in the fire and flood, you'll just keep struggling to hold all the pieces together yourself."

Marie looked down at the floor between their feet. An image came into view, a picture: clouds and shafts of sun pouring over a wheat field. She focused on the words that seemed to go along with the image. *Strength for the day, comfort for the tears, and a light for the way.* She looked back at Margaret, "What's that verse?"

"What verse?"

"Fire and flood. The verse. I can't remember."

Margaret stepped back and recited the passage from memory: "When you pass through the waters, I will be with you; and through the rivers, they shall not overwhelm you; when you walk through fire you shall not be burned, and the flame shall not consume you."

Marie listened. "Yeah. That's it. I know. I thought about it in Kabul. I just can't . . ." Her words trailed off into silence.

"You just can't hold on to it."

"Yeah."

"I know. That's the hard part." Margaret lowered her voice. "Promise me. Promise me now. Promise me you'll write that letter just as soon as Carolyn leaves."

Marie sighed. "Okay. I promise."

Margaret clapped Marie's shoulders. "Good! Now, call everyone to dinner. It's time."

24

Dinner with the three Dutch boys was a noisy, multilingual, entertaining affair, and Marie enjoyed the chaos. Eventually, though, the boys disappeared into the living room to watch a movie on a laptop, and the adults fell into serious conversation.

"What are you all hearing from Kabul?" Doc asked as if to the entire room. It fell quiet.

Edmond rephrased the question. "Does anyone know what really happened?"

"No," Dave said. "The men were never caught."

The group returned to its uneasy silence.

"So what does this mean for us now?" Marie asked.

Dave and Edmond looked at each other. Obviously, they'd discussed this. Dave offered the summary. "We don't know. Some Afghans reacted and condemned the murder, but others didn't. The religious leaders didn't. That's troubling. That means the mullahs have given permission to kill a foreign aid worker. Obviously, that's a problem . . ." After a pause, he added, "for all of us."

Marie focused on breathing while the others remained silent.

Dave leaned back, took a deep breath, and shifted the focus. "The Kabul killing shows us what's possible, but the situation with the Uzbeks and the governor here is probably more immediately significant for us."

Marie froze in her seat.

"I'm collecting information." Dave went on. "It doesn't look good. Maybe it'll pass, but I doubt it. It's an old feud."

Marie folded and refolded her napkin while in her imagination, she saw the man on the street in the brown jacket, jeans, and pointed shoes. *Is he tracking me? No. I'm just rattled. Paranoid. He could be anyone.* But then there was Char Ab and the village she'd come to love.

Marie put her napkin on the table. "I think the elder of one of our literacy communities is involved."

"In the feud?" Both Dave and Edmond responded simultaneously.

Marie struggled to inhale. "Yeah. Char Ab." She gave the commander's name quickly. "Ahmad Rasul Khan." She looked directly at Dave.

Dave looked at Edmond. The Dutchman offered the piece he knew. "Yes. We know that name. He is a friend of the governor. Family."

"Yes." Doc cut in. "And a friend of my boss, the director of the Ministry of Health. They are all family."

Dave focused on Marie. "You go there, to Char Ab?"

"It's the location of one of our literacy classes. They've welcomed us."

"This could be important." Dave exhaled slowly, rubbing his graying beard. "Never tell anyone when you're going, Marie, just your driver; and only when you go, not ahead of time. Okay?" Dave added.

Suddenly, she felt like an errant child sitting through a lecture. "Yeah, that's what I do," she said, with a slight edge in her voice.

Dave's eyebrows rose. He had his own responsibilities, and Marie's impatience didn't help. "And text me, Marie. When you leave town, arrive in the village, leave the village, and arrive in town."

"*Okay*," she said, exasperated.

"Marie, you have to take this seriously. It could be very important. You don't want to get caught up in some local feud."

"I know. I get that. I'm collecting information, too."

"Good. Keep me posted."

Marie picked up her napkin. *I'll go back,* she thought. *It's okay. I can go.*

Doc shifted his weight. "My boss is preparing his house for a wedding party. I believe it will be soon."

A wedding party. Marie heard Bibi-jan's voice in her ears. *"My niece is getting married. Tomorrow night is the henna party."*

"The party is at his house?" Dave studied the doctor's face.

"Yes," he said, in thick German-accented English. "It's just over there." He motioned beyond the walls. "It's the new concrete house. Three levels." The three-story, pink, yellow, and orange house towered over the walls on Zia Gul's street. Doc went on, "He is preparing it for a wedding. I think the party will be this week."

Marie cut in. "If it's the wedding my village friend told me about, then tomorrow night is the henna party and the wedding will be Tuesday."

"You know these people?" Dave's voice was tight.

"Yes." Marie was careful. "A relative of the villagers, but I don't know if it's the wedding Doc is talking about."

Dave looked at him.

"I don't know," Doc said. "It's a relative, but I've not heard the name."

"You'll go?" Dave's question was for the doctor.

"But of course. The director of the Ministry of Health is my boss and my friend. How could I not go?"

The reality of the situation settled into Marie's heart. *A wedding. One side of a feud. A target.* She imagined the men, the farmers trading their soiled clothes for crisp shalvar kameezes, wool vests, and jackets. All the men of Char Ab. She looked at Doc. *Of course he would go,* Marie thought. *He'd have to.*

Dave looked down at his empty plate then directly at Marie. "You will not go, Marie, even if it's your friend's family."

She thought of Bibi-jan's invitation. She would have to go. It would be a great insult if she did not. She looked up at Dave, then Doc, then back to Dave. She found a way out. "It's okay. If there's a wedding, the women will have their party elsewhere."

"Of course. If there's trouble, it'll happen at the men's party." Dave nodded.

The room fell into silence, each one pulling on the threads that impacted them the most.

Finally, Margaret broke the tension. She stood abruptly. "Dessert? Coffee?"

Marie looked up and immediately began gathering empty plates. She and Margaret left the table and busied themselves preparing dessert. Margaret had prepared a special treat for the occasion, one of Carolyn's favorites: homemade apple pie. By the time they returned, their trays full of steaming cups of coffee and plates of pie, the conversation had changed. Marie sighed, grateful.

That night, Marie didn't sleep. She awoke to the sound of her dogs barking, fell back to sleep, and awoke again to the sound of a window rattling in the wind. *Wind?* She crawled out from under her Chinese blankets and jammed a piece of folded paper into the window frame. *Wind. Tomorrow, it'll be clear and cold.* She looked into the darkness through the plastic-covered glass. She could see nothing.

When she returned to bed, her thoughts swirled. She imagined Carolyn on the dustway saying good-bye. She pushed the image away. Then she imagined the waterfall in the village breaking its banks and washing the teacher's house down into the valley below. She shook her head. Getting up, she drew a glass of water from the water filter in the kitchen and drank it before returning to bed. She drifted into dreams. She stood in the waiting room at Kabul airport. Suddenly there was an explosion. Glass tore her skin. She awoke, startled.

She lit her headlamp and checked the clock. Three forty-two. She found her backpack, unfolded her laptop, shoved her earplugs into the jack and turned it on. She found an old TV show on her hard drive. Somewhere during the episode, she fell back to sleep.

DAY 3

CHAR AB, AFGHANISTAN

25

The next day Marie awoke in bitter cold. Winter had arrived. She drank her morning coffee huddled beneath her blankets and wished the day was already over. Then she remembered Char Ab and Bibi-jan's invitation. She would go back to the village. Soon, the snows would fall and the road would close, or Dave would decide it was too dangerous and demand she stay in town.

Marie dressed in her best Afghan clothes: a long beaded shirt, burgundy-and-gold striped, with matching burgundy tombones. The plastic beads scraped the soft skin of her neck, but the long johns she'd added against the cold protected the rest of her body.

She met Carolyn in the hallway. "Mari-jan, look—you have a wedding invitation."

Marie took the large envelope from Carolyn's hand. It could only be an invitation. She pulled the large card from the envelope, looking at the flowers around the edges and studying the handwritten, stylized Dari that recorded the details. Marie couldn't read the script. "Thanks. Who brought it?"

"I don't know. Some guy knocked on the gate. Omed didn't know him. Who's it from?" Carolyn was concerned. "When is it?"

Marie shrugged. "I can't read it, but it's probably from Bibi-jan." She looked at the date. "I think it's tomorrow."

"Is it your Bibi-jan, from Char Ab? Where is it?"

"I don't know. I'll ask Faiz Muhammad to read it to me."

Carolyn looked at Marie's clothes. "Where are you going now?"

Marie followed her friend's eyes. "Char Ab. They're having the henna party tonight, but I'm just going to lunch to celebrate."

"Char Ab?" Carolyn tried to hide her alarm.

"Yeah." Marie reasoned. "It's okay. I'll go for lunch and be back by the afternoon. Don't worry about it."

Carolyn looked down at the tiled floor. "And the wedding?"

Marie shrugged. She tried to decipher the swirling handwritten Dari invitation, but couldn't. Still, she knew it was from Bibi-jan. "Yeah. We'll see. It won't be with the men." She looked up at Carolyn. "I'm sure it'll be fine. And anyway, I'll be Bibi-jan's guest. She's the woman of honor in that family. I'll meet all her relatives in one day. It's perfect!" With that, she pulled on her long winter coat, wrapped a thick navy-and-white striped scarf around her head, and headed out the gate, the invitation still in her hand.

Faiz Muhammad was waiting for her in the alley. "Congratulations. You have a wedding invitation."

Marie slipped into the backseat and handed her driver the card. He pulled it out of the envelope, read the careful script, and smiled. "Congratulations. You have become invited."

"When is it? Where? Who?"

Faiz Muhammad slipped the SUV into gear and backed out of the alley. He gave the address of a house in town. "Tomorrow at noon, but you should go at one."

"The big new house?"

Faiz Muhammad laughed. "No, no. I will show you tomorrow. It is not this neighborhood."

Marie nodded, relieved. "Who is it?"

The driver shrugged. "They are the family of Aga Rasul Khan. You have become a friend. It's an important wedding. You must go."

Marie studied the card until the SUV backed into the intersection. She looked up the street. Two young men in jeans and Western-style winter coats walked toward the German base at the far end of the road. A woman in a light blue burqa walked with a boy of about twelve. Three schoolgirls in black jackets, matching black slacks, and bright white scarves walked together, chattering. The old man sat alone in his shop, wrapped in a thick Chinese blanket.

Marie looked to the left. She caught her breath. Two men stood beside a wall, talking. One of them was the one she had noticed before, but his brown jacket was gone. He wore a dark gray winter coat and an orange-and-blue watch cap. Marie pursed her lips and leaned forward. "Faiz Muhammad-jan. Do you see those men?"

The driver looked without turning his head. "Yes, Mari-jan."

Marie spoke in a whisper. "I've seen that one before. The one with the gray coat. He had a brown jacket."

Faiz Muhammad nodded. "Yes, Mari-jan."

The SUV passed the men. "Do you know who they are?"

"No." The driver considered. "I've seen the man before today, too. Perhaps he is secret police."

Marie nodded.

"Perhaps not."

She looked at her driver in the rearview mirror. "What do you think?"

He shrugged. "Trust in God."

Marie leaned back. *"Trust in God." It's what Afghans say when they're helpless.* She ground her teeth and watched the town's walls and gates give way to open fields. By the time the silent grave pennants came into view, Marie had forgotten about the man with the gray coat. She'd also forgotten to text Dave.

When the SUV descended the steep cliff and crossed the last small bridge into the village, a group of men emerged from the small, un-painted, mud-brick building to meet them. This time, they had no farm tools in their hands. The men welcomed Faiz Muhammad and quickly drew him into the building. They sent an old man to lead Marie up the long path to Bibi-jan's.

The air in the village was cold and sharp, but the jagged, snow-covered mountains beyond the scoop-faced hills rose bright and clear. Marie snapped a quick photo with her phone and smiled. *Char Ab. God, this is beautiful.*

The path was steep and long, but the effort to walk it felt good in Marie's legs. She imagined Bibi-jan standing in her casement window, laughing, her belly rocking up and down; and Shukria, in the open face of the barn, welcoming Marie's outstretched hand.

Marie followed the old man easily. When they entered the orchard, she listened for the cascading water and found it. She inhaled the dense scent of decomposing leaves and listened as they crunched under her stiff shoes. At the narrow alley between the orchard and Bibi-jan's arc-walled compound, the old man stopped, nodded, and disappeared the way they'd come. Marie realized he'd not spoken a word. *These are good people,* she thought. *Respectful.*

She stepped through the next gate and looked up at Bibi-jan's house. There was no plastic sheet across the woman's sitting room window. Marie loved the view and the unfiltered light the glass al-lowed into the room. She looked for Bibi-jan in the casement, but saw no one upstairs.

Shukria emerged from the shadows of the barn and met Marie in the middle of the yard. She clasped Marie's hands warmly. Marie marveled at the change. The two exchanged greetings quickly. Marie heard a click and a scrape. Bibi-jan appeared in the casement window. She'd thrown the window open and now leaned out into the cold.

"Come in, come in. Drink tea. You will eat lunch. We are having a celebration. Come!"

Marie smiled and followed Shukria across the yard, through the dark, hay-strewn barn, and up the staircase that led to the second floor. She pried off her shoes in the upstairs hallway, pulled the carved wooden door open, and pushed the heavy, brown wool blanket aside.

Bibi-jan was waiting at the door. "Welcome, welcome. We will celebrate. My house is your house. Have we not become friends?"

Bibi-jan enveloped Marie's hands, and Marie kissed the older woman's cheeks. She wondered what the celebration would look like, but lost the thought in Bibi-jan's welcome and the sharp scent of burning wood charcoal. *A sandalee.* The window side of the room was covered with thick blankets draped across a square frame. A sandalee was such a wonderful thing. Many Afghans used them, but usually not until the winter cold made them necessary. It was still early, but Bibi-jan had already set hers up.

Bibi-jan nudged her guest toward the blanketed corner. "Come. I have a sandalee. We will become warm and drink tea."

Marie lifted the heavy blankets, sank down onto a thick, cotton mat, and pulled the blanket up over her shoulders. The heat from the small dish of coals underneath the square wooden frame penetrated the cold of her coat, her clothes, even her long johns, and finally her skin itself. She delighted in the gift. The old woman sat down at the corner next to her. Their knees tucked against each other's, the warmth of the sandalee, their community. Marie unbuttoned her coat and pried it off of her shoulders without allowing even the slightest wisp of cold to slip out from the thick blanket. She looked at Bibi-jan. The old woman's eyes were shining.

Bibi-jan was full of conversation. "You will eat lunch. We will share stories. Today has become good."

Marie smiled. "Then I will visit the literacy class."

Bibi-jan clapped her hands underneath the blanket. The sound was dull and soft. "No, no. Today is a party. We will not learn today."

"Tomorrow?"

"Bah! Tomorrow we will have a wedding. You will come. Did you receive the invitation? My son gave it to your guard."

Marie acknowledged her receipt of the invitation. "May you live forever."

"Good. Then you will come!"

Marie beamed. "If God allows."

Just then, Shukria entered the room with a tray of tea and treats.

Bibi-jan smiled at the young woman, and Marie watched with surprise. *Has there been some thaw between these two?* When Shukria left, Marie tested the subject. "How is your daughter-in-law?"

The old woman slapped the blanket-covered table. "She's lazy. She doesn't know how to work." Then the roughness of her voice faded. "She is my daughter-in-law." She held her hands palms up in the air. "What can I do?"

Marie wondered if her story of the farmer, his fields, and the salty well had encouraged the change, or if the short reading from the New Testament had spoken to Bibi-jan's heart. Perhaps it was just the upcoming wedding lifting her spirits. Whatever it was, it was good.

Marie and Bibi-jan chatted for about an hour. First, Bibi-jan told the story of her nephew who would marry her niece and the planned wedding party where the young women and girls would dance. Marie's eyes lit up. She loved Afghan women's dance.

"Will you dance, Bibi-jan?"

"Bah! I am old. Do you see this scarf?"

Marie laughed, acknowledging the white scarf the older woman wore, a symbol of age and honor.

"I will not dance! But you must!"

"I'm a foreigner. What do I know?"

"Hah. Shukria-jan will teach you."

Shukria-jan? This was the first time Marie had heard the old woman use the ending that showed endearment. "Shukria-jan?"

"Ah, this daughter-in-law doesn't know anything. I have to teach her everything. She is a town girl." Her tone was dismissive but not altogether harsh.

Marie started to respond, but Bibi-jan interrupted her with the story of a cow that had stopped giving milk. They had slaughtered it and would eat some of the meat for lunch. Marie told Bibi-jan about the other classes back in town, but the older woman didn't care. Her world existed within the semicircle of her village and the Shamali-Tajik extended family within whose identity she lived. Bibi-jan returned to the subject of the upcoming wedding. "You must wear henna. Do you have henna?"

Marie smiled. "I'll get some. Don't worry." She imagined the dark orange paste and the designs she'd paint on the back of her hands.

When Shukria returned, she spread the brown, yellow, and orange cloth across the floor in the opposite corner of the room. She brought three plates heaped with rice laced with raisin, carrots, and spices, each heap topped with a small cluster of pressure-cooked beef. Marie and Bibi-jan left the warmth of the sandalee and sat down around the plates of steaming food.

The young woman poured warm water over their hands, collected it in a basin, and handed them a towel to share in turn. She left and returned again with a thermos and four glass cups.

Marie counted the cups, looked around, and wondered who else would join them. When no one arrived, she lifted her hands, palms upward, and prayed for the meal, the household, and the family's upcoming wedding. When she was finished, she swept her fingers over her face to seal the prayer. As soon as she did, she heard the deep voice of a young man.

"*Khosh amaden.* Welcome."

Startled, Marie turned to see the face of a youth, his beard nothing more than a thin mustache across the top of his lip. Marie bowed her head, put her hand on her heart, and spoke her salaam.

The youth sat down on the floor opposite her. Marie noticed he had a crooked foot. Bibi-jan made the introductions. "This is my *kinja*. My youngest child."

Marie looked at the young man. *So this was the husband of Shukria, the boy who had been injured.* "I've become very happy to meet you. Your family has welcomed me. Thank you. May God bless you."

The youth received Marie's kind words. "You are welcome in my home. Please, eat."

Marie relaxed, only then aware that she'd tensed at the young man's presence. She gathered a ball of rice with her fingertips and pushed it into her mouth with the back of her thumb, careful not to drop too many grains on the floorcloth.

The young man spoke between mouthfuls of food. "You are a good person. You brought a literacy class for our women. We have become happy. Now, you will celebrate our wedding."

"Thank you. For me, the class is a blessing."

The youth corrected her. "For you, it's sawab, credit with Allah."

Marie considered. She'd heard this many times before but was never sure how to respond. She chose her words carefully. "God has told us we should love our neighbors, even if they are different from us. You are my neighbor. Yes. I believe God is pleased with our work."

The young man nodded. "Allah is merciful."

Marie let the conversation go.

The group ate their meal in silence, Shukria joining them in the corner closest to the door. Marie was aware of the sharp cold air against the back of her neck. She was grateful for long johns but wanted to be back under the sandalee. Two subjects gnawed at the edges of her thoughts. First, the location of the men's wedding party; second, the young man's injury, his friend, and Shukria. She considered each. She knew it would be completely inappropriate to ask after the men's party; there would be no way for her to justify such a question. But the young man's story, that she could ask.

When they finished eating and Shukria had poured tea into glass cups, Marie braved the question. "Brother Jan. Your foot has become broken. What happened?" She asked her question lightly.

The young man wasn't challenged. "Yes. I fell from a roof."

Bibi-jan slapped the floor next to her knee. "I told him not to fly kites from the roof. But he was a boy. Boys don't listen."

Her son smiled sheepishly and nodded. "Yes, yes. My friend and I were flying a kite. He tried to take it from me. We fought. I fell and my foot became broken."

Marie thought for a moment. When she had heard the story of the two boys fighting, she had assumed it was a real fight, not some childish wrestling over a kite. And where had they been? Surely they didn't fly kites from roofs in the village. "Where did this happen? Here? In the village?"

The young man laughed out loud. "No, no. In town. My cousin has a car repair shop. I was his apprentice. My friend was my classmate in school."

"Where is he now?"

The young man shrugged, clearly sad. "He has become dead. His brother, also."

Marie hesitated. *So it was true. The young man's friend was one of the brothers the police killed.* Slowly, the blood drained from Marie's face. *And Shukria-jan's brothers.* She looked at the young woman, and she swallowed the groan that rose within her.

Bibi-jan put her hand on Marie's knee. "We have all eaten bitterness."

Shukria fled the room.

The young man lifted his hands and prayed the meal-ending blessing in Arabic.

Marie hoped it was time to retreat to the warmth of the sandalee, but the young man didn't stand up to leave. Instead, he rubbed his chin as if thinking of something difficult.

Marie waited.

26

The young man began. "Missus, we are small village. We are far from Kabul, but we are good people."

Marie thought, *But Shukria, her brothers?* The young man's words didn't fit into Marie's thoughts. She looked down at her hands.

He went on. "We believe there is one God and Muhammad is His prophet."

Marie felt a slow, thick tension spread across the tops of her shoulders and down along her spine. She nodded. "I, too believe there is one God."

The young man wasn't interested. "Yes, yes. Of course." He rubbed his chin again. "We think you are a Christian. Is this true?" At this, he leveled his eyes at Marie.

Marie nodded and caught sight of Bibi-jan from the corner of her eye. The old woman was looking down at her tea. Marie inhaled deeply. *There's no way out now.* "Yes. I am a follower of the Honorable Jesus Messiah. He is my Savior and my Master." She had no idea what the young man's intentions were, but she would not deny her faith. If he told her to leave his house and his village, she would accept that. She didn't expect anything worse.

The young man swept away her words. Clearly, there was something else that held his interest. "We have no stores in our village. You understand this?"

"Yes." Now, Marie was utterly baffled. *Had he changed the subject? No. Not likely.* She waited.

The youth rubbed his chin even harder. "Our mullah is a *qazi,* a judge. He has studied Sharia law at university. He is very wise."

"Yes." Marie knew that many village mullahs had only studied under other mullahs; they weren't educated, so to have a mullah who had studied was a gift. She recalled meeting the village mullah on her first visit to the village. She remembered his dark beard and hooded eyes. He had welcomed them. "That's a great honor. God is good." Whatever the young man wanted, he would unfold it in his own time.

"Yes, yes. Allah is kind." The young man paused as if choosing which rock to step on next as he crossed a river.

Marie forced her shoulders to relax. Bibi-jan plucked grains of rice from the carpet. Shukria was still gone.

Finally, the young man resumed his purpose. "Do you read your holy book?"

The question was direct but not confrontational. Marie responded easily. "Yes. I read my book every day. I pray and I try to obey what God has taught."

"We accept four books as having come from God: the Taurat, the Zabur, the Injil, and the Glorious Quran. That is the last and final book."

Marie nodded, mentally translating the young man's words. The Taurat was the Torah, the first five books of the Old Testament. The Zabur was the Psalms and the Injil, the New Testament. She expected the youth to ask her if she accepted the Quran, but he didn't. Instead, he once again changed directions.

"Afghanistan is a Muslim country. Before we became Muslims, our forefathers worshiped fire. Now, we are Muslims. Praise be to Allah! We believe that the Honorable Jesus Messiah is a prophet of God. This is in the Glorious Quran."

Since she didn't know what to say, she simply prayed silently and waited.

The young man continued. "Our mullah is a judge. He has read many books about religion. He would like to read the book of Jesus."

At that, Marie stopped her internal praying and looked directly at the young man. *Is he asking me for a New Testament? What do I say?* She thought of the small, green-covered volume in her backpack, the one that Bibi-jan had seen, and chose her words carefully. "It's good to read the Injil."

The youth waved his hand as if pushing her words away. "You read our language?"

"Yes. I am literate."

Bibi-jan reentered the conversation. "You see. I told you. The foreigner is literate."

The young man nodded. "Do you read your book in our language?"

Ah, Marie thought. *He has made his meaning clear. He does want a copy of the New Testament. Now what?* She prayed silently. "Yes. I read my book in your language. I know my book, so when I read it in your language, I learn words."

The young man considered that idea, but again swept it away as irrelevant. "You have a book of Jesus in our language?"

Marie didn't want to present herself as someone who simply distributed New Testaments. That, she knew, was illegal and to many Afghans, deeply offensive. "Yes. I have the Injil in your language for my own reading. I read it every day."

"Hmm." The young man rubbed his chin. "Perhaps, our mullah who is a judge could see your book."

Marie nodded. She knew the way forward. "Yes. He can look at my book. Then, he can return it to me."

"You have only one?"

Marie recognized the opening step of a bargain. "They are expensive and difficult to find."

"Perhaps another could be found."

"Perhaps."

"You have friends?"

"Yes." Marie added. "Perhaps a friend has a book and does not read it."

"Perhaps your friend doesn't want his book of Jesus in my language."

"Perhaps."

"Perhaps your friend will give you his book of Jesus and then, you will have it again."

Marie hid her smile. She heard the word *again*. This man was hoping to leave the room with a copy of the New Testament in Dari. Marie looked at Bibi-jan and knew the old woman had told her son about the green-covered book. She prayed silently. Finally, "Yes. I think a friend will give me the book of Jesus in your language. Then I will have two, but I don't need two. I only need one."

The young man clapped his hands. "Then we are agreed. Our mullah can read your book of Jesus in our language."

Marie reached into her backpack and pulled out the small, green New Testament. With a smile spread across her face, Marie handed it to the young man. "May God bless your mullah who is a judge."

"Yes. May Allah help your friend." He slid the small book into his jacket pocket and rose from the floor. "You must come to our wedding tomorrow. It is not difficult. It is in town. You have received the invitation?"

"Yes. May you live forever."

"Good. You will come." He spoke his good-byes and left the room.

Marie looked at Bibi-jan. The old woman just shrugged. "He is my son. He's a good man." With that, she drew Marie back to the wonderful warmth of the sandalee. Marie was delighted to be back under the heavy heated blankets. She had a dozen questions for her friend, but she hesitated, wondering where the conversation would go.

Bibi-jan surprised Marie when she sighed deeply, then spoke. "In the days of the Russians, my house was full. I had many sons. They were strong and smart. Now I have only one son." Marie looked into the old woman's averted face. She wondered at the depth of sadness revealed in her words. She waited.

The old woman continued. "I had a daughter-in-law then. She was the daughter of my husband's sister. She was a good girl. I knew her when she became born. She grew up in this village. When she was small, we agreed I would take her." The woman's words trailed into silence.

Marie watched, but only the silence remained. Finally, Marie chose a question. "What happened to her?"

Bibi-jan sighed. "She became pregnant, but the birth was filled with pain. The men were fighting. We were bound in this village. They could not take her to the doctor."

Marie asked her next question gently, softly. "Did she die?"

The old woman nodded.

"And the baby?"

Again, Bibi-jan nodded, her eyes filling with tears.

"I'm sad for you." Marie chose a phrase not normally used to console a person when experiencing a death. Bibi-jan looked directly into her eyes, but said nothing. Marie prayed for words and spoke. "This story is very sad. It's very hard. In your grieving, may God comfort you."

"We all eat bitterness." The woman swept the words away with her hand.

Marie thought for several moments, such a powerful phrase—*we eat bitterness*. Finally, she found words. "In this world, everyone eats bitterness sometimes."

Bibi-jan nodded, the tears now gone from her eyes.

"Still," Marie said. "God is with us."

Bibi-jan locked her jaw, narrowed her eyes, and shot a silent rebuke directly at Marie.

Marie prayed silently, again. This was tender territory, and she knew her words could wound or salve. "Mother-jan. God has protected you from many things. God has protected you from many evils. God has not protected you from all evils. Still, God loves you."

Again, Bibi-jan swept Marie's words away with her hand. "Allah is kind." She sighed and looked across the room, her eyes unfocused.

"Yes. God is kind, but we are not always kind. We do not always follow God. Sometimes we choose war instead of peace. Sometimes we choose to buy weapons instead of building roads and bridges. Sometimes we choose our own customs instead of taking women to doctors. God gives us permission to choose."

Bibi-jan turned and focused on Marie, considering. "Perhaps."

"I've heard Afghans say this life is a test."

"Yes." Bibi-jan engaged with the idea.

Marie offered the common Afghan explanation, which she knew was taken much more seriously than its equivalent was in America. "There is an angel on my right shoulder. He speaks to me. He tells me the right things to do."

Bibi-jan continued the illustration. "Yes. And there is a bad angel on our left shoulder. He tells us to do bad things."

"And you and I, we choose. We make decisions. Sometimes we walk the way of righteousness. Sometimes our paths are crooked."

"Hah!" Bibi-jan snapped. "Afghanistan is full of crooked paths!"

Marie nodded, then added softly, "The world is full of crooked paths."

"Yes." The old woman's word was decisive.

"Perhaps, if there had not been war, your daughter-in-law would have lived."

"Yes." Bibi-jan nodded. "And my grandson."

Marie spoke her next words with certainty. "And God has given you a new daughter-in-law and a new grandson. These are gifts of God."

Bibi-jan growled. "This girl? Who is this girl? She is not my family. Here she is. I don't know this girl."

Marie smiled gently and leaned toward the old woman. "Mother-jan. She is a gift from God. Receive her. Welcome her. She is God-given."

A look of absolute loss spread across Bibi-jan's face.

"You cannot compare the two, Mother-jan. They are different. In God's garden, there are many kinds of flowers. Some are big and bright. Some are small. Some are red and some are white. God created each one. God says each one is beautiful."

Bibi-jan shook her head slightly. "Maybe."

Marie was firm. "Mother-jan. You and I are flowers. God created us both. We both belong to God. God loves us both."

At this, the old woman looked into Marie's face. Her eyes were soft, rounded, and heavy; her lips, relaxed, turned down at the edges. She cocked her head sideways. "Do you think so?"

Marie knew her words were working. *This,* she thought. *This is why I'm here.* Excited, she prayed silently, careful to choose her next words well. She thought of phrases from Scripture and translated the meanings. "When your mother was young and you were in her womb, God knew you. When your mother brought you to the world, God called you by name. When you were small, God taught you to walk. When you were hungry, God fed you. When you were thirsty, God gave you water. When you were naked, God gave you clothes. God is with us. Even in this room. God is with us."

The old woman looked around the room, then back at Marie. "Really?"

"Really."

In a flash, Bibi-jan's face closed. She snapped, "Allah is everywhere. Allah is great."

Marie responded patiently. "Yes. And God is here. God is here and He loves us."

"Perhaps." Bibi-jan locked her jaw.

A woman called out from the doorway, pushed the heavy, brown curtain open, and leaned her burqa-covered head into the room. "Bibi-jan? I am here." In midsentence, the woman saw Marie. "Teacher, you have come! We have been sad; we have been forgotten. But we have no class today—today we will cook." She disappeared before Marie could respond.

Bibi-jan grabbed Marie's hand under the sandalee. "You will stay the night. We will have a party. We will eat, we will put henna on our hands and feet, you will dance. Stay the night."

Marie smiled and pushed herself out from under the blankets, excusing herself. "It has become late. With your permission?"

Bibi-jan rose with her. "You will come tomorrow. The wedding is in town. Come."

Marie hesitated. "Bibi-jan, it's not good for me to go to a wedding alone."

Bibi-jan laughed and smacked Marie on the shoulder. "No, no; it's not good to be alone. You must bring a friend! Come."

Instantly, Marie chose Zia Gul. "Yes, yes. I will come." She took Bibi-jan's hands, kissed her cheeks, and stepped toward the door. At the landing, Marie slipped into her shoes, grabbed her walking stick, and hesitated. "Bibi-jan, is it possible to say good-bye to Shukria-jan?"

Bibi-jan huffed with impatience, but shrugged. She cried out the woman's name in a loud voice. Within a moment, Shukria appeared at the bottom of the mud-brick stairs, the boy squirming on her hip. Marie clasped the younger woman's hands and kissed her cheeks. "Shukria-jan, I am sad for your loss. May God give you comfort and peace."

The young woman looked down at the hay-strewn ground.

Marie put the palm of her right hand on the boy's capped head. "Son, may God bless you. May God protect you."

Shukria looked directly into Marie's eyes. "Thank you. Please— come. Anytime. Please."

Marie released the younger woman's hands and looked back up the stairs at Bibi-jan. "May God keep you safe. May God bless your party."

The old woman responded. "Come tomorrow. We will eat and you will dance."

27

Marie waved, turned, and walked through the barn and across the walled-in yard. This time, there was no one waiting for her at the orchard gate. Marie enjoyed the silent walk, the early afternoon breeze, and the view from the hillside. She felt a lightness in her step, an ease in her breath. Pictures from her visit, fragments of conversation wove in and through her thoughts; the thaw in Bibi-jan's attitude toward Shukria, the small, green-bound New Testament in the youth's hand, the words of God's love spoken around the warmth of the sandalee. She looked up and smiled at the hillside. *Char Ab. Beautiful.*

When she rounded the last hill, she saw Faiz Muhammad's SUV between the small bridge and low house beneath her. She knew he was inside, probably drinking tea and sharing conversation with the village men. She remembered the wedding, the three-story pink, yellow, and orange house, the Uzbek men, the gray-coated man on the street, and Dave's concern. She stumbled on the rocky path, then caught her footing. *Father, please protect them.*

In a flash, she realized she'd forgotten to text Dave. She stopped, pulled out her phone, and sent the message: "In the village. Leaving now." She started to put the phone back in its pouch, then opened it again: "Sorry." She wasn't used to informing him of her movements. If she went missing, her driver, Carolyn, or her guard would know where she'd been. Still, he'd asked—demanded, really—and there was no reason for her not to comply. Anyway, a late message was better than none.

Faiz Muhammad was waiting for her when she reached the valley. He had seen her descend, and he had left the small room where he'd been waiting and emerged in the company of a group of bearded Afghan men. Marie studied the men as she walked toward them. One, she recognized, was the lame son of Bibi-jan. The man next to him, she thought, was the mullah. The others, she didn't recognize at all. A sharp tension spread across her shoulders and through her hips and knees. She focused on the path and prayed.

Faiz Muhammad stood back as Marie approached the SUV. As she passed the men, she put her hand over her heart, bowed her head slightly, and muttered a respectful "Salaam alaikum."

The men offered their responses in rough unison, but said nothing more.

Marie slid into the SUV, closed the door, and relaxed. Faiz Muhammad drove up the steep hillside, and Marie formed a question. "Faiz Muhammad, how did your day pass?"

The driver stroked his beard and looked in his rearview. "Very good. Very good."

"Were you with the men all day?"

"Yes. They are good men."

Marie understood that her driver had answered the question she'd only implied. "Good. Will we come back?"

"Yes. We will bring more literacy books. We will check on the class. You will visit your friends. It's a good village. The people are very good."

"Thanks be to God."

Faiz Muhammad agreed.

Out the window across the wide, arid plain, the cluster of grave markers, with their faded red, green, and black pennants snapped in the cold afternoon breeze. The scene shifted in her imagination; the sky darkened and the wind kicked up. The pennants strained to hold onto the mounts. Marie shuddered and closed her eyes, but the image remained.

Faiz Muhammad's question cleared Marie's unease. "You will go to the wedding, yes?"

Marie's head snapped toward the rearview. *Wedding?* "Yes. Yes, it is the wedding of my friend's niece and her cousin."

"Good. It will be a good marriage."

Marie smiled, then remembered she needed to invite Zia Gul. She asked her driver to take her to her friend's house.

Marie stepped inside Zia Gul's familiar yard. In the pale green sitting room, her friend was surrounded by three visiting women from the neighborhood. Marie knew the women, but not well, and she wanted to tell her friend about Shukria, her Uzbek brothers, and the lame man. She wanted to tell her about the New Testament and the village mullah, and she wanted to invite her to the wedding of the most powerful family in town, a family wrapped up in a dangerous feud. She needed her friend's advice, not on what to do—there was nothing to do, nothing to change or fix. No, she needed her advice on what to feel, how to make sense out of the story, how to interpret a reality completely foreign to her own understanding. But there were visitors, strangers from the neighborhood, women Marie couldn't trust to guide her wisely. Marie would wait. She took her place on a cotton floor mat and settled into the newsy conversation that dominated Afghan women's concerns.

The visiting women chatted about a cousin's child who had been sick but was now well and a niece who had given birth to twins; they complained about the price of wood and their expectations for a long, cold winter; they talked about a son who had joined the Afghan National Army and another who had slipped across the border to Iran; they complained about the price of flour and told the story of a local bread maker who had been arrested for selling lightweight loaves.

The conversation drifted on. Finally, as the day waned, the visitors asked permission and rose to leave. Marie looked at the darkening sky and stood up as well. She walked with the visitors and Zia Gul to the inside of the gate, but waited with her friend until the women left. "Zia Gul-jan. There is a wedding tomorrow. You will come with me?"

Zia Gul clapped her hand. "You have an invitation?"

Marie pulled the card from her backpack.

"Yes, yes. I will go. My husband is going to the men's party."

Marie narrowed her eyes. She thought of Doc and the three-story concrete house. She remembered Dave's concern. *Hah!* She thought. *If Zia Gul's husband is going, it must be safe.*

Zia Gul's question broke into her thoughts. "Do you know the family?"

Marie cocked her head sideways. "Yes. They have a literacy class in

Char Ab. Your husband knows the family?"

Zia Gul leaned forward. "Yes, of course. Ahmad Khan is building the new mosque." She pointed toward town.

Marie looked toward the top of Zia Gul's wall, but she couldn't see the dome of the new mosque. A motorcycle rickshaw whined, rumbled, and whined again. Marie turned back to her friend. "Ahmad Rasul Khan?"

"Yes." Zia Gul nodded. "He is a good man. Very powerful, very rich. It is sawab for him."

"To build the mosque?"

"Yes. Very great sawab. God is pleased. The man will have credit. Many people will pray for him."

Marie nodded, then remembered the wedding. "You will go with me?"

"Yes. I will go. Come early and we will prepare. We'll put henna on our hands, and I will arrange your hair."

An image of herself in sparkly clothes, glittery eye shadow, hennad hands, and hair curled and piled high on her head made Marie laugh. The party itself would be just like Carolyn's engagement party, except that instead of drinking tea with milk, they would eat cake. Plus, the wedding might have a singer or a tape player. And now, Zia Gul would come with her. It was perfect. Absolutely perfect.

The two promised to dance and mocked each other's skills and elegance. They laughed about the brilliant but revealing clothing some of the older girls would wear, and the subsequent conversations that prospective mothers-in-law would have as they considered brides for their own sons. For Marie, the laughter felt good, easy—a reprieve from all the unanswered questions, the hard stories and dangerous conversations. By the time their laughter subsided, the last of the evening light had nearly disappeared from the sky.

Marie followed Zia Gul's young son along the darkening street toward her home. As she walked, she thought about the visit. *But there was so much I wanted to tell her. Shukria and her brothers. Still, it was a good day. So rich, so full.*

A dark blue Toyota Corolla drove past Marie and the boy she followed. The car didn't slow down. Marie looked at the darkened windows. She tried to imagine the men inside, and an image of the now gray-coated, blue-jeaned man appeared. She gulped. *Paranoid.* She pushed the fear away, but just as suddenly, the image of the grave markers, their pennants straining against the wind, snapped into view. She shook her head.

I have to think. Pray. It's too much. She rubbed her eyes. *Bibi-jan and Shukria; the brothers, Uzbeks, dead; the wedding, the New Testament, the mullah.* She looked around. The last of the afternoon light was completely gone. *But the parties are okay. They have to be, even the men's. Zia Gul's husband is going. He wouldn't go if he thought it was dangerous. Unless—*

Marie's legs suddenly went numb. She stopped. *Yes, he would. He'd have to, just like Doc. It's such an important family. He'd have to honor them.* Possibilities spun through Marie's mind. Her legs buckled. She grabbed the wall beside her. *Breathe. It's fine. There'll be guards. They're strong; they won't let anything happen.* She forced herself steady, released the wall, and followed the boy up the alley. *Besides, they wouldn't attack us. Nobody cares about the women.*

The boy banged on her gate.

Home. You're safe. She greeted her guard and her dogs. Her heartbeat slowed and steadied. She walked across the dark yard and into the hallway. With a shock, she banged her shin on something solid and hard. The hallway light flickered and vanished, then flashed on. Marie looked down at a large red Pullman suitcase. She cursed under her breath.

Carolyn appeared, tears in her eyes.

Marie stopped.

The young woman stood before her. "I've packed everything I want. Only my carry-on's in my room. Two nights." She surveyed the hallway. "Two nights and I leave."

Marie followed her eyes. Two large black suitcases sat side by side, each carefully packed. Waiting.

"Now what?" Carolyn was lost.

Marie didn't know what to do. She wanted to retreat, hide in her room, put all the pieces together, make sense of it, and settle down. She looked up into the face of her friend. *Carolyn.* She felt a groan deep in her stomach. *Carolyn.*

She focused on the other woman's needs. "Come on," she said. She walked to her room, dropped her black backpack on the floor, and pulled a large piece of white paper from under her foam mattress. She grabbed a pile of colorful markers from her desk and dumped them onto the floor next to the paper. She wrote a heading on the white page in thick bright pink: "You know you've been in Shehktan for too long when . . ."

"What's this?" Carolyn asked.

Marie added another line to the top of the page. "Top Ten." She thought for a minute, picked up a bright green marker, and wrote: "You see that new sparkly fabric at the bazaar and just have to buy some!"

Carolyn laughed, knelt down on the floor, and added her own. "You see a woman walking down the street with bright yellow pointy shoes and ask her where she bought them."

Marie's turn: "You can recognize your friend even though she's wearing a burqa."

Now both women were laughing.

When they finished that list, they started another: "Things I don't like about Shehktan." This time, they each wrote at the same time, giggling as they did. When they were finished and the paper filled, they leaned back and read their thoughts.

Things I don't like about Shehktan:
Head scarves.
Kalashnikovs.
Mud.
Electricity going out.
Slow Internet.
Pajama bottoms under my skirts.
Tying my hair up all the time.
Security updates.
Bitter tea.

Their list went on and on, a juxtaposition between the extreme and the trivial. And they laughed. Finally, their emotion spent, they went into the kitchen to prepare dinner. Carolyn kept her list going aloud. "Lousy cooking pans. Ovens that threaten to explode when you light them. Tough meat. Cleaning stones out of rice. Boiling hot water to take baths."

Marie pushed her own complaint list out of her mind and spoke to her soul. *I'm staying. Think.* And she did. She thought of Bibi-jan, Shukria, her staff, and Zia Gul. She thought of the mullah and the lame boy and the small, green book. The "reasons to leave" litany was just for Carolyn's sake. *I belong here.*

They cooked a light meal of scrambled eggs, fried onions, and cubed potatoes. Marie sent the night guard to bring back one loaf of round Afghan bread. She ached for this long, wrenching good-bye to end and at the same time dreaded its aftermath.

The two women talked through the details of Carolyn's journey out of country: Kabul guesthouse one night; then Dubai, two nights; London, three hours; New York, passport control; three hours to Denver—home. They talked about the Kabul guesthouse and Chad and Casey. They talked about the airport checkpoints and searches. They talked about the waiting area and segregated seating—men everywhere, women clustered in a corner. Carolyn spoke of all the foods she could eat along the way: ice cream in Dubai, sushi in London, Starbucks in New York, and then anything she wanted.

Marie looked up. "What's tomorrow?"

"Lunch with Aziza and Khadija. Dinner with Dave and Margaret."

"This is our last night together?"

Carolyn looked down. "Yeah."

Marie knew something was missing. Something important. Significant. "I'll be back in a minute." She left the sitting room, returning with her Bible, a single glass, and a small carton of yellow mango juice.

Carolyn looked at the Bible, the cup, and the juice and understood.

Marie opened to the book of John and began reading. As she did so, the two interlaced their prayers with the words of Scripture.

"'As the Father has loved me, so have I loved you. Abide in my love.' Lord God, you've loved me forever. You loved me in America, and You've loved me in Shehktan."

"You stayed by my side, rejoicing over me with singing; quieting me with Your love."

"If you keep my commandments, you will abide in my love, just as I have kept my Father's commandments and abide in his love."

"You've taught me through your Word."

"You've guided me by your Holy Spirit."

"You helped me walk with you, day after day in this dark place."

"You've opened my eyes to see your love for the people around me."

Suddenly, Marie interrupted their prayers. "I gave a New Testament away today."

Carolyn was shocked. "What?" Marie told the story.

"Wow. That's so beautiful." Carolyn's voice trailed off wistfully.

Marie returned to their prayers. "You picked me up when I fell down."

"You've forgiven me when I've failed." Carolyn clipped the end of the last word and began weeping. "I wanted to do so much. I hardly did anything. I could barely even speak the language." Her tears turned to sobs.

Marie laid her hand on Carolyn's knee. "Carolyn. Listen." She returned to Scripture: "These things I have spoken to you, that my joy may be in you, and that your joy may be full."

Carolyn nodded. She prayed through her tears. "You've comforted me in the hard times."

Marie continued. "You've given me laughter and shown me beauty."

Carolyn took the Bible from Marie's lap and read the next verse: "This is my commandment, that you love one another as I have loved you."

Marie looked at her friend. "Carolyn. You've loved well. Really."

The young woman nodded, her cheeks still stained. She prayed. "You've given me friends, Afghans and foreigners."

"You've allowed me to see you reflected in the people around me."

"You've loved me. Every day."

Marie retrieved the book and read the next line. "Greater love has no one than this, that someone lay down his life for his friends."

Carolyn drove the heels of her hands into her eyes. "You've given me your life."

"And shown me how to live mine."

"You are my friends if you do what I command you."

"You never call me stranger or foreigner."

Carolyn opened her eyes and set her jaw. She repeated Marie's prayer. "You never call me stranger or foreigner."

"You said we're your friends, like we're friends with one another, but more faithful."

"Forever faithful."

Their prayers turned into celebration. They recalled conversations, prayers, healings, and revelations of God's love to their staff, friends, and the people they'd met along the way.

"You've given us the privilege of seeing others come to know you and fall in love with you."

They read on, turning their hearts to God and to one another.

"You helped us love one another even when we've disappointed each other."

"Even when we've angered each another."

"Outside, we've faced hatred and fear."

"And you've been with us."

"We've seen your people kidnapped and killed."

"And beaten and imprisoned."

"We know you've chosen us."

"We're yours."

"This hasn't been an easy journey, but you've been with us every step of the way."

"Always, every step, every breath."

"Sometimes you've led us to the cross."

"Sometimes to the resurrection."

They opened their eyes into hushed darkness and sat in the quiet.

Finally, Carolyn broke the sacred silence. "Hah! No electricity. Another thing I won't miss."

They laughed. "Shehktan."

Marie lit a wooden match and turned the knob on a gas lantern. A low roar filled the room. She held the match-flame beside the lantern's round mesh mantle. The flame jumped, grabbed, and engulfed the top of the lantern. Marie turned the knob slightly and the flame retreated, settled within the soft mantle, and popped, glowing bright orange. She adjusted the gas again and light circled the floorcloth, the open Bible, and Marie and Carolyn's faces and folded knees.

Marie tore the edge of the carton of mango juice and poured its deep yellow contents into the glass cup. She placed the cup on the floorcloth among the dirty plates, empty cups, and solitary piece of broken bread.

She picked up the fragment of bread. She broke it in half and handed a piece to Carolyn. "Take and eat. Jesus said, 'This is my body, broken for you.'"

Carolyn reached out her hand, received the broken bread from Marie, put it into her mouth, and ate it. Marie did the same with the other half.

Outside, a dog barked. A distant car honked. A man pounded on a neighbor's gate.

Marie picked up the cup of mango juice, their stand-in for grape juice or wine. "This cup is the new covenant of my blood, poured out for you." She handed the cup to Carolyn. "Take this. Drink it."

Carolyn took the cup, drank half its contents, and handed it back to Marie.

Marie finished the cup and set it back down in the circle of light on the floorcloth.

The two sat in silence for several moments.

The dogs outside barked. A gate creaked open, and the voices of two men clashed in indecipherable argument.

Carolyn sang the opening line of a very simple song. "Sing hallelujah to the Lord."

Marie joined, their voices rising in unison. "Sing hallelujah, sing hallelujah."

The argument outside ended. The dogs quieted.

"Sing hallelujah to the Lord."

Marie gathered the empty cups and plates and carried them into the dark kitchen. Carolyn cleaned and folded the floorcloth, picked up the gas lamp, and left the room to settle into the darkness.

PART 4

DAY 2

SHEHKTAN, AFGHANISTAN

28

All night long, the wind blew. The plastic on Marie's windows snapped, tore, and shredded as Marie tossed and turned beneath the fading warmth of her thick Chinese blankets. In the morning, she rose to bitter cold. *One more day. One more day and Carolyn will leave. One more day and I'll take my home back, move into the empty spaces. Make it my own again.*

She thought through the upcoming day. *Morning at home. Zia Gul's before lunch. Henna and hair. The wedding. Carolyn will come home late. We should play a game.*

She crawled out of her blankets, pushed herself up from the floor, and stepped into her day.

Task one: get warm.

Turning the valve on the diesel heater, she watched the liquid pool in the bottom of the canister. She lit a wooden match and dropped it carefully. The tiny flame caught and spread. She pulled on Western clothes: blue jeans, fleece socks, a long-sleeved shirt, and a beige cable knit sweater.

Task two: coffee.

She wrapped a thick Chinese blanket around her shoulders, slipped her feet into a pair of thick-soled house boots, and walked into the hallway and listened. Silence. Carolyn was still asleep.

She made her morning cup of coffee, returned to her room, and flipped open her laptop. She wasn't going to the office, but it was still a work day. She started with email, filtering her inbox for security reports. There were over thirty, each gathered from a different part of the country. She clicked through them, looking at the provinces involved, the types of incidents described, and, for a few, the assessments.

On an Afghan news aggregator, she skimmed the headlines. There were several local reports. A district police station had been attacked; a police checkpoint had been bombed; two Afghan men had been killed while visiting a village unrelated to their family; two villages were fighting over a land dispute. *Normal.*

She thought of the brothers, the Uzbeks, and Char Ab. Whatever they were fighting over, it had nothing to do with her. She thought of the gray-coated man. *Secret police? Probably.* She told herself, *nothing for me to worry about.*

She filed the security messages.

Finally, her inbox was left with only a handful of personal emails. Most were full of stateside family news. So-and-so is getting married; our daughter-in-law is pregnant with our first grandbaby; they're laying people off at the office; we're preparing for Thanksgiving.

Marie responded to each, amazed once again at the distance between their lives. Most of her friends had completely forgotten the events in Kabul, just two weeks previously. Some mentioned it in passing, mostly with gratefulness that Marie had left the city. Several recognized the loss of Carolyn but considered it no more than a sad event. After all, people in America come and go all the time.

Marie saved her closest friend's email for the end. She knew that one would be different.

My dear Marie,

I'm so sorry for your loss. And now, one on top of the
other. I know I can't imagine it. I don't have any words. No
wisdom. I just know he's enough. You have to find him in
all this. You have to stay close to him. I can't even begin to
tell you how to do that. I just know it's important. Please
take care of yourself. I'm worried about you.

Love, Debbie

Marie read the email several times over. She thought of Margaret's
words. "Christ is enough." *Is that what she said? Wasn't there more? "Go
back and ask God where he's been in the journey."* She read her American
friend's email again. "I can't even begin to tell you how to do that. I
just know it's important."

Yesterday's worn clothes were draped over the closed aluminum
trunk. A stack of folded black long johns sat on top of a red carry-on
suitcase. The posters she and Carolyn made the night before curled
against the front of the suitcase. The floor was littered with markers, a
pair of socks, and a scarf of navy blue and white.

She found the burgundy-framed photo of her four friends and her,
all smiling in the dappled light of a dense green tree. Marie remembered the scene. It was spring and they'd gone out of town for a picnic.
Faiz Muhammad had found the place: a grove of trees with a spring,
and a small, deep pool of water. The women had taken a large piece of
dark green carpet to cover the brown earth, a pot of lamb palau, two
thermoses of tea, a bowl of tomatoes and cucumbers, and all the plates,
cups, and silverware the picnic required. They'd broken bread beneath
the trees, their privacy guaranteed by the hills that rose steeply around
them, and Faiz Muhammad in his vehicle on the dirt road just beyond.

They had laughed and played and taken turns splashing in a cool,
spring water pool. They'd lain on the carpet and watched the leaves
dance in the breeze until their clothes dried. Then Faiz Muhammad
had come and taken the picture.

Ah, she thought. *Shehktan.*

She looked back at her friend's email. "You have to find him in all this." *How?*

She looked at her clock. Eight eleven a.m. Forty-five minutes until she'd go to Zia Gul's. She put her hands to the keyboard.

Hey Debbie,

Thanks for your email. Yeah, it's hard. Carolyn's leaving tomorrow. The whole house is in chaos and winter's here. It's already crazy cold! I keep thinking I'll get used to all these changes, but I don't. It's just so hard to keep up.

Still, there's so much good stuff. All the literacy classes we started are going well. I've visited all of them, but there's one that's really captured my attention. It's out in a village, and I'm getting to know the whole family. They're really amazing, and their lives are so full of stories layered on stories. I'm going to a wedding with them here in town today. The men's party has probably already started. Zia Gul and I will go to the women's party around 1:00 p.m. I'll meet all the women relatives. I can't wait.

The leader of the family is a really important man. Apparently, he's powerful and owns a lot of land. And get this, he and his people are in the middle of some kind of feud. I don't know what it's about, though.

The women have their own feud going. The leading woman is old and kind of harsh, except that she's welcomed me in a big way. Her daughter-in-law is a blood bride, taken to pay for an injury done to the old woman's son, now the girl's husband. The old woman lost her other daughter-in-law giving birth and doesn't like this new one. It's crazy no matter how you look at it. I hope I never get used to this kind of thing. Oh, and the village family are feuding with that bride's relatives. I have no idea how any of that will play out, but they're such nice people and I got to give them an NT yesterday. So God's doing something, and I get to see it.

Oh yeah, and the village is beautiful, with mountains and waterfalls and cultivated fields. Along the road there's these grave markers from the war. Their pennants are beautiful in a haunting kind of way. I took some pictures. I'll send them later.

I've got lots of work to do—the literacy project and the other little projects. I have to take over Carolyn's part in all that, but I can do it. Anyway, I'm glad for this work. It's helping people. I really think it's worth doing.

Please keep praying for me. I feel like one of those little pennants in the wind. The ropes and knots holding me on just keep getting more and more frayed. Really, I think that's the hardest part. So pray, yeah?

Love, Marie

She pressed send, leaned back against the cold wall, and thought about the projects. She tried to tally the full number of unique beneficiaries. She counted. *Maybe six hundred fifty. Yeah, that's worth doing.* The looked through the now-shredded plastic that covered her window. She saw her dogs, jostling against one another in the yard. She smiled. *Hah! I can do this. See. It's not so hard. I just needed to remember what I'm doing and keep moving.*

When it was time, Marie unburied her sparkly royal blue and bright white party clothes and matching scarf. She folded them carefully and dropped them inside a cloth rice bag. She would change at Zia Gul's. She stepped out into the hallway to find her beaded dress shoes and walked straight into Carolyn.

"Hey, going to the wedding?"

Marie stopped. She felt an instant pang of guilt. "Yeah. It's your last day. Want to come?"

Carolyn pulled her brown sweater tighter around her body. "Nah. I packed my wedding clothes."

"You're taking them home?"

Carolyn pushed a lock of disheveled morning hair out of her face. "Yeah. Maybe I'll wear them to my engagement party or my bachelorette party. That'll be fun. Little of Afghanistan in America." She looked down and stepped backward, letting Marie pass.

Marie had a vision of Carolyn standing fully covered in sparkly pink amid strapless Western black dresses. "Sure. If you want."

Carolyn shrugged. "Maybe. Anyway, it's packed and I'm going to Aziza's."

"Yeah. Good." Marie looked down the hallway. *No beaded shoes.* She turned, then stopped. "I thought tonight we'd play a game or something after you get home. You know, keep it light."

"Yeah, the waiting's killing me." She shivered against the cold.

Marie looked into her friend's downturned face. "I'll go with you to the airport tomorrow. Wait for the plane with you. See you off."

"Yeah. Thanks."

In her room, Marie dug through another pile, found the missing shoes, and dropped them into the rice bag with her wedding clothes. She pulled her long, navy blue skirt from the pile of worn clothes draped over the silver trunk, then grabbed a set of long johns from the floor and found a clean pair of black tombones folded neatly on the shelf. She dressed, adding a tan sweater on top. In the hallway, she added her long, wool winter coat, thick blue and white scarf, and slip-on cleated shoes.

Outside, she stepped through her gate and into the narrow alley. She saw a small girl, no more than six years old, walking away from her along the wall. The girl balanced a large aluminum tray on her hand and shoulder. *Bread dough,* Marie thought. She looked at the girl. *I certainly wasn't working that hard at age six.* Her shoes slipped in the mud. Her hand caught the wall. She steadied, found her balance, and kept walking.

Her thoughts drifted to the village. *Shukria-jan. Bibi-jan. Two women trapped in a relationship neither wanted. Afghanistan!* Marie locked her jaw. *Tribal justice. An eye for an eye; a girl for a foot.* Her eyes narrowed. She watched the small girl with the aluminum tray disappear into a gate in the alley. She imagined the heat of a fire-filled tandoor waiting for the bread dough of a six-year-old girl. *It shouldn't be like this. A girl should be allowed to be a girl!*

Marie felt the weight of an imaginary sledgehammer in her hands. She felt herself swinging and swinging and swinging as hard as she could—the satisfactory thud when the mud brick cracked and shattered. Then, with another blow, a gaping hole. Again and again and again. She stopped walking, squeezed her eyes tight. Shut out the image, the violence. Another scene appeared: an Afghan woman, surprised; a bucket of soapy water at her feet. A wad of khaki Afghan clothing in her hand. A girl hiding behind her skirt. Marie, a stranger, standing before them with a sledgehammer in her hands, her eyes filled with indignation. *No, Marie. You can't fix it. It's Afghanistan. This is the way it is. Stop. Breathe. Look around. See.*

A woman in a light blue burqa, head bowed, followed a young boy beside a mud-brick wall across from the alley's opening. They disappeared. Marie kept walking. The alley was deserted. Her thoughts were her own. She saw Bibi-jan sitting on the carpet in the room with the large glass window that looked out over the valley; Shukria seated next to the door, her knees pulled tight against her chest; the black-bearded mullah with his soft, kind eyes. The lame son shuffled closer, excited, speaking rapid words. *"Come back. Come back."* Bibi-jan standing at her window, her fists on her hips, scolding. *"Where have you been?*

Come. We will—" Her words lost in a roar of wind—fierce, wild wind.

Focus. I'm going to a wedding. She felt the weight of the rice bag with her wedding clothes swinging from her hand. The rough edges of the beaded sandals banged rhythmically against her knee.

She adjusted the backpack draped over her shoulder. *It's light. Why?* She remembered. She'd left her laptop at home. *A wedding party.* She knew better than to take it with her—too many guests, too easy to lose. She shuddered at the thought: all her contacts, documents, everything sold or given into the hands of someone bad. A laptop had to be protected, but she didn't remember thinking about that—deciding and intentionally leaving it behind.

She reached for her phone and found it tethered to the loop on her backpack. She knew her wallet, her passport, and her packet of US cash were all tucked where they belonged. She rewrapped her heavy blue and white scarf with her free hand. *It's okay.*

She exhaled, focused on the wedding, measured her steps and observed her world. A tree, its brown leaves curled in the early winter cold; a boy with a white skullcap, a cloth-wrapped bundle pressed against his chest. Another and another. Boys were walking home from the mosque, home from Quran class. The old man sat in his wooden shop. A burgundy motorcycle rickshaw bounced down the road. And a man with a dark gray, Western-style coat and an orange-and-blue watch cap squatted against a wall halfway up the road. He took a cell phone out of his pocket, pushed a button, and began speaking.

Marie bit down hard, stood up straight, and continued walking. The young man pretended not to watch. Marie passed him on the opposite side of the road, turned, and looked up at the pink, yellow, and orange concrete house towering over mud walls in the distance. She could see the shapes of men clustered in front of the gate. *Guards? Guests?* She imagined both. She felt her ribs pressing hard against her heart. She shook her head. *It's too much. God, it's too much.* She slipped through Zia Gul's gate, relieved to be off the street.

29

Marie found Zia Gul squatting on the ground next to a tin water tank, a bright blue plastic bucket full of dishes at her feet, her hands covered with ice cold, soapy water. Zia Gul was cross. Her daughter had gone to visit a cousin and hadn't returned. The dishes were the girl's job.

Marie squatted on the ground beside Zia Gul. She wrapped her knees in her arms and listened to a mother's annoyance with an errant child. She shook her head sympathetically with every complaint, but her thoughts were crowded, fragmented, uneasy. She watched Zia Gul fill the kettle with water, drop it on a gas burner in the outdoor kitchen, and light a match. The simple actions—water splashing into a kettle, the scratch of a match, and the soft roar of blue flame—quieted Marie's mind.

She followed Zia Gul into the pale green sitting room. The two sat down, cracked almonds with the bottom of a glass cup, and drank tea as they talked about the laziness of children, the amount of work a woman must do, and the damp cold that made everything so much more difficult.

"You are happy. You have no husband. No children. Your life is easy!"

They teased each other.

"Your children are healthy. You will have grandchildren. You will be rich."

"Bah! They are too much work. They make a woman crazy. 'Mother-jan, Mother-jan, Mother-jan.' Hah! A mother can't think!"

Marie dropped her blue and white scarf onto the floor. Zia Gul moved behind her, untied her hair, and began brushing her long auburn locks. "Your hair is so soft. Not like mine."

The brush in her friend's hands felt so gentle, so sweet. Marie picked up her cup and looked down at a tube of brownish-orange henna paste on the carpet before her and imagined the designs they'd paint on one another's hands: vines, flowers, paisleys. She held her glass cup under the nozzle of the air thermos. The hot tea tumbled, steaming, into the cup. She was looking at the henna paste, thinking about designs, feeling the brush in her hair and her friend's hand on her head. *Peace.* If she had stopped to find the word, that's what she would have said. Peace.

Suddenly, a deep, fierce boom sounded, sharp and loud, and Marie felt a hard, flat blow, as if a heavy board had slammed against her chest.

The window buckled, shuddered, and smacked back into its frame. The cup fell. Winded, Zia Gul slammed Marie against the floor. They gasped and pushed themselves upright, wild-eyed, mouths gaping. Marie didn't notice the orange-brown henna paste staining the fibers of her tan sweater or the sharp pain across her left hand where the steaming tea had scalded her skin.

Zia Gul jumped to her feet. She cried out the names of her children. The three smaller ones rushed into the room and clung to their mother. Two children missing. She cried out their names, louder and louder. Marie sat frozen, transfixed, lost in the still trembling window glass. Her phone rang.

"Marie. Where are you?"

She recognized Dave's voice, rushed and agitated.

"Zia Gul's. I'm fine."

"Stay there." The call went dead.

Zia Gul's oldest daughter ran breathless into the room. "It's at the wedding! The wedding!" She shouted over and over, her eyes full of terror, her face covered in tears.

Marie looked at the heavy mint colored drapes and sheer, white curtain, but the window faced the street, not the towering pink, yellow, and orange house. She focused her thoughts, smelling dust and something sharp, acidic. Men shouted. Vehicles gunned and crashed over the rough road. Zia Gul pushed the smaller children into Marie. Calling out the name of her oldest son and her husband, she fled the room.

Marie held the children in her arms, their bodies trembling. Seeing her cell phone still in her hand, she called Dave. Busy signal. She held the phone in front of her and sent him a text: "Wedding."

She heard Zia Gul outside, standing within her walled yard, scolding. She heard the boy's voice, defending. Then silence. Zia Gul returned to the pale green room. She gathered her smaller children into her arms and hugged them tightly. She stared hard at the edge of the ceiling where the green-checked fabric disappeared into the painted plaster. Finally, she found words. "It's okay," she said firmly. "It's okay. Father-jan is safe. My son is safe." She covered the heads of her smaller children with kisses. "My children are safe."

Marie spread her hands, palms upward, and whispered. "Thanks be to God."

Zia Gul looked at her older daughter, still standing stock-still in the pale green room. She shook her head and scolded, "Where were you? You should have been here!" Suddenly, Zia Gul convulsed. Her whole body shook with heavy, wracking sobs. Marie pushed herself from the floor and knelt beside her friend, wrapping her and the smaller children into her own arms. The oldest daughter joined their embrace.

Inside the pale green sitting room Marie, Zia Gul, and the children huddled tightly against the chaotic sounds and scents intruding from the street. Men running, trucks loaded with sloshing buckets of water screeching to a halt, boys furiously pulling and pushing the bright metal rod on the neighborhood water pump, torn hands throwing shattered concrete and splintered beams into careless piles.

She imagined men carrying men, some bleeding, groaning, and cursing, some silent.

At the German base, only two blocks away, young, blue-eyed soldiers snapped alert, their weapons in their hands: ready, waiting for whatever chaos the day would bring them. She pictured Dave inside his house, collecting scraps of news, reading text messages, pacing his wide hallway.

Carolyn. God, where's Carolyn? She pulled her phone from its pouch. "Carolyn."

Her friend's voice was frail, more like a child's than her own. "The driver's coming for me. Then you."

"Carolyn?" Marie's voice was steady, strong. "Are you okay?"

"Yes. Just . . . Just . . ." Her words tapered off. "I'm fine. At home. In the hall. It's okay. The driver's coming. You're still at Zia Gul's, right?"

Marie could hear the fear in her friend's voice. "Yes. I'm here. Carolyn, are you all right?"

"Yeah, yeah. Fine. I pulled the blankets over me."

"What?"

"I'm in the hall. My window's so big. I'm in the hall. I pulled the blankets over me."

"Did the window break?"

"No. No, it just shook. I was about to get dressed. The driver's coming."

"Where are we going, Carolyn?"

Carolyn's voice was nothing more than a squeak, but Marie understood. "Dave and Margaret's."

Marie stayed steady. "Okay. I'll be ready. We'll be there soon. It's okay."

"Yeah."

"Do you want to stay on the phone?"

"Yeah."

Marie let go of Zia Gul and the children. "Okay. I'm here. I'm with Zia Gul. I'm going to speak in Dari, okay?"

"Yeah."

Marie looked at Zia Gul. "Nazanin's alone at the house. Our driver's coming to get us both." Her friend nodded, wiped her face, and stood up.

The oldest daughter grabbed a small towel and blotted the spilled tea from the carpet. That's when they noticed the henna, dark orange across Marie's chest. They looked at the children, their shoulders stained. Zia Gul's back, the carpet—all stained.

Marie apologized, but her words faltered into English.

Zia Gul waved them away, as if to say, *It doesn't matter. It doesn't matter that the clothes are ruined. That the carpet is ruined. That the day is ruined.* Then she spoke.

"The father of my children is alive. My children are alive. My friend is alive."

Marie and Zia Gul leaned side by side against the cold-green wall, the children huddled around them. They waited in silence, keenly aware of the chaos at the concrete house less than a block away.

Zia Gul inhaled a deep breath. She caught Marie's hands in her own and squeezed hard. They kept their hands clasped tightly. Marie could hear Carolyn breathing into the phone. She was sure her young friend was crying. "Carolyn, is the driver there yet?"

Carolyn's voice was still too high, too light, too weak. "Yeah. Omed just knocked. I have to go."

"Okay. Let's hang up. Miss-call me when you get here. Okay?"

"Yeah."

Marie held the silent phone in one hand and Zia Gul's hand in the other. *Soon,* she thought, *the phone will ring again and I'll have to leave.*

Marie leaned into Zia Gul. She didn't want to leave, but she wanted to be with Carolyn. *Couldn't she just come here?* But Marie knew the protocol. There'd been an event, a crisis. They would have to lock down somewhere safe. Dave would collect information. He would call the police, the secret police, other foreigners, and the Afghans he knew in the government. He would assess the situation and make decisions. Marie would have no part in making those decisions; but whatever they were, whatever he decided, she would do. Her phone rang twice, then stopped: Carolyn's miss-call.

Marie kissed the heads of each of the smaller children.

Zia Gul stood up and pulled Marie to her feet. The two embraced, kissed each other's cheeks, and walked hand in trembling hand to the gate. Inside the gate, Marie tied up her hair. Zia Gul buttoned Marie's long navy blue coat and wrapped Marie's blue and white scarf around her friend's head. They kissed again, wiped the tears from their own faces, and parted; Zia Gul to her house and her children, and to her husband and her son, who were far too busy in far too brutal a chaos; Marie, to the home of Dave and Margaret, to Carolyn, and to conversations just as full of chaos.

Marie slid into the backseat of Faiz Muhammad's SUV. She hugged Carolyn, her precious, trembling friend. Faiz Muhammad warned her to hide. She lay her head down on the seat, her arms still wrapped around Carolyn. She felt the road rock beneath them both.

30

Marie pushed Dave and Margaret's door open and stepped inside to the sound of an animated children's movie floating down the hall, then the voices of two men. She called out a greeting and heard Dave's reply. It was oddly cheerful, maybe for the sake of the children watching the movie or maybe because she and Carolyn had arrived safely. Marie slipped out of her shoes in the hallway, pulled her scarf down to her shoulders, and untied her hair. The women shrugged out of their heavy coats and found thick, Western-style slipper boots under a low bench. Marie slid her feet into one pair, relieved to have something more than socks between her soles and the tiled concrete floor.

Dave called out again. "Marie, Carolyn. Come in."

She wondered where Margaret was and wanted to find her first, but Dave was insistent. She walked into the main sitting room and found Dave and Edmond sitting opposite one another on the green, Western-style furniture. With a shock, Marie saw the furniture vanish, its place taken by the outline of a green pennant, shredding in the wind. She grabbed the doorjamb, steadied herself, and focused. The room returned to view. She forced herself across the room toward an empty chair and sat down.

She heard Dave's voice. "We're reviewing security."

Aware of a tightness locking the sockets of her hips, the cold from the floor shot through the slippers and into the soles of her feet. "Do you know the details?" Her voice was flat.

"We're working on it."

Marie narrowed her eyes and shifted into business mode. "Was there a target?"

Edmond spoke, his English accented but otherwise perfect. "Yes. The target was the commander, Ahmad Rasul Khan, but he was not killed. Some of his men were killed. Many were injured. But he was not."

Marie felt thin blades of icy cold shoot through her ankles and up to her knees. She pictured the lame son and Bibi-jan wailing. She shook away the image. *No. He's alive. Shukria's husband—Bibi-jan's last living son—must be alive.* "What about the governor?"

The Dutchman looked at Dave. Dave shook his head. "He'd already gone."

"Was he injured? The commander?" Somehow, she thought that would matter.

Dave responded. "Yes. Many men were injured. We don't know

how many. The commander was injured, but not badly. Four people died. At least. They took two to the main hospital in the city. Doc called. He said one of them might live."

Marie looked at the wall. "Doc? Is he okay?"

"Yeah. He's at the local hospital. Working."

Marie looked over at Carolyn.

The younger woman sat still, her backpack on her lap. "How?"

Edmond leaned forward and pressed his forearms against his thighs. "A suicide bomber. He came as a guest."

"And there was no security?" Marie's question hurled like an accusation.

"Yes. There was security." Edmond sat back. "The guards searched the guests at the gate. That's where he blew himself up. At the gate."

Marie imagined a line of clean, crisp wedding guests—all men, standing in twos and threes, smiling and laughing. She pictured the farmers and the mullah standing between the low building and the last little bridge to the village. She saw the guards with Kalashnikovs at the gate, greeting the guests, clasping hands, pressing beards to beards. Inside, Zia Gul's husband, Shukria's husband, the commander, the doctor—all sitting on the floor, eating palau, drinking tea, chatting. Then the blast. She remembered the solid shock of sound against her chest. The window buckling. The hot tea scalding her hand. Zia Gul wrapped around her. The carpet against her cheek. She pushed the images aside and looked down at the deep orange-brown henna stain on her chest. *Focus.* "What's the assessment?"

"That's where it gets tricky."

Marie tried for sarcasm. "You *think*?"

Dave responded in patience. He spoke his words slowly. "There will of course be retributions. If there are retributions, there will be more attacks. In a sense, we are caught between two groups who will *never* get along."

"They don't have to get along." She paused, looked around the room, and searched the plastic-covered windows. "They just have to stop killing each other." Her last words trailed into a whisper.

"Not gonna happen." Dave was abrupt.

"Okay, but what about us? We're nongovernmental, non-combatants. And this has been going on forever."

Dave and Edmond looked at one another. Clearly, they'd been discussing the situation. Dave spoke. "Here's the thing. The violence is escalating. They've attacked a major figure on his own territory. We can't guess what's next."

Marie pushed Dave's concerns away. "Dave, it's not our fight. Besides, our neighbors accept us. They wouldn't allow anything to happen to us."

Dave mimicked her tone: "You think?" He looked directly at Marie. "What about Kabul?"

Instantly she saw the blue room, the broken venetian blinds, the young Afghan men standing behind their mismatched desks. "Kabul?" she whispered.

Dave pressed his point in excruciating detail. "Someone powerful must have approved that. It couldn't have happened otherwise." He narrowed his eyes. "The point is, Marie, it could happen here."

Marie shivered. "Winter is coming. The kings will go home from war." Still, she wanted a way out.

"Maybe, but this isn't the Taliban. These are personal feuds." Dave grew impatient. "Anyway, that's not the only problem."

Marie leaned back. She put her backpack down on the floor. "Okay. I'm ready."

Dave tucked his elbows into his knees and spoke softly. "Marie, like you said, winter is coming." Marie's heart tumbled in her chest. The image of the empty airport floated into view. She saw the low building covered in snow; then the dustway, white and trackless. Dave went on,

"When the snows fall, the plane won't be able to land. You know we can't go to Kabul over the road anymore. We can pay men to clear the field, but if we have to evacuate quickly, we won't be able to."

Marie sighed. "So, what are you thinking?"

"That's what we're trying to decide."

"Okay, where are we now?"

Edmond rubbed his short hair catching the light filtering through the plastic-covered windows. "I will have to take my family away."

Marie heard the edge of a song from the DVD in the other room where Margaret and the children watched a movie.

Edmond continued. "I've got three boys. And we're tired. I can't—"

Marie acknowledged him with a nod.

"Look." He opened his hands. "If something happens, how will I get my children out? My wife?"

His words fell dully, heavily, like misshapen forms falling at Marie's feet. Still, a decision to leave was difficult, and it helped to have affirmation. "Yeah. Makes sense. Yeah."

Dave was more encouraging. "It's the right thing. The risk is too high. When are you thinking of going?"

"I should call, see if there's room on Carolyn's flight." Startled, Marie looked at Carolyn. The younger woman's arms were wrapped around her backpack. She seemed to be barely breathing. Edmond pulled his phone from his pocket.

Marie only heard Edmond's half of the conversation. Still, it was clear enough. "Flight to Kabul . . . tomorrow, if possible . . . yes . . . security . . . I understand . . . yes . . . two adults and three children . . . yes, luggage . . . uh—one minute." He turned to Dave. "Do you all want to go?"

Marie leaned forward, her jaw fell open. *Tomorrow?*

The ice from the floor shot from Marie's knees to her hips this time and her hands trembled. "It won't snow for a few more weeks at least. We can shut down. Say good-bye. Leave well."

Dave nodded slowly, his eyes fixed on a corner of the room. "Yeah.

Gives us time to wrap up the office. Pack. Get out before winter." He looked at Edmond. "Carolyn's still on tomorrow's flight. The rest of us will leave in two weeks. I'll call them later to book the flight."

Marie forced a slow, shallow breath. She pressed her lips together, forced the air all the way to the bottom of her lungs. *Two weeks.* Two weeks. Oh, God!

Edmond returned to his phone call. "No, that's all . . . Thank you."

"What about Doc?" Marie's knees and hips ached.

"He'll call us later, when he's done at the hospital. But I doubt he'll leave now. He's the responsibility of the Ministry of Health. A doctor. Who kills doctors?" Dave looked down at the floor. "I think he'll stay." He looked back to Marie. He saw her locked jaw, her narrowed eyes, her flexed fingers hovering over her thighs. "Marie, I'm sorry. There's nothing we can do." He paused. "We'll sit out the winter. You can go home for Christmas. We'll come back in the spring. You know, assess things first. See what the deal is. Come back, restart the projects. If things settle down, we'll come back. What can we do?"

Marie leaned forward and rubbed her thighs with the heels of her hands. Ice-cold, though she knew the room was warm. The big German diesel heater in the corner made sure of that. She looked down at its glass window. The flames were bright, leaping red and orange. *It should be warm.* She rubbed her knees. "I know. I know. I get it." Her words were short, clipped.

Dave heard her exasperation and matched it. "You can't stay here alone, Marie. You just can't do it."

"Yeah, yeah. I know. I get it. I'm just . . . I'm just not ready."

Dave softened his voice. "We'll leave in two weeks. Maybe longer. Before the snow. We'll have time. You can say good-bye. We'll shut things down. It's best."

Edmond added, "Marie, if you don't leave, you place not only yourself in danger, but your Afghan friends, too."

Marie knew without foreign coworkers, she couldn't stay. "I know. It's okay. I get that. Stuff happens." Her words took on a tone of rebuke. "I've been here long enough, too." She threw her hands in the air. "If we have to go, we have to go. I'll deal with it."

"Yeah. I'm sorry." Dave folded one of his hands and pressed it in hard against the palm of the other. Marie licked her bottom lip, scraped the moisture off with her teeth, and focused her still-narrowed eyes hard on the worn carabiner that tethered her cell phone pouch to her backpack. *Cell phone, backpack*—she realized she'd left her laptop at home. She wanted to check the news; she needed to write home to her family and friends before they awakened to yet another Afghan crisis.

"Yeah." She looked directly into Dave's eyes. "Okay." She sprang up from her seat and headed out of the room. "I'm going back to my house. Fine. I'll deal with it. It's what we have to do." She slung her backpack over her shoulder in one practiced movement. "I'll write a shutdown plan for my projects. I can deal with this."

Dave stood and held his hand out as if to stop Marie. His words were soft, patient, almost embracing. "Marie, please. Sit down."

Marie locked her knees. "We're done." She threw her free hand in the air, her fingers flexed. "We've got a decision, and that's it. Let me go!"

Dave waited. Marie took one more step toward the door before stopping. After a moment, she turned and looked back at Dave. "Marie." Dave's voice was calm. "This is a serious situation. Just be patient, okay?"

Marie sighed. "Okay." She turned and sat back down, her backpack cradled in her arms. The conversation continued without her.

Marie sat perfectly still in the room with its green upholstered couch and two matching chairs; a wooden bench with a woven seat;

a large, square wooden coffee table, its bottom shelf full of books; a dark green cotton floor mat in the corner; blue carpet, no pattern; green-and-white striped drapes; and smiling family portraits with a cake-smeared grandchild and two children on a swing.

The phone rang, more words spilled and swirled. The sound of the DVD came from the other room. *A boy's voice in Dutch? English?* A dog barked. A neighbor's voice spoke outside. Marie remembered the street. She'd looked up and down the road when they jumped out of the SUV. *Where were the children? They should have been on the street. I should've seen them.* She rubbed the side of her head. *I have to make a plan. Resource the literacy classes. Give them everything they need to work up to level three. Give Aziza salary money for the teachers—we can transfer the money; Aziza can get it at the bank. No, Fawad will get it. Fine; he'll give it to Aziza.* Marie rubbed her head again.

I have to say good-bye. Can I say good-bye? Will we leave quietly? I'll just say I'm taking a break. Oh, the village. She looked up at Dave. "I'll need to go up to the village to say good-bye. Maybe go to the funerals."

Dave and Edmond looked at each other. "Marie. We'll talk about that later. Right now, I don't know." Marie launched her argument, but Dave waved his hand. "We'll talk about it later. Not now. Okay?"

Marie pressed her lips together. "Okay." Suddenly, she recalled the brown jacket and the gray coat, the man she'd seen too many times. *Did I tell Dave? I meant to.* Her jaw fell slack. *There was no time.* She rubbed the side of her head. *It's all unraveling so quickly.* "Dave!" The sound of her own voice surprised her.

"Yeah?" Dave stopped mid-sentence and looked at Marie.

Marie kept her feet on the floor while her words tumbled out. "There's been a man. Following me, I think—I'm not sure. He had a brown jacket but it got cold. I saw him again, I'm sure . . . I think in a gray coat. Maybe secret police. Or that's what Faiz Muhammad said; I don't know. I meant to tell you. It all happened—everything's been happening—so quickly. I wasn't sure until this morning. Yeah, it was this morning. I was walking to Zia Gul's with my wedding clothes."

She remembered her sparkly blue and white clothes and beaded sandals tucked into a rice bag. She could see the bag clearly, sitting on the burgundy cotton floor mat in Zia Gul's pale green sitting room. She lost track of her own words, of the faces around her, of what was happening.

Margaret entered the room with a large silver tray, a pot of coffee, and several mugs. Marie looked up into her friend's face, gentle and soft. Like her mother's face. She lost sight of Margaret in the vision of her mother. Saw her mother walking into her bedroom with a silver bowl and a bright white cloth. *When was that? I was a child. Sick. Maybe Mom remembers it.* She had sat on the edge of Marie's bed, put the bowl on the table, and lain the cool, damp washcloth against the fire in Marie's forehead.

Marie took in a breath, aware that she hadn't been breathing well. She drew another breath, this one deeper. She registered Edmond's voice. He was saying something.

"Probably."

She looked over at him. "Probably what?"

Margaret put the tray on the coffee table, poured a cup, added milk and sugar, and handed it to Marie. She examined the cup as though it were a stranger, an odd, uninvited guest, but one that should be welcomed. Margaret never mixed her coffee. Marie cocked her head sideways and looked into Margaret's face, but still saw someone else; her mother, holding a cool, white washcloth. Marie took the cup.

Dave spoke. "Thank you, Marie. It probably was the secret police. We know they've been watching us more than usual. It's another thing we're considering."

Suddenly, Dave and Edmond were on their feet. Marie watched them embrace. She looked at the hot coffee in her hands, Margaret still in front of her.

The older woman tugged at Marie's elbow. She leaned forward, placed her hand on the top of Marie's head. "Come," she said, her voice soft, softer than Marie had ever heard it before. "We need to say good-bye."

"What?" Marie looked up at Margaret, her eyes wide, her jaw soft.

Margaret took the coffee out of Marie's hand and placed it on the floor next to the heater. She took Marie's backpack, slid it off Marie's knee, and allowed it to fall slowly to Marie's feet. "We need to say good-bye."

Marie shook her head, looked at Margaret, Dave, then Edmond. "Now?"

"Edmond and Tanja are leaving tomorrow with Carolyn. We won't see them again. We need to say good-bye."

Marie pushed hard against the locks in her knees and hips. They protested, but gave way as she walked over to Edmond. She knew she should find words, and she had them, but there were too many: indecipherable, jigsaw puzzle pieces falling onto a tabletop, only fragments of colors and shapes. She reached for one, then another. But she found no sentences and finally wrapped her arms around Edmond.

Neighbors in a hurricane. Sheets of plywood, nails, ladders. Huddled together when the trees crashed, electricity vanished, wind tore the clapboard and pounded, full force against a trembling frame. Did I dream that? Marie held Edmond tightly, a circle of defense. But no, this was no storm. This was Shehktan. Shehktan, a storm in itself.

She let go of Edmond, stepping back. Shoved her hands into pockets she didn't have. Felt them fall, lost. Picked them up. Locked them together. Nodded. *Breathe.* Commanded herself. *Breathe.* And her breath came jagged. She pulled it in deep, wrapped it into her ribs. Took another. Easier. Another. Firm.

She looked up into Edmond's face. Nodded again. Pressed her lips together. "Travel well." It was a weak offering, but at least it was words. She looked down at the floor, put her hands on the back of her hips. "It's the right thing to do. Yeah. It's the right thing to do."

DAY 2

Edmond collected Tanja and the boys as Marie, Carolyn, Dave, and Margaret watched and waited. When the boys were ready, they all spoke their brave good-byes. Marie forced her lips into a smile. She picked up the youngest boy, kissed his cheek, and ruffled his blond hair. "Say hi to your grandma for me." Her voice was light as she could make it. Light enough. The boy smiled.

She held the other two, kissed their foreheads. *Tomorrow?* They were good boys. *It's the right thing to do.* She embraced Tanja. "You've done well here. It's time."

The woman nodded, caught a quick breath, and pulled her oldest son to her hip. "Yes. It's time."

Marie didn't follow them out the door. She stood beside Margaret and Carolyn in the cold hallway, wordless, just present.

She heard a car door, then another and another. The starter screamed, the engine rumbled, and evened out. Voices, then a metal scrape. She heard the clunk as the gear engaged; more voices; then the metal scrape again. She heard the steel rod that locked the gate snap into place. Then silence.

31

Margaret guided Marie back into the sitting room, back to the heat from the German diesel heater, back to her Western-style chair, and placed the coffee cup into the cradle of Marie's hands. She sat on the very edge of the chair Edmond had just been in, a chair he was not likely to ever fill again. Marie noticed how Margaret sat—with her hands folded on her lap and her back straight, her lips pursed, her eyes staring across the room, dimly lit through the hard plastic-covered windows. Carolyn was back on her chair, her backpack once again wrapped in her arms.

Dave returned, and the four sat in silence. Marie sipped her coffee; Margaret sat straight, lost in the window pane; Dave leaned forward, elbows on his knees, forehead in the heels of his hand. Carolyn hugged her backpack.

The journey's not over. Marie tried to concentrate. *Not yet. Two weeks; two weeks.* She looked at the carpet. Its blue nap, soft and even, shifted into gray; then faces appeared. A room full of literacy students, their dark eyes shining, their lips forming words that couldn't reach her. She strained to hear but just saw silent rounded curves and flashing smiles. Another class, and another. Her coworkers. Aziza chiding her. *Why is she chiding me?* Words without sounds. Bibi-jan—her head thrown back, laughing; her belly rocking up and down. Shukria—her scarf pulled over her mouth but a smile in her eyes. The lame son; the green New Testament; the mullah; the scoop-faced hills; the houses carved into the face of the hillsides; the mountains rising up beyond the village; and the brown valley below with its darker brown serpentine river cut into curved irrigation channels. Faiz Muhammad reflected in the rearview mirror; the railless bridge buckling under their wheels; and the grave pennants flapping and straining in the wind.

Marie pushed the heels of her hands into her eye sockets. She rubbed hard, hard enough to register pain. The spell was broken.

She stood up. "I have to go. I've got to get started. There's work to do."

Dave's words came as another unwelcome surprise. "Marie. We're on lockdown." A decision she had not been a part of.

"Oh." Why hadn't she thought of that? Of course they were. They would have to be. "But we lock down at our own houses." She looked over at Carolyn, but the younger woman said nothing.

Dave sat down. He leaned back and rubbed his hands against his knees. "Carolyn's leaving in the morning. You'll both stay here with us." His voice was soft, but full of warning.

"Here?"

Margaret stepped in. "Carolyn will stay in the guest room next to our room across the hall. You can stay upstairs in your old room. It's all set up."

Marie pictured the room she had lived in for three months, though not with Dave and Margaret; that was before they came. She shook her head no. "I have stuff to do. I have to go. The guard can walk me home, or Faiz Muhammad can come back for me." She looked at the empty doorway. "*They* just left."

Dave nodded. "They don't belong to me."

The finality in his voice awakened her. She closed her mouth, pulled her lips together, and drew a deep breath. *So the storm's not over. Of course not. Maybe the worst is over. Maybe we're on the backside. Or maybe . . .* She looked up at the wall behind Dave.

He spoke. "It's probably over for now, but we can't know. I'm collecting information. No one knows. Some men were arrested. Maybe we'll know more later. Maybe tomorrow."

Marie nodded. "Okay." She sat back down.

The four sat in silence. Several minutes passed before anyone moved again. It was Margaret who broke the spell with a practical concern. Always practical. "There's no heater up in the room, so I put some extra blankets on the bed."

"I'll be all right."

"The guard hasn't covered the window with plastic yet, either. It'll be cold."

Marie shrugged. "It's okay. The plastic on my window shredded last night. I'll be fine."

"In the morning, we'll get Carolyn to the airport. I'll make some calls and we'll assess the situation," Dave added.

"What about Omed, our guard? He expects us back."

Dave waved his hand, the exhaustion in his face obvious. "I already sent word."

"I see. You didn't want me to argue before I got here?"

"Nope."

Marie felt her heart bang against her ribs. They had so little control over their lives; now even what she'd had was being taken out of her hands. A small snarl entered her voice. "I could've grabbed my tooth-brush."

"I needed you here."

Marie clenched her jaw, then forced herself to relax. "Yeah, but listen. I need my laptop. We can't leave it there."

"Your laptop—?" Dave looked up, alert.

"It's at home. All my files, all my contacts—everything. We can't leave it there."

Marie watched Dave process this new piece of information. "Yeah . . . You're right. We can't leave it there."

Carolyn jumped in. "I need my suitcases."

Marie looked at her friend. She couldn't remember hearing Carolyn's voice since the phone call. *Did we even talk in the car?* The reality of Carolyn's situation hit Marie. *She was alone, and now she's leaving tomor-row, and all this is happening. This isn't right. This isn't the way it's sup-posed to be.* Suddenly, Marie wanted to talk with Carolyn, just Carolyn and her. She turned to Dave. "We'll get our stuff and come back."

"No." Dave was firm. "I'll go."

Marie and Carolyn followed Dave out to the yard. They gave him instructions: the laptop and power cord on the floor, maybe . . . somewhere. Grab suitcases in the hall, the overnight bag in Carolyn's bedroom, the toothbrushes. Please remember the toothbrushes. They watched Dave climb into his car, back out onto the street, and drive away.

Marie took Carolyn's hand. They embraced but found no words. They just wept. They wiped their tears and returned to the blue and green sitting room.

A few minutes later, Dave returned with everything but the tooth-brushes. Marie slid down on the cotton floor mat, unfolded her laptop, and turned it on. She was desperate for something, anything else to focus on.

Margaret watched her young friend. She could see that the shock had passed. She collected the coffee cups and left for the kitchen. Dave and Carolyn followed her.

Alone, Marie looked around the empty room, and the fragment of a song formed.

"I shove my prayers in the cracks / I got nothing to lose / No one to answer back."

She pushed the song aside, looked at the screen. *I have to write a plan.* She opened a blank document, listed her projects, then stopped. Nothing more came. She rubbed her eyes and tried again. She typed out headings—salaries, materials, food—then . . . blank. Again, she looked around the room. The haunting melody of the song returned. *I shove my prayers in the cracks. I shove my prayers in the cracks.* She looked again at the page on her computer screen and typed more words: notebooks, reading books, pencils, erasers. She stopped. *Yeah, the classes would need notebooks and reading books, but they already had erasers, pencils, sharpeners, and dry-erase markers.* She deleted the page.

From the kitchen the voices of the others could be heard, but she couldn't make out their words. She went online and opened a news page, selected the international tab, and scanned the articles for some report of the attack. There was none. She searched for Shehktan, but again, nothing. She folded her arms and looked at the screen. *Shehktan,* she thought, *is irrelevant.*

She opened her email and found the security report. It was brief. "Attack on a wedding . . . Ahmad Rasul Khan targeted . . . One suicide bomber . . . Multiple fatalities . . . NGO workers are advised to restrict movements . . ."

She closed her laptop and looked up. The plastic-covered windows were dark. *What happened to the day?* She smelled the diesel from the heater, then something savory and warm. *Dinner?* She became aware of hunger gnawing at her stomach, then immediate nausea. She tried to swallow and recognized thirst. Across the room, Dave was tapping at his laptop. She looked over at Carolyn's chair: empty. "Carolyn?"

Dave looked up. "She went to lie down."

Marie slipped her laptop back into her backpack. She stood up but didn't know where to go or what to do. "Margaret?"

"In the kitchen."

Marie looked at the black backpack still in her hand. She put it down on the blue carpeted floor and walked on stiff legs across the sitting room and the tiled hallway and into Margaret's warm kitchen.

Marie slid silently into a chair at the small wooden table. The older woman didn't notice. She was standing at the cabinet pulling plates onto the counter. Marie listened to the scrape and click of glass plates on the concrete countertop.

Margaret turned and left the plates on the counter and sat down opposite Marie at the table. "How you doing?" Her voice was soft and weary.

Marie formed a word in her mind, rejected it, formed another, and gave up.

Margaret sighed. "Another coffee?" Marie looked up. "I'll get it." Margaret squeezed her hand and went back to the stove to prepare the coffee. Water poured into a kettle. Gas roared softly from an unlit burner, a match scratched, popped, and burned. Gas became flame.

Margaret sat back down. The kitchen was warm and full of scents: garlic, sulfur, gas, bread, and something savory. Hunger spread across Marie's abdomen. "Are you making dinner?"

"Chicken with vegetables and almonds. Hungry?"

Marie nodded, but although she felt hungry, she wasn't sure she could eat. She looked at the stove and saw a large aluminum pot with a blue cotton cloth wrapped around its lid. "Rice?"

"Yep. No salad, though. Nothing fresh."

Marie smiled weakly. She leaned back. "Nothing fresh. Thank God!"

Margaret nodded—it was a relief to hear nothing new. "It's been quite a day."

"Think it'll stay that way?"

The kettle whistled.

"I don't know."

Marie watched Margaret turn off the gas, lift the kettle onto the concrete counter, fill a French press with ground coffee, and pour in steaming water. She felt her shoulders unlock and relax downward. She looked at her hands lying loosely on the table. *Coffee,* she thought, and sighed. *A gift.*

"I don't know, Margaret. It's all too much. Carolyn, the village, the attack. When I was with Zia Gul, it felt like something slammed against my chest, but it was just the blast. Knocked the wind out of me. Just crazy. It all happened so fast."

Margaret nodded, but said nothing.

"We were getting ready. Zia Gul was brushing my hair. She wanted to style it." She smiled. "I was pouring tea from the air thermos. We were going to henna our hands. Go to the wedding." She paused and took a sip of coffee, its warmth spread through her body. "Not the men's, you know. We wouldn't have been there. The women's."

Again, Margaret gave Marie space to talk.

"Bibi-jan invited me. I invited Zia Gul. We were going to dance." Her eyes filled with tears. She pushed her thumb and forefinger into her sockets to push away the tears before they fell. "I left my wedding clothes at Zia Gul's. Her husband and son were there. At the wedding. They're all right." Marie sighed deeply. "They're all right."

Margaret rose from the table. Turned the oven gas off and pulled a pan of simmering chicken from the oven box. She set it on the counter and returned to the table. "Marie, how do you feel?"

She shook her head, at a loss for words.

"How do you feel?"

"I—I don't know. I have no idea. Numb, I guess." She looked into Margaret's waiting face. "Like—ah, it's too much. Too many . . ." Her words trailed off.

"Too many what, Marie?"

Marie focused on the blue flame under the rice pot, took a deep breath, and turned back toward her friend. "Too many. Too much of everything. Like all these pieces flying around so fast I can't . . . I don't know. Like I'm trying to hold on, but I can't. And all these pieces keep flying past me." She stopped.

Margaret covered Marie's hand with her own. "Good." She got up from the table.

"Good? How's that good?" Marie jumped to her feet.

Pushing a stack of plates into Marie's hands, she smiled. "It means you know where you are. That's enough. Now let's eat dinner."

Marie found Carolyn lying with her eyes open on the bed in the main-floor guest room. Carolyn stared at the ceiling and whispered the one thought that had apparently been plaguing her mind. "I should have left last week."

Marie stood still in the doorway. "Yeah, I'm sorry."

"You're sorry? For what?"

Marie sat down at the foot of Carolyn's bed. "I don't know. Sorry I wasn't with you during the explosion. Sorry you didn't get out before all this. Sorry you're packed and ready to go and now you've got to wait for a plane. I don't know, just sorry."

A small carved door decoration hung from a nail on the wall behind Carolyn. Marie thought of Bibi-jan's rich, deeply carved sitting room door, and she looked back down at Carolyn. "I'm sorry I wasn't paying attention. I got so lost in my own world."

Carolyn swung her feet over the side of the bed and sat up. "Yeah.

We've been going in different directions." She rubbed her shins, then stretched her back. "I'm leaving tomorrow."

"Yeah."

"You should leave, too."

Marie dug her hands into her hips, caught a quick breath, and shook her head. "Yeah, probably, but I'm not, and I don't want to."

"I'm sorry, Marie. It's just—" Carolyn's words gathered strength. "It's just, I can't imagine leaving you here in all this chaos."

Marie caught her breath. "Well, I came to tell you dinner's ready."

Carolyn grabbed Marie and hugged her tightly. Marie's body convulsed. "Oh, Carolyn, I'm so sorry." Their apologies blended together in tear-filled whispers.

Marie stepped back and wiped the tears from her face. She searched for words, some way of making sense out of the fragments of emotion swirling in her heart. She wanted desperately to stay, to continue in Shehktan, but could she? Should she?

Carolyn's eyes fell on the orange-brown henna stain across Marie's tan sweater. "What's that?"

In a flash, Marie recalled the tube of henna on Zia Gul's floor. She smiled, remembering. "Henna. I fell on it when the bomb went off. Got it all over Zia Gul and the kids, too. Everywhere."

The two women laughed just slightly, just enough to break the tension. Marie lifted her left hand. "Spilled tea, too." Showing red colored fingers and knuckles.

"I just sat on the floor behind my suitcase and waited."

"Yeah. I'm sorry."

"Me, too." Carolyn took Marie's other hand in her own. The two women walked together into Margaret's dining room.

Dinner passed slowly and quietly. They filled the space with Margaret's warm food and gentle small talk. When the meal was finished,

Carolyn, Margaret, and Marie dropped the dishes into a pan of water and returned to the living room with its plastic-covered windows. Dave was already there, reading news on the Internet. Margaret tapped him on the shoulder, and he instantly understood her expression. "We should pray."

The four foreigners gathered into a small circle in a Western-style room on the forgotten backside of Afghanistan. Outside, the night was dark, cold, and silent. Inside, a single small LED lamp, run off of a backup battery system, cast dark shadows over their faces. They held one another's hands—something they didn't normally do, but that now seemed appropriate, natural. They bowed their heads and unfurled each scrap of chaos, fear, and confusion before the only one who could make any sense of it. They asked for wisdom to light their path through the darkness and for protection from a storm they could neither control nor track. Three of them asked for a future in a place they'd come to love, and one asked to get home safely.

Behind Marie's closed eyes, a faded green pennant, tied to its pole, snapped against the wind. Suddenly the pennant tore, was lifted in the air, and tumbled end over end across a littered field. Marie pushed the image away, but the green reappeared. This time it was a green shirt, torn and tangled, amidst splintered, white clapboard and twisted, gray asphalt shingles. She shook her head and the image faded.

She offered her next prayer silently, privately. It wasn't much, but it was everything. *Lord, help.*

When they finished praying, Marie leaned back and stretched. Yes, there was a storm, but it was out there—beyond the plastic-covered windows, beyond the mud-brick walls. In this place, in this circle, she was safe.

Marie walked upstairs to the bedroom she'd slept in when she first came to Shehktan. It was different then, before Dave and Margaret arrived and took over the house. In those days, when Marie first landed, the room was filled with her own things: the two suitcases and the clothes they carried, a small collection of books, electronics, and personal products she'd thought important enough to bring with her from DC to London to Dubai to Kabul to Shehktan. That was a long time ago. Since then, she'd learned that off-the-shelf long johns were completely inadequate, clogs would break her ankles on the rocky streets, and her suede winter boots would be a disaster in the mud and rain. Since then, she'd also learned that a good vegetable knife is worth its weight in gold and that a pile of brightly colored markers would help her shape her experiences into thoughts clear enough to understand.

In those early weeks, she'd slept on a mat on the floor next to a sawdust heater that burned quietly through the night. Now, the room contained a mattress and box spring covered with a pile of thick, fuzzy, Chinese blankets, a wooden dresser complete with a mirror on top, and a corner area full of dented cardboard boxes. The air was thick and musty, like an attic cluttered with the things of an abandoned life.

Marie took off her long Afghan skirt, but kept on her long johns, tombones, shirt, and stained sweater. It was cold and she had no hot water bottles, no diesel heater, and no thick winter curtains over the thin, unglazed windows. She also had no toothbrush, no toothpaste, and no headlamp. Home was just three blocks away yet unreachable. She turned off the switch that controlled the backup LED light nailed to the door jamb and plunged the room into darkness.

She pulled the light summer curtain away from the window and looked out onto the street below the wall. The view was clear from the darkened room. *Empty.* Marie tried to locate the top floor of the pink, yellow, and orange concrete house on Zia Gul's street, but she couldn't find it. Instead, her eyes fell on the concertina wire outline of the German base on the other side of her own house. She could see the sharp outline of the corner guard towers against the softer, nearly starless night. She imagined the guards, Afghans at that level, cradling their Kalashnikovs in gloved hands. She let the curtain fall.

Marie slid underneath the pile of thick blankets on the bed, her slipper-boots still on her feet. She unwound her heavy blue and white scarf from her neck, wrapped it around her head to ward off the cold, and listened to the silence without the hum of electricity. She felt the soft, velvet darkness like a cocoon and pulled the blankets higher. *Two weeks. I can do this. I'll go to the village one more time. I'll visit all the literacy classes. It's not good-bye. Just until spring. We'll come back when the snow's gone. Aziza and Faiz Muhammad will deliver the materials while I'm gone. No problem. I'll pack. I'll check the lists taped inside the cabinet: fast evac, slow evac, and permanent move. This'll be a slow evac. I'll have time. I'll get it right. It'll be okay.*

Finally, she surrendered to exhaustion.

PART 5

DAY 1

SHEHKTAN, AFGHANISTAN

32

Something flat, solid, and hard slammed against Marie's back. Her eyes snapped open, only to be blinded in a flash too extreme to be a dream. *An explosion?* Glass shattered and slashed through her blankets, then her scarf. She felt a tear across her cheek, cold, then hot and fierce.

A rocket? A bomb? Automatic gunfire sounded a fast staccato.

Marie bolted upright and threw the blankets off. Again she was blinded—a shock of light engulfed the room, then left it in sudden utter darkness.

Another blow struck her—this one like a sledgehammer pounded against her ribs. She fell and rolled, and rolled again. *What hit me? Glass? Metal?*

A rapid pop-pop-pop. *Gunfire? Definitely gunfire.*

She heard her name, yelled in a panicked voice she barely recognized. *Where am I?* She grabbed her backpack, caught the lightweight skirt draped over the loop, and was gripped with pain. *Glass?* She pushed to her feet, but her thigh slammed against something. She tripped and fell again. Her knee—her left hand—piercing agony. *Nails? Glass?*

That voice again pierced the darkness. "Marie! Are you all right?"

Bolting half-upright, she slammed her face into the wooden door. Groaning, she found the knob and pulled. The darkness faded into shadows. Stairs. *Stop. Think.* She braced herself against the wall.

Again, that panicked voice. "Marie!"

Breathe. "Yeah. I'm okay, I think."

"Get to the basement!"

"I'm coming."

More automatic weapon fire, then explosions, some farther away. Marie grabbed the wall, tried to orient herself. *The German base. Definitely. They're attacking the German base.* But something else, too. Someplace farther away. *Toward the other side of town.*

She felt for the stair with her foot. Found it. *Careful. Concrete stairs. Break your neck. One, two. How many stairs are there? Three. A landing.* She kept her palm on the wall, fingers pressing into a smooth surface that gave no catch-hold. Another step. Another. Marie counted. Shadows appeared. She had reached the first floor hallway.

That voice, still panicked. "Marie!" It was closer now, ricocheting around the concrete stairwell.

"I'm coming. I'm coming." Another stairwell. Another hallway. "Where?"

Marie held the wall, feeling half a dozen sharp fragments between her flesh and the smooth concrete surface. She found the doorway and held its wooden frame.

"Get down," another voice commanded.

Marie dropped to her knees—more throbbing. She steadied herself. *Dave.* She crawled toward him. *Glass. It has to be glass in my knees.* She stopped crawling. "Dave? Margaret? Carolyn?"

"Over here."

Marie located their voices, half-crawled toward the wall, favoring her knees, and huddled against it.

"What happened?"

Dave sounded calmer now. "Are you okay?"

"I think the window broke. I'm sure the window broke. There's glass everywhere. I think I've got glass in my knees and my hands. But I'm fine."

Marie heard Margaret on the floor breathing hard, drawing closer. She felt her hand on her shin. Margaret held a small light close to Marie's leg, moved it over the black cotton tombones to her knee, her thigh, her face, all sprinkled with blood. Margaret gasped.

"I'm okay. I'm okay. I think it's just glass. I'm fine."

The automatic gunfire continued outside, close by and far away.

Marie heard Dave make a phone call. "Edmond? You guys okay… all right. Keep your phone with you. I'll make some calls."

"Carolyn?" Marie heard her own voice come out high-pitched and tight. "Where's Carolyn?"

"I'm here. I'm here."

Marie felt a sharp pinch against her cheek. She winced. "What are you doing?"

"Shush," Margaret soothed. "I'm pulling splinters."

Tweezers? No, fingernails. Marie braced against the sharp stabs of nails on soft cheek. She strained to hear. "What did he say? What's going on?"

"Be still!" she commanded. A circle of light blazed in Margaret's hand where she held a tiny headlamp. Her fingernails were searching, digging, prying; tiny trails of moisture crossed Marie's cheek.

Dave's words, rushed. "They're fine. I don't know." He pushed another number. This time he spoke in Dari.

Breathe. Breathe. Marie closed her eyes.

Dave's words slowed into sentences—full, patient, clearly articulated. Suddenly, he switched to English. "They're attacking the German base and the main police station. It's coordinated. We need to be still."

"Who?" A twisted demand from Marie.

"They don't know. They assume the Uzbeks. I have to call the others."

Dave spoke to Edmond with the same words: "Uzbeks, coordinated attack, German base, police station."

Marie pictured the German base, with its concertina wire and guard towers. *Too close.* The police station was eight blocks beyond. She put the pieces in order. *The first rocket must've been aimed at the German base, and the second at the police station.* As she thought, automatic weapon fire continued, interrupted by loud, harsh booms.

Marie listened to the hum of rotating blades. *One helicopter? No, two.* Light swept across the room. Marie looked up. The window, high in the wall above their heads, flashed white, then back to black. During the far too brief glimpses of their basement refuge, Marie took in what she could: storage boxes against the wall, a large wooden storage cabinet, open shelves, books, tools, blankets.

Dave took the headlamp from his wife, cupped it in his own hand, held it against the floor, and crawled out of the room.

Marie sat in the darkness, Margaret on the floor by her knees. Carolyn, shivering, drew up next to Marie.

"What happened?" Marie heard her own voice too high-pitched, confused. She already knew the words—rockets, gunfire, attack, base, police station, broken window, glass—but she couldn't string them together to make sense.

Margaret kept her hand on Marie's shin. Her voice trembled. "The window in your room broke?"

"You're on the first floor, protected by the wall. I was on the second." Marie began, still untangling the offense, putting fragments in order.

"Yes. And the guard nailed plastic across all the windows on the first floor last week. The ladder's broken. He had to borrow another. He was going to do it today."

"Today?"

"Today."

Marie felt the cold in the basement, but not as sharply as in her room. She smelled the musty boxes and coughed. A light swept across the window and shone on Margaret's face. It was worn and puffy but soft. Her eyelids drooped at the corners. "Margaret? Are you all right?"

Margaret's voice was thick with sadness. "Yes." She gave words to her experience of the event. "I wasn't asleep. I don't sleep well anymore—age. I was half awake, praying. Dave was snoring. I was thinking about packing. I heard the explosion and the glass." Her words shook free of the mesh into fragmented, misshapen pieces. "I thought—you—I'm so sorry."

"Sorry?"

Margaret's words rushed. "If you—Carolyn—home—didn't stay here . . ." Finally: "I was afraid for you."

"I'm fine. I'm fine. It was the right thing to do. We couldn't know. And anyway, would it be better if we were home? The German base is closer to our house." Marie felt Carolyn press into her shoulder. She looped her arm around Carolyn's, found her hand, and grabbed it. The glass bit. Carolyn, trembling, pressed tighter into Marie.

A thin shaft of light fell across the doorway. Dave's face appeared, half in light, ghostlike. His hands were full of something he was dragging; Marie couldn't figure out what. He entered the room. "We need to go into the hallway. There's no window there." His voice was calm. He was all business, back in control.

Marie felt the glass still biting her hands. She looked up at the gray window over Carolyn's head. *Of course. Glass.*

Margaret moved. Marie could see her crawling. She scrambled forward, avoiding her glass-studded knees as much as possible while keeping low against the thinly carpeted floor. She realized the loop of her backpack was still tight in her hand and wondered at the instinct that had made her grab it before she fled the glass-shattered room. She crawled, Carolyn at her hip. They met the light at the doorway, passed through, and leaned against the far wall.

Dave shut the door. He lit a battery-operated LED lantern and returned Margaret's headlamp. A circle of light engulfed them.

Three doors, all closed. A stairwell. Isn't there a window in the stairwell? Marie thought. *No, not on this side of the house.* The pounding of automatic fire continued, but dully, the sound muffled by the walls. Then a heavy thud, distant but strong. Finally there was silence for the span of a few minutes.

"They're done."

Marie's words were swallowed by another heavy thud. "Okay, they're not done." She felt herself smile and realized she had to fight the urge to laugh—wild, crazy, manic laughter.

Margaret opened a white plastic box. Marie studied its contents in the light of the lantern. *A first-aid kit. Bandages, gauze, packets of alcohol-soaked swabs. Something silver—tweezers.* She felt Margaret's hand on the top of her head, pushing it gently backward, and then the cold, sharp edges of the tweezers.

The metal pinched and scraped, disappeared, then pinched and scraped again. The tiny spotlight from Margaret's headlamp forced Marie's left eye closed. With her right, she watched a profile of Dave with his phone in his hand. He pushed buttons, asked questions, gave information, pushed buttons again. Marie felt the cold bite of alcohol and flinched.

"Be still."

Marie obeyed. The cold spread across her cheek, but most of the bites were pointed. Only one felt long.

Dave looked toward Marie, but not into her eyes. He spoke, softly, his voice rising from someplace far away. "How is it?"

Now Margaret was the controlled one. "A stitch would be good, maybe three, but it's fine." She held a piece of gauze against a weeping wound. "Find me a butterfly." Dave's hand disappeared from Marie's view. She heard paper and plastic scraping while Dave fished around for a butterfly bandage.

Margaret. "Cut one end. It's close to her eye."

She felt Margaret's fingers pinch her cheek, the nails catching her eyelash. She felt cold adhesive and release.

"I need another one."

More rustling. Another snap of scissors. Another pinch and then release. Marie instinctively reached for her cheek, but Margaret pushed her hand away. "Don't touch."

Carolyn swung around, her face floating before Marie's eyes, too close.

Marie wanted to know the damage. "What do you see? Is it okay?"

Carolyn nodded, still trembling. "Yeah, yeah. It's okay. Thank God it didn't take your eye."

Margaret cut a piece of gauze and tore a strip of adhesive tape. She taped the patch to the side of Marie's face. It was large, too large. "How bad is it?"

She saw Margaret smile in the circle of light, her brown eyes warm and reassuring. "It's not bad at all. You might have a little scar."

"Why's the gauze so big?"

"There's just a lot of small cuts. Very small, nothing to worry about. You must've had your face turned away from the window."

"Yeah. And the blankets and my scarf were over my head."

"Good thing you sleep away from the window," Margaret said, keeping her tone light.

Margaret unwrapped Marie's scarf, balled it up, and set it aside. She untied Marie's hair and ran her fingers through the strands, searching her scalp for shards, but she found nothing. She crawled back into the storage room and returned with her arms full of blankets. "Lean forward."

Marie and Carolyn, side by side, obeyed in unison. Margaret dropped a blanket behind their backs and wrapped it around their shoulders. Marie felt the comforting warmth. *Thank you.* A blanket. Such a small gift. *So good.* "Carolyn. Are you all right?"

"Yeah." Her voice still trembled. "Yeah. Just . . . scared." She paused. "And my window didn't even break."

The gunfire and rockets continued in the distance. The hallway, Marie knew, was safe. *We're not targets. Just nearby. Just caught up in something we've got nothing to do with.*

"Marie, give me your hand," Margaret said, still in control.

Marie stretched out her right hand, saw the blood, and shuddered. Margaret cradled Marie's open palm and searched the soft flesh for flickering shards of light. She plucked out pieces, quickly but carefully. She wrapped the palm of Marie's hand in bright white gauze. The effect struck Marie as comical. *That's my hand?* She spoke. "Just scratches, huh."

"Yep. They'll close before morning."

Marie knew that was an exaggeration, but it wasn't bad, really. In fact, the tea burn on Marie's left hand was more tender. She braced herself, watching Margaret pull out glass, clean the wounds, and wrap her palm and fingers in gauze. When the older woman turned her scissors to Marie's black cotton tombones and black long johns underneath, Marie protested.

Margaret chided her. "You can buy new ones."

Sporadic gunfire continued beyond the walls. Dave continued to make phone calls, asking questions and sharing information, in Dari and in English. Marie leaned into Carolyn and drifted into shallow sleep.

33

Marie awakened abruptly to the sound of a strange man's voice from the doorway above. Gray, early morning light illumined the hallway. She was still sitting up, but her knees were pressed against her chest, draped in a blanket. She stirred, looking around. Dave was already halfway up the stairs. Margaret was awake, looking at the opening through which her husband had left.

Carolyn still shared the blanket with Marie, but was wide-eyed and still. "What's happening?" Marie asked.

Carolyn blinked, looked into Marie's face, and smiled. "You slept."

"Yeah. I guess I was tired." Marie flexed her shoulders and extended her still-slippered feet.

Margaret turned to the younger women. "Exhausted, more like it."

It was quiet in the hallway, save for their whispers and the full voices of Dave and the strange man above. "What's going on?"

"It's the guard. Someone's come to the gate."

Marie searched her mind but found no answers. "When did the fighting stop?"

"I think we heard the last gunshots around four o'clock."

"Two and a half hours long?"

"Yeah."

"Did you sleep at all?"

"A little. Not much."

Marie studied the heaviness in Margaret's face. She pushed the blanket off her shoulders and forced herself to stand. Her back, knees, and hips protested. "I'm going up."

Carolyn grabbed Marie's forearm. "Why?"

"I need the bathroom."

Margaret smiled. "Yes, of course. But could you wait till the guard leaves? You're not dressed."

They all looked down at her black legwear with the gaping holes in each knee and chuckled. Finding her long, dark blue skirt still looped around the strap of her backpack, she stepped into the storage room, shook out her skirt, and pulled it on. The voices from the hallway upstairs disappeared. She heard the slap of the front door shutting.

Marie wrapped her arms across her chest and tucked her hands into her armpits, to keep out the cold, as she climbed the stairs. She saw a dark stain as if brick-red crayons had scratched along the flat blue surface of the stairwell wall. She trembled and looked at her gauze-wrapped hands.

In the first-floor hallway, everything looked normal: shoes were piled at one end, coats and scarves hung above them. Even the lights on the modem blinked and the bulb on the backup power supply glowed solid red. She entered the stairwell that led to the room she'd fled. Along the wall, she saw the same trail of dried blood, dark red against pale blue. She followed it.

The blankets from her bed hung by only a corner, the rest gathered across the floor. Broken glass littered every surface. The light summer curtains floated in the morning breeze. Marie pulled the curtain aside and saw the gaping hole in the window. One corner had been blown out by the concussion of the first blast. *If there'd been a hard wind barrier outside the window, it wouldn't have broken.* But in the cold air, what remained of the brittle glass held only half tight in the window frame.

A misshapen round stain marred the light blue carpet where she'd fallen. There were other stains, too. Those were from her knees. She thanked God for her house shoes, thick-soled slippers to protect her feet from the cold radiating through the carpet-covered concrete. They had protected her from more than cold.

She stood in the middle of the room. *Disarray, broken glass, a little blood. Still,* she told herself. *Nothing extreme enough to justify that blind terror.* The house was still standing. Margaret, Dave, Carolyn—they were all okay. *We weren't the target. Not like the wedding house, not like the foreign woman killed in Kabul.* She looked around. *Just a room with some broken glass and blankets on the floor.* She looked at her hands. *Cuts, that's all. Nothing more.*

She heard Margaret's voice and retreated to the stairwell. Moments later, she found Margaret in the kitchen. On the stove, a kettle of water for the morning coffee slowly heated. *Such a normal thing, water for coffee.* She saw the silver tray, the four cups, the bowl of sugar, and the tiny cardboard box of milk. *Mundane. Normal.* "Where's Carolyn?"

"Getting dressed. Getting her stuff together. She's going to the airport, you know?"

"I'm going with her."

"You can't."

"No, I have to. I have to say good-bye."

"Marie." Margaret's voice was soft, but heavy. "Look at your clothes."

Marie looked down. "So what? It doesn't matter. Look, my skirt covers my knees. It's okay."

Margaret turned away and poured boiling water into the French press. "Dave will go with her. Say good-bye here."

Marie looked around the kitchen. Last night's plates were still sitting, unwashed in a tub of water and soap. She stepped forward and reached for the dishcloth. Margaret grabbed her wrist. Marie looked down at the bright white gauze and cartoon bandages and relented.

The four foreigners gathered in the same room they had joined for prayer the night before. It seemed exactly the same, but now the half-light of morning filled the space. Marie looked around as if there should be evidence, as if, perhaps, the furniture should be overturned, the windows broken. Something to show for the chaos. But there was nothing. Just a normal room, four ordinary people, and four cups of steaming morning coffee.

Dave didn't speak about the visitor until they'd nearly finished their coffee. Instead, he led them to debrief their harrowing experience. He had awakened to the explosion. The window next to him and Margaret had buckled from the force, but it didn't break. They heard the shattering glass from above. They jumped and bolted. Margaret caught Carolyn along the way, and the two ran to the basement. Dave crouched in the hallway and called for Marie. By his account it took her forever to respond. He was about to run up the stairs when he finally heard her voice. He told her to go to the basement and ran down the stairs ahead of her. It all happened so fast.

Carolyn had heard the blast and the shattering glass and lay paralyzed with fear under her blankets. Suddenly, someone grabbed her hand and she jumped, terrified; but it was Margaret. The two ran to the basement, to the back room. There was no time to think.

That was the thing they all agreed on. It happened so fast.

Finally, the last of their coffee finished, Dave explained the latest news. "The governor sent a hand-delivered letter. That's who came this morning. I have to go to his office."

Marie watched the weariness settle into his face. "What does he want?"

Dave shrugged. "I don't know, but I'm sure it's important. I called the driver. He's coming for me."

"Faiz Muhammad."

"Yes."

"What about me?" Carolyn's voice was weak, nearly empty.

"Edmond's coming for you. They're taking the same flight."

Marie was startled. "I want to go with Carolyn. Say good-bye at the airport."

"No."

Marie sat up, looked hard into Dave's face. His voice softened. "There's no room, Marie."

"Okay, but I'd like to go to my house. I need clothes. A toothbrush—"

Dave already had a plan. This time, there would be no discussion; Marie would have to comply. "Yes. We'll drop you at your house on the way to the governor's office. Say good-bye to Carolyn here. Pack your evacuation bag. We'll get you and bring you back here. You can't lock down at home. Not this time. We'll lock down here, maybe just for a few days. We'll figure it out."

Lockdown. One night was bad enough, but this? Marie felt her legs buckle. *Lockdown. Get inside the thick mud-brick walls of your compound, lock the gate, hide from the men with Kalashnikovs out on the street.* Marie knew the drill, but she wanted to go home, lock down in her own space. She was prepared for that; she'd done it so many times, even before Carolyn arrived.

Dave interrupted her thoughts. "I'll call you from the governor's office when we leave. Be ready."

Marie wanted to protest, to counter, but Dave's tone prevented her. Instead she simply asked, "When?"

"Now."

Now! Marie jumped up to go, but Margaret stopped her. "Sit down, Marie. We need to pray." Her voice was surprisingly light.

The four joined hands, one pair covered in bandages. They bowed their heads, closed their eyes, and spoke their thoughts, hopes, and fears to the God they trusted above all. When they breathed their last *amens,* they sat in silence awhile, each staring at the space between their feet. Finally, Dave nodded. "Okay, let's do this."

Marie grabbed Carolyn—Carolyn, her friend, her companion, her sister—and held her tight. "I'm sorry I can't go with you. I'm sorry."

Both of them wept in each other's embrace, Carolyn's departure finally upon them.

After a few moments, Marie felt Dave's hand clamp down on her shoulder. "Now. He's here." When neither woman moved, he gently pulled Marie back.

Marie and Carolyn locked eyes—a flash of shared panic.

Dave pulled again. "Marie."

Wincing, Carolyn turned away and walked out the door.

"We have to go."

An outrage spread across Marie's abdomen, filled her chest, and tore at her throat. She forced herself to swallow. She grabbed her back-pack, pushed her feet into her shoes, took one of Margaret's scarves, and followed Dave out the door. The two hesitated at the gate. Looked right. Looked left. *Quiet. No children. There should be children.* They stepped forward. Marie slid into the backseat of Faiz Muhammad's SUV. Dave took the front. The gate beside them closed. Marie heard Dave speaking.

He was calm. "Do know where your evacuation lists are?"

Marie pictured the white cabinet in her hallway. Inside the door were three lists: fast evac, slow evac, permanent move. "Yeah."

"We won't be long. Get your stuff. Fast evac. That's all. Okay?"

She wouldn't need much, just a few days' worth, maybe, just her backpack. They would lock down, wait for things to settle, and go back to normal. Then, two weeks, and they'd leave for the winter. She'd pack for that later. No need to think about it now.

Omed met her at the gate, both relieved and agitated. They exchanged rushed greetings, and Omed nodded, offering his help.

The shape of her smile felt stiff and awkward in the muscles of her cheeks. "Thank you. You're kind." She entered the house alone. Everything was as she'd left it, except that Carolyn's two big suitcases were gone from the hallway. Again, Marie thought it should look torn up like a house after a storm had splintered the trees and torn away the roof, but nothing was out of place. Everything was as she'd left it. She stood in the middle of the hallway, confused. She knew she should be doing something, but couldn't think of what.

She prayed just one word: "Lord?"

Suddenly, she pictured the three evacuation lists taped to the inside of the white hallway cabinet. She pulled the door open and tore one list off the wood: "Fast Evac." She scanned the list and ran. She gathered items and threw them into a pile on the floor of her room: passport and cash; laptop and power cord; phone and charger; MP3 player, backup jump drives, camera, USB cable; hairbrush, toothbrush and toothpaste, handful of toilet paper; two pairs of underwear, two pairs of socks, one change of clothes; water bottle, aspirin, first-aid kit; family photos.

She dumped the contents of her backpack, removed everything that no longer belonged, and packed it again. It didn't all fit. She pulled the memory card from her camera and tossed the camera aside. Still too tight. She threw out a pair of socks and the zipper closed. She filled the water bottle from the filter and shoved it into the outside pocket. Done. She looked at the time on her phone: fifteen minutes. *Dave said he would call by now.*

She dug out her toothbrush and toothpaste, brushed her teeth, and put the supplies back into her bag. She dug out her brush, untied her hair, untangling the knots that matted the base of her skull. She returned the brush to the bag.

No phone call.

She put the bag outside the front door and returned to the house. Twenty minutes. She changed into a clean pair of long johns and tombones, shedding the torn ones and leaving them in a pile on the floor.

Still no phone call.

She ran to the hall and grabbed her brown, gold-trimmed scarf. It was too light for the cold, but at least it was clean and glass-free—and hers.

At last, the phone rang. "Yeah," she replied, "I'm ready."

"Marie."

"Yeah, I'm here. Got my bag. You at the gate?" She was rushing. Not listening.

"*Marie.*"

"Yeah."

"Listen." His command was strong, abrupt.

Marie stopped in place. "Okay. I'm listening."

"We have to leave."

Dave's words echoed in her mind. Marie grabbed at them, slowed them down, and turned them over in her mind. *We have to leave. We have to leave.* She knew they were leaving. What did he mean? *Leave.* "Leave?"

"Yes." Dave's voice was decisive.

Through the phone, Marie could hear the engine of the SUV and the rumble of tires against a road. He'd already left the governor's office. "When—where?"

Dave spoke clearly. He could not be misunderstood now. "Margaret is packing us. We'll pick you up in ten minutes, fifteen at the most."

Disoriented, confused, Marie reeled, the hallway convulsing around her. *Stop. Focus.* "How?"

"Their plane's waiting. There's room for us. We'll take it."

In a flash, the scene unfolded before her imagination: her packed evacuation bag, the piles she'd left in her room, Omed in the yard, her dogs, the small white plane that would sweep them away.

"Marie?"

Not thinking, she shifted into action.

"Marie?"

"Yeah, I'm here. I understand; I got it." No time for good-bye. *Move.* She clicked the phone closed and ran back to the white cabinet. She pulled the second list from inside the door, but the words on it were blurry. She realized her eyes were full of tears. She wiped them away, set her jaw, and focused. The words cleared. She grabbed her green carry-on suitcase from the floor of her room, unzipped it. Dumped its contents and spun around, opened boxes, threw their contents across the floor, and plucked out what she wanted most. She pulled piles of clothes from cabinet shelves. Scattered them, grabbed items, and let the rest tumble into chaotic heaps.

The phone chirped. She growled. "Come on! That was just a minute!" She caught the time before she pushed the talk button. It had been thirteen minutes. "Yeah?"

"We're almost in your alley. Be ready."

She scanned the list. She'd grabbed everything. She was ready.

No. She wasn't ready at all. She shoved everything into the suitcase, her clothes and supplies tangled together. She pushed, zipped, pushed, and zipped again. She grabbed the suitcase and dashed out of the room, stopping at the doorway to look around. *What did I forget?* There were piles, colors, shapes everywhere. She grabbed a photograph off the wall—the five women smiling in the dappled shade. She held it fast in her hand and ran the suitcase to the door. The dogs pushed, circled, and snapped at each other. The dogs! *Omed will have to care for you.* She called to the guard and he came, grabbing the small suitcase and the backpack in one smooth motion.

Within moments, she was sitting in the backseat of the SUV beside Margaret, her suitcase in the back, piled on top of theirs; her backpack at her feet; a framed photo clutched in her hand.

34

The SUV rocked backward out of the alley. Margaret reached across and slipped her fingertips between the framed photo and Marie's hand. Her grip bit into the small wounds, but Marie held tight.

Faiz Muhammad called back from the front seat as he swung the vehicle backward into the wide, unpaved road. "Mari-jan, it is best if you do not become seen."

Instinctively, Marie hid her head in Margaret's lap. The older woman curled over Marie's back. Marie felt Margaret's chin dig into her kidney. Her phone rang. She groped for it and looked to see who was calling. She called out to the front seat. "Dave, it's Aziza. What do I tell her?"

"Tell her we're fine. Tell her we're going to Kabul. Tell her we'll be back in a few days. No—don't answer. Call her later."

Marie blinked. *A few days . . . Really?* She closed her eyes and saw a faded green scrap of cloth spin, swirl, and disappear. She snapped her eyes open and through the sliver of window she could see the concertina wire, the watchtower, and the Afghan guards with their Kalashnikovs ready.

The vehicle pushed through the intersection, turned, and traveled through town. Margaret and Marie huddled in the backseat. Nausea like a sharp blade pierced Marie's back. She wanted to ask Margaret to shift. The vehicle rocked, slowed, turned, and rocked harder. Marie tried to breathe. She pictured the street, the park with its low wall, the glass-fronted shops, the boys and men sitting on scraps of carpets piled high with used clothes, the bank, and the open stalls of the bazaar. *Zia Gul.*

Faiz Muhammad called back. "Mari-jan. We have almost arrived at the airport."

Marie and Margaret sat up, disoriented. Wide, empty brown fields stretched to the right and left, then a low wall, gaping, uneven. Taller walls appeared. The last neighborhood.

"I forgot my camera." Marie still gripped the framed photograph in her hand.

"What?"

"I forgot my camera. I took it out because there wasn't enough space in the backpack. I didn't put it in the suitcase."

Margaret shrugged. "You can buy another one."

"Maybe it'll be here when we come back."

Margaret gazed over at her friend. "Maybe we'll come back."

The vehicle swung right, and Marie saw the small white aircraft sitting on the dusty runway. The vehicle slid in the gravel and recovered. A man in a white shirt and blue trousers stood outside the extended door ladder of the plane. Another man stood next to him, a man in Afghan clothes with a pancake-shaped wool cap on his head. *Edmond.*

The vehicle bounced, jerked, paused, and jerked again. They came to a stop on the edge of a graveled parking lot beside the low concrete airport building. Edmond and the copilot reached the vehicle just as Marie slid to the ground. Dave threw open the back of the SUV, and the men grabbed the suitcases. They dashed the thirty yards or so to the aircraft.

Faces peered at them through the windows. Marie couldn't make them out, but guessed: Carolyn, Tanja, a child, perhaps the doctor. She grabbed her backpack and jogged the distance, her hand still clutching the framed photograph. She flew up the stairs, bowing at the entrance—then remembered. *Faiz Muhammad-jan!* She turned, but Margaret was behind her. Faiz Muhammad stood just ten feet beyond, but she couldn't get to him. She called out, waved. Her faithful driver placed his hand over his heart and said something, but his words were swallowed by the aircraft's engine. Marie turned and slipped into the first empty seat, the one directly behind the pilot, and buckled her seatbelt automatically. Margaret nearly fell into the seat across the aisle.

In a flash, Edmond, Dave, and the copilot were on board, the door was closed, and the aircraft was taxiing. Marie searched the window for Faiz Muhammad, but she couldn't find him.

Margaret grabbed her arm. "Marie, where's your coat?"

Marie looked around, looked out of the small airplane window to the vehicle, and then remembered. "At your house." Her voice was laced with defeat.

The aircraft took off quickly, a cloud of dust in its wake. It circled, ascending. Marie watched the dustway, the small town, and the cultivated fields beyond disappear from sight. *Shehktan.* They rose southward, toward the hills and snow-covered mountains. Marie looked for Char Ab, its four waterfalls and river, but from this angle she couldn't find the village that had so captured her heart.

And then all of it was gone.

Over the years, Marie had experienced so many different kinds of prayer: fighting, lamenting, arguing, demanding, begging, shyly asking, praising, laughing—even dancing prayer. But buckled into the seat of a small white plane rising over the hills and mountains of Shehktan, Marie fell into the prayer of silence, her soul leaning into the presence of God. She wept.

There were so many things she didn't know. Was there any connection to the Kabul killing? What happened at the governor's office? Why were they fleeing so quickly? When would they return? Would they ever return? And where were they going? Was there a plan? Had arrangements been made? She'd forgotten her coat, her camera—what else? She looked down at the photograph in her hand: burgundy frame, smiling women. She traced their faces with her fingertips. Khadija, the youngest, quick to laugh, almost always optimistic. But then, Marie remembered her tears when Carolyn announced her news. Marie groaned. *What will she do now?* And Aziza, so wise and mature. Marie pictured her at Carolyn's engagement party—gracious and in charge. She smiled wistfully. Zia Gul. *My friend, my sister.* And Carolyn. Marie turned her eyes to the ceiling of the small plane.

The questions within Marie churned, ascended, twisted, and collapsed like dark fragments, shards of painful images, flickering candles of hope. She knew the questions were themselves a kind of prayer that rises, inarticulate yet more real, more honest, more desperate than carefully formed sentences born of reasoned thought. A phrase whispered, a response breathed. "I am with you always. I'm here. I will never leave you." Aching for courage, for comfort, for answers, Marie leaned her beating heart, her churning, nauseous body, her half-formed, fragmented questions into the arms of the God she knew surrounded her.

She remembered the words of a friend, spoken so long ago. The context was lost, but the words were pure. "Sometimes, breathing is the most faith-filled thing we can do."

High above the snow-covered mountains of Afghanistan, a small white plane carried Marie from the mud-brick houses, the scoop-faced hills, and the serpentine waterways of her Afghan home. She bid farewell.

Marie closed her eyes. For the moment, she let go, leaning her head into the seat back, exhausted.

Marie felt fingertips on her forearm as it rested on the armrest. *Margaret.* The older woman was nodding from across the narrow aisle, saying something Marie couldn't register. She heard clicks, shuffles, a woman speaking in a foreign language. *Tanja.* A small boy's question. The engines of the plane were silent. *We must have landed.*

She unclipped her seat belt, turning to watch the three Dutch boys walk past her seat, then their mother. Marie looked up into the young woman's face; it was drawn, almost gray.

A heavy hand on her shoulder. *Doc?* His lips were tight, folded downward. The edges of his eyes under his glasses matched.

Carolyn appeared next, white-faced.

Then she felt Margaret's hand again, firm on Marie's forearm. More words she could not understand though she heard them, saw them in her mind, searched for their meanings, but gave up. She watched Margaret unfold herself from the small seat and pull her black leather tote bag from beneath the frame, her expression resigned.

Then the copilot was beside her. She looked up at him, tall and stooped in the low cabin. Blue trousers, white button-down shirt, close-cropped, blond hair, brilliant blue eyes, straight smile. The normalcy of his clothes, his face, and his manner struck Marie as odd, out of place, incongruent.

She realized it was her turn to leave the plane. She forced herself to follow.

The Kabul sun, bright and sharp, blinded her as she stepped down the small metal ladder. The cold air bit through her thin, brown scarf, her stained, tan sweater, and her navy-blue skirt. She remembered her coat hanging quietly on a hook in Margaret's hallway.

The men were moving, collecting suitcases, exchanging information. Marie stood beside Margaret and Carolyn. She watched with backpack slung over her shoulder, picture frame in her hand. When the men walked across the tarmac toward the airport building, Marie followed. When they held the door open for her, she passed through. When they talked with the Afghan guards, she waited.

Marie thought of a river, tumbling rough and fast down a mountain cliff, pooling behind light tan boulders and tumbling free again. Eventually, it reached a flat valley, widened, and smoothed. Still, its force, its smooth-surfaced current, flowed inescapably toward the sea. Marie felt both the smoothness and the force.

On the taxi ride through the city, sights slid by: faces of urban dwellers, shop fronts, racks of fruits and vegetables, meat hanging from hooks. At intersections, the traffic slowed, jammed; cars honked. Blanket-wrapped men wove crosswise through clogged vehicles; women in light blue, face-screening burqas floated past, guided by watchful boys at their sides.

Marie choked on exhaust-filled air. Narrow icicles of pain shot across the side of her head and through her eyes. With the pain came gradual awareness. First, she registered her overfilled backpack, its misshapen edges jamming down into her lap. Next, the picture frame, her fingers locked around it. Then Margaret's thigh, pressed against her own in the tight backseat of the taxi. And Margaret's hand, wrapped even tighter, her rings cutting into Marie's fingers, digging into the bandages. Her hand, white-gauzed, white-taped, and cartooned. Carolyn pressing into the other side of Marie, her arms wrapped around her own backpack, her eyes wide, searching.

Dave sat in the front seat. His own pancake-shaped wool pakol cap was rolled over his head; a purple-and-white checked man-scarf around his neck; a dark gray winter coat, almost blue, and shiny. The driver next to him had salt-and-pepper hair that disappeared into a black-and-white scarf. A police officer waved their vehicle through an intersection. A bus packed tight with women covered in scarves or burqas, young men with clean haircuts, and older men with small turbans, pulled beside them, then fell behind. A row of tailors displayed bright women's dresses on hangers in their windows. *Kabul.*

The driver stopped in front of an unmarked, gray double gate. *The guesthouse. It's too soon to be here. Not even winter yet, really. The snows haven't begun to fall.*

Marie followed Margaret out of the taxi and stepped over a culvert edged in ice. She heard the guard's words of welcome, recognized them, and responded in Dari. She walked through the gate and stopped just inside. She looked around. *Where's Faiz Muhammad?* She remembered. She'd left him on the dustway in Shehktan.

Dave gave her instructions, and though she heard, she didn't take them in. She followed the guard, who carried her suitcase into the building she'd slept in on her previous visit, but not into the same room. Instead, he led her to the white-walled sitting room with the five-gallon canister of clean water and the dark, dusty TV screen.

She looked at him questioningly.

"Mari-jan, I'm sorry. The other room, has become damaged. You and Nazanin will sleep here." His words were clear, comprehensible, delivered in patient and gentle Dari.

Marie nodded, looked at the room and hid her disappointment. "Thank you, Coco-jan."

The guard tilted his head sideways. "Mari-jan?"

"Yes?"

"You have fled."

Marie narrowed her eyes. She recognized the word for *fled*: it meant "to escape." The Afghans used that word all the time. "The Russians came and we fled." "The Taliban came and we fled." "The flood came and we fled." She managed to nod.

"Saber."

Marie translated. *Saber:* "Wait. Be patient." A word spoken to the grieving when a loved one has died. She said nothing.

"God is good."

She remembered. This man was a believer. He was testifying to the goodness of God, speaking so much more than mere kindness. "Yes. Thank you, Coco-jan. God is good."

35

The man left. Marie stood alone in the white-walled sitting room and surveyed the peach curtains, the blue-and-white checked ceiling fabric with its tiny blue flowers, the new wide, ceiling-to-floor mud stain covering the far corner; the swirling red and black carpet, and the darker red floor cushions lining the walls. She looked at the dark gray TV screen used for watching DVDs, the player mounted on a shelf beneath it, their wires and cables all covered in dust. Beside the power strip, on the floor, sat a dark orange metal voltage stabilizer, smacking like roller skates in response to the fluctuating Kabul electricity.

She dropped her backpack onto a cotton mat just inside the door and caught her reflection in the mirror mounted behind the water tank. She stopped and stared. Shook her head slowly from side to side and looked away. She could not put words to the weariness she saw reflected back at her.

She dragged her suitcase to the far side of the room and pulled a fuzzy blanket from a pile in the corner. She dropped down onto one of the cotton mats, unfolded the blanket around her, and slipped into a deep, exhausted sleep, the burgundy frame still held tight in her hand.

The sun moved bright and cold across the mid-afternoon sky. As Marie opened her eyes, she saw Margaret sitting across from her on a cotton mat, her folded body wrapped in another blanket, a book in her hands, half-glasses perched on her nose. She saw Carolyn's two oversized red suitcases and small carry-on and her own black backpack and green carry-on. She stirred and felt the corner of something hard and pointed jam against her upper arm. She pushed the blanket aside and retrieved the framed photograph.

Margaret looked at the frame, then up at Marie. "I took measuring spoons."

"What?"

"Measuring spoons. I took them in my hands when we fled to Pakistan. I didn't realize I had them until I put my children to bed. I kept them in my hand all day."

Marie nodded, setting the picture next to her on the mat. She sat up and wrapped the blanket around her knees. "Are we at the guesthouse?"

Margaret slipped a light blue cloth bookmark into the pages of her book. "Yes. We'll be here for a few days, probably longer."

Marie looked across the room at Carolyn's red suitcases.

"Yes, Carolyn's here, too. She's leaving tomorrow morning."

Marie rubbed her eyes and coughed the Kabul dust from her throat. Questions crowded the back of her mind. She chose one. "What happened?"

The older woman was patient. She'd been here before. "What do you remember?"

Marie raised her eyebrows, opened her mouth, and shook her head. "I certainly remember the firefight. I remember the glass and the basement hallway. I remember packing. Getting on the plane. I think I said hi to the guard."

Margaret nodded. "Dave went to the governor's office. Do you remember that?"

"Yeah. I packed to go back to your house. Then he said we were leaving. I packed fast."

"You forgot your coat."

"Yeah. It's at your house."

"The governor told him we had to leave." Margaret's words were flat, matter of fact, just information.

"Why?"

Margaret pulled a breath deep into her lungs. "He said he can't protect us. He expects more violence. He said there was a threat."

"A threat?"

"Yes."

"Against us?"

Margaret nodded.

"Why?"

"I think because we were in the middle . . . The governor said they had information."

"What kind?"

Margaret shrugged. She paused. "We'll debrief later."

"What kind of threat?"

"Dave will tell you more."

"Tell me *something*!" Marie insisted.

Margaret looked at the heavy peach curtains hanging unevenly across the window behind Marie. She spoke softly. "Apparently, they wanted to kidnap one of us."

"For money?"

"Not exactly." Her voice clear.

Marie focused. "Why?" She wanted to understand.

This time, Margaret insisted. "Dave *will* explain."

There was more she wanted to know. More that she thought Margaret would tell her but she nodded and said, "Edmond, Tanja, the boys? Doc?"

"Yes. They're all here, in Kabul, but not at this guesthouse."

"Where are they?"

"They went to stay with others." She added. "Edmond and his family are leaving tomorrow. Same plane as Carolyn."

Marie pulled the blanket tighter around herself. She realized there was a diesel heater in the room and the air was warm. Perhaps she didn't need the blanket at all. Still, she kept it. It felt good wrapped around her back and knees, her hands tucked safely beneath.

"Who's here, at the guesthouse? The guard said it was full."

Margaret nodded. "It's just that the room you stayed in last time is damaged. Part of the mud roof fell in. It has to be fixed."

"Okay, is anyone here with us?"

"Yes."

"Who?" Marie wondered why Margaret hesitated.

Margaret pressed her lips together. "The new couple, Chad and Casey, and their little boy, Simon. They're staying here until they finish language school. Six months."

Marie looked across the room. The image of the young American couple sitting on the Western-style furniture in the large sitting room of the main house floated into view. Chad: tall, broad-shouldered and narrow-hipped, looking like the Texan he was. Casey: blonde, blue-eyed, all jeans and T-shirts. Little Simon: full of energy, banging on the wooden highchair. A knot formed in her stomach. "They just have all the answers," she said cynically.

Margaret winced. "Yeah. Like you. Or like you used to be before all this."

Marie pressed her lips together. She wanted to deny it, to look wiser in comparison, more mature, but she knew Margaret was right. That was what really bothered her about the newcomers. Chad and Casey were so sure of the path before them. Their answers were all so simple, so clear. *Were mine, at the beginning?* Marie sighed. "Yeah, maybe."

"And we have no answers, and the not knowing is terrible to live with."

Marie took a deep breath.

Margaret went on. "Listen. In Kabul, everyone is still talking about the woman who was killed. What happened in Shehktan is far away. You have to be patient."

Marie shrugged.

"You know, in a way, we're refugees. Displaced. Disoriented. We don't know what will happen next. We don't know if we'll ever go home, although we certainly won't go back any time soon. We don't know what we'll do or where we'll go."

Marie picked up the word, as if holding it in her hand, and studied it. But it was impenetrable, hard and closed. "Refugees?"

"Yes. I've been here before. It's like the ground is swirling underneath us. It'll take us a little while. We'll have to find it."

Marie found her own metaphor: it felt like trying to walk across a storm-soaked field covered with debris. No clear footing, just jagged edges and sinking earth. "Yeah." She felt the bandage on her cheek with her fingertips and picked at the edges of the adhesive tape. "Yeah, that's the word, *refugee*." She put her hand back under the blanket. "I don't like that word."

Margaret laughed. "Nope. No one does."

"And Chad and Casey?"

"Be patient with them. They've never been here before."

"Yeah, me either."

"You're here now." Margaret leaned forward, her voice soft, wise, and encouraging. "Marie, the ground will settle; we'll find our way. The important thing, the only really important thing is to remember, always remember: God is with us." She tilted her head sideways, pulled the half-glasses from the bridge of her nose. "Do you hear me?"

"Yeah. I hear you."

"Good." She spoke with finality. "And I'll remind you. You're going to forget. Trust me. You'll forget, and that's okay. But I'll remind you. And you can remind me if I forget." She shook herself free of the blanket and stood up. "Now, come on. It's time to get something to eat. They're waiting for us."

"Wait." Marie didn't stand. "What's next? I mean, not dinner. What's next?"

Margaret picked up the blanket and folded it into a large, heavy square. She placed it on top of the cotton mat where she'd been sitting. She retrieved her paperback. "Tonight, after dinner, we'll debrief.

Then we'll keep gathering information, thinking, and praying." She paused. "Figure it out, I guess."

Marie turned Margaret's words in her mind. *Figure it out?*

The two women walked across the open compound to the kitchen. Inside, Marie sat down on a low plastic stool and began pulling cartooned bandages from her fingers. The wounds were small, dark red pricks. She pulled the adhesive from the palms of her hands. Those wounds were longer and deeper, but still, nothing important. All but one had formed a scab.

Dave walked in. "Good to see you. Glad you slept."

Marie looked up. His face was worn, heavy. "Yeah, thanks. Sorry about . . ." She trailed off, not really knowing what she was sorry about. She was just sorry.

"You did fine, Marie. You did what I asked. That's what I needed. Don't worry about it." He slipped out the door.

Margaret cleaned the one still-open wound on Marie's palm. "Do you feel any glass?"

Marie opened and closed her hand several times. Another wound, a small gash on the heel of her hand, spread open.

"Okay, stop that." Margaret ran an alcohol swab across each of the marks. The liquid bit into the deeper scratches, but not badly. She put a new butterfly bandage across the two open gashes. "Yeah. It'll take a while for the bigger cuts to close. Just because of where they are."

"Yep." Marie remembered the stained stairwell wall. "Lot of blood for cuts so small."

"Thank God."

"Thank God for a lot of blood?" Marie teased.

Margaret pulled the gauze from Marie's cheek. The adhesive tore at the soft skin. "One's healing nicely."

"What's it look like?"

334

"Rakish." The older woman smiled.

"I want to see."

"Shh." Margaret wiped the scratches with another cold swab.

This time, the alcohol bit sharply. Marie suddenly thought of her mother again; she saw a white cloth and felt cool water on her burning head. *When was that?* But the memory faded before she could catch it.

When Margaret finished cleaning the accessible cuts, Marie walked through the hallway to the bathroom to clean the others. She passed Carolyn and Casey, sitting on the floor of the living room, building plastic blocks with little Simon. The younger woman called out a greeting. Marie waved and went on.

She studied her face in the bathroom mirror, counting nine small cuts and one noteworthy gash. Still, it was nothing much. The gash was no longer than an inch, cut straight across the high point of her cheek. It had already started to knit together; the two butterfly bandages had seen to that. Marie ran her fingertip across the tear. The edge was rough where a scab was forming. She looked down at her hands. Both were covered with small star-shaped scabs and several longer scratches. The ones on her palm and the heel of her left hand were deeper. Still, they would heal quickly and disappear.

Maybe it was all an overreaction. We weren't the targets. Just caught up in someone else's battle. We'll go home. It'll be okay.

She pulled her knees free of clothes and bandages and began cleaning them with alcohol pads. They weren't bad, either. Not much to show for so much drama.

Suddenly, Margaret's words echoed in her mind. *Kidnap one of us. Kidnap?* She stood up and looked at herself in the mirror. *That can't be right. Can it?*

Marie grabbed the edge of the sink to steady herself. *That's what Margaret said—they wanted to kidnap one of us.* Marie's knees buckled. She nearly fell but caught herself against the closed door. *Steady,* she told herself. *Slow down.* But her heart kept racing. She took a breath, then another and another until her legs strengthened and her hands steadied. She looked at the small wounds on her knees. *So this isn't all of it.* She covered the cuts and dressed again. Dave will tell me.

When she left the bathroom, Marie heard Dave's voice and smelled the savory fragrance of hot lamb kebabs. Marie drank in the aroma of roasted meat and spices and fresh, hot Afghan bread and realized the hunger gnawing deep in her stomach. The seven foreigners—Chad, Casey, Simon, Dave, Margaret, Carolyn, and Marie—sat down at the dining room table to share an unexpected meal together. Three of them were just beginning their journey, one of them was ending hers, the rest just confused.

The conversation drifted around the mundane. Marie knew Dave wouldn't discuss what had happened until they had a chance to debrief the experience in private. She ate silently, her thoughts dull and unfocused.

She looked around the room at the faces of her friends. Margaret was patient, quick with affirmation and encouragement. Margaret looked at people as though she genuinely saw them.

Dave was always thinking, always planning, always in control. He took his responsibilities seriously. Marie imagined he'd been on the phone all day, collecting information, assessing situations, making plans. In a way, she and Dave were similar. They both knew how to work, how to focus, how to get things done. But they were different, too. Dave was consistent, a man of rhythms. He kept regular hours, ate his lunches with the male staff and his dinners with Margaret. For him, the lines between work, family, and relationships with Afghans were clearly drawn. Marie was the opposite. She lived for the interactions, the conversations, the shining eyes and quick smiles of Afghan women. For her, if there was a chance for tea and conversation, work could wait.

And Carolyn, so young, so vibrant and capable. The Afghans delighted in her, loved her. Carolyn, leaving for the life she was dreaming of; leaving with memories that would both delight and pain her for years to come.

Marie looked at Chad, young and earnest, so full of confidence in himself; and Casey, so full of energy and excitement. Casey caught Marie watching her and took it as an open door. Her words came rushed, with a teenage quality. "Wow, Marie! That's so crazy. I can't *believe* it. Must be such a relief to get out."

Marie caught Margaret's quick, silent warning. She looked at her plate, seeing there instead her sparkly wedding clothes, royal blue and bright white lying on Zia Gul's swirling red carpet. She shook her head and looked for words, but Casey kept talking.

"You said you never know what could happen, the last time you were here. Remember? I mean, that's so crazy. I'll bet you're glad to be out. I mean, praise God you're out."

Marie looked down at the cuts on her hands and mumbled her response. "It's my home. Shehktan. It's my home." Her voice was deep and soft, full of confusion and doubt. She looked at Casey and found her full voice. "It's my *home*," and in that, the meaning she was searching for. *It's my home; therefore, I am not glad to be out. It's my home; therefore, it's where I want to be. It's my home; therefore, I'm lost. Confused.*

This time Margaret gave Casey a gentle warning look and Dave changed the conversation.

After the meal, Margaret placed a gentle hand on Marie's shoulder. "Carolyn's leaving in the morning. We all need to debrief, talk through what happened. Together. Casey and Chad will clean up."

36

The four left the main house, walked under the mulberry tree, and retreated to the white-walled, peach-draped room in the back of the compound. Marie sat down on the cotton mat she'd slept on earlier. She wrapped the thick Chinese blanket around her shoulders and knees. Carolyn lit the diesel heater, then sat beside her. Dave and Margaret sat down on the mat opposite, where Margaret had waited earlier for Marie to awaken.

Dave started. "We have to talk through what happened. How each of us experienced the event."

The event? Was there one event? Marie pictured Bibi-jan and then Shukria, the village, the lame son, and the mullah. She saw the man with the brown jacket who traded it in for a dark gray winter coat. She saw Zia Gul and her children. The pink, yellow, and orange house; the towers and concertina wire on the German base; her dogs, her guard, and her room; everything in chaos.

"We should start with the bomb. The wedding. Carolyn?"

The young woman looked down at the carpet before Dave and Margaret. "I was at home, getting dressed. Going to Aziza's house. They were making me lunch. The sound was huge. Loud. The dogs went nuts." Her voice was thin. "I grabbed my phone. Ran into the hallway. Pulled a blanket over myself and scrunched up on the floor behind my suitcases. I didn't know what to do."

Marie felt Carolyn tremble next to her. She unfolded her blanket and wrapped it around Carolyn's folded knees.

Dave spoke. "You did great."

Carolyn nodded, but tears pooled in her eyes.

Dave looked at Marie. She picked up her piece. "I was at Zia Gul's, pouring tea." She looked down at her left hand. The skin across the back of her fingers and knuckles was still bright red. She sighed. She told them about Zia Gul's panic, screaming for her kids, her husband, the daughter, the son, the words they'd heard and spoken. Finally, she stopped.

Margaret told her part. "I was in the kitchen, washing the breakfast dishes, thinking about dinner. Carolyn was coming, and I'd sent the guard for chicken and vegetables. He was out." She talked about the sound, the fear, and Dave rushing into the kitchen, the phone in his hand.

Dave talked about the phone calls. "I found out it was at the wedding, the Minister of Health's new house. The guard rushed in, terrified, a bag of chicken in his hand."

The group laughed suddenly at the unexpectedly funny image amid the retelling of their shared trauma.

"I'd called the liaison officer at the German base. He was talking to me when the guard came in. I didn't know who to pay attention to. Then the guard ran out, the bag of chicken still in his hands." Dave shook his head.

"The German officer didn't know any more than I did. I called you two, made arrangements to get you. It was too close. Faiz Muhammad was already on his way to your house, but he was on the other side of the city with his family."

Carolyn picked up the account. "I heard the explosion. I was in my room getting ready to change clothes. I grabbed a blanket and hid in the hallway next to my suitcases. I didn't know what was going on." Her voice trembled. She talked about Omed banging on her door, Faiz Muhammad pulling up in the alley. "I called you two and made arrangements to get you. It was—it was too close."

When they'd each finished recounting their parts of the crisis, they looked down at the swirling red carpet between them and waited. Margaret began to pray. Each spoke their words of thanksgiving: for the lives not lost, for their safe gathering at Dave and Margaret's, for their passage from a terror that had knocked them, breathless, to the ground.

Their stories went on—the long afternoon, the conversations, dinner, the prayer afterward. They reached the middle of the night— the first blast, glass, the basement, gunfire, and more blasts. They put the pieces of their shared experience in order. Occasionally, they stopped to pray. The sky outside the peach-draped guest room darkened into night. Finally, their stories reached the meeting at the governor's office that morning. Marie had been waiting for this.

Dave rubbed his gray beard. He spoke slowly, carefully. "The attack on the wedding and the middle of the night firefight were connected."

Of course, Marie thought.

Dave went on. "A vehicle carrying two injured men, the driver, and some others hit an IED on the road to the main hospital. Five men. They were all killed. There'll be retribution for that."

Instantly, Marie pictured the village farmers and the mullah standing with Faiz Muhammad before the low house in Char Ab. Dave's words brought her back to the present.

"Also, and very importantly for us, the police stormed a house. They killed three men and arrested seven others. Uzbeks."

Marie sighed.

Dave took a deep breath and watched Marie's face as he spoke. "Those men provided intelligence. Some of it was about us."

Marie's eyes widened. "Us?"

"Yes, us. They told me at the governor's office." Dave continued. "The commander, Ahmad Rasul Khan, supports the governor. They're all family. The commander was the target of the bombing, but the real target was the governor. These guys want to destabilize the governor and push him and all his supporters—Ahmad Rasul Khan and the Minister of Health—out of power. The bombing and the attack on the German base and the main police station were all part of that. It looks like kidnapping one of us was a part of it, too. Part of the plan."

Marie sat upright. *There was a plan? Something concrete?* She thought of the brown-jacketed man who'd reappeared in a gray coat.

Dave continued. "The governor said if they grabbed one of us, the American military would come in with guns blazing. It would show that the governor had no control. That would be the end of him. He and his entire family would be discredited. Shamed."

Dave kept talking. "That was the plan, anyway."

Again, Marie pictured the brown-jacketed man on the street, standing next to another on a motorcycle. She pictured him again, this time with a gray coat on another street corner. *So I wasn't paranoid. He really was there.* "And they were watching us?"

"Yeah. They knew all about us, Marie. They knew when I went to the office, when I went to the bank, when I went home. Everything."

Marie tilted her head. "They knew about you?" She wondered if the brown-jacketed man had followed her at all. It didn't make sense.

"Yeah, but that wasn't the really disturbing part."

Marie sat unable move.

With grief in his eyes, Dave looked directly into hers. "Marie, they knew where all your literacy classes were. They were mapping *you*. It sounds like they thought you were the easier target." Dave's voice was filled with sorrow.

She whispered. "We've escaped a trap." Marie imagined a wire loop, lying in the mud of her alley just outside of her dark green gate, just in front of her next footfall.

The four sat in silence for several moments.

Dave cleared his throat. "There's more."

Marie watched Dave press his fingers into his temples and asked, "What is it?"

Dave looked down at the carpet. His voice came from far away. "They've implicated our translator. They think Fawad is involved."

Instantly the man's face flashed into Marie's mind. "Fawad . . . ?" Her stomach convulsed. "He helped me with the stamps and signatures last time we were in Kabul." She realized she wasn't surprised. Just sickened.

Dave nodded, took a deep breath. "They say he was being paid." He shook his head, his mouth tight.

"*Fawad?*" Marie remembered the man standing beside her in a blue-walled room, venetian blinds across a window, slants of dust-filled light. "Fawad?" She thought back to when she had seen him in the official's office. *What had the man said? "But they may steal you in*

Shehktan, too. You can't trust anyone." "Fawad!" She saw him behind his office desk, asking her for the addresses of all the literacy classes, wearing an expensive new suit jacket. Something about him was off and she'd known it. "Paid? For what?" As soon as she asked the question, she realized she already knew.

Dave looked into Marie's eyes. He whispered. "For you." He took a deep breath. "He was tracking you, Marie."

"No!" Marie whispered, cold running through her limbs and weakening her body. *No.* She had complimented him on his new suit. Had the suit been the price for her own freedom? *He smiled and thanked me.* She trembled.

She looked up at Dave and saw deep sorrow in his eyes.

"I'm sorry, Marie. I trusted him."

Marie nodded. "We couldn't know."

"No."

Marie sighed deeply. "What about the man on the street? Brown jacket? Gray coat?"

"I met him. He was secret police. He was protecting you. They didn't know what was going on, but they had some warnings."

The group fell into silence.

Marie rocked, ever so slightly, forward and backward. She looked up at Dave, his gaze distant, unfocused. She looked at Margaret, her eyes glassy, heavy. She felt Carolyn beside her, still. "Did they arrest him?"

"Not yet. They can't find him." Dave shook his head.

Marie knew it didn't matter.

Margaret began to pray.

Marie stopped rocking. She sat up straight and interrupted the prayer. "We were about to step into a trap. It could've been chaos. I mean, that's my biggest fear—getting kidnapped. I thought someone was watching me, following me. But then I decided I was just being paranoid, hyper-vigilant, frightened. I thought the thing here in Kabul had spooked me. But we were being stalked? I was being stalked?

Hunted. And now we're here." She paused. "Alive. In Kabul. Safe."

Dave studied the carpet. "I knew something was wrong, but I hoped it didn't have anything to do with us. I kept collecting pieces of information, but nothing fit together." He looked over at Marie. "I didn't want you to go to the village or walk to Zia Gul's or visit the classes, but I wasn't sure why. Not until this morning."

Marie saw the weariness in his face. "You got us out. I couldn't see."

Dave swept away Marie's half-formed apology. "You didn't have the information. That was my job, and I didn't have it all either. But we're safe now."

Margaret waited until Dave was finished. Then she lowered her head and began a song. Dave joined, then Carolyn. Finally, Marie added her voice. The four sat in a peach-draped room in a Kabul guesthouse and called their voices together. They sang, and in singing, they drew breath and strength.

Marie felt her shoulders unlock. She leaned back.

The song ended.

Marie opened her eyes. She looked straight at Dave. "So, we can't go back. Not even to say good-bye to our friends."

"No—we can't go back."

Marie felt tears against the backs of her eyes.

Margaret spoke. "Marie. You'll find your way through this. You'll find your way."

Marie looked down at the swirling carpet beyond her folded knees. She felt Carolyn, stiff and silent beside her. "Yeah, time heals all wounds." Her words were bitter, sharp-edged. "Next week, we'll all be fine."

Margaret shook her head. "Marie, we've been here before. Remember that."

"*I* haven't." She saw the photo sitting beside her feet. Five smiling women. She thought about Margaret's measuring spoons and her flight to Pakistan with her children. "I know you have . . . I'm sorry."

Margaret leaned toward her. "Marie. Remember this; time does *not heal* all wounds. Time *seals* wounds. It doesn't heal them."

Marie looked into Maragret's soft face.

"Marie. Christ heals all wounds. Next week, you will not be fine, but you will be better." Margaret continued. "The most important thing here is to find Christ in this experience."

Marie looked down at the smiling faces in the burgundy framed photo.

Margaret went on. "We've walked with God in this place. You too, Carolyn. All of us."

Marie felt Carolyn stir.

"Now, we have to remember. We have to recall who he is, who we are in him. Where he's been with us in Shehktan."

Marie formed a half-smile as she listened.

Margaret noticed. "What are you thinking, Marie?"

Marie inhaled heavily. "I just feel like that's what you've been telling me all along. I have to find Christ in the journey. I mean, I know he's here. Of course. He's everywhere and he's always with us. But sometimes, that's just good theology. Something my mind knows, my mouth says, but my heart . . . I don't know . . . doesn't really believe. No, I believe it. Of course he's here, but I don't really know where or how; it's like I've just been holding on, and now there's nothing to hold on to."

Margaret nodded, but there was no condemnation in her face, only the sadness of understanding.

Marie pressed her hands together. "But how?" She looked into Margaret's eyes. "I know how to work. I know how to keep busy. I know how to drink tea and talk with women, but how can I find Christ in all of *this*?" She looked down at the swirling red carpet beneath her feet. "It's like all my thoughts and prayers are jumbled. Just a mess, like the room I left behind."

Margaret nodded. "Ask God to show you, Marie. You'll figure it out with him. We all will—differently—but we'll find him."

Marie looked up at the white walls of the sitting room. She imagined them covered with posters full of colors and words. *Yeah, I could start there.* She had a task, something she could do, a way forward. *I can map this,* she thought. *I can find Christ in this crazy journey.* She looked back at Margaret. "Yeah."

Margaret and Dave left Marie and Carolyn sitting side by side in the small room. Marie found her aluminum water bottle. She filled it from the five-gallon water tank and caught her reflection in the mirror. *Calm yourself.* She looked again, and walked down the hallway with her toothbrush, toothpaste, and water bottle. The curtained window still stood at the end of the hall, and she felt the weight of her water bottle in her hand. Her shoulders were relaxed, her steps easy.

When Marie returned to the small room, Carolyn was already in her pajamas. Marie changed clothes and curled up under the thick Chinese blanket that had warmed them both before. Carolyn turned out the light and took Dave and Margaret's cotton floor mat. The two lay in silence across from each other for several moments.

Carolyn broke the silence. "Why did you bring that picture?"

"What picture?"

"The one from the Easter picnic?"

The Easter picnic. That's what it was. Marie smiled. She could see the day clearly. They'd laughed and sang and told the story of the Honorable Jesus Messiah and his final days on earth. "Easter. Yeah. I'd forgotten that."

"I thought about it when we prayed and celebrated Communion the other night. You know, we were reading in the book of John, the Last Supper. Do you remember?"

"Yeah, but it seems like an eternity ago."

"Yeah, I know. It was just Monday."

Marie shook her head. "What's today? Wednesday?"

"Yeah." Carolyn fell silent for a moment, then returned to her story. "When we were praying, I thought of the Easter picnic." She explained. "The two of us and Zia Gul, Aziza, and Khadija went to that grove that Faiz Muhammad found for us. We each told part of the Easter story. We ate our picnic and told each other what Jesus said that last night."

"Yeah. Khadija was amazed."

"She'd never heard the story."

"Then we celebrated Communion." Marie saw a piece of broken bread in her hand. "With the leftover bread, broken for us."

"Yeah. Then the really hard part."

Marie nodded in the darkness. "Khadija cried."

"Yeah. She didn't want to believe it."

"Zia Gul and Aziza convinced her it was all true."

"But we said the story wasn't over. Told her to wait." The two women paused. Marie remembered the dust and the green hills and the sound of water and the hot sun. Carolyn brought her back to the story. "Then we wrapped up the pots and plates and cups."

"Yeah, and we told the last part when three days later, Jesus was raised from the dead."

"And Khadija clapped. She loved it."

Marie smiled. "Yeah, and Aziza loved it that the women went to the grave and saw his resurrected body first."

"We told that part and then we swam in the little pool."

"The spring, yeah. The water was so clean."

Carolyn picked up the thread. "We stretched out on the carpet and let our clothes dry in the sun, then took the picture."

"Faiz Muhammad came to carry our stuff. He took the picture in the shade of that big tree." Marie could see it all: the dark green carpet, the food, the pool of water, the tree. "We were so happy and the hills were brilliant green, all covered with new grass."

"Yeah." Carolyn closed the story. "It was Easter Sunday and we were celebrating."

The two women fell into silence. Marie listened. Carolyn's breathing deepened. The transformer relays slid and clicked. Outside, two cats snarled, one screamed, then nothing. In the distance, a pack of dogs barked. Marie didn't bother to count them.

FAREWELL

KABUL, AFGHANISTAN

37

In the morning, Marie awoke to the sound of a zipper. She sat upright, rubbed her eyes, and looked around. Carolyn stood over one of her two oversized red suitcases. "It's time," she said.

Marie shook herself awake. "Time?"

"Yeah, taxi's coming."

Marie jumped up, dressed, wrapped her brown and gold scarf around her head, and grabbed one of Carolyn's big red suitcases. She followed her friend out to the yard. Dave and Margaret were waiting. The four clasped hands and prayed.

When the gate opened, Marie grabbed Carolyn and hugged her tightly. They wept on each other's shoulders.

Dave drew close and whispered. "Carolyn. It's time."

Marie let go. She wiped her face with her still-torn hand. "Carolyn. Don't forget. It's been a good journey."

"I won't." She walked through the gate and was gone.

Marie turned. *Easter. It was Easter.* She remembered—five women smiling in dappled light. *We celebrated the resurrection.* Suddenly, ideas, images, and words cascaded through her mind. She walked to the sitting room. She had a plan. She grabbed her backpack, hooked her yellow cell phone pouch to the strap, and headed out the gate.

The sky was bright and clear. She jumped over the ice-trimmed culvert and walked toward the wide paved street just a block from the guesthouse. She knew what she wanted—a stationery store: markers, poster board, and tape. She walked past a group of meat sellers, the half carcass of a butchered animal hanging from a steel hook. Another animal stood bound nearby: a shaggy black and gray goat with dark eyes. Between them, a pool of dark blood melted into the hard Kabul ground.

Two Afghan men, one gray-bearded, the other, barely an adult, stood silently in the wooden shop between the live goat and the half butchered carcass. They stared at Marie as she walked by.

Marie looked at the suspended carcass, the pool of blood, and then the living goat. She wanted to buy it, cut it loose, and find a shepherd to lead it back out to the high pastures.

She jumped the culvert again and this time, climbed up onto a concrete sidewalk. She walked to the first glass-fronted store and stepped inside. The store sold cell phones, top up cards, and chargers. A young man in Western-style blue jeans with too many zippers, a gray-and-black sweater, and slicked back hair greeted her from behind the counter. Marie asked for a stationery store.

The young man pulled a flip phone from inside the glass case and set it on the counter. "This is a good phone." Marie smiled and again asked for the stationery store. The young man shrugged and gave her directions.

Marie walked past a row of glass-fronted stores and crossed through the traffic-clogged street to the other side of the road. The stationery store was easy enough to find with its window full of ink cartridges, notebooks, and drafting instruments. She chose thick markers: blue, green, red, and black; masking tape, and a set of multi-colored, thin, drawing markers. She asked for poster board or flip-chart paper, but had to settle on a forty-eight-inch-wide roll of white kraft paper. She bought a glue stick, a pair of scissors, and a small yellow pad of paper. It was all more than she needed, but she didn't care. She had a plan, something to do, a way to make sense (or at least begin to make sense) of everything that had happened. *Maybe*, she hoped, *a way to find Christ in all this confusion and loss.*

She returned to the guesthouse, to the white-walled sitting room with the peach drapes, and went to work. She unrolled the kraft paper and cut three long pieces. She taped them, one above the other, to the widest, bare, white stretch of wall in the room. She drew a long, serpentine, black line from the top left corner to the bottom right. She counted the days: fourteen. Just fourteen days.

In thick black marker, she wrote a title: "Fourteen days and my life disintegrated." She sat down on the dark red, cotton floor mat where just an hour before her friend's suitcase had sat. She looked at the legend she'd written. "Fourteen days." *Crazy.* She marked the days on the timeline starting with day 14.

She picked up the small yellow pad of paper. On each page, she wrote the milestones. "Foreign worker killed." "Carolyn says she's leaving." "Home to Shehktan." "First trip to Char Ab." "Start in-town literacy classes." "See stranger on the street." "Meet Bibi-jan and Shukria." "New Testament." "Last dinner with Carolyn." "Wedding bombed." "Firefight." "Evacuation." "Debrief." She unpacked the glue stick and fixed each yellow milestone page onto the timeline.

She remembered the image of the green pennant struggling to hold on in the fury of a dust storm. Then another kind of storm. Climbing out of a basement; twisted gray asphalt shingles and splintered white clapboards; a green shirt caught, tangled in jagged boards and torn asphalt.

She stood, took a thin red marker, and began to write the images. The descriptions weren't enough; they were too thin, too dry, too quiet. She tossed the marker down, grabbed her scarf and laptop, and walked quickly to the Internet café.

She collected her ticket from the boy at a scratched wooden desk, sat down on a badly upholstered black-flowered couch, and turned on her computer. She needed pictures to tell the parts of the story that were too dense for words.

She searched the Internet for images, pasted them into a document, and paid the boy behind the scratched desk to print them for her. Sheaves of paper in hand, she walked back to the guesthouse, oblivious of the staring men on the street, the choked buses packed with faces, the sharp odor of human refuse flowing through the culverts, or the biting, early winter cold. In their places, images drifted: community and laughter, storms and destruction, rescue and new hope.

Marie sat down on a dark red cotton floor mat, her brown and gold scarf, still wrapped around her head. She cut each tiny rectangular picture with the scissors she bought at the stationery store. She grabbed her glue stick and a thin green marker. She began pasting the images to the timeline. Above each image, she added a caption, an explanation, a clarification.

She looked at the clock and thought of Carolyn sitting on a plane, watching the mountains of Afghanistan retreat beneath her. She imagined Carolyn's family, waiting for her in Colorado. She pictured Brad, the guy whose name she so seldom used, and Carolyn walking in a meadow. She glued a picture to the timeline: two women crossing a gorge on a rope bridge. *We had to do it. We had to walk this ending together and we did. We walked it together.*

She added more pictures: the hand of a young woman wrapped around the hand of an older woman. She thought of Bibi-jan and Char Ab. *It was like visiting a woman trapped in a nursing home. No way out. Nothing left but to learn how to live.* Immediately, she was transported to the sitting room with the warm sandalee and the glass window with its view of the valley below and the plateau beyond. *I went there. I sat with them. I loved them.* The last words she wrote caught her attention. *I loved them. With my hands and my feet and my words and my smile, I loved them.*

Suddenly, she saw the face of Jesus, smiling—not an image, but a realization. Jesus healing a sick woman. Jesus teaching on a hillside. Jesus calming an angry sister. The words of Scripture wrapped around her. "For this is the love of God, that we keep his commandments."

Love: the kind that compels the healthy into the home of the sick; the kind that shops for groceries for a shut-in. The kind that holds a crying child in the middle of the night. Not spectacular. Nothing for the evening news or a Hollywood movie. Just love. Patient, kind, generous love.

Marie smiled. *Jesus.* She breathed a prayer for Bibi-jan, for Shukria, for the lame son, and the mullah. *Love.*

In the next picture, a tattered flag strained against an invisible wind. That image, so familiar. Hanging on. Just hanging on. *Were you in the wind or the ropes of the flag?* The next images: a great cloud of dust moving across a plain; black-robed women fleeing; another woman, stopped, looking over her shoulder; the corner of a house exploding into the wind. *Were you in the wind?* A man, viewed through crosshairs, standing in the wreckage of a bombed-out street. *No. You weren't in the wind or the bombs or the bullets. You weren't in the violence of the storm, but you were with me in it. In the middle of it all, you were with me. You knew the storm was coming. You knew I was being tracked, hunted. You saw what I didn't see. You grabbed me and pulled me away.*

She pasted the image of a helicopter, two rescue workers plucking a woman from the roof of a house. *You were in the rescue. You gathered us up. You carried us away. I didn't want to go, but you knew I had to. You protected me. You delivered me.*

Marie read the words she'd written in thin green marker on white kraft paper. She looked at the images: friendship, laughter, fear, violence, and escape. *Fourteen days and my life disintegrated.* She leaned her forehead against the wall, her fingertips on the picture of the helicopter. She spoke her next prayer out loud. "I was never alone. You were right there with me, even in the confusion. In the fear. In the blindness. You were right with me. All the way through, you were with me."

She searched the deeply cracked no-longer-white wall in the other room and found it—a tiny plaque with clouds and shafts of sun pouring over a wheat field. She stepped carefully through the mud and around the collapsing ceiling fabric. She plucked the plaque from its nail and read the simple words aloud.

God didn't promise days without pain,
Laughter without sorrow or sun without rain,
But God did promise strength for the day,
Comfort for the tears and a light for the way.
And for all who believe in his kingdom above
He answers their faith with everlasting love.

Her voice filled the rain-and-mud-damaged room. "This is what you've been trying to tell me all along. I wasn't listening. I couldn't see, but you've been with me. Right in the midst of it all."

The surface of one wall had collapsed onto the floor in a tangled heap of white plaster and mud. The wall hooks where she'd hung her long brown coat and scarf had fallen and lay half-buried in mud. One end of the bronze-colored curtain rod swung downward, the hem of the heavy yellow drapes buried in thick mud. The white sheers were brown and rust-streaked. The bed was gone.

The plaque's bottom corner, beneath her thumb, was stained with mud. She wiped away the stain and smiled. "Isaiah 43:2." *There it is,* she thought. She heard the verse in her mind and prayed it back to God. "I passed through raging flood waters, and you were with me. A rushing river knocked me down, stole my breath—but only for a moment. You didn't let it overwhelm me. When the firestorm swept over me, you didn't let me get burned." She nodded. "Yes. You're with me. You've always been with me, even in the storm, even in the loss."

She cradled the little white plaque to her chest and returned to the sitting room with the peach drapes and the story of her journey mapped out on white kraft paper taped to an Afghan wall. The sorrow and pain were clear, but so were the laughter, the comfort, and the love. She spoke her next memories out loud. "There's a village—Char Ab, Four Waters. I had a literacy class, way outside of town, cut into the face of the beautiful scoop-faced hills of Shehktan, Afghanistan. Farmlands lay in the valley below it. Snow-laced mountains beyond. So beautiful. And the people, they were just precious. Bibi-jan. Shukria. The teacher. The mullah and the lame son. I only got to go a few times, but I went, and we laughed. We loved. We drank tea and shared meals and touched each other's lives."

With the small plaque in her hand, she picked up a purple marker and added new captions to her timeline. "Love in our community. Sorrow in our loss. Grace in our grief. Hope in our words. Comfort in our songs. Companionship in our steps. Love in our moments. Protection in our storm. Deliverance in our danger."

She scooped up the burgundy framed photo of five women smiling in the dappled light of a dense Shehktan tree. She studied each face, remembered the story they'd told one another, and the meal they'd shared. "It was Easter." She smiled. "Khadija cried through the Passion. Aziza, Zia Gul, Carolyn, and I knew the end."

"Because Christ was on Golgotha with the mocking crowds and weeping women. Because he stood before Pilate when the elders and people demanded his execution. When all hell was breaking loose, He was right in the middle. Right there. Right in the circle of accusations, condemnations, humiliations, beatings, everything. He was right there. Right in the middle of it all." She paused, then went on. "Because he knew the end."

"Aziza, Zia Gul, Carolyn, and I—we waited for it. Khadija found it. And when it came, we celebrated." Marie remembered stepping down into the cool, spring-fed pool. They'd giggled and splashed one another. They'd laughed like small girls, free of headscarves and watching men.

"Christ in the water and Christ in the sun. Christ in the joy, in the laughter, and the love." She wrote one more caption at the very end of her timeline: "Resurrection." Under that she wrote, "My story's not over."

When she finished, she sat down on the cotton floor mat, looked at her experience in color and words and pictures, and began to weep. This time, her tears were full of comprehension, exhaustion, and relief.

Late in the afternoon, Marie left the red cotton mat in the peach-draped guest room whose wall carried the story of her journey. She walked across the yard to the main house, entered the kitchen, and scooped little Simon into her arms. She kissed the startled boy and put him back down on the floor. Margaret and Casey stared.

"I'm going to the Internet café." And she was gone.

She walked the few short blocks to the café, received a ticket from the boy behind the scratched desk, and sat down on the black-flowered, spring-shot couch.

She opened her laptop, connected to the Internet, and began writing.

> Dear friends,
>
> I'm camping out in Kabul. I'm not sure what's next, but it's clear that we can't return to Shehktan. Security in the area deteriorated, and we got caught in the middle of a crazy tribal power struggle. Thank God, my friends and I got out safely. We had to evacuate quickly. The Afghans have a saying. "We left without sandals on our feet." What they mean is that they ran as fast as they could in the face of whatever disaster was crashing in on them. That's what happened to us. Leaving like that is always difficult, but its success leads to a future. I've met so many people in Shehktan who fled their homes in the face of things far worse than what we encountered. Like them, I don't have any idea what my future is. Still, I'm grateful for the journey.

At this point, I think it would be best to go home to America, catch my breath, regroup, and seek the Lord for whatever's next. Of course, I could return to Afghanistan and work someplace else in the country. I don't want to do that unless I know for sure that it's what I should do. I need time to figure it all out.

I also need time to rest. The last two weeks have been so extraordinarily difficult. Now, I need to say good-bye. I can't visit my friends to say farewell personally, but I can call some of them. I'll do that. I'll also wrap up and close down my projects. Then I'll book a flight home.

I can't thank you enough for walking this journey with me. You've blessed me more than I can say. I hope you'll continue with me as I figure out what's next.

In Christ, Marie

Marie reread the email. She thought about cutting the paragraph about going home to America, but realized she'd made that decision. She pressed send and bought a set of airline tickets: Kabul, Dubai, London, DC. Home.

She wrote two more messages, one to her best friend, and the other to her parents.

I'm coming home. I'm tired, but my heart is good. I'll be home in time for Thanksgiving.
Love, Marie

She attached the flight details, closed her computer, and paid the boy behind the scratched wooden desk. She was going home.

EPILOGUE

Over the course of the next week, Marie said her good-byes. She wasn't able to call Bibi-jan or Shukria or the village teacher. Those women didn't have cell phones. So she asked Faiz Muhammad to deliver a message for her. The driver agreed. She spoke her message and added a blessing, a simple one that Faiz Muhammad would be comfortable delivering. "Please tell them, 'Mari-jan says, God loves you. He's with you. And he will show you the right path.'"

Faiz Muhammad was delighted, but reminded Marie that he would have to tell the son, and the son would tell the wife and mother, and the mother would tell the teacher. Marie smiled. *Ah, Char Ab. Four Waters.*

She made arrangements for the final supplies to be delivered to each literacy teacher. They could finish the courses or not as they saw fit, but at least they would have the materials. She talked to Aziza and Khadija and shut down her other projects. Those phone calls were painful. She could hear the sense of betrayal in the voices of the other women. The finality of those conversations drove the reality of Marie's flight from Shehktan deep into her own heart.

She called Zia Gul, and the two women wept. Marie pictured her friend in the pale green sitting room with the burgundy cotton floor mats, mint-colored drapes, and swirling red carpet. She remembered the henna stain on the carpet and her wedding clothes in a bag. She tasted, again, hot tea and the easy comfort of lazy afternoons spent in warm conversation and shared prayer. She felt Zia Gul's hands around her own, then the weight and scrape of her friend's gate. She knew she would never walk back through that gate, but she could hold on to Zia Gul's friendship. Like her friend's brother working in a faraway land, Marie could call Zia Gul on the phone, hear her voice, and trade their news. It wouldn't be the same, but it was something.

After each phone call, Marie breathed her short prayers. She knew that although she'd left Shehktan, Christ was still there, still in the streets and homes, still speaking his love and truth into the hearts of the people he had invited her to love along with him. She knew that would have to be enough.

Marie spent time with Margaret and Dave, praying about the things they'd experienced, the work they'd done, the people they knew, and the paths before them. Those hours were bittersweet. Marie knew she'd miss her friends, especially Margaret, whose wisdom and grace had been such a gift to her across the years. Leaving is never easy.

Marie crossed paths with Casey several times over the week. The younger woman, still full of naïve enthusiasm and ill-timed questions, no longer annoyed Marie. *Casey's young,* Marie thought. *Her enthusiasm and faith are beautiful.*

Once, while Marie was sitting with Margaret over tea, Casey bounded into the room with a great plan. There was an NGO on the other side of Kabul that needed staff. She wanted Dave, Margaret, and Marie to join.

Margaret just smiled. Marie leaned back on the heels of her hands and said, "Oh, to have faith yet unscathed!"

Casey was unsure. Perhaps Marie's words were an insult, perhaps a compliment.

Marie smiled. "No, I appreciate your enthusiasm. Thank you."

"But you could work here in Kabul."

"Perhaps. Of course, there are many possibilities. We'll each figure it out." And that was it.

Three days before Thanksgiving, Marie folded and repacked the clothes, equipment, and personal items she'd brought with her in her flight from Shehktan. She carefully pulled the three forty-eight-inch-wide posters with the story of her journey in color, pictures and words from the white wall of the guest room. She folded each length into a small rectangle. Between the pages, she slipped a framed photograph of five women, smiling in the dappled light of an Easter Sunday afternoon. Finally, she added a mud-stained, wooden plaque of a sun-sprinkled wheat field, with a simple poem and a great promise: "When you pass through the waters, I will be with you." Marie smiled. "Always."

She zipped her suitcase closed, swung her black backpack over her shoulder, and surveyed the room: white walls, peach drapes, red cotton floor mats, thick Chinese blankets, and a swirling black and red carpet. She whispered her thanks into the cool air.

She walked past the five-gallon water canister and paused at her own reflection. She lifted the edge of her brown-and-gold striped headscarf and spoke into the mirror. "In America, I won't wear a scarf. I'll let my hair down whenever I want." She smiled. "In America, I'll . . ." She shook her head. "I have no idea." She shrugged, looked down, then returned to the face in the mirror. "In America, I don't know, but it'll be okay." She smiled again and stepped through the doorway.

From the hallway, she glanced into the wrecked bedroom. Already, the mud had been cleaned away. The blue-checked ceiling fabric had been removed and replaced with light blue flowers. The heavy yellow drapes and bronze-colored curtain rods were gone. The once damaged wall was whole, clean, and bright white. A new green carpet covered the floor. She closed the door.

She dragged her carry-on suitcase and her overstuffed backpack across the yard to the inside of the gate. Along the way, she scooped little Simon into her arms, hugged him close, and put him down. At the gate, she added her hands to a circle. Dave, Margaret, Marie, Chad, Casey, and even little Simon bowed their heads and prayed.

Marie wept, unashamed of her tears. She hugged each person, said her good-byes, and released them.

Before the guard, she placed her hand over her heart, bowed her head, and spoke blessings over his family. He did the same, and Marie climbed into a waiting taxi.

The ride to the airport was too brief. Marie watched the shops, the fruit stands, the cloth sellers all slip by. She saw women in scarves and long coats and others in light blue burqas that floated behind them as they walked. She saw men in turbans with wool blankets wrapped around their shoulders and others with Western-style winter coats and watch caps. She smiled at honking horns and gray and green clad soldiers and police. She chatted with the driver about the weather, the latest news, and the condition of the Kabul streets.

She passed through the airport checkpoints, trading hellos and jokes with the women who were meant to search her, but didn't. She showed her ticket, her passport, her black backpack, and green carry-on suitcase over and over. And when it was time, she boarded a commercial airplane. The engines turned, the aircraft taxied and took off. The snow-laced mountains of Afghanistan disappeared beneath the clouds.

Marie was going home.

A NOTE FROM THE AUTHOR

In 2010, my Afghan neighbor called me to his home. We sat, his family, my foreign friends, and I, and shared tea and stories of floods and orchards and fields destroyed. After forty minutes, my host reached his purpose. "Men have come to our mosque. They've asked us to throw rockets at you." That was the beginning of the end.

A month later, a team of medical workers, Afghan and foreign, were executed in the mountains of northern Afghanistan. A month after that, a member of our foreign community was kidnapped with his Afghan driver. Both were eventually released, but by then, the reality of our situation was clear. We had to leave.

This book is not that story. So much of what really happened to our little community of foreign aid workers cannot be written. Security prohibits the telling. Instead, I've told a story that tells the truth of our experiences in a context drawn from events gathered across my years in Afghanistan. The pieces of this novel are true, but they are not all mine.

Farewell, Four Waters opens with the events around the killing of Gayle Williams on October 20, 2008. Marie's reaction to Gayle's execution are my own. The story of the Friday fellowship following Gayle's death is also true, but I don't recall the Scripture we read that day.

Shehktan is not the town in which I lived. The true identity of my own "Shehktan" has been hidden. Char Ab is also a pseudonym. Zia Gul, Bibi-Jan, Shukria, the lame son, the mullah and Faiz Muhammad are all based on real Afghans who I loved deeply. Fawad is based on a man I barely knew, but his story is true.

The experience of Shukria and her brothers comes from a different part of the country. It, too, is painfully true. The history of the

Shamilis is also true. The battle between the Uzbeks and the Tajiks is very real, but located elsewhere.

The long firefight is based on the experience of a group of brave young American aid workers who were living in another town. They were my friends and my family. Their terrifying night and forced evacuation broke all our hearts.

Chad, Casey and little Simon are based on a family I met in Dubai. The true family is still in Afghanistan and doing amazing work. I'm proud to have known them. Dave and Margaret are also based on a couple I knew. They, too, are amazing, godly people. Carolyn is not based on any single person; however, Marie's attachment to her is based on my own attachment to several coworkers who left the field before I was ready.

The Easter picnic is based on two picnics combined. Both were glorious days.

The poster Marie made in Kabul is my own. However, I made it in two parts; first, in a cabin in America after my kidnapped friends were released. Then later, I added the pictures at a retreat I took on the Chesapeake Bay. The process of making the poster helped me find Christ in the journey, and that has made all the difference.

The plaque, with its simple poem, hangs on the wall of my American home. It's my touchstone, my reminder of the floods and fires I've passed through.

Here is the truth: I have known the companionship of Christ in the darkest places. I am who I am because of the journey. I wouldn't trade any of it. In the deepest, most honest ways, *Farewell, Four Waters* is my story.

ACKNOWLEDGMENTS

My publisher encouraged me to write this story as a novel. I was skeptical, until I started. However, as the pages multiplied, I found the freedom to explore truth, struggle, meaning, and hope. Some days, I walked away from my computer with deep sorrow in my heart. Others, with peace and gratefulness. The writing took me back to my own Shehktan and my own losses. It also took me back to Christ. Jesus, thank you. You are so good to me. Always.

I'm immensely grateful for Moody Publishers and especially for Deb, Janis, and Michele. You've welcomed me, encouraged me, and guided me along every step of the way.

I'm also grateful for my editor, Cara, who took a messy manuscript and turned it into a coherent book. Thank you for your hard work, patience, and the endless questions that helped me clarify the story I wanted so badly to tell.

Dr. Namaan, of Moody Bible Institute, and Lisa, my former neighbor in Afghanistan, thank you. You championed the first book and opened the door for this one.

So many of my "foreign friends," American, British, and beyond encouraged this second book. Thank you, as well. Debbie, Mark, Cindy, Amy, Brian, Mike, Elaine, Mary—your friendship is strength to my bones. Thank you! A hundred times, thank you.

To all the Afghans I've known and loved; I wish I could show you this book. I'm so sorry I can't. May you know the grace of our Lord, the Honorable Jesus Messiah. May you find a future filled with his love, joy, and peace.

Finally, my prayers are for you, the reader. May you, also, find Christ in your own experiences. May you know his presence even in the darkest, hardest valleys of your own life journey.

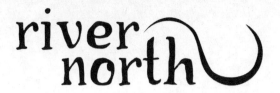

IMPACTING LIVES THROUGH THE POWER OF STORY

Thank you! We are honored that you took the time out of your busy schedule to read this book. If you enjoyed what you read, would you consider sharing the message with others?

- Write a review online at amazon.com, bn.com, goodreads.com, cbd.com.

- Recommend this book to friends in your book club, workplace, church, school, classes, or small group.

- Go to facebook.com/RiverNorthFiction, "like" the page, and post a comment as to what you enjoyed the most.

- Mention this book in a Facebook post, Twitter update, Pinterest pin, or a blog post.

- Pick up a copy for someone you know who would be encouraged by this message.

- Subscribe to our newsletter for information on upcoming titles, inside information on discounts and promotions, and learn more about your favorite authors at RiverNorthFiction.com.

midday connection

Discover a safe place to authentically process life's journey on **Midday Connection**, hosted by Anita Lustrea and Melinda Schmidt. This live radio program is designed to encourage women with a focus on growing the whole person: body, mind, and soul. You'll grow toward spiritual freedom and personal transformation as you learn who God is and who He created us to be.

www.middayconnection.org